Praise for Lisa Wingate's contemporary romance

Texas Cooking

"Takes the reader on a delightful journey into the most secret places of every woman's heart.... A book that all women, young and old, will remember always."
—Catherine Anderson

"Lisa Wingate dishes up fun and charm."
—*USA Today* bestselling author Rachel Gibson

"Wingate has cooked up a practically perfect romance: soft, sweet, often uproariously funny, alive with people you'd want to know and places you'd like to be."
—*Detroit Free Press*

"*Texas Cooking,* first in a planned trilogy, will have readers drooling for the next installment.... Beautifully written mix of comedy, drama, cooking, and journalism."
—*The Dallas Morning News*

"*Texas Cooking* is a delightful love story."
—Janice Woods Windle

"Lisa Wingate's *Texas Cooking* is delicious! This novel has a spiritual dimension devoid of preachy righteousness, and the characters have a psychological depth that doesn't come across as too heavy.... Wingate's style ranges from humorous to searching to achingly tender scenes. She perfectly portrays every moment, investing her characters with deep emotional lives. Her writing is wise, witty, and compassionate."
—*Romantic Times* (Top Pick)

continued ...

Tending Roses

"A story at once gentle and powerful about the very old and the very young, about the young woman who loves them all. In Kate, Lisa Wingate has created a wonderful character. Richly emotional and spiritual, *Tending Roses* affected me from the first page."

—Luanne Rice, *New York Times*
bestselling author of *True Blue*

"Stop what you are doing and experience *Tending Roses*. . . . A rich story of family and faith."

—Lynne Hinton

"You can't put it down without . . . taking a good look at your own life and how misplaced priorities might have led to missed opportunities. *Tending Roses* is an excellent read for any season, a celebration of the power of love."

—*El Paso Times*

"Wingate's touching story of love and faith proves the old adage that we should take time to smell the roses and try to put our modern problems in perspective."

—*Booklist*

"This novel's strength is its believable characters. . . . Many readers will see themselves in Kate, who is so wrapped up in her own problems that she fails to see the worries of others."

—*American Profiles Weekly Magazine*

"Get your tissues or handkerchief ready. You're going to need them when you read Lisa Wingate's book *Tending Roses*. Your emotions will run the gamut from laughing loudly to shedding tears."

—*McAlester News-Capital & Democrat*

LONE STAR
Café

Lisa Wingate

AN ONYX BOOK

ONYX
Published by New American Library, a division of
Penguin Group (USA) Inc., 375 Hudson Street,
New York, New York 10014, U.S.A.
Penguin Books Ltd, 80 Strand,
London WC2R 0RL, England
Penguin Books Australia Ltd, 250 Camberwell Road,
Camberwell, Victoria 3124, Australia
Penguin Books Canada Ltd, 10 Alcorn Avenue,
Toronto, Ontario, Canada M4V 3B2
Penguin Books (NZ), cnr Airborne and Rosedale Roads,
Albany, Auckland 1310, New Zealand

Penguin Books Ltd, Registered Offices:
80 Strand, London WC2R 0RL, England

First published by Onyx, an imprint of New American Library,
a division of Penguin Group (USA) Inc.

First Printing, September 2004
10 9 8 7 6 5 4 3 2 1

REGISTERED TRADEMARK—MARCA REGISTRADA

Printed in the United States of America

PUBLISHER'S NOTE
This is a work of fiction. Names, characters, places, and incidents either are the
product of the author's imagination or are used fictitiously, and any resem-
blance to actual persons, living or dead, business establishments, events, or
locales is entirely coincidental.

To Sharon K,
friend to authors, artists,
and lost pets . . .
May God bless all the labors of love
you left behind on this Earth.

Chapter 1

Cross•road (kraws'rod) *n.* an intersection; a place where two roads meet traveling opposite directions; a place to move across; a place of crossing; a gathering place.

IN the dictionary, *crossroad* is an unassuming entry between *crossfire* and *crosswise*. It is a word with a plainspoken feel, one that means exactly what you'd think it would mean. No mystery to it, just two roads converging, then moving apart again.

Yet the mystery *is* the road. Not the one you're on, but the one you pass by as you slow at the stop sign, then hit the gas and move on to the next ordinary mile of an ordinary day. You don't notice the road, don't gaze down it and wonder, What would happen if I went the other way?

Not on an ordinary day.

For me, the extraordinary came by way of voice mail. I didn't know it then, but I was slowly drifting onto the other road, the one that traveled far from all that was familiar. The one that was a mystery.

The voice mail alert made me jump in my seat, and I didn't answer it right away. Less than an hour before, I'd been told that I might as well turn off the cell during my commute to Austin.

"There's no cell phone service on the old road," my assistant had told me as I was getting in the car to begin my drive to the office. "Now don't panic, Ms. Draper." Her voice took on a playful, pacifying tone. I could tell that, as usual, she was going to tiptoe merrily over the lines of strictly business behavior and try to lighten the moment with a joke. "You can do this. If you start to have withdrawals, you can pick up the cell phone and rub it against your cheek and pretend it's working."

"Very funny," I muttered, more impatient than usual with Kristi's teenagerish personality. I'd been in Texas a month, trying to push the first issue of *Texcetera* magazine to press on time, and so far nothing was going right. The fact that my assistant here was a bubbly twenty-three-year-old fresh out of college didn't help the situation. At thirty-six, fifteen years into a career editing magazines, I knew that when the magazine doesn't go to press on time, heads roll. I also knew that the publishing company wouldn't have pulled me from my editing job in Richmond and sent me to Austin unless they were desperate to launch *Texcetera* on schedule.

"Are you sure the interstate is closed?" I'd already asked her that once. I couldn't believe that with everything else we had to worry about, we now had to worry about the main road to Austin being out of service. "How can they close an interstate? That just doesn't happen." *It doesn't happen in Richmond.* Lately, in Texas, nothing surprised me. So far, my trip had been like an episode of *The Twilight Zone*.

"It's been on the news here in Austin, like, all morning? A bridge fell down last night. Just poof." She paused, and I pictured her illustrating the *poof* with hand motions. "Now they've found cracks in ten other overpasses, and they think maybe the contractor that built them cheated on the materials. They've been talking about it on every channel. Don't you listen to the news?"

"No time this morning." I didn't want to admit that I'd been at my computer obsessing about the upcoming issue since four-thirty A.M., and I did that every night because I didn't want to think about the other things that kept me awake. I didn't want to wonder why Dale had chosen to stay out of the country on another assignment for *Time* instead of coming home to Richmond, or why my father, who was supposed to have been living in a retirement condo in Killeen since my mother's death, had run away to the abandoned family farm. It was easier to worry about the magazine.

Kristi let out a playful *humph* on the other end of the phone. "OK, I just looked at the inbox on my computer, and I can tell where *you've* been all morning. Thanks for the huge to-do list. Don't guess I'll be going to lunch today. Don't you ever sleep?"

Normally, a comment like that would have irritated me, but I'd learned that whatever went through Kristi's mind tumbled right out her mouth. She wasn't far off the mark, anyway. Lately I didn't sleep.

Kristi went on talking, her Texas drawl stretching one-syllable words into two. "There's a heck of a storm coming. I don't know if you'll run into it on your way or not, but it looks bad here." The phone went dead for a moment, and then Kristi's voice returned midsentence. ". . . hear that? Gee whiz, thunder just shook the whole building, and the power blinked."

"Is it that bad?" My mind began spinning ahead, worrying, as I backed out of my father's unused retirement condo and watched the garage door close.

Kristi must have known what I was worrying about. "I'm sure the storm will blow over before time for the Rose Garden tours in Austin. Anyway, if you don't get going, you'll never make it here for the cover shoot. It's a ninety-minute trip on the old road, at least."

"You're kidding." Glancing at my watch, I realized that in slightly over two hours, we were supposed to be shooting the first *Texcetera* cover—the first lady of the United States and the first lady of Texas together conducting the Rose Garden tour near the state capitol. That picture would sell thousands of magazines and bring *Texcetera* onto the market with a splash. Dale had pulled all kinds of strings to get me and my photography team fifteen minutes alone with the first ladies before the tours began. Even from as far away as the Middle East, Dale still had the power to make things happen. After three years together, and despite all of the recent problems between us, that fact about him still impressed me. In his long career in freelance journalism, Dale had made contacts in almost every facet of print and politics. I couldn't believe who Dale knew and who knew him, and how far people were willing to go for him.

"All right, I'm gone. I'll go straight to the Rose Garden for the shoot and interview. Call the photography team and tell them not to be late. You're sure that all I do is stay on this . . . what number did you say it was . . . FM 47-B? And that will take me all the way to Austin?"

"That's it." She paused, and I heard the office computer's battery backup beeping as the phone cut out and then came back. "Just get on 47-B and head south. There's no place to get lost. FM 47-B doesn't even cross a major highway or go through any real towns or anything. It crosses a few county roads that don't go anywhere. No one uses old 47-B anymore, except locals, and sometimes the army guys from Fort Hood, but I imagine there will be a lot of traffic today, with the interstate closed down and all. The radio said that 183 is jammed bumper-to-bumper coming into Austin, so don't try that way."

"All right," I said. "Thanks for calling to give me the warning. I would have ended up trapped where the interstate is closed, I guess." I was grateful for Kristi's loyalty, especially since I'd known her only a month. No one else on the magazine staff would have bothered to warn me. Actually, they probably would have loved it if I got stuck on the interstate and couldn't make it to work.

Kristi snorted into the phone. "No, you'd probably drive around the barricades and flash them your press pass." She giggled, delighted with her own joke.

"All right, that's it. You're fired." Kristi's sunny disposition was as hard to resist as it was to put up with. I caught myself going along with her jokes, even when we didn't have time for them.

"I know." She sighed, almost as if she wished that were true. "Oh, don't forget to get gas before you start out. Hardly any gas places on old 47-B. Not that are open, anyway. If you get desperate, stop at the old Lone Star Café at Crossroads Store. They sell gas. But don't ask to use the bathroom."

I didn't inquire as to what that meant. She finished the sentence with a conspiratorial giggle that worried me.

An hour later, Kristi was on my voice mail, and the giggle was gone. Completely. Pressing the cell phone to my ear, I tried to hear through the static as I crept along with other commuters on a two-lane road that hadn't seen so much traffic since LBJ was president. In nearly an hour of driving, I'd seen only a couple of ranches and the rusted-out carcasses of a few old gas stations long ago abandoned by humankind.

For the first time since I'd known her, Kristi sounded panicked. "Laura, there's a problem with the . . ." Static obliterated the rest of the message, leaving my imagination to conjure all sorts of terrible scenarios.

I groaned under my breath and looked for a place to stop to try the voice mail again. Beside me, the shoulder of the road dropped off steeply into a thick tangle of wild sunflowers that covered a deep ditch. No place to pull off. Ahead, the cars and trucks were stopping at what looked like an intersection.

I could probably pull off there. Stretching in my seat, I tried to see past the vehicles coming to a halt one by one at a faded stop sign. Beyond the intersection, it looked like there might be an abandoned gas station or old grocery store. Hopefully, when I got there, the cell phone signal would kick in again, and I could pull into the parking lot long enough to get the message off my voice mail.

The tower signal on the cell phone disappeared as I came to a stop at the end of the long line of cars backed up at the intersection.

"Crud," I muttered, shaking the phone as I counted the cars. *One, two, three . . .* all the way to twenty-three, plus one livestock trailer, and a gold Mercedes ahead of me. This would take a while. The woman in the Mercedes slammed her cell phone on the dashboard and threw her hands in the air, then pounded on the horn. In front of her, the cows stuck their noses through the trailer bars and mooed in reply. She waved her hands at the windshield, trying to shoo them away, but didn't honk the horn again. Absently, I read the gold-lettered decal in her back window, *Shaw Real Estate,* and the custom license plate, HOUSHNTR. Cute.

Drumming impatiently on my steering wheel, I inched closer to the stop sign. Stop, inch, inch, inch, stop . . . And on the cell phone, no signal, no signal, no signal . . .

Please let there be a signal at the top of the hill. One little bitty bar on the tower indicator. Please . . . It's amazing what you'll pray for when you're stuck in traffic on an unfamiliar back road at nine in the morning, when you have to be in Austin by ten and your assistant has left a frantic message on the cell phone, and you don't know what it says. *And please, get this traffic moving . . .*

I knew better than to pray for things like that. I really did, but at the moment I was desperate.

Ahead, the traffic crept forward at a snail's pace. I ground my teeth, gripping and ungripping the steering wheel, watching the digital clock change: *9:04, 9:05, 9:06.* Inch, inch, inch. Stop.

I turned away from the clock and looked out the window, squinting at the stop sign that was causing all the trouble. Clinging to a crooked post by one nail, it swung lazily back and forth, shaking its head at the traffic.

Leaning back in my seat, I tried the deep breathing I'd learned before dropping out of yoga class back in Richmond. Closing my eyes, I tried to imagine ocean waves coming in and out on a tide. *Inhale, exhale, inhale, exhale,* said a soothing voice in my head, and then, *If you don't get to Austin by ten o'clock, Laura, you're dead meat . . .*

Inhale, exhale, inhale, exhale . . .

The honk of a horn startled me and I bolted upright. Ahead of me, HOUSHNTR had moved three feet forward, and, while meditating, I had failed to close the gap. The guy in the pickup truck behind me was mad. I fought the urge to give him what my mother called "the naughty finger." In Texas, the naughty finger was best kept out of sight, because many of the pickups had at least three rifles on the back-window gun rack, and "shooting the naughty finger" took on a whole new meaning.

The guy behind me honked again, and I realized that the cars ahead were moving.

The livestock trailer rolled forward, and I saw the reason that the traffic jam was clearing. In the intersection, a guy in a cowboy hat was waving traffic through. He looked fairly official, wearing some kind of uniform shirt, white with a badge or something, with blue jeans and boots. He was standing next to a pickup with lettering on it.

Thank God. Finally. Leaning forward, I tried to read the letters on the side of the pickup as we crept closer to the stop sign.

Two school buses rounded the corner on the cross-road just as HOUSHNTR and I were finally getting to the front of the line. The traffic cowboy put a hand up to stop us, then motioned for the school buses to move around his pickup and onto the highway.

"Oh, great," I muttered, combing loose strands of blond hair away from my face, frustrated with the delay.

HOUSHNTR wasn't pleased either. She pulled into the intersection and the cowboy motioned for her to stop, so she slammed her hands on the steering wheel and rolled down her window to complain. He smiled and said something that must have been charming, because HOUSHNTR threw her head back and laughed, then backed up her car until she almost hit mine.

The cowboy glanced at me and shrugged apologetically as the buses passed by; then he signaled for our line to move along. HOUSHNTR leaned out the window and said something as she passed. He shook his head and grinned, his teeth an even white row beneath the shadow of his hat.

Raising my hand in a cursory wave, I slowly moved forward, absently reading the letters on his truck. *Tri-County HAZMAT,* it said. Whatever that meant. Trash collector, maybe? At the moment, I didn't care. He was a hero to me. I was going to make it to Austin on time.

The voice mail beeped again on my cell phone. "Yes!" I heard myself squeal. My elbow hit the horn as I scrambled for the phone, and HAZMAT jumped back like he thought I was going to run him over. *Crazy lady in a rental car.* I raised the hand with my cell phone in it, then ducked my head apologetically, hoping he might understand the sign language.

He shook a finger playfully at me as I rolled past.

Pressing the phone to my ear, I tried to hear as static garbled the voice-mail menu, then cleared. Behind me, the pickup honked again, and I realized I had slowed to a crawl, holding my breath, hoping the voice mail wouldn't fuzz out before I could get the message.

"Laura." That was definitely panic in Kristi's voice. "There's a problem with the cover shoot for this morning." A fist twisted in my stomach, and I tried to imagine what she meant by *problem*. "And . . . ummm . . . there's a problem with the Hometime feature." Now I felt sick.

The pickup driver honked twice more, and I moved off the road, toward the overgrown parking lot of what had once been a gas station or store, now nearly hidden among a tangle of vines, scrubby Texas trees, and underbrush. Ahead of me, HOUSHNTR veered sharply to the right, cutting me off as she too pulled into the parking lot, talking on her cell phone and gesticulatingly wildly.

I stopped under the shade of one of the trees as Kristi's voice continued serving up the bad news. ". . . got word that the hailstorm this morning wiped out the Rose Garden at Zilker Park. The electricity is out all over Austin, and now we heard there was a tornado on the ground at Round Rock. That's not too near us, but still, it's scary. The governor's aide called and said the first lady has gone on back home and they're leaving for Washington tonight, so there's no way we'll be able to shoot the cover." A long pause, during which Kristi actually emitted a sigh of despair, something I'd never heard her do before. "And when the power went out, it crashed my computer. It wouldn't come back on the battery backup. The whole thing is fried." Another long pause, and then, "And . . . the only copy of the finished Hometime feature was on there. I'm . . . ummm . . . I can probably get another copy of the original, but it took me three days to get it put together the first time. The thing

was a mess the way Mrs. Bronstad sent it. I didn't want
to say anything, but it was only, like, a bunch of notes.
She may be great at doing crafts on TV, but I don't think
she knows how to write a magazine article. Anyway, as
soon as we get power back here, I'll get another copy
and get started on it again." Her voice trembled as she
finished the sentence, and I wondered if even Kristi had
finally reached the breaking point. "I'm sorry, Ms.
Draper. I hope you get this message before you get all
the way downtown."

The cell phone beeped and an electronic voice said,
"End . . . of . . . messages." I rubbed the growing ache in
the center of my forehead and tried to think of a way to
salvage the situation. *Think of something, Laura. There
has to be a way. Think of something.*

Staring past the bridge of my fingers, I studied a rusty
Moon Pie sign that hung on the weathered limestone
wall of the old store. Sunlight glinted off the M as a
breeze puffed through the parking lot, rattled the sign,
then disappeared into a passing dust devil.

A hailstorm wiped out the Rose Garden. . . . How
could that be happening in Austin when it was only
partly cloudy here?

*The weather in Texas always borders on the impossi-
ble. Lots of things in Texas seem impossible. The plants,
the wildflowers, the differences in terrain, cows with
horns spanning six feet, the largeness of the sky, the sheer
distance across the state. It is a place you learn to love for
its idiosyncrasies. . . .*

The words from an article I'd read a few days earlier
came into my mind. An article written for *Texas Today*
by my old college friend Colleen Collins, who had left a
reporting job in D.C. to move to San Saline, Texas, get
married, and run a small newspaper there. Back in college, Collie, my twin sister, Lindsey, and I had been in-
separable. Collie had called to tease me about being

sent to Texas to temporarily fill the editorial position at *Texcetera,* and she'd told me to call her if there was anything, *anything,* she could do to help.

"Collie," I whispered in a moment of eureka. Now was the time to take her up on that offer. Picking up the cell phone, I quickly dialed the office number. Busy signal, which meant the power outage had brought down the phone system. I hung up, dialed my e-mail server, pushed the button to compose a message to Kristi, and spoke as clearly as possible into the cell phone.

"Got your message. Call Colleen Collins at the *San Saba County Review* and ask if she has the rights to that photo she showed me of the first family at the ranch in Crawford. Tell her we'd like to buy it for the cover of *Texcetera.* Also, ask if she has anything we could use for the Hometime feature. I'd take a reprint of something from her newspaper if it's ready to go and has the right feel for the column." I paused, then said, "Send," which, as usual, the voice-recognition software didn't recognize. I repeated, "Send . . . send . . . *send!*"

Finally the phone beeped, and I moved it away from my ear, watching the screen as the message scrolled by. The software had garbled the message, but Kristi would be able to decipher it.

Beside me, HOUSHNTR finished her cell phone call and made a wide circle around the parking lot, looking curiously at the old stone building. Slowing as she passed the windows, she studied something behind the cloudy, dust-covered glass. I wondered what was in there.

HOUSHNTR continued her circle, but gave a long glance over her shoulder, like she was thinking about going back for another peek. I chewed a fingernail, watching her car come closer to mine, wondering if I should honk the horn, or if she would turn around and look before she ran into my rental car. I gave the horn a polite tap, just in case.

HOUSHNTR started, noticing my car, then smiled and
waved as she passed, like a beauty queen in a parade.
Lifting my fingers on the steering wheel in reply, I
looked at the building again. What did she see in there?
The old stone structure appeared abandoned. . . .

My cell phone rang, and I jumped, dropped the
phone, then fumbled on the floor, trying to get to it.
Grabbing it somewhere near the gas pedal, I pressed the
button, hollering, "Hello . . . hello . . . I'm here!" even before I could get the phone to my mouth.

"Laura?" I recognized Dale's voice.

"Dale?" The line fuzzed, then cleared as I pressed the
phone against my ear. "Dale, is that you? I'm here." For
an instant, the familiarity of his voice was comforting,
like snuggling into a warm blanket. Then a sliver of apprehension needled me. Dale was still in Saudi Arabia,
not due home until early next week. He never called
home when he was busy on an assignment. "Dale,
what's wrong?"

"Don't panic, Laura. Everyone's fine." There was
something different in his voice, something about the
way he bit out my name, heavy on the L, clipped at the
end. I sat mute, not sure how to react.

"Laura, are you there?" That sounded more normal.

"Yes." I took in a breath and let it out. The stress of
the day was getting to me. "Sorry. It's been a seriously
bad day so far. You won't believe what's happened
this—"

"I heard about the Rose Garden shoot," he interrupted, and I fell silent again. It wasn't normal for him
to cut me off, especially when we were talking about
work. That was one thing we'd always had in common.
Dale and I could talk magazines all day long. "I called
the *Texcetera* office earlier. Your assistant told me about
the hailstorm ruining the shoot." Rushing the words, he
cut the sentence abruptly in a way that said it wasn't the

shoot that he wanted to talk about. "I was sorry to hear about that."

I was sorry to hear about that. No, *Hang in there, baby; it'll be all right.* No, *Let's crack open a bottle of wine when we get home and make the world go away.* Just, *I was sorry to hear about that.* It was the kind of thing you would say to an acquaintance, a colleague. Not to your soul mate.

"Oh." I was probably being too sensitive. Anyway, I didn't want to argue. "Well, you won't believe where I am right now. Stuck on some back road between Killeen and Austin. A bridge fell down on the interstate, and now the whole thing is closed. The whole interstate. Can you believe that? Kristi rerouted me on this old FM 47-B. Anyway, as far as I can tell, there's only one spot on this whole highway where the cell phone will pick up a signal, so here I am, marooned in the parking lot of some abandoned gas station. If you'd called a minute later, you wouldn't have gotten me."

He didn't answer, which usually meant he was either not in a talkative mood, or was distracted by his laptop. Either way, there was no point going into the whole story about my detour. "Well, I can tell you all about it when we're back home. The magazine goes to press on Friday. I need to handle some distribution issues and work on the balance sheets this weekend and early next week. I'll get a flight out of here next Wednesday or Thursday and be there in time to meet with the Realtor Friday. When do you think you'll be getting in?"

There was a long pause that let me know I'd hit on the reason for the call. He wouldn't be back in Richmond next week.

"I'm not coming." Three little words that could have meant a myriad of things.

"You mean not next week?" A whisper of irritation crept up my spine and tightened the muscles in my shoulders. If I had to cancel another appointment with the real estate lady because Dale was delaying again, the woman was going to think I was nuts. "I've got the real estate lady all set up to show us some houses in the country outside of Richmond. A couple of them sound nice—house, an acre to two, exactly what we were looking for."

The silence on the other end was deafening. I wondered if the signal had cut off and he wasn't there anymore. "Dale, what's going on? Are you still there?" The words were sharp—the tone that our conversations seemed to take lately.

"I'm here." I heard papers rustling in the background, and he took a deep breath, his words coming fast, sounding impatient. "Meet me in Rio, Laura. Get *Texcetera* in the bag, catch a plane, and meet me."

"You took another assignment over there, didn't you?" Frustration made me come to the point. I was sick of hailstorms and closed highways and conversations with hidden meanings. I was sick of Dale making excuses to delay coming back to Richmond. In the past ten months, he'd taken every overseas assignment he could get his hands on. Between his freelance work and my employer sending me here and there on emergency jobs, we'd barely seen each other in the last three months. He'd even managed to be out of the country for my mother's funeral. "You know what, Dale, I don't want another set of tickets to Europe or anyplace else. I want to go look at houses *together,* like we said we were going to. Are you going to be home next week or not?"

He exhaled a long, weary sigh that changed to a huff at the end. "Laura, I'm not coming. I've been trying to find a way to tell you. It never seemed like the time was right. I didn't want to make things any harder on you."

"Things?" I repeated, stunned.

"Your mother's illness. Her passing away. All the trouble with your father. I didn't want to add our problems to it." *Our problems.* He said the words as if this thing, this *problem,* had existed for months without my knowing it.

"I don't understand." My mind raced back to our last conversation, a week and a half ago. "I didn't think we had a problem. The last thing I knew we were talking about traveling less, getting a house, moving to the country, and trying to make some time for each other. I had the real estate lady set up to show us houses next week. I told you that. We talked about that last week." The emotions of the day came rushing from the pit of my stomach, swirling through my head like smoke, making the conversation, the rumble of the car engine, the distant growl of thunder seem unreal, like part of some bad dream from which I would awaken any moment. I killed the engine so I could hear myself think.

"*You* talked about that last week, Laura." His voice held the eerie calm of words rehearsed ahead of time. "You talked about it. Lately you've been doing all the talking."

I blinked hard, killing the engine, staring out the car window as the wind picked up, pelting the windshield with loose leaves. The Moon Pie sign clanged against the building, the sound hollow, empty. I studied the uneven cream-colored stone blocks around it, staring until the thick mortar lines started to blur. "What do you mean, *I've* been doing all the talking? You were right there, telling me it was all right to set things up with the real estate lady. You were right there talking about getting a house, getting married, maybe even starting a family. You were the one who brought up the idea of adopting in Romania. Don't you remember that? How can you say that was me?"

"It *was* you, Laura," he insisted. No emotion. No hint

of the churning tide I felt within myself. "That was all you. In the first place, I never said I wanted to move to the country."

"You did." I felt like we were talking from opposite sides of the moon. "You said you could make your home base anywhere."

"Good Lord, Laura, that was a passing comment that *you* turned into shopping for a house in the country. I mentioned that they'd taken the significant-other clause out of the health insurance, and *you* turned that into a reason to get married. I mentioned the *story* I was going to shoot on the orphanages in Romania, and you turned that into some kind of save-the-world fantasy of adopting kids overseas."

"What are you talking about . . . ?" I choked out, my mind racing back in time, trying to determine if I could have been so blind, so busy, so self-deluded that I hadn't noticed our conversations were one-sided. "How could . . . how could you let all this time go by without saying anything?" I stammered, trying to put words to the thoughts careening through my mind.

"I don't know." For the first time, he sounded guilty. "I don't know, Laura. I guess I thought if I gave it time, it would go away. I thought you'd turn back into yourself, into the person you used to be."

"What would go away?" I heard myself scream, my voice echoing through the car, blotting out the noise of the rising wind outside as storm clouds blew in with frightening speed. "What did you think would go away?"

He didn't answer right away, and I could tell we'd gone beyond the words he'd rehearsed, into what he was really thinking. "This whole home-and-family, biological-clock thing. This whole thing that started a year and a half ago when your friend Collie quit her job and moved to Texas. It's as if you couldn't stand it that first your twin sister and now your best friend were going the marriage-and-mommy route and you weren't."

"That's not true," I spat bitterly. "And how could you bring my sister into this? She's a divorced single mother, for heaven's sake. I feel bad for her. I'm certainly not jealous of her, or Collie." But somewhere deep inside, I wondered if there could be a grain of truth in what he was saying. Was I trying to compete with Lindsey and Collie? Was that why my life—Dale and me, living together, pursuing our careers, doing our own thing—didn't seem like enough anymore?

"Yes, Laura, it is true." His voice became steady again, practiced, back to the lines he had rehearsed. "And then when your mom died you went completely nuts about it. All of a sudden, you're desperate to get a little pink house in the country and hide from life."

"I'm not hiding from life, Dale. I'm trying to make a life."

"Oh, come on, Laura. You've been over the edge ever since your mother died. You're trying to get over your guilt by molding yourself into something that would have made her happy."

"I don't feel guilty over my mother's death." Did I? "She had a stroke, Dale. It wasn't anyone's fault. It just . . . happened."

Dale exhaled a breath of frustration, his voice softening. "Yes, you do, Laura. You're full of guilt over it, and you shouldn't be. Everything in this world is not, I repeat *not,* under your control. You've done more for your parents than your brothers did or than Lindsey did. You're still doing it. The only reason you didn't put up a fight about going down there to work on *Texcetera* was because it was a convenient excuse to check up on your father. And now there you are trying to control whether your father stays at the retirement home or out at the farm. Leave it be and come to Rio."

Righteous anger kindled in my chest. How dare Dale,

who didn't even speak to his family, tell me how to care for mine. "For heaven's sake, Dale, my father has a bad heart. Of course I'm worried. He shouldn't be staying out at the farm alone. The place has been sitting empty since the last renters moved out. The house is practically falling down. It's full of old furniture and other junk my brothers use when they go out there on their hunting trips. Dad doesn't eat. He doesn't take his medications. Half the time he doesn't turn on the air conditioning. It's a hundred degrees in there, and he's wrapped up in a blanket. Yes, of course it bothers me to find him like that, when we thought he was living at the retirement condo and dealing with Mom's death all right. I wonder how long this has been going on. I wonder whether he stayed at the condo at all after my brother moved him down here. He didn't come back to Texas because Mom is buried here, Dale; he came back to cash it in on the farm where he was born. He always said he'd die there, and now here he is waiting to follow Mom to the grave."

"Lindsey and your brothers don't agree with you, Laura. They all think he's trying to manipulate you, and that you're making the problem worse by falling for it. They all think you've lost perspective since your mother died. You never used to let him do this to you." Dale was steady, confident in his argument, speaking to me in slow, measured words, as if I were a child. "Why is it that you're the only one who can't see what's going on?"

"There's nothing to see!" I exclaimed, angry that Dale had been talking about *me* with my siblings. "I am not losing my mind. . . ." Everything that had happened in the past two months came crashing down on me—my mother's death, Dad convincing my brother to help him move into a retirement home in Texas, me finding Dad wasting away at the farm, the problems with Dale and me, the growing sense that there was something wrong with my life. I lowered my head into my hand, trembling, sobbing out words that were barely words. "How can you do this to me, Dale? How can you do this to me now? On a cell phone? How can you do this?"

I wanted to be angry, to say, *If you could do this to me now, when I need you, after three years together, then you're not the man I thought you were. You're not a man at all. I don't need this. I don't need tickets to Rio, or any other vacation spot. I need time at home to relax. I need someone to talk to, someone to lean on.*

I don't need you.

Instead, all I could do was cry.

Thunder rumbled outside, and wind buffeted the car, a mirror of the emotions within me as he answered, "Laura, there's a lot more going on with you than the problems between you and me."

"Stop analyzing me!" I screamed, my mouth filled with bitter tears. "Stop it!"

He let out a long breath and paused, determined to keep his cool. "All right then, I'll tell you how things are from my perspective, and then I'm going to hang up. I'm a forty-six-year-old man. I'm at the top of my career. I'm financially comfortable. I like my life. I like my condo in Richmond and the Corvette in the garage. I like my golf days and my sailboat and all the traveling my job involves. There's no room in my life for baby seats and diapers. I have two grown children. I've done the house-and-family thing, and I'm not looking to go back. I'm not looking to move to a house in the country and mow lawns and rake leaves. I want to go to Rio and have a nice time and get back to our normal lives. This is me. This is who I am. You knew it when we got together. I'm ten years farther along in life than you are, Laura, and maybe that makes a difference. I'm not likely to change. You can think it over. You can cuss me out, call me a jerk, never speak to me again, or call me tomorrow and tell me you're ready to fly to Rio, but really think about it, Laura. Really think about whether my life, *our* life, is the kind of life you want."

And then he hung up. The line went dead and I sat there holding the phone, listening to silence through one ear and the storm through the other. I stared out the window through the haze of tears as the first drops of rain fell on the glass. Outside, the trees leaned in the wind, branches whipping wildly toward the north, allowing a view of the old store building. A deep crimson oleander bush caught a gust of wind and parted, revealing a faded sign painted on the ancient blocks of weathered white limestone.

I squinted to make out the words.

Crossroads, it said.

You are here.

Chapter 2

I don't know how long I sat there, staring at those words as the leaves shuddered apart and together. Rain misted the windshield, then began falling in earnest, forming tiny rivers on the glass, changing the letters from faded black to watery gray.

A gust of wind caught the car broadside, rocking it like a boat in a storm. Somewhere in me there was the thought that I should start the car and go someplace safe.

Someplace safe? What place would be safe now?

I wasn't safe. I was alone in an oncoming storm. Why wasn't I crying or screaming or beating my hands against the steering wheel? Why didn't I feel anything but numb? Why was there a voice inside me saying, *You knew this was coming. You must have known. . . .*

I tried to block the questions from my mind, taking a deep breath, holding it, then exhaling, taking another, trying to breathe my reality into the howling wind and watch it disappear. I stared at the space where the oleander bush was leaning in the wind, and I read the words over and over again.

Crossroads, Crossroads, Crossroads . . .
You are here, you are here, you are here. . . .

Those four words. Simple, yet complex. A watery

summation of things. A peeling-paint metaphor that brought back the echo of Dale's accusations.

You've been over the edge. . . .

Over the edge . . .

House-and-baby thing . . .

Come to Rio. . . .

Why didn't I want to? Was there really anything wrong with that life that had seemed so perfect? Was I just reacting to the tactless way he'd stated his priorities—job, house, car, Laura . . . in that order? Could a few words change the way I felt, or had the way I felt been changing all along? Had I been slowly erasing the picture of Dale as he was, penciling in changes that made him fit some murky, undefined need I'd had since the loss of my mother?

A droplet of ice struck the windshield like a bullet, punctuating the question. I focused outside the window again, into the present, where the rain was turning to hail, pummeling the hood of the rental car and bouncing like Ping-Pong balls onto the parking lot. The window glass rattled, raising a deafening noise, hailstones threatening to punch through any moment.

The car could get damaged. The windshield could break. The voice in my head sounded like Dale's, scornful and parental, like a reprimand.

I don't care, I thought. *I don't care. I don't. It's only a car.*

A flash of movement outside distracted me, and I jerked upright as the back door of the building blew open. Swinging free on its hinges, it hammered against the post that supported the rust-streaked metal awning overhead.

I had the strangest urge to leave the car and run inside for shelter. Would that be a safer place?

As if in answer, a single lightbulb flickered to life in the darkened doorway. A figure in a dark, hooded rain slicker stepped onto the porch and waved an arm in a circular motion, beckoning. Or was I imagining it? Tree limbs blew together like a curtain around my car, hiding the store from view. Squinting through the rain, I tried to catch a glimpse again, but the branches bent lower, narrowing like the tunnel closing around Alice as she fell into Wonderland.

Around me, the storm buffeted the car back and forth as branches scraped the paint, raising long, high-pitched squeals like fingernails on a blackboard. A hailstone struck the front window, leaving a tiny, star-shaped crack that should have alarmed me. Instead I closed my eyes and leaned my head against the headrest, drinking in air, surprised, at first, that it felt foreign in my throat.

I knew why. I had been holding my breath for months, waiting for this to happen, knowing that Dale and I were falling apart, knowing that this was coming sooner or later. Now that it had, I could finally breathe again.

Breathe deep. It'll go away in a minute.

Outside, the storm quieted, seemed farther away, the volume inching lower, lower, lower, until only the calming rhythm of the rain and the gentle melody of the wind remained, just a soft whisper, like a child trying to whistle. I took long, slow breaths, tasting air for the first time in months.

Better. That's better. My heart slowed its hurried rhythm, beat slower and slower. My mind drifted back, past the frantic events of the morning, past the tangle of funeral arrangements and arguments with Dad that had consumed the past months, past all the phone tag and hurried rendezvous with Dale, back to some quiet place I could barely remember. . . .

My body jerked fitfully, and I realized I was falling asleep. Opening my eyes drowsily, I caught a quick glimpse of the HAZMAT truck slipping past my car and disappearing around the corner of the old building. My eyes, leaden and raw, fell closed again. How long had it been since I'd slept?

Just for a minute. I'll just close my eyes for a minute. Then I'll go on to the office and straighten out the mess at the magazine. We'll put it to bed on Friday, and next week I'll go back to Richmond and figure out what to do with my life. I just have to think it through. Really think . . .

My mind slipped away and settled somewhere dark and quiet, drifting like an unmanned boat on its way to anywhere. The problem with Dale and the trouble with the magazine floated away like chaff cast upon the current. It felt good. Peaceful.

I let go and sailed away. . . .

Someone was knocking right beside my ear. Knocking on the hull of the boat. Someone out there in the water, invading the silence with knocking . . .

I flung my eyes open and jerked upright, sucking in a startled breath, then choking on the hot, damp air. Blinking the fog from my eyes, I felt reality slip under my feet as the boat became a car and the ocean a parking lot, and the peaceful breeze only a dream.

Only the knocking was real. I jerked sideways and looked toward the driver's-side window as it came again. Outside, someone leaned close, the face hidden beneath a dark rain slicker. Was I still dreaming? A nightmare, where the grim reaper appeared at my car window bearing more bad news?

"Yes?" I said, my voice hoarse, not nearly as forceful as I would have liked it to be. I realized my cheeks were wet, and I reached up and wiped them, pretending to be rubbing my eyes. The movement was clumsy, my muscles cold and sluggish. How long was I asleep?

The figure outside lifted a hand and motioned for me to roll down the window, the sleeve overhanging so that only the ends of the fingers, an old person's fingers, were visible.

I opened it partway and repeated, "Yes? Can I help you?"

"Thought it could be you needed help." The voice was a woman's, slightly clipped and unfriendly, coarse with age.

"No," I said, looking around. No cars nearby. Had she come from the old building? "I'm fine."

She leaned closer and peered at me, the end of a hawkish nose protruding from the shadows of the hood. I couldn't see her eyes, but I felt her looking into mine. Finally she straightened and said across the top of my car, "Hasselene, she says she's fine."

Someone moved near the passenger-side window. I glanced in that direction, then back at the driver's-side window, then back again. Surrounded by old people in mysterious rain slickers. This *had* to be some kind of weird dream.

In terms of dream analysis, what would something like that mean?

The second onlooker studied me like I was a Martian just landing on the planet. "How can she be fine? She's been sittin' out here for hours."

I opened the passenger-side window a crack and started to defend my fineness and apologize for trespassing on their parking lot, if indeed this was their parking lot, but what she'd said stole the words from my mouth.

Hours? I glanced at the car clock. *Four-forty-five P.M.* How could that be?

"Hours?" repeated the woman at the driver's-side window. "That can't be right. I didn't see her out here."

"Well, you know, you can't really see this spot here because of the tree," the other replied.

I sat staring at the clock, thinking, *Four-forty-five.*

Four-forty-five! The office will be closed for the day. Everyone must be wondering where I am.

Meanwhile, the conversation continued across the car, the two women completely ignoring my presence. I followed the volley with my eyes, like a spectator at a tennis match.

"Do you mean to say she's been sittin' here under this tree since the hailstorm this morning?"

"Since before the storm, Mernalene. That's what he said. He said he saw her pull up here right before the storm started."

"And here she still is. That's a shade past unusual."

"He thought it was. He said he meant to mention it earlier, that he'd passed by her when he pulled his truck around front and came in to get out of the storm. But he thought she was someone we knew, so he didn't get too concerned over it."

"I don't know her. Maybe we should call the county sheriff."

"Oh, Mernalene, for heaven's sake. Don't be such an old grouse."

"Well, could be she's lost, or deranged or something." Mernalene, the one on the driver's side, leaned close to the window again to see if I was, indeed, deranged. Her hood drew back so that I could see the dim outline of her face, which was angular, wrinkled, and ancient-looking, with high cheekbones. "Are you lost?"

I had the urge to say yes, since the alternative was deranged. *Yes, I'm lost. I don't know where to go from here.*

Tears crowded my eyes, and I wasn't even sure why. *Please don't let me start crying now.* I swallowed the lump in my throat and finally choked out the word "No" in a voice so thin I was sure she could see right through it. "I'm sorry; I pulled in to use my cell phone, and"—*and I lost my magazine cover, and my Hometime feature, and my soul mate, but other than that everything is fine*—"and I guess I fell asleep."

Water dripped from the old woman's hood and ran in tiny streams down the inside of the driver's-side window as she cocked her head incredulously. "Lands! Surely you couldn't have slept through that hailstorm. You've got cracks in your windshield, for heaven's sake. Surely a person couldn't sleep through that."

I could tell she was fairly certain I was, indeed, deranged. "I did, I guess. I was"—I searched for a word, and finally finished lamely with—"tired."

She bobbed her head to one side and gave me the same skeptical look my sixth-grade English teacher used—the look that said, *Don't feed me that line of hogwash, young lady. I know what you've been up to.*

As had always happened with Mrs. Raddle, the look dissolved all of my pretenses, and forced me to face the truth. I let my head fall back against the headrest and rubbed my forehead, muttering, "I'm just really, really tired." I was exhausted—physically, emotionally. I was teetering on the ragged edge of some breaking point I'd never experienced before.

I used to be so together. Where did all of that go?

Tears crowded my eyes and dripped down my cheeks, the taste making me wonder how long it had been since I'd eaten. "I'm sorry," I whispered, feeling idiotic. "I'm sorry. I really . . . I really should get going. . . ." Going where? To the office? Dad's retirement apartment? Home to Richmond? Where?

"Oh, Mernalene, now you've made her cry," Hasselene reprimanded from the passenger-side window. "She's in no shape to drive; that's certain enough."

"Well, I'm not blind, Hassel," Merna snapped.

"You are so, actually." Hasselene pressed an aged hand against the window, trying to touch me through the glass. "I have to apologize for my sister. Merna can't see a thing without her specs, and sometimes she doesn't see too well with them, either."

"Oh, Hassie, for heaven's sake."

Hasselene ignored her and looked at me. "Why don't you come on into the store and have a cup of coffee? Looks like you could use a little time to clear your head."

I rubbed my eyes with the heels of my hands. "I . . . I should get going." I felt the oddest temptation to say yes, to leave the familiarity of the car and follow these two women into the unknown. *If this were a dream, Laura, you'd do it. You'd go with them and see what's on the other side of that wall. . . .*

"Surely, if you been sittin' here all day, you haven't got anyplace real important to be," Hasselene countered. "You've got time to come in for a minute or two, surely."

"Oh, Hassie, let her be," Mernalene barked, anxious to be rid of me. One less deranged person taking up the parking lot. "Can't you see she wants to get on the road?"

The other woman stood back but kept her hand against the window glass, holding me there. "Cup of coffee will do her good," she countered, then added in a lower, slightly conspiratorial tone, "Can't you see she's here for a *reason*?"

I'm here because this is where my cell phone picked up. But I didn't say it. I sat there crying, acting like a complete idiot.

"I'm sorry," I choked out. "I don't . . ." I intended to say, *I don't have time to come in for coffee,* but instead I said, "I don't know what's wrong with me." *Except that I'm falling apart. Right here in some parking lot, in the middle of nowhere, on a Monday, a workday. I'm falling apart and I don't know why I can't stop it.*

Hasselene pulled back her hood. "It's a known fact around here that our coffee cures a multitude of ills." Her eyes, the clear gray of a dawning sky, met mine, beckoning. "Come on inside for a minute or two before you're on your way."

I studied her face, drawn by something I couldn't identify. There was a timelessness there, a benevolence that offered comfort. Her deep olive skin was softly wrinkled by age, the corners of her eyes and mouth marked with the evidence that she smiled often. Her cheekbones and chin were high and prominent, speaking of beauty long ago. Yet even now she was beautiful, fascinating in some way I couldn't put into words. Her eyes, so bright against her dark skin, compelled me to say yes.

"Yes," I whispered, and for reasons I couldn't explain, I unlocked the car and got out, balancing unsteadily on stiffened legs.

The rain had stopped.

Squinting at the sky through swollen eyes, I watched the dark clouds melt into the distance, trailed by a rim of puffy white thunderheads. On the nearby circle of hills, rain was still falling. From where I stood, the view seemed to stretch for miles. I imagined that I could see all the way to Austin. Where I should be. Right now.

"Oh, if you leave now, you'll only drive right back into the storm," Hasselene said, answering the unspoken question. "See, there's a storm blowing around the Spanish Rim. It won't come over our way like the one this morning did. We don't ever get weather from that direction. Our weather has to come up the gap like the storm did this morning. Other than that, we watch the storms go by for miles around."

Mernalene stepped closer to me and pointed toward the storm as she pulled back her hood. "Storms come and storms pass. Not a one of them lasts forever."

I barely heard what she said. Instead I looked at Hasselene, then back at Mernalene, then back and forth
again.

Hasselene gave me a knowing smile and patted my
arm. "Don't be alarmed, hon. We're twins."

"Oh," I replied, uncertain of why that fact shocked
me, since I was a twin myself. Lindsey and I, however,
were anything but identical, in looks or any other fashion. Perhaps it was the women's age that made their
identical looks so surprising. They must have been . . .

"Eighty-one." A twinkle lit Hasselene's eye, and she
gave a quick, knowing wink. "That's the second question folks always ask. 'Are you twins?' And then, 'How
old are you?' "

"Oh," I said again. "Well, I wasn't . . . I mean, I
didn't . . . I'm sorry for staring. I'm just not . . . with it
today. I'm sorry."

"Oh, no need for the sorries. Come on in and sit until
the storms blow around the rim. Things'll look better in
thirty minutes or so." Thunder rumbled not far away,
and lightning crackled sideways across the frothy white-
tipped thunderheads.

I jumped like a nervous cat.

"Don't worry. It won't come here," Hasselene
soothed as they slipped their hands under my elbows
like they planned to carry me into the store.

"I'm OK," I assured them, politely trying to move out
of their grasp. Their eagerness to get me inside sent
warning bells through my head. Maybe leaving the
safety of my car wasn't such a good idea. Then again, it
wasn't like I was in much danger from two little old
ladies. At the worst, they might try to sell me Avon or
religion, and that I could handle, even on my worst day.

They hung on to my elbows, guiding me through the
maze of puddles in the gravel parking lot. As we passed
the side of the building, I looked at the oleander bush.

The wind had stilled, allowing the branches to fall back into place, covering those prophetic words: *Crossroads. You are here.*

I stared into the leaves, wishing I could catch a glimpse of the letters, prove they existed. Perhaps they weren't real after all. Perhaps none of this was real.

The sisters noticed me looking at the wall, but neither said anything. From the corner of my eye, I thought I saw them exchange quick, conspiratorial smiles.

Chapter 3

As we rounded the corner of the building, I realized that my car was actually parked in the back. The front was slightly better kept, though it, too, could have been mistaken for an unused building—some ancient relic of a bygone time when country stores were built with high false fronts and shed-style porches where passersby could sit in the shade, sip sarsaparillas, play dominoes, and listen to the lazy whir of ceiling fans.

The store looked as though it had been waiting too long for those bygone days to return, the passage of time having nearly absorbed it into the landscape.

It was a place as crackled and faded as the washed-out lettering on the old, wavy plate glass windows. I squinted, trying to make out the words. *Lone Star Café,* they said, or maybe whispered was a better term. The letters were more of a whisper now, as if the place no longer merited a name. At some point, someone had squeezed in *Daily Special* before and after *Café.* The *Dai* had faded, so that the whole thing blended together to look like it read *Lonely Star Café . . . Special.* The name seemed appropriate. The high frontispiece, constructed of white limestone blocks and thick sand-colored mortar, had been overcome by a tangle of trees. The intertwining of branches and building gave the

sense that the place had been there for a very long time
with its back turned to the highway, opting instead to
serve the road less traveled.

My mind conjured images of early-day automobiles
stopping at the old-style gas pumps that now sat rusting on
the side of the parking lot, looking like they should have
been carted off to some antique shop long ago. Hanging on
a wire between the gas pumps was a rusted metal sign with
the hand-lettered words now barely visible:

> DO NOT TIE HORSES TO GAS PUMPS
> PLEASE USE HITCH RAIL

An arrow pointed toward two decaying wooden posts
near the wide front porch. Vines had wrapped around
the posts and the porch railing, like the camouflage nets
my father's army units once used to hide secret en-
campments. Even from the county road, the building
would have been hard to spot—one of those places you
had to be looking for to find. A trio of enormous live
oak trees grew in the center of the gravel parking lot,
their gnarled trunks perhaps five feet in diameter, their
limbs stretching thirty feet in all directions, forming a
thick canopy over the parking lot and hiding the building from view.

Beneath the trees, several vehicles were parked. I recognized the white HAZMAT truck, and beside that, the
Mercedes with HOUSHNTR on the license plate.

"When did she come back?" I hadn't meant to ask the
question out loud, and I wasn't sure why I asked, except
that I remembered the way she had cruised slowly past
the store looking in the windows. "I mean, I thought I
saw her pull back onto the road just before . . ." I
paused, realizing I was pointing out that I had been
asleep, or dazed, or having a breakdown in their parking
lot for hours.

"We've had people in and out of here all day," Mernalene answered, her eyes narrowing to silver strips against her weathered sandstone skin. "*Surely* you noticed that. That bad weather chased in fifteen, maybe twenty people—all came rushing in to wait out the storm, hopin' the trees would keep the hail off their cars. Had more traffic today than we usually get in a week. A real commotion. Folks rushin' in, talking on their portable phones. One fella asked me could he plug his little computer into my phone line—said he didn't think he'd even bother trying to get through the storms to Austin. Said he'd do his work over the phone with his computer, and I guess that's what he's doin'. He's been in there for more than an hour, peckin' away at that thing, tyin' up the phone." She grumbled the last words irritably.

Hasselene batted a hand at her. "Now, Merna, don't get cross. We weren't expecting anyone to call, and anyhow, he's a real nice young fella. He said he owned a couple of restaurants in Austin, and their biscuits weren't near as special as ours. He asked if I'd share the recipe and tell him what we put in our coffee to give it that little something extra."

Eyes widening, Mernalene rammed her fists onto the ample swell of her hips. "Well, you didn't *tell* him what's in the coffee, did you?"

"Of *course* not!" Gasping, Hasselene slapped a hand to her chest. "That's a secret. It's *always* been a secret. I did give him the recipe for the biscuits, though."

Her sister snorted. "Well, why'd you do that? That was Mama's recipe."

Hasselene lifted her chin indignantly, and for a moment I thought they were going to have a slapping match. I had a feeling they had forgotten I was there. "Yes, and Mama would have been happy to share it. It would have pleased her greatly to hear that young fella say her biscuits were special. *Special,* that's what he called them."

"Well, all the same, you shouldn't go handing things out to folks we don't even know, Hassel."

Crossing her arms over herself, Hasselene clenched her fists. "Well, I guess *you* can go on in there and ask for it back, Mernalene. His car's still here. Go on in there and tell him your addlebrained sister isn't fit to make a decision for herself, and you want the recipe back."

"I didn't say I wanted it back."

I took a step backward, out of the line of fire.

"Then why the devil are you fussing at me?" Hassel leaned closer to Merna, her cheeks ruddy and hot. They stared each other down inches apart.

"Well . . . well, sometimes you're too generous with folks, that's all."

"Better that than stingy."

"You let folks talk you into things."

"Guess it'd be better if I was a grouchy old woman who didn't *talk* to folks at *all.*"

Merna's eyes flared, and she shook a craggy finger at Hassel. "Just remember, they'll all be gone as soon as the interstate opens up." Her voice rose to a shriek, startling a flock of sparrows from the tree overhead. Raindrops fell from the leaves and showered around us, cooling Mernalene's temper. Sighing, she shook her head, her shoulders sagging. "They ain't gonna keep coming back because you give them a biscuit recipe or send them off with a free jar of jam."

Hassel nodded, but the corners of her lips turned upward in a private smile, as if she knew something we did not. "I know," she said quietly. "This is more excitement than we've seen in ten years."

"Reckon so." Merna started to say something else, then seemed to realize I was still there. "Can't believe *you* didn't see all the commotion."

I shrugged my shoulders, not sure what to say. Given all the activity they were describing, I couldn't believe I'd sat there all day thinking I was alone. A twang of panic went through me at the idea that I hadn't noticed a thing and could remember nothing. Had I simply been exhausted, or was it something worse? Could I be having some sort of breakdown? How could I completely miss work, sit in some parking lot in the middle of nowhere, fall asleep at the wheel and not wake up for hours? Maybe I'd blacked out. . . .

The ladies frowned at me in unison, like reflections of each other in a mirror. Like me, they seemed to be wondering, What is wrong with this woman?

Confusion must have been evident on my face, because Hasselene felt the need to reach out to me again. "We should go inside and get you a cup of our Crossroads coffee." She swished her hands forward, trying to drive me like a sheep. When I didn't move, she reached for my arm.

. . . *you didn't tell him what's in the coffee,* ran through my mind, and I jerked away without meaning to. Hasselene missed my arm and stumbled to one side, then the other, wobbling like a toppling bowling pin.

"Ohoooooooooooooh!" she gasped, stumbling backward, tripping on an overgrown vine as I reached out and tried to catch her. Wobbling three more steps, she landed hard against me, knocking me toward the tangle of grapevines and overgrown bushes in the front flower bed. I scrambled to keep my footing, trying to prevent both of us from falling into the bushes, as Hasselene screamed again, "Ohoooooooooooooh!"

And Mernalene cried, "Oh, Hassie! Oh, look out!"

I plunged rear end–first into the rain-soaked tangle of

vines, and Hasselene, who must have weighed well over a hundred and sixty pounds, landed squarely on top of me. Breath rushed from my lungs with an audible "Woooof," and I felt the vines wrapping around me like spiny tentacles, clutching my silk suit, pulling tighter, breaking our fall, until finally Hasselene and I hung suspended a foot or two off the ground.

"Oh, heavens," I heard Mernalene say from somewhere above. "Are you all right?"

From where I was pinned, I could see neither Mernalene nor sunlight, only leaves and the flowered fabric of Hasselene's dress a few inches from my face, sinking lower as she wiggled and grunted, trying to free herself, muttering, "Blamed grapevine, I ought to . . ."

Rainwater rattled loose from the vines and fell into my face. I blinked and shook my head, trying to clear my vision, wondering how my day had come to this, and thinking that I heard something small crawling in the bushes not far away.

"What happened?" a man's voice asked from somewhere above.

"Hasselene fell into the grapevines again," Merna answered flatly, like this was not an odd occurrence.

"Is she all right?" a younger woman's voice inquired, ending in a gasp that was filled with exaggerated concern.

Mernalene answered quickly, "I think so. Are you all right, Hassie?"

Hasselene snorted irritably. "Just get us out of here. These cursed vines are all hooked around our darned clothes!"

"Here, let me help you out of there." The man's voice held a hint of slow Texas drawl. A shadow blocked the sunlight, and I thought I heard the faintest laughter as he leaned closer. "I'm sorry." The tremble in his voice as well as the apology confirmed that he was trying very hard not to laugh. The shadow moved back and forth overhead, and I saw hands slipping into the vines, pulling the flowered housedress free. "Who else is in there?"

Mernalene answered for me. "The woman from the car out back. The one you asked about. We were going to bring her in for a cup of coffee, and Hasselene knocked her into the bushes."

"I hope she's all right," the younger woman said again. "Here, let me see if I can help you get these vines loose." A second shadow blocked the sunlight, and more hands grabbed the vines, working free the fabric of Hasselene's dress. "See if you can get up now."

Hasselene's weight lifted from my stomach, and I caught a full breath, then opened my mouth to tell all of them I was fine, just as the vines yanked the old woman off balance again and she landed back on my stomach, forcing the words out of me: "I'm . . . wooooof."

"Just a minute," the man drawled, choking on laughter. "Let me get this undone." There was a faint sound of fabric tearing. "Now try. Here, put your arms around my shoulders, Aunt Hassel."

I caught my breath as her weight was again removed from my stomach. A burst of sunlight followed, and I blinked blindly, twisting around so that I could yank my suit free of the vines.

"Here, let me help you," he said, and I could see him helping Hasselene to her feet and coming back for me.

"No. I'm fine," I replied, determined to salvage what little dignity I had left. Pushing one arm against the ground, I heaved myself from the bushes amid the sound of ripping fabric. One wet, dirty suit down the drain, which didn't really matter. I didn't want to ever again see the suit, or anything else that would remind me of this day.

Bending over, I retrieved my sandal, put it on as

gracefully as was possible under the circumstances, and dusted off my clothes, hoping to look moderately composed as I stood up and turned to face them.

"I think I'll live," I concluded. A whiff of breeze caught my chest and traveled the length of my stomach, and I realized there shouldn't be a breeze on my stomach, and that meant my shirt was hanging open . . . flapping in the wind with the three top buttons undone. Gasping, I snatched at it, and wrapped it around me, hoping no one had noticed.

When I glanced up, all of them were staring at me. The old ladies blushed, and so did I. Beside them HOUSHNTR was trying to seem concerned while pretending she hadn't noticed my shirt, and at the head of the pack, the HAZMAT man was standing with his hands suspended in midair, trying to look as though he hadn't been about to step in and render aid before he noticed I was only halfway dressed.

Hasselene recovered first. "Are you all right? It was all my fault. Terrible to be old and fat. You shouldn't have tried to catch me like that, should have let me fall. Oh, and my goodness, your suit. It's all ruined. You shouldn't have climbed out of there on your own. Graham could have helped you get loose." She glanced at HAZMAT as he lowered his hands and stuck them in his pockets.

Wait for the HAZMAT man to save me? Not on your life. "I'm fine," I assured them, wishing I could wiggle my nose and disappear. Anything to get out of this ridiculous situation. "Really."

We stood there in silence, none of us able to think of the right thing to say after a rescue from marauding grapevines. The door slammed on the front porch, and a man stepped out. The five of us turned toward him in unison, grateful for the distraction.

He gave Hasselene and me a quizzical look, then

shrugged and proceeded down the steps. "Guess I'd better get on the road now," he said, like he couldn't see the bloody scratches on Hasselene's arms, or me holding together my soggy, torn suit. "Thanks for letting me plug my laptop in." He waved with his computer case. "And thanks for the biscuit recipe."

"You're welcome," Hasselene chirped, giving her sister a self-satisfied smirk. "Stop in again sometime."

Nodding, he opened the door to his SUV and set his briefcase inside. "I'd still like to know what's in that coffee."

"Not a chance," Mernalene grumbled, and her sister elbowed her in the ribs.

HOUSHNTR took a step backward and hurried toward the SUV. "Let me give you my card," she said, pulling a silver cardholder from her suit pocket. "I'd be happy to show you those commercial properties in Killeen, if you decide you're interested. Killeen's a fast-growing city. Lots of retail potential there." Her words jingled like a string of bells, the syllables running together on a thick lace of flirtation. "Lots of young army families, and Lord knows, they don't cook."

The man nodded, taking her card. "Thanks." He gave her a quick smile that said he was more interested in a date than real estate. "I'll be in touch."

"Good." She clearly realized he was interested. In something, anyway. "Call me if you need anything."

"I'll do that." Climbing into his SUV, he started the engine and made a loop around the parking lot, slowing at the far end to look into the trees, studying something there.

Shading her eyes, HOUSHNTR watched him as she walked back to us. She stopped beside HAZMAT and angled her posture slightly toward him, ready to resume some unfinished conversation. He didn't seem to notice.

I realized he was looking at me. His eyes, a deep,

ocean-water blue, held a look of concern that drew me in. "You're a little scratched up." He motioned to the side of my face, and I realized there was a soreness there I hadn't noticed right away. "Can I get you something for that?"

I winced as I touched the dampness of fresh scratches. "No. I'm fine. Really," I answered, embarrassed by all the fuss. "This'll be hard to explain at work tomorrow."

HAZMAT smiled slightly. "Just tell them you were in the tornado." The smile lessened the severity of his short, military-style hair.

I found myself smiling back. There was something I liked about him—something I couldn't quite put a finger on.

There was something HOUSHNTR liked about him, as well. She moved a little closer, so that the conversation became a threesome.

Neither of us turned to her. "That might work." For a moment I forgot to be embarrassed, or stressed, or anything else.

Hasselene leaned close to examine my cheek, breaking the spell. "Oh, my goodness, you did scratch your face. Come on inside and let me put something on those. My goodness, I'm sorry. I'm so clumsy these days."

Holding my shirt together, I backed away. "No, really. I'm all right. I've got to get going."

"But you haven't had any coffee yet," Hasselene and Mernalene protested in unison, and then Hasselene finished, "At least come in for some coffee."

"No, really," I said, moving my free hand back and forth in front of myself like a referee signaling *No play, no play.* . . . "Thank you, and everything, but I really have to get back to work."

Hasselene met my gaze with concern. "Are you sure you're all right?" She knew I wasn't.

"Yes," I lied. This day had been as far from *all right* as

it could get. I couldn't even see *all right* from here. "I'm fine. Thanks again for worrying about me, but I'm fine." Spinning around, I started across the parking lot before they could take me prisoner again. Behind me, I heard the conversation continuing.

"Guess I'd better be getting on the road, too, Aunt Hass," HAZMAT said.

"Oh, must you?" Hasselene replied. "We'll be serving up dinner soon. It's meat loaf night. You haven't stayed for dinner even once since you've been back in town. You used to love our meat loaf when you were little. Remember, Punky? You could eat a half a meat loaf all by yourself. You were such a round little thing."

Punky gave a quick, embarrassed cough. "Can't tonight. I've got a couple asbestos inspections to do in Austin yet. Thanks for the coffee and the pie, and lunch."

"Oh, goodness, we're glad to have you back here again. Thanks for putting a board in that windowpane that got broken by the hail." To my surprise that was Mernalene's voice, sounding unusually warm and affectionate.

"That's all right," he replied. "You save me a slice of that meat loaf, Aunt Merna, and I'll come by in the morning to put a new piece of glass in the window."

The sound of traffic on the highway masked the ladies' reply. I realized I had stopped a few feet short of my car, listening. I couldn't imagine why.

Shaking my head at myself, I walked the last few steps, climbed into my car, started the engine, and circled the parking lot, ready to leave the Crossroads behind. But which way to go—right toward work, or left toward Killeen and home? It was after five o'clock. Most of the staff would be gone from the office by the time I got there, and even if they weren't, I wasn't ready to face the office. The entire staff already resented my

being there, and now I'd been absent all day without explanation. It wasn't like me to do such a thing, especially
when we were up against deadline. Normally, when I
traveled on jobs, my mind was on the *job*. I was focused,
excited, turned on about taking some small publication
that Landerhaus Publishing had bought, and creating an
upscale glossy worthy of the Landerhaus name. The bigger the challenge, the better. I loved it—every part of it,
from coming up with a new look for the magazine to
going over the advertising revenues. It really didn't matter how many hours of overtime it took, or how little
sleep I got. When you love something, you just dig in
and run on adrenaline.

So why was I exhausted now? Where was the rush I
usually got when we were close to putting out the first
issue? Why was I dreading going back to the office?
What was different this time? Was it just the problems
with my father and a lingering grief over Mom's death?

Maybe it didn't matter what caused it. I had to make
sure it didn't happen again. If I fell apart, *Texcetera*
would too, and there would be hell to pay when I got
back to Richmond. I wouldn't be their miracle girl anymore. Miracle girls have to keep their heads together.

I waited for a break in the traffic, my mind already
clicking into gear. When I got home, I'd call the office
and leave a voice-mail message, give some vague explanation for my absence so that no one would be worried
about me. I'd tell them to expect me first thing in the
morning, give the impression that things were right on
track. I'd call my friend Collie, and see if Kristi had gotten in touch with her about using the picture of the first
family as our cover photo. I'd also find out whether Collie had any features from her newspaper that we could
use as our Hometime column. Collie was always digging
up good stories about people and places in the hill
country—"Texas fluff," she called it. She had a flair for

fluff, which was pretty funny, considering that I had given her that first Texas fluff assignment, and she had argued bitterly that she was a D.C. reporter, *Washington, D.C.,* she'd said over the phone. *D.C. stories, you know, real stories?*

And now there she was living in San Saline, Texas, happily making a living writing small-town news and Texas fluff.

Hitting the gas, I pulled into the line of commuters heading toward Killeen. At the intersection, the stop sign shook back and forth, appearing almost human in the late-afternoon shadows, disappointed that I was leaving. I felt a twinge of regret, a vague sensation I couldn't put into words, even in the privacy of my own mind.

I wish I would have gone in for coffee, I thought. *I wonder what's in the coffee. . . .*

I remembered the sadness in Mernalene's eyes, and the loneliness in her words: *They'll all be gone as soon as the interstate opens up. They ain't gonna keep coming back because you give them a biscuit recipe or send them off with a free jar of jam.*

Drumming my fingers against the steering wheel, I looked at the old store in my rearview mirror and considered taking a left at the intersection, going back long enough for a cup of coffee. Long enough to postpone the call to the office and my nightly argument with Dad, and all of the questions about Dale and the rest of my life.

Sitting at the Crossroads sipping a cup of coffee sounded good compared to all of that. It sounded . . . quiet, peaceful. *It's a known fact around here that our coffee cures a multitude of ills.* Oh, how I wished there were such a drink.

"Cut it out," I muttered to myself. "Get a grip." The

guy behind me punctuated the sentence with a long blast on his horn that said, *Nowww!*

Get a grip. *Now,* I told myself, then hit the gas and left the Crossroads behind.

Chapter 4

THE cell phone started ringing as soon as I reached the outskirts of civilization. I answered, my mind rushing ahead, trying to conjure up something to say if it was someone from the *Texcetera* office.

"Hello?" a woman said.

I let out a breath. "Yes? This is Laura Draper."

"I'm trying to reach Hardy Draper," the woman on the other end of the line said.

I cringed. If someone was trying to reach my father through my cell phone, that could mean only one thing: He wasn't answering the phone at the farm again. "He isn't here. Can you tell me what this is about?"

"This is Hillside Pharmacy. We wanted to let him know we still have his Coumadin refill waiting here. The pharmacist was concerned because the old bottle should have run out by now."

Dad! I hollered in my mind, because in our minds was the only way we were ever allowed to holler at the sergeant major. "I called to refill that three days ago. He hasn't come to pick it up yet?" Which meant he'd been off his blood thinner for three days and never said a thing about it to me.

"No, ma'am. We've tried to call him several times." She paused, and then added, "I'm sorry," like she understood what I was dealing with. "We close in twenty minutes, if you want to come by and get it."

I rubbed my forehead, exhausted. "All right. It'll probably take me about that long to get there. Please don't close up before I get there."

"We'll be here until six-thirty," she repeated, meaning, of course, that if I got there at six-thirty-one, I was out of luck.

At six-twenty-nine, I raced into the pharmacy parking lot. The clerk was locking the security bars on the drive-through when I pulled up to the window. Frowning at me, she considered whether to open for me or not, then slid the window up behind the bars and said, "May I help you?"

"I'm here to pick up the prescription for Hardy Draper."

Relieved that I wasn't asking for anything new, she grabbed Dad's prescription off the counter and handed it to me through the bars. Hurriedly, I paid the tab and pulled out of the pharmacy, heading toward a showdown with Dad.

The drive to the farm wasn't long. As I pulled onto the gravel road, I began preparing myself for another argument. I'd tell him he'd been out of blood thinner for three days, and he'd argue that I was wrong, and then he'd clench his jaw and turn away and tell me he didn't need it anyway, and let out a string of cusswords about doctors. The evening would degenerate from there, while I tried to get him to eat something and hoped to interest him in something on TV, and he sat listless in his chair, staring at the wall.

The muscles in my back tightened, sending tiny spasms up my spine. *I can't deal with this today. I just can't.*

The cell phone rang on the seat beside me. Startled, I grabbed it and barked, "Hello?" into the receiver.

"Wow, what's wrong with you?" my sister, Lindsey, replied.

I sighed, stretching my neck to one side and then the other, working the kinks out. "Nothing. I'm on my way to Dad's."

"Ohhhh," she said, as if that explained everything. "You going to cram some Coumadin down his throat? He called this afternoon and told me he was out of his blood thinner." She gave a little huff into the phone. "Like there's something I can do about it from a thousand miles away in Denver."

"Geez," I muttered, a spear of worry needling me. "He's really lost it. You've been back home in Denver for a month and a half. Do you suppose he forgot you're not here anymore?"

Lindsey gave a sarcastic little laugh. "He didn't forget, Laura. He's only trying to manipulate everyone. He wants us all to be right there, watching his little pity party."

One thing about Lindsey, you could always count on her to say exactly what she thought. She'd always been that way. She was the tall, athletic, dark-haired twin who took after my father, and I was the quiet, studious blond-haired one, only five-foot-four. Lindsey never took any lip off anybody, not even my father. And, of course, he loved that about her. Lindsey could do more with Dad than my brothers or I could, but Lindsey wasn't inclined to let family problems interfere with her work at the Colorado Museum of Natural History.

"Lindsey, that's kind of harsh." I didn't know why I was bothering. Lindsey's mind was made up. She'd tried pandering to Dad for two weeks after Mark helped him move to the retirement home in Texas; then she'd thrown up her hands and gone home. "Dad's having a hard time right now."

Lindsey laughed ruefully. "Dad's just yanking your

chain, Laura, and he's going to keep doing it as long as you keep hanging around there playing nursemaid."

Grinding my teeth together, I clenched the steering wheel, trying to keep my temper. Lindsey, Mark, and Daniel were all in agreement that what Dad needed was a dose of tough love. Their contention was that if he had to get off the couch and take care of himself, he would. But I was the one seeing Dad every day, and I knew what kind of shape he was in. "For God's sake, Lindsey, he can't even keep himself fed and his clothes clean."

The phone fuzzed as I went down a hill, so all I heard was ". . . telling you, he's going to stay that way as long as you let him. You need to go home, Laura. All of this isn't good for you, and it isn't good for Dad. You both have to let Mom go and get on with life. Real life. Back in Richmond."

I started to tell her about the phone call from Dale, but instead said, "I can't go home right now. I'm at *Texcetera* at least through next week."

Lindsey was in the mood to argue. "Why'd you let them send you down to Texas, anyway?" She emphasized *Texas* as if it were a dirty word. Lindsey still resented the fact that Dad had chosen to move to Texas, near Mom's grave and the old farm, rather than into the quaint retirement center she had picked out for him in Denver.

"You know what, Lindsey?" My patience snapped like a frayed thread. "I don't want to talk about this right now. It's been a horrible day and I'm not in the mood to analyze my life, all right?"

The line was silent for a minute. Lindsey wasn't used to me biting her head off. "Well . . . what's wrong?"

Raw emotion prickled in my throat, and for a moment I couldn't talk. Finally I said, "Dale and I had a . . ." I wasn't sure what to call it and finally finished with, "A fight."

"You and Dale?" Lindsey was clearly stunned. "You mean a real fight-fight, or just a should-we-go-for-Chinese-or-Italian-takeout fight?"

I laughed. Lindsey could always make me laugh. "No, the real kind. The I-think-we're-over kind." I realized there should have been more emotion in those words.

"Laura, that can't be." Lindsey's voice was filled with disbelief. "You and Dale are the perfect couple. You two never fight."

"We never *see* each other, at least not lately," I corrected. "It's easy to avoid fighting when you're both gone all the time."

Silence held the other end of the line as Lindsay tried to digest the news. "What was the fight about?"

I bit my lip. "A lot of things." The last thing I wanted to do was tell Lindsey that Dale had accused me of being jealous of her and Collie. "Lindsey, listen, I'm almost at the farm, so I'd better go."

"Oh." Lindsey sounded reluctant, like she wanted to fix things from a thousand miles away. "Well, listen, call me later if you want to talk, or want to let me know about Dad, or have a general man-bashing session, all right?"

I chuckled. Since Lindsey's divorce five years ago, she didn't miss many opportunities for man bashing. "A minute ago you were telling me what a great guy Dale was."

Scoffing into the phone, Lindsey said, "That was before he made you cry. I might have to classify him in the same genus with all of the rest of them now."

"I think he probably fits there." I pictured Lindsey in her office at the museum, surrounded by paleontology charts, sticking Dale's picture squarely in the same category with the dinosaurs.

"All right, then, he's officially a lower life-form."

I chuckled again. Something about Lindsey's no-

nonsense approach to life made me feel better. In Lindsey's world, things were always black-and-white. No messy gray areas. I wished I could be more like her.

"OK, Linds," I said, "I have to get out and open the farm gate now, so I'm going to sign off. Dad has the place locked up again."

"And he isn't supposed to do that either," she reminded me. "In case he has one of his heart spells and the ambulance needs to get in."

"I know." I sighed.

Lindsey wasn't ready to quit. "You know, if he can figure out how to call me here in Colorado, and navigate through the museum's automated phone system, he can get to the pharmacy for his medicine and remember to leave the front gate unlocked. He does this stuff on purpose."

"Could be." Lindsey did have a point, but she wasn't the one watching Dad waste away. She wasn't the one who'd found him hiding out at the farm, not interested in food, or the TV, or anything else, waiting to follow Mom to the grave.

"Don't let him get to you, Laura."

"I won't." But I knew I would. The minute I arrived, Dad would start manipulating, and I would start dancing like a puppet on his strings. "See you later, Lindsey."

Setting the cell phone down, I climbed out of the car and fiddled with my keys, singling out the one for the padlock on Dad's front gate. Slipping the key into the lock, I turned it to the left. Nothing. I tried turning it to the right. Nothing. I yanked on the lock. Nothing.

A sound between a sob and a growl started somewhere deep inside me and found its way to my lips. "Dad!" Bracing my foot against the gate, I jerked on the chain, once, twice, three times, foolishly hoping that the lock would open or the chain would break. Of course it didn't, and I knew why. "He's changed the lock again,"

I muttered, yanking my keys out of the lock and dropping them in my pocket. "I can't believe it. He's changed the lock again."

Clawing my fingers into my hair, I stood for a moment, looking down the quarter-mile driveway to the old farmhouse that was now only a derelict relic used for my brothers' occasional hunting trips. I considered getting back in the car and driving to the condo, turning off the phone, climbing into bed, pulling the covers over my head, and ignoring all of it.

Maybe Lindsey's right. Maybe Dad is just manipulating me.

I turned around and walked to the car.

Maybe he needs to be left alone, to be forced to take care of himself.

Sliding into the driver's seat, I put the key into the ignition, started to turn it, then let go, then started to turn it again, then let go.

Maybe I'm hurting by helping.

I looked out the window at the house, squinting through the long evening shadows.

But maybe he's lying on the floor, alone, having a heart attack.

Yanking the keys out of the ignition, I muttered a string of curse words worthy of a truck driver as I grabbed my purse and the pharmacy bag, and headed toward the gate.

"I can't believe this," I muttered, climbing over the gate like a trained monkey. "I really can't believe this. This is ridiculous. Lindsey is right. When I get down there, I'm going to . . ."

I continued muttering bitterly to myself as I half walked and half slid down the slope of the gravel driveway, my purse clutched against my chest. By the time I reached the house, I had worked up a full head of steam.

Pausing, I counted to ten when I reached the front porch. Was that the television I heard inside?

When I opened the door, the house was silent. "Dad?" I called, even though I knew where I would find him—in his recliner. And how I would find him—lights turned out, no television, staring at the wall.

Which was exactly where and how he was when I stepped into the living room. He didn't turn to look at me, just acknowledged my presence with the slight raising of an eyebrow.

Most days I ignored that. I knew he only did it to aggravate me, and I was determined not to play his game.

"Dad," I said, more irritably than I meant to. "You've got to quit locking the gate. I had to walk all the way down here, and if an ambulance needs to come or anything, they won't be able to get in."

Pulling on the blanket wrapped around his shoulders, he cocooned even tighter, despite the lingering heat of the afternoon. "I don't need any ambulance." Stubbornly, he tipped his chin up and away from me.

"Well, that's good. Glad to hear it," I bit out, my usual annoyed-Dad-with-cheerfulness voice failing, and the stress of the day coming out instead. "But you've still got to quit locking the gate."

A spark lit Dad's eye. I could see it from across the room. It meant that he knew he was getting to me. "I can lock my gate if I want to. I don't want people getting in here."

I laughed ruefully, "What people?" then immediately wanted to pound myself in the head. He wanted an argument and I was giving it to him. "There aren't any *people* here. There's only you and me. I had to walk down from the gate with your Coumadin prescription." Crossing the room, I stood by the TV, trying to force him to look at me. "I shouldn't have to walk in from the gate, Dad. I shouldn't. I'm sick of it. Quit changing the damned lock."

Dad craned his head and rolled his eyes back like an egret zeroing in on a fish. I thought he might say something about my torn suit, but instead he barked, "You watch your mouth in this house, young lady."

Any other time, the absurd statement and the term *young lady* would have made me laugh, but this time I hit the end of my chain with a twang. "You know what? I don't have to!" I screamed. "And I don't have to go pick up your prescriptions, and I don't have to deliver all your laundry and groceries, and try to make sure you get something for supper, and come here every evening to watch you sit there in the dark in your chair, and . . ." I set the prescription on top of the TV with the intention of pointing a finger at him and adding a few more things to the list, but something stopped me. The something was warmth. A warm spot on the top of the old console television. I turned to look at it, holding my hand there a moment longer to make sure.

All at once I realized that what I'd heard coming in really *was* the TV. Dad wasn't sitting in the dark all day waiting for me to come. He was *watching TV*. And down there beside his chair, poking out from beneath the skirting, was . . . *a pizza box?* Where did he get a pizza box?

Dad's just yanking your chain, Laura. Oh, God, Lindsey was right. Dad was leading me around like a puppy on a leash.

I opened my mouth to say something, then closed it, then finally said, "You know what? I'm not going to argue with you. It's been a horrible day and I'm tired. Here's your medicine. There's lunch meat in the refrigerator. Find yourself some dinner. It's been a horrible"—tears pressed my eyes, and I swallowed hard, determined not to cry in front of him—"horrible day," I finished, feeling betrayed and hurt, the same way I had felt when Dale called my cell phone that morning.

"I'm going home." I turned and walked across the room, noting his wide eyes and his mouth hanging agape. I'd finally managed to shock him into silence. I stopped at the door and pointed a finger at him, something I had never dared to do before. "And if you lock that gate one more time, I'm going to search that barn and gather every one of those old locks and throw them in the trash!"

Dad coughed like he had a chicken bone stuck in his throat, and for once he couldn't think of a response. At least not quickly enough. Turning away, I headed out the door, victorious. From the rack on the porch I grabbed the gate key off the hook where Dad always kept it, and headed up the driveway.

The sense of victory faded as I trudged back up the hill to the car, stopping periodically to empty pea gravel from my sandals. In the quiet of the evening, the events of the day played in my head like a movie. The day seemed unbelievably long, impossibly complicated, completely unreal.

Exhaustion washed slowly through my body, slipping over my skin like the long shadows of the live oaks. I didn't want to talk to anyone or think about anything. All I wanted to do was go back to the condo, lock the door, go to sleep, and ignore all of it.

But when I got to the condo, the message light on the answering machine was flashing like crazy. I stood with the doorknob in my hand, not wanting to go in.

The sound of voices nearby forced me inside. The other residents of the retirement village were always coming by, bringing casseroles and cookies and sympathy. They asked after Dad with sad, worried faces. They told me I had to get Dad out, get him involved in activities, get him back into life, as if I had some kind of magic to make that happen.

Skirting the living room, I pressed the button on the

answering machine, then turned up the volume and started down the hall to the bedroom to change clothes.

"You have eleven messages," the machine announced gleefully.

"Great," I muttered, imagining that the office had been calling all day long, trying to find me.

I wasn't prepared for Dale's voice on the phone. "Laura, this is Dale. It's about nine A.M. your time. Need to catch you today. I'll try your cell phone." My mind flashed to the conversation with Dale as the machine played on, "Ms. Draper? This is Kristi. You must be gone already this morning. I'll try your cell phone."

"Mrs. Draper? This is Marleen McCormick, with Addison Realty. I was calling to see if we could push our appointment to look at houses back about an hour next Friday. Could you and your husband make it at about three? Let me know."

Me and my husband . . . Something twisted inside me. Unbuttoning my suit, I started down the hall, trying to shed the day like the ruined clothes.

The answering machine continued on. "Laura, this is Collie. I called to—" The machine beeped suddenly, cutting off the message and starting the next one.

"Laura, this is Kristi. The power just—" Again the message cut off, the machine gave a long beep, and the electronic voice announced, "End of messages."

"No!" I growled, half running, half hopping to hit the replay button as I slipped off my slacks.

The machine beeped and cheerfully said, "No messages."

I faced it as if it were a lion, and I was a lion tamer. "No!" I scolded, pounding the button. "No! No! No! You can't lose my messages. Not today."

The machine merely chirped, "No . . . essages," with a little skip in the middle as I hammered the button one more time.

Slamming both fists on the countertop, I tried to imagine what messages the machine had lost. I wished I had Kristi's home number. I wasn't even sure where she lived. *Maybe I should get dressed and head for the office, try to get things under control before the staff shows up tomorrow.*

I glanced out the window, thinking. Three gray-haired golfers were on the eighteenth green, staring at me hammering on the answering machine in my underwear.

I spun around and headed down the hall to the bathroom. No matter what, I wasn't going outside again. This day was definitely cursed. I was going to stay home, where nothing else could happen.

Slipping my robe on, I leaned close to the bathroom mirror and examined the red spot on my cheek from my altercation with the vines.

You're a little scratched up. The deep, resonant sound of HAZMAT's voice was so clear that I stopped and looked over my shoulder. Then I turned back to the mirror, staring at myself, the scene at the Crossroads playing out in my mind.

I could imagine what I must have looked like. A nutcase, for sure.

Rubbing the bridge of my nose, I pictured us in the bushes, me hanging suspended by my suit, Hasselene floundering around like an overturned turtle.

I started to chuckle. My mother always said that when things go wrong, all you can do is laugh or cry, and it's better to laugh. If she could have heard the story of the Crossroads, we would have both laughed until we cried.

I laughed with her in spirit, looking into dark blue eyes and an oval-shaped face with a smattering of freckles barely visible on the bridge of the nose. There in the mirror was my mother, smiling, young, as I remembered her from my childhood, when she probably wasn't any older than I was now, but had already celebrated seventeen anniversaries with my father, raised my two brothers into their teenage years, and was beginning all over again with the surprise arrival of twin girls.

Life takes some unexpected turns, she used to say.

I realized the phone was ringing in the other room, and the answering machine wasn't picking up. I didn't feel like talking to anybody, but the phone stubbornly kept ringing, so finally I walked down the hall and answered with a "Hello" that sounded less than welcoming.

"Hello?" The male voice was familiar, a hint of Texas accent stretching *hello* into almost three syllables.

"Yes?" I sounded hoarse, tired. "Can I help you?"

There was a long pause, and I wondered if the caller was trying to decide whether he had dialed a wrong number. Finally he cleared his throat and said, "I . . . think I met you this afternoon . . . at the Crossroads?"

The HAZMAT guy? I stood staring blankly at the wall, not quite sure how to answer. I hadn't given him my name. I hadn't given any of them my name. How would he know where to find me tonight?

A finger of apprehension crawled up my spine. "Yes?" I said again.

He seemed to understand the hidden meaning behind my silence. "This must seem really strange."

"A little," I replied, feeling suddenly at ease, though I couldn't imagine why. *The way my day is going, he's probably an insane stalker, or . . .*

"I have a checkbook here belonging to a Hardy Draper. We found it by the bushes in front of the Crossroads store right after you left. We tried to come after you, but you were already gone."

Or a nice man who happened to find the checkbook I didn't even know I had dropped.

"We figured it was your husband's or something."

"My father's," I rushed. "It's my father's checkbook. Sometimes I carry it when I'm shopping for him."

"Oh." He sounded pleased, and for an instant I thought he was trying to flirt with me.

"I'm not married," I heard myself say; then I thumped myself in the forehead, trying to kick my brain into gear. What in the world was I doing?

A noise that sounded like construction machinery rumbled on the other end of the line. He covered the phone for a moment and spoke to someone, then came back on, and I could tell he needed to wrap up the conversation.

"Well, listen," he said. "I'm sorry to bother you so late, but I didn't want you to be worried." He paused, then added, "About the checkbook."

"Thanks," I said, then felt the need to add, "Really." I rested the phone on my shoulder, suddenly wishing I could keep him on the line. I wasn't sure why.

He chuckled, a deep, throaty sound that made my skin flush like I'd slipped into a hot bath. "You looked like you had enough to worry about."

I groaned, then, to my surprise, laughed softly. "It wasn't my best day."

He chuckled again, a friendly, comforting sound. "I suspected that." The line was silent for a moment; then he added, "Everything all right now?"

"Yeah," I replied, but the laughter in my throat was tightening into a knot of tears. "Fine."

"Good," he said. Some unspoken nuance in that single word told me he didn't believe me. He seemed to think for a moment, then sighed and said, "I wondered—" A loud clang in the background interrupted his sentence, and he covered the phone and spoke to someone again, then finally said, "Well, listen, I'll take this checkbook by the Crossroads in the morning and leave it there for you."

"That would be great. Thanks." I sounded as alone as I felt.

"No problem." He paused, reluctant to hang up.

I wasn't ready for him to hang up. His voice was like a hand reaching through the darkness to pull me out. I knew as soon as it was gone, I would be on my own in the storm again. "Wait, I . . ." I began, then forgot what I was going to say, and finally finished halfheartedly with, "I didn't catch your name. I'd . . . I'd like to know who to thank."

"Graham." I liked the sound of his voice. "Graham Keeton."

"Thank you, Graham Keeton," I said.

"Not a problem," he repeated. "Have a good night . . . ummm . . ."

"Laura." I filled in the blank.

"Have a good night, Laura."

"Thanks," I whispered, choking on the tears in my throat. "You too." Then I slid the phone away from my ear and held it against my chest for a minute, trying to ward off the loneliness I knew was coming.

Walking to the couch, I sank into the cushions, wrapping the afghan around me. It smelled like Mom—the faint, comforting scent of perfume and white flour and Tide. That was how Mom always smelled. God, I missed her. No matter how much time went by, I continued to miss her—not so much every moment of the day now, but in quiet moments, the pain was intense. Even at thirty-six years old, all grown-up and independent, without her I felt like an orphan in the universe.

Pulling the afghan up to my face, I drank in the soft scent, closing my eyes. My thoughts began to drift into calm, quiet water.

Have a good night, Laura, Mom's voice whispered into the still air.

Strange. That was the same thing Graham Keeton said to me on the phone....

Have a good night, Laura, I heard him say as I let go of the day and floated into sleep again.

I dreamed about the Crossroads. The day was clear and quiet. The air was filled with the soft scent of honeysuckle and the music of a brook nearby.

Dimly, I felt my lips twitch into a smile, and I burrowed into the pillows, unwilling to be awakened again. It felt good to be back....

Chapter 5

THE sense of peace lasted until morning. Opening my eyes, I blinked drowsily at the clock, then jerked upright and looked again.

"Six-fifteen!" I gasped, my throat raw and dry. "Six-fifteen!" I never slept past five A.M. Actually, since coming to Texas, I hadn't slept much at all.

Stumbling to my feet, I ran to the bedroom, grabbed a red pantsuit from the closet, and threw it on the bed, muttering, "I can't be late again."

With that last sentence came the realization that I hadn't been late the day before; I had been nonexistent. AWOL. I could only imagine what all of them must have been thinking yesterday when hour after hour went by and I didn't show. Kristi must have been panicked.

I pictured Kristi trying to keep things under control at the *Texcetera* office, taking messages, telling everyone, "Oh, I'm sure she'll be here any minute," frantically trying to call me on the cell phone, wondering if I'd been in a car accident, or even caught in the tornado.

Should I try to come up with something to tell her— some story about getting caught in the storm—or just go into the office and try to play it low-key? The staff here didn't know me well enough to know that I would *never* be out of contact for an entire day right before deadline. I was always where I was supposed to be when I was supposed to be there, and I was always on top of a deadline. I was back at work the day after my mother's funeral, because we were sending a magazine to press.

A cold sweat broke over my body and something that felt like panic started in my stomach and bolted through my body. In the cold light of morning, I realized how out of character yesterday had been, and what a monumental screwup it was. *This has got to stop,* I told myself. *Get it together and get going.*

Grabbing the cordless phone, I hurried to the bathroom, punching in Dad's number as I went. I hurriedly put on makeup as the line connected.

He answered on the first ring, sounding anxious.

"Hi, Dad. It's Laura."

"Well, where are ya?" He was trying to be a curmudgeon, but something in his tone that told me he'd been waiting for me to call. I guessed maybe after last night he thought I wouldn't.

"I'm at the condo. I have to be at work early this morning, so I'm checking on you by phone."

Dad was silent. Every morning for the past month, I'd gone by to make sure he had something for breakfast and to try to talk him into coming back to the condo.

"Make sure to take your pills," I went on. "Especially your Coumadin. You've been off it for a few days, and that's not good."

"I don't know which one is the Coumadin." His voice started in a bark and ended in a thin, pitiful sigh. "I can't read the darned print on these labels." He punctuated the sentence with an audible *humph.* I could picture him slumping back in his chair with his arms crossed over his chest.

My head started to pound. "Yes, you can, Dad. You know which medicines are which. You can read the bottles fine."

"Cannot. They're too small. Can't open them either. Got arthritis in my hands this morning. Don't need all these medicines anyway." Which translated to, *If you don't come hand-feed them to me, I'm not going to take my pills.*

I stopped putting on my eyeliner and stared at myself in the mirror, my hands clenching and unclenching on the edges of the counter. I'm not sure what happened at that point, but I feel sure that my skin grew deeper and deeper red, and giant drops of sweat squeezed from my forehead and ran onto the floor, and steam exploded from my ears. I heard the whistling sound that Elmer Fudd hears when Bugs Bunny has run him around the rabbit hole one too many times.

The next thing I knew, I was hollering into the phone, "Well, then ask the pizza-delivery boy to read them for you when you call for a pizza this afternoon!" I pressed the disconnect button and slammed the phone down on the counter, then picked up my eyeliner and violently lined one angry blue eye and then the other. Grabbing my hairbrush, I combed it through my hair, which was in haphazard crinkles from sleeping wadded up on the sofa. No sense trying to style it into the usual shoulder-length bob. I'd traveled so much in the past couple months, it had grown long and out of shape and lost the highlights I used to be so careful to keep up with.

I pulled my hair back in a clip and frowned at myself in the mirror. I looked tired and uninspired—*thin,* Mom would have said. *Laura, you're too thin and pale. Are you eating all right?* Then she would have said, *Are you happy, honey?*

She was always worried about whether I was happy, and I never could figure out why. I'd answered her question many times over the years. *Yes, Mom, I'm happy. I really am. Why do you keep asking me that?*

She would only shrug and shake her head, as if she saw something inside me that I couldn't see myself.

Now, looking in the mirror, I caught a glimpse of the lost soul Mom saw in there. I looked into the face of that tired, uninspired, thirty-something woman in the mirror and wondered, *Where does she go from here?* Unfortunately, the mirror didn't answer. Mirrors only reflect what you already know. And I didn't have any answers.

Turning away, I left the bathroom, and my mind began spinning, rushing ahead to the day and everything that needed to be done. Thursday, and there was so much to do before the magazine went to press late Friday.

"I can do this," I muttered, slipping into my favorite red pantsuit and heading for the door. In my red suit, I could do anything.

I was halfway to the interstate before I remembered that the interstate was closed. At least, I assumed it was still closed, and a quick check of the local radio station confirmed it. Mentally, I considered the various other routes available, and which would be the fastest.

Then I remembered the checkbook at the Crossroads. I remembered the conversation with Graham Keeton, and Hasselene and Mernalene, and the bushes, and all the crazy things that had happened the day before. I found myself smiling at the ridiculousness of it all as I turned the car around and headed toward FM 47-B.

My cell phone rang, and I answered it, a hint of laughter in my voice.

"Well, you sound amazingly cheerful for an editor with no magazine cover and a gaping hole in your Hometime feature." I recognized Collie's voice immediately. Like a typical reporter, she cut right to the chase.

I chuckled. Something about the way Collie said it made my predicament seem funny. "So I guess Kristi called you."

"Yeah, she e-mailed me this morning. She said you want my picture of the first family at the ranch for the first *Texcetera* cover." She seemed surprised. "I'm honored."

"I'm desperate," I admitted.

"Well, in that case, I'm not so honored," Collie quipped.

I chuckled again. "You know I didn't mean it like that, Coll."

"Yeah, yeah, you only love me when you can't get another date."

Pausing for a moment, I checked for oncoming traffic as I pulled onto FM 47-B. "You know I love you, Coll. We need to get together before I leave Texas. I want to see the baby, and besides, I could use some girlfriend time."

Collie didn't answer right away, and in the background I heard the muffled sound of her baby daughter fussing. "Sorry about that," Collie said when she came back. "They learn young that if they really want something, they should make noise when you're trying to talk on the phone. So, anyway, is something wrong?"

"No." *Not something, everything.* "It's a long story." And I wasn't ready to get into it this morning, not even with Collie, who had been my best friend since college.

Collie waited to see if I would expound, then finally said, "Well, listen, you can tell me about it over lunch. I have to come into Austin today for a doctor's appointment, so I thought I'd just come by your office and bring the picture."

"Oh, Collie, you're the best." I felt better already. There is something about knowing you have one true friend that makes even the hardest day easier to bear.

"I know," she quipped. "It's lucky that your assistant e-mailed me this morning before I left."

"This morning?" I repeated, realizing Collie had said

that earlier. "You mean she just got in touch with you about the cover this morning? I asked her to do that yesterday."

"Don't panic, Laura." Collie was quick to pick up on the edge in my voice. "She said she would have gotten in touch with me yesterday, but between the storms and the power being out, there was no air-conditioning in the office building and they sent everyone home for the day. She said she never even saw you yesterday before they closed the place up."

If the office was closed, then no one knew I wasn't there. "I . . . didn't make it in," I muttered.

"You what?" Collie now knew something was wrong. Me not making it into the office was unheard-of. Collie knew that even if it were a hundred and ten degrees in the office, I would have been there working.

The phone conveniently began to fuzz. For once, I was glad. "Hey, Coll, I'd better sign off. I'm heading down FM 47-B to Austin, and there's no cell phone reception on this road."

"All right, but"—the sound of static, and then—"tell me what happened yesterday. Over lunch, all right?"

The phone disconnected before I could give an answer, which was convenient, since I didn't have one.

I tried to work it all out in my head as I drove along the old highway, winding slowly through the hills, past the yuccas and live oaks and the tumbledown gas stations. The commuter traffic was lighter this morning, because it was earlier, and the trip to the Crossroads seemed to pass more quickly than the day before. I had a strange sense of arrival when I saw the crooked stop sign ahead. I felt the breath go out of my lungs in a long, slow sigh, the way you do when you're at the end of a journey, and you know you've finally come to a place you can rest.

I paused to look at the stop sign, remembering how

crazed I had been the day before, trying to get through the intersection. Oddly, none of that was with me today.

There was just a sense of peace, of having all the time in the world. No rush. No worries. No stress.

Today I think I'll try the coffee, I thought as I pulled into the parking lot.

When I drove around to the front of the store, I realized I wasn't the only one who'd had that idea. Perhaps a dozen vehicles were parked in the shade beneath the trees. I circled to the back of the lot, surveying the cars, wondering why so many would be there that early in the morning.

HOUSHNTR was there again, and the restaurant guy who'd ferreted out the biscuit recipe. Maybe he'd decided to take HOUSHNTR up on her offer to look at restaurant properties around Killeen.

Or maybe they'd come back for the coffee with the secret ingredient Hasselene wasn't supposed to divulge. I wondered what, exactly, was in the coffee, or if it was really anything special, and if the restaurant guy would convince the old women to tell their secret.

A sense of mystery tingled inside me as I parked behind HOUSHNTR and the restaurant guy, and got out of my car, heading toward the store. Most of the vehicles looked like they were probably from Austin or Killeen—clean foreign models not more than a year or two old. In front were a couple of old pickups that appeared to be local.

I walked slowly closer, not realizing what I was really looking for. A twinge of disappointment went through me, and I knew why, even though I didn't want to admit it. I wanted one of the pickups to say HAZMAT on the side.

I just want to thank him personally for returning Dad's checkbook, I told myself. *That's all.* But I found myself self-consciously smoothing the stray wisps of blond hair into my hair clip and wishing I didn't look like I'd been thrown together in fifteen minutes that morning.

Something in the bushes caught my eye as I reached the steps to the front porch. A butterfly, I thought at first, and then I realized it wasn't a butterfly at all, but a piece of my no-longer-in-existence green suit.

I had a sudden vision of how I must have looked dragging myself out of the bushes the day before, my suit torn to ribbons, hair sticking up in all directions. I felt myself flush from head to toe at the unflattering image, and I put my hands over my face, groaning under my breath. On second thought, it was probably a good thing that HAZMAT wasn't here. I was embarrassed enough, having to see Hasselene and Mernalene and the real estate lady.

The sound of whistling coming from around the corner caught my ear. Listening, I stood for a long moment, my mind transported back to some long-ago Saturday, my dad in the garage, whistling as he drilled and planed and sanded, putting together some table or bench or rocking chair he would take to the swap meet on the posh end of town and sell for what Mom called his "poker money." She didn't seem to resent the fact that, even though she'd asked him for years, he never built anything for her. Instead, his creations went to the swap meet, where he could watch strangers fawn over them, and he could tell the story of how he'd learned furniture making from his father, who had died at the beginning of World War II. If people would listen long enough, Dad would go on to tell how he himself had lied about his age and enlisted when he was barely sixteen and had made a lifelong career in the army.

What he wouldn't mention was that he joined up against his mother's wishes, and left her home with his younger brother to raise, and they nearly starved to death without him there to help. Dad had a way of seeing honor and duty on a grand scale, and never close to home. It never seemed to matter to him that we spent our lives moving from one home to another, always leaving behind friends and schools. He never thought twice about being gone from home for months at a time. He always wanted the assignments that would be most advantageous to his career. Only in our last few years of high school, when he'd finally made sergeant major, did we finally stay in one place for more than two years. He was about to retire by then, home for good. But by then it didn't matter. We didn't know how to be together, even when we were in the same room.

I slid my foot from the porch step, walking slowly toward the corner of the building, compelled to follow the sound, or the memory, I wasn't sure which. My mind slipped back in time as I tiptoed closer, leaning forward, like my six-year-old self trying to peek around without being seen. I could see my father in his woodshop, hear him whistling that same tune. . . .

Chapter 6

I was around the corner before I spotted the HAZMAT truck and came face-to-face with Graham Keeton. Startling, I jumped back, my mind returning to the present in a dizzying rush.

Caught off guard by the near collision, he stepped to one side. His arm moved with the lightning speed of a trained reflex, pointing a gun at me like he meant to use it.

We stared at each other for an instant. His eyes traveled from the sights of the gun to me, and back. Then he realized it was a caulking gun, and so did I.

A chuckle puffed from my lips. "Don't shoot."

He gave me a sheepish look and slid the caulking gun behind his back. "Sorry," he apologized. "Habit."

He needn't have told me that. I would have recognized the military-style firing stance anywhere. "Caulked anybody lately?" I teased.

His lips lifted into a wide, slow smile, genuine, not the kind put on in a rush to impress somebody. "Just a window and myself today." He held up his other hand, which was covered with a gray gluelike substance. He'd tried wiping it here and there on his coveralls, so that now he looked like a kid playing in finger paint.

"Does the window look any better than you do?"

He pretended to be offended, then grinned again. "Quite a bit, ma'am."

Ma'am. Another militaryism I hated. My father called everyone *ma'am,* and on the rare occasion that he got involved in disciplining us, he called us *little ma'am,* and not in a nice way, either.

"Laura," I corrected. "It's Laura."

"Yes, ma'am," he replied, then grinned, met my gaze with a wicked twinkle, and repeated, "Laura."

I rolled my eyes, because I knew he was toying with me. The surprising thing was, I liked it.

The twinkle in his eyes said he knew that.

As I stood there with Graham Keeton, it occurred to me that I should be saying good-bye and heading for work. Why did I find that thought disappointing? "So, I didn't mean to bother you. I heard someone whistling when I pulled up, and I walked around to see who it was. Is my father's checkbook in the store?"

Nodding, he walked a couple of steps to his truck, fished a rag from the clutter in the back, and started wiping his hands. "It's no bother. I'm done back here." He sat on the edge of the tailgate and crossed his long legs in front of himself as if he intended to be there a while. "I was replacing a couple of the windows the hailstorm broke." Glancing up, he gave me a quick wink, then went back to wiping his hands. "Earning my meatloaf dinner."

I nodded, then fidgeted some more, trying to think of something to say. He didn't seem to share my discomfort. He seemed perfectly at ease sitting there wiping putty from his hands.

All right, Laura, tell the man good-bye and be on your way. Time to head for work.

Instead, I looked aimlessly around and noticed a tall stone wall nearly hidden by trees and ivy, only a few feet away. I realized that we were actually standing in an alley between two structures.

Stepping closer to the wall, I gazed up through the trees. The structure was built of enormous limestone blocks, rising perhaps two stories, the lower story windowless, and a row of arched windows on the upper level, the broken windowpanes reflecting the dappled shadows of the live oaks.

"What's this?" Curiosity tickled the back of my throat—the kind of curiosity that comes with working in the magazine business. I had a feeling there was a story here, and Graham could tell me what it was. Taking a step closer, I peered into the thick curtain of foliage.

"Old gristmill." I heard his cowboy boots crunch on the gravel as he crossed the space between us. "It used to be quite a landmark around here, but the trees and the mustang grapevines have pretty well taken it over."

"Amazing," I breathed, astonished that the building could be so well hidden by the foliage.

"It's so overgrown now, if you didn't know it was there, you'd never find it." Graham stepped to my side and reached into the curtain of vines, pulling them back to give me a better view. "We played many a game of knights and castles, and cowboys and Indians in there, that's for sure. All of us kids who grew up down the road in Keetonville used to get on our bikes and ride up the old river-bottom road to play here." He paused for a moment, looking thoughtfully at the old wall. "Guess even the kids don't come here anymore. Too busy watching TV and playing Nintendo."

A sense of magic filled me at the thought of finding something ancient and secret. "It's really well hidden. I sat right over there all day yesterday, and—" I cut off the sentence abruptly, realizing what I had said. *For heaven's sake, Laura, don't bring up what a nutcase you were.*

He had the good grace not to ask. Instead he pushed the branches aside a little further and pointed. "Look down there."

Separating a few strands of honeysuckle, I wiggled through the narrow gap in the tightly braided vines until I could see what was on the other side. "What in the world? It's built on the side of a hill." I realized the building had been constructed against the face of a steep cliff, and HAZMAT and I were standing on the edge. The part of the building we were looking at was the mill tower, and below, the rest of the building flowed down the rocks, intertwined with the vines and the contours of the cliff, so that it appeared to have grown there like a living thing. "It must be three stories tall."

"At least." His voice was soft, filled with wonder like mine, intimate in a way that sent a soft shiver down my spine. "We rescued a damsel or two from that tower."

Gazing at the building, I squeezed a little farther through the vines, my mind transported through time, filled with little-girl images of knights and enchanted castles. "It looks like there's a path over . . ." I moved to point toward a narrow trail down the cliffside, and the vines slipped from under my hands, slapping me in the chest. Surprised, I jerked upright, and the foliage grabbed my clothes with a dozen corkscrew-shaped fingers. I had visions of the day before. "Oh, shoot," I groaned. Which wasn't what I felt like saying at all.

Sir Lancelot had the nerve to laugh. "Hold on a minute. This is going to take a little finesse."

"No, I've got it," I insisted, twisting around, trying to reach the little grippers that were holding my shirt. When that didn't work, I wiggled backward, hoping to slip free.

"Hang on a minute. You're making it worse."

"I think if I just pull this way—"

"Hold still!" It was half laugh and half command. "Kind of like a fish on a string, aren't ya?"

I couldn't help myself; I started to laugh. Suddenly the whole thing seemed incredibly funny. The jostling only made things worse.

"Hold still."

"Sorry." Laughter bubbled in my stomach, and I squeezed my eyes shut, trying to be patient—and motionless. Unfortunately patience is not my strong suit, so I took some deep breaths, counting silently—*one, two, three,* in through the nose, *four, five, six,* out through the mouth, *one, two, three . . .*

"What in the world are you doing?" he asked.

"Yoga." Even that seemed funny, and I started to laugh again.

"Yoga?" he repeated. "You're not from around here, are you?"

"Richmond," I answered. "Virginia."

"Mm-hmm," he muttered, like that explained everything.

I had a feeling that Richmond and I were both being insulted.

From somewhere behind us, I heard a faint click, then a *whoosh,* like a door or a window opening.

"Well, what in land's name is going on out here?" Mernalene's hard-edged voice was unmistakable.

Oh, no. All of a sudden, the situation ceased to seem funny, and moved into the realm of embarrassing.

"Graham, are you all right?" Hasselene sounded concerned. "Who in the world is that in the bushes?"

Oh, no. This really can't be happening. . . .

"It's Laura . . . from yesterday." Graham pulled free the last of the little grippers on the grapevines.

I stumbled backward three steps, flailing my arms, then popped to an upright position with my hands askew in the air, looking ready to say, *Ta-da!*

I settled for a chagrined, "Sorry to bother you this morning." And forced myself to smile, as if getting stuck in the bushes were an everyday occurrence.

Come to think of it, lately it was.

Mernalene gave me a narrow-eyed, questioning look.

Hasselene smiled, poking her head through the window. "Well, look at you!"

Yes, look at me. Let's not.

"Ummm . . . good morning," I said. "I just came by to get my checkbook." *Thought I'd fall in the bushes again while I was here.*

Mernalene nodded. "Oh, yes, the one we found yesterday. You know, it's a good thing Graham figured out who it belonged to. We probably never would have guessed it was yours, being as it's your husband's name on the account."

"I'm not married," I blurted out, then gave myself a mental kick and finished with, "It's my father's checkbook."

Hasselene and Mernalene glanced at each other, and both said "Ohhhh," at the same time, then turned back to Graham and me with calculating expressions, sizing us up like they were pairing up lost socks.

Graham seemed to sense it, too. He cleared his throat and moved away from me, closing the tailgate on his pickup. With another step toward the driver's-side door, he tipped his hat to the ladies, even though he wasn't wearing a hat, then proceeded to do an extremely poor job of excusing himself. "Well, I'd better be on my way. I've . . . uhhh . . . there's a chemical spill site I'd better check on at . . ." He glanced at me, then at the barracudas in the window, then took another step toward the truck, and finished lamely with, "Somewhere."

"Hasselene leaned out the window as if she intended to grab him. For a moment I thought she might come tumbling through the opening. Mernalene snatched at the shoulder strap of her sister's apron.

Hasselene didn't seem to notice. "Well, can't you come in for a cup of coffee, Punky?"

"Or a biscuit," Mernalene added with surprising enthusiasm. "We've got your favorite homemade jam. Mustang grape."

Graham pulled his keys from the pocket of his white cotton coveralls. "No, ma'am." He reached the safety of the driver's-side door, opened it, and turned back to flash the ladies what I was sure was his most charming grin. "But I'll be back tonight for my meat-loaf dinner."

He winked, and Hasselene giggled like a schoolgirl. Mernalene fluttered her lashes.

I rolled my eyes.

Graham seemed to realize he'd gone from prey to predator. He looped an arm through the open truck window and leaned confidently on the door frame. "Better leave that window alone for the rest of the day, Aunt Merna." He motioned to the windowpane over their heads. "It's not dry yet. I put plenty of caulking on it."

The picture of Graham holding me up with the caulking gun crossed my mind, and I chuckled under my breath.

Graham ducked his chin and shook his head slowly back and forth.

The ladies went back to mentally pairing up socks, while rubbing their chins in unison.

A lump traveled from my throat to the pit of my stomach. *Gulp.*

Graham climbed into his truck. "See you later, Aunt Merna, Aunt Hass," he said, making it clear he didn't intend to be a pawn in whatever game they were playing. "I think tonight when I come back I'll bring a flashlight and a hatchet and go check out the old mill."

"Oh, certainly," said Hasselene.

"Why would you want to do that?" barked Mernalene. "Nobody's been in there for years."

Hasselene elbowed her. "For heaven's sake, Merna, don't you remember that was always their special place when they were little? Remember when the kids were here, you couldn't find a towel in the house, nor a mop with a handle on it, because they'd be out there with the towels all wrapped around like capes and using the mop handles for swords. Remember that? They were so cute."

Graham rolled his eyes. "See y'all later." He started the truck, then leaned out the window, delivering another charming grin and a "Have a good day, ladies," before driving away.

I watched the truck disappear up the alley, then looked toward the old mill, curious, wishing I could be there when he went inside. I wondered what he would find. . . .

But in the back of my mind there was a still, small voice. The one Pinocchio hears when he meets Jiminy Cricket. It was telling me that I didn't have time to be curious, that I had work to do at the office. I could still get there ahead of everyone else, try to clean up some of the disasters caused by the power outage and my absence yesterday. I needed some lead time this morning to assess the situation and come up with a salvage plan. I had to have my head on straight before our nine-o'clock staff meeting, so that I could create a viable time line for getting the magazine to press by Friday. Come hell or high water, as my father would have said, I was going to keep the press date. That was why I'd been sent here in the first place, and, even if my personal life was in shambles, I still knew my job.

My head began to spin with everything the day would require. Final copyedits, page layouts, style sheets, print deadline, cover reconfiguration, tag lines, budgets, advertising space, Hometime feature.

The Hometime feature. Panic gripped me. Collie hadn't said anything about coming up with an article for the Hometime feature. Had Kristi forgotten to mention it to her? "Crap," I muttered.

The sound of an "Ahem" reminded me that I wasn't alone.

I glanced sheepishly at the ladies. "Sorry. My mind is already at the office."

Hasselene nodded and gave me a look of sympathy or pity, I couldn't tell which.

Mernalene was less forgiving. "Well, aren't you gonna come in and get your checkbook?"

"Oh." I had completely forgotten about the checkbook and my reason for stopping in the first place. "Sure."

I walked back to the front of the building, noticing that two new cars had parked behind my Lexus, and a flatbed farm truck now sat beside the old gas pumps. A man in greasy coveralls and a cowboy hat was filling the tank. I didn't realize I was staring until he turned and looked at me from beneath the brim of his hat. "Yeah, the old pumps work. You'd be about the third one to ask me that since I been standin' here fillin' up my truck."

"I never would have guessed that those old things were still operational," I admitted. "Sorry for staring."

"It's all right." Shrugging, he removed the nozzle from the gas tank and hung it on the pump. "We aren't used to so many city folks stoppin' by the place." He paused as a black Audi zoomed up to the front of the building and slid to a halt inches from the broken hitching rail. "No one in such an all-fired rush around here normally."

"Guess not," I said, feeling the perverse need to apologize. "I'll bet you'll be glad when the interstate opens again and the crowds leave."

He thought about that for a minute, then shook his head and answered, "Naw. Not really. As the official mayor of Keetonville, I'm glad to see some life around the old Crossroads again. Lone Star Café doesn't look quite so lonely these last few days. Maybe some of this business will trickle down the road to the shops in town. It all kind of reminds me of this place back in its heyday."

"Really? How long has this place been here?" Curiosity made me move closer to him, as the newest customer climbed out of his Audi and rushed into the store.

The official mayor of Keetonville leaned against his truck and crossed his arms comfortably, not in a rush to be anywhere, and clearly happy to talk up his town. "Long as any of us can remember. Well, longer than that by quite a bit. Let's see. . . ." Pushing his hat back, he scratched his forehead. "My mama was born in 1900, the year Keetonville was incorporated as a town, and she remembered the Crossroads always being here. So it's at least that old. Now, the sisters will tell you it's older than that by quite a bit, but you can't listen to everything they say. They got a lot of that from their pappy, and he was a whoppin' big storyteller."

"I never would have guessed this place had been here that long." I squinted over my shoulder at the thick limestone frontispiece. There was an ancientness to it, yet at the same time, each block was solid and square and true. No cracks in the sand-colored mortar, no crumbling corners on the stones, as if the passage of time had no effect here.

"Course, it wasn't a gas station way back then," the mayor went on, and I turned back to listen to him. "Crossroads was the only general store for thirty miles around. Folks come from all over to trade goods and to bring grain loads to the mill. Course, I don't remember back that far. I only heard about it from my mama. In World War Two years, they used to show movies in the mill building, for the GIs from Fort Hood. Old films and newsreels mostly." He gazed past me into the soft canopy of live oaks, inclining his head to one side, listening to voices I couldn't hear. "Lot of history in this old place."

For the blink of an eye, I thought I heard them too, those voices of long ago, of so many people who had come and gone, leaving behind the stories that whispered softly among the leaves of the live oaks.

The screen door behind me slammed, and I jumped as the driver of the black Audi rushed down the steps clutching a cup of coffee and a biscuit wrapped in a cloth napkin. Holding the biscuit between his teeth, he opened his car door and climbed inside.

Which was exactly what I should have been doing. Shaking off the warm fuzzies, I waved good-bye to the man at the gas pumps. "Thanks for the conversation," I said, and trotted up the steps.

The screen door was just settling back into place as I grabbed the handle next to a faded McCaughey's Better Bitters sign that looked like it was the only thing holding the door together. Through the screen, I could hear the hum of conversation.

I opened the door and stepped inside, standing in the square of sunlight as my eyes adjusted to the dim interior.

The inside of the store reminded me of a Norman Rockwell painting, the colors muted by age and dust. The walls were whitewashed limestone block, interrupted every ten feet or so by thick, hand-hewn support pillars. Overhead, heavy, rough-cut timbers held up a beaded wood ceiling that looked like it might have once been white and perhaps before that a pale shade of green. The hues had long since faded, leaving the boards only slightly tinted with the evidence that someone had once cared enough to paint them.

Stretching toward the ceiling on three sides of the room were tall shelves cluttered with everything from charcoal and lighter fluid to canned goods, motor oil, tools, fuses, a box of Moon Pies, stick candy, three bolts of fabric, and a display of ladies' underwear. The bolts of fabric were gingham, in three different colors. They had been sitting so long that the folded ends were sun-bleached white. The underwear display with its smiling pinup girl in briefs looked like it had been there since 1950.

In front of the underwear and the dry goods, a long counter ran the length of the room. On one end the case had a glass front, and on the other were rows of small display drawers with nuts, bolts, washers, and various plumbing supplies visible through the thick green-glass fronts.

A surprisingly modern cash register sat atop one end of the counter, the display case beneath it cluttered with a strange assortment of watches, pocketknives, at least twenty different kinds of chewing tobacco and snuff, and a box that said, *Lost keys*. The keys looked like they had been there a while and no one was coming back for them anytime soon. Behind the counter and the cash register and the keys were a pair of saloon doors, swinging slightly to the sounds of clanking pans, clattering dishes, and an off-key rendition of "Amazing Grace."

Noises on my side of the room caught my attention, and I surveyed the row of six tables by the front windows. The thick, wavy plate glass diluted the sunlight to a dusty shade of gray. Old gingham café curtains shielded the bottom half of the windows, and along the top, the words *Lone Star Café* were more clearly visible from inside than from outside. The painted letters colored the sunlight orange-gray and cast odd shadows across the rough wooden picnic tables and the benches, which were old church pews perhaps three feet each in length, and still sporting tiny wooden crosses and carved communion chalices on the ends.

The odd combination of furniture didn't seem to bother the customers—mostly commuters like me. They made a strange picture against the antique backdrop, yet they seemed oddly comfortable there, those businessmen and -women in their crisp new suits. They leaned back in the church pews, partaking lazily of coffee, biscuits, and varying amounts of conversation. At the table closest to me, HOUSHNTR and the restaurant guy were huddled over a pile of real estate listings and a basket of biscuits.

HOUSHNTR noticed me and gave a quick smile and a beauty-queen wave. I waved back and turned away, hoping she wouldn't mention the day before.

My attention caught for a moment on the underwear display. I frowned at the cardboard pinup girl, who smiled back at me, her hands braced on her impossibly thin waist, and her shoulders twisted coyly to one side. I tried to decide how long she had been there, though I wasn't sure why I wanted to know. Antiquities were my sister's department, not mine. Still, there was the fascinating sense of a time capsule about the Crossroads.

I realized that Mernalene was looking at me as she refilled a basket of biscuits on the counter. She glanced at the underwear display, and for a mortifying instant I thought she was going to ask if I wanted to buy some underwear.

Giving myself a mental nudge, I hurried across the room as Mernalene leaned through the saloon doors into the kitchen. "Hassel, where's this lady's checkbook?"

Hasselene appeared in the doorway. Untying her apron, she handed it to her sister, saying, "Here, go mind the griddle. Lands, we'll have to prepare better tomorrow. I've used up all the eggs and most of the breakfast casserole. That batch of biscuits in the oven is the last of the dough. Tomorrow we'll have to make half again as much."

"They might not be back tomorrow," Mernalene groused as she tied on the apron. "Not if that interstate reopens. They won't be back after that. It'll be just locals again—just our kind of folks."

Hasselene made a *tsk-tsk* sound through her teeth. "Oh, Merna, these are nice folks." Her ample bosom rose with a long intake of breath as she surveyed the crowd. "It's good to see the tables full again." Chuckling, she winked at her sister. "They sure like our coffee. Lordy, looks like some of them are running out, and . . ."

The saloon doors squeaked open and slapped closed, and her sister was gone before she could finish the sentence.

Frowning at the doors, she shook her head with a long, pensive expression. She realized I was still watching, and leaned toward me, whispering in a conspiratorial tone, "Merna's a little constipated today. She had potatoes for dinner last night, poor thing."

"Oh . . . uh . . . uh-huh," I muttered.

"I heard that!" Merna hollered from the back room.

Hasselene grabbed a coffee cup and a pot of coffee and set them on the counter in front of me. "How about if we start you off with some coffee this morning while I finish putting out these biscuits?"

"Oh, I can't stay," I told her, glancing at my watch. "I have to get my checkbook and head for work."

I got the impression that she was disappointed. "Well, all right then. Let me go see if I can find your checkbook." She glanced over her shoulder, wagging a finger at the coffeepot. "Carry that out to the dining room after you fill your cup, and see if anyone needs a refill, would ya mind?"

I watched her for a minute, then, with a helpless

shrug, wandered out to the dining room with the pot in hand. "Ummm . . . anyone need any coffee?"

Cups slid to the edges of all five tables, and I walked along with the pot, unintentionally eavesdropping on paperwork, laptop screens, and conversations as I passed. One doctor, one insurance salesman, two computer programmers, a college student, two nurses coming off the night shift, and a grade-school teacher checking spelling papers.

None of them seemed to think it was the slightest bit odd that a lady in high heels and a power suit was serving up the coffee.

I finished and walked away, feeling strangely invisible, or completely at home, I wasn't sure which. Hasselene was waiting at the counter with Dad's checkbook and a cloth napkin with biscuits wrapped up in it.

"This will get you started on your day." She smiled and handed it across the counter.

"Thanks," I replied, glancing around the counter for something to put the biscuits in. "I don't want to take your napkin, though. Is there a paper one around here someplace?"

Hasselene drew back. "No! No, no. Paper napkins dry them out. Take this one."

I didn't want to be obligated to return the napkin, so I pushed the bundle back across the counter. "I'd better not. I'll just take the coffee. I don't know when I'll get the chance to—"

Hasselene grabbed my hands in hers, pushing the bundle back to me. "It's all right." Her eyes, the welcoming gray of a summer evening, met mine, and a warmth spread from the bundle beneath our fingers into my body.

"It's all right," she said quietly. "You'll bring it back."

Chapter 7

THE rest of the trip into Austin was shorter than I had anticipated. In only twenty-five minutes, I was pulling into the *Texcetera* offices in the Wardman Building. The place was fairly quiet, which was pretty typical for eight A.M. The staff had a habit of dialing up from home in the mornings, skipping rush hour, and coming into the office sometime around nine-thirty for the staff meeting.

In the early-morning hours, Kristi and a couple of others held things together for the other fifteen members of the staff. The schedule had been set up by the previous editor, and since I was there only temporarily and had enough ongoing battles, I chose to leave it alone. If the home office in Richmond found out, they wouldn't be happy about it, but it was one of those things best left for whomever they hired as a permanent editor for *Texcetera*.

Kristi was waiting nervously by my office door when I arrived. She didn't make her typical morning jokes. That should have worried me. Strangely enough, I wasn't worried. My stomach wasn't tightening into the usual knot, and I didn't have perspiration dripping down my back. My mind wasn't spinning and my head wasn't pounding.

About halfway through my cup of Crossroads coffee,

all of that tension had melted away. I was more relaxed than I'd been in months, which made me realize how keyed up I'd been lately.

Kristi pushed open my office door so that I could make it through with my half-empty coffee cup, my laptop, briefcase, and my bundle of yet-uneaten Crossroads biscuits wrapped in the blue gingham cloth.

"Thanks," I said, wishing I could shut the door and block out Kristi and whatever bad news she was about to deliver. What I really wanted to do right then was finish my cup of coffee. In peace. Which wasn't like me at all. Usually I couldn't wait to dive right in and work like a crazy woman. The bigger the challenge, the more fun my job was.

Kristi was on my heels like the shadow of doom as I walked into the office. "I'm sorry about yesterday." She reached out to help me untangle my jumble of possessions. "I didn't know what to do. First we got that power surge that fried my computer, and then there were tornado warnings all over the news, and then the power was out, and there was no air-conditioning, and it's August. It was, like, a hundred and twenty degrees down here, and the building-maintenance people finally came down and said we had to leave because it was too hot in the building. I tried to get in touch with you, but I couldn't, and so finally we all left." She paused to take a quick breath, then said again, "I'm sorry. I know we're already way behind and yesterday made it worse. I couldn't work on the Hometime feature at home, either, because the power was out. It came back on sometime during the night, I guess."

Shrugging my briefcase off my shoulder, I set the rest of the things on my desk. "It's all right." I took another sip of coffee, feeling incredibly calm, inexplicably sure that we would recover from yesterday's disasters in time to make our print deadline. "We'll get it all straightened out."

She stood looking at me with her arms hanging slack and her mouth open. "O-OK" No doubt she couldn't believe I wasn't running around frantically shouting orders.

She glanced at the gingham-wrapped bundle on my desk, and I pushed it closer to her. "Want a biscuit?"

Brows knitted, she gaped like my head had just jumped from my body and rolled across the floor. "Ms. Draper, are you all right?"

"I'm fine." I smiled, and her astonishment grew. It made me wonder how much of a harpy I had been this past month since I'd come to Texas. "Have a biscuit." I moved my briefcase out of my chair and sat down to think.

Kristi picked at the knot in the gingham napkin as she took a seat. "These smell good. Look. There's a tiny jar of jam in here and a spoon and everything. Gosh, I'm starving." Opening the jar, she slathered jam on half a biscuit, then took a bite. "Oh, these are good. Where did you get them?"

"Long story." As much as I hated to ruin Kristi's breakfast, I knew we needed to get down to business. "So what else did we lose yesterday, besides the Hometime feature and the cover?"

The question evaporated Kristi's moment of biscuit bliss. "Only those two things. Everything else was on the zip drive from auto backup the night before. We'll have to do a restore this morning." Sighing, she sank into her chair and set the biscuit on the edge of the desk. "I'm sorry about the Hometime feature. I should have backed up all the work I was doing on it."

"You should have *told* me about all the work you were doing on it," I pointed out, and Kristi slumped in her chair.

"I know. I didn't want to get anyone in trouble. The article really was a mess when Mrs. Bronstad sent it in.

I thought I'd take care of it, get it ready to go, and talk to you about it later, or . . . talk to whoever takes over as editor here." Looking at her hands, she picked nervously at the chips in her neon-blue fingernail polish. "I thought I could save you some stress."

"Thanks for trying." I felt another twinge of guilt for not having been there the day before. "Anyway, accidents happen. We'll work something out for Hometime. Did Collie Collins say whether she had anything we could use for the column?"

"She said she didn't have anything with the right length and tone, nothing she hadn't already sold to another magazine, anyway."

"That's not good."

"I know."

"We've got to have something by tomorrow."

"I know."

Unzipping my laptop case, I took out the computer and set it on my desk, muttering more to myself than to Kristi, "There isn't time to assign it to somebody. . . . Hmmm . . ." An idea lit in my mind, and I turned to Kristi again. "We've got the pile of new submissions. We might get lucky and find something in there. It would have to be fairly perfect, because we don't have turn-around time for rewrites." I stood up and grabbed my modem cord. "You start looking through the snail-mail submissions, and I'll start checking the ones on-line. Maybe we'll get lucky."

Kristi rose slowly. "What if we don't?"

"Then I'll lean on Collie when she comes by to bring the cover pic at lunchtime. She'll dig up something if she knows I'm desperate."

Kristi seemed buoyed by that possibility. She turned around with the usual bounce that made the ringlets of her dark hair bob like ribbons on a package.

"Don't forget your biscuit," I said.

" 'Kay," she chirped, then backed up three steps without turning around. Glancing at me from the corner of her eye, she frowned, the look on her face saying, *What are you doing?*

"I'm having a biscuit," I explained, as if she couldn't tell that by looking.

"Sorry." She ducked her head sheepishly. "It's just . . . I've never seen you bring anything to eat before. It's kind of like a joke around here—you never eat and you never sleep."

The words gave me a quick mental image of how the staff viewed me. *Dragon lady.* "Geez, that's comforting to know."

She winced. "Oh, I mean, nobody means anything by it. You look better today—like you feel better, I mean. I mean not so . . ." She faded off and looked around for a hole to crawl into, then finally finished with, "I'll just go get to work now."

"Don't forget your biscuit," I said again.

Kristi grabbed the biscuit and ran from the dragon lady's lair.

I sat shaking my head, imagining word spreading in whispers among the gray burlap cubicles: *The dragon lady brought biscuits. In a little gingham napkin. She actually ate one. See, she doesn't sleep in a coffin at night. . . . She's human after all. . . .* That's what Kristi's look had said.

I don't know why that bothered me. The company hadn't sent me here to win friends. They'd sent me to whip the magazine into shape, to turn a disaster into full-color glossy perfection, and a disorganized, under-motivated staff of reporters into a team capable of producing a magazine that would rival any in the state. The home office expected me to do whatever it took. I'd done it before, in other places. Why was I having such a hard time with it here, now?

Taking the last sip of my coffee, I stared into the cup. Empty already. *Looks like it's going to be a long morning.*

I couldn't have imagined how long. The morning was filled with problems—a snafu in restoring the computer backup, a staff meeting in which everyone wanted to shout questions and no one wanted to come up with answers. Kristi and I followed the staff meeting with a completely fruitless search for a new Hometime column.

By noon, my head was pounding and I was jumping around like a cricket on a string. My Crossroads coffee and my newfound nirvana had completely worn off.

I bumped into someone as I was rushing out of my office with an armload of layouts. "Sorry," I muttered.

"Well, you should be. You almost spilled the cappuccino on your new cover photo."

"Collie?" I sounded like a drowning sailor hollering, *Land ho!*

"Yeah." She punctuated the word with a chuckle. "What's wrong with you?"

"You want the short list?"

"I don't know. How long is the short list?" Collie quipped. "I have a hungry baby and takeout Chinese food here, so I'm a little pressed for time."

"Oh." I realized that I hadn't even taken the time to give Collie a decent greeting. "Oh, Collie, you brought the baby." Holding the papers to the side, I leaned close to the baby carrier as Bailey gurgled a spit bubble, then smiled at me.

"Yes, and I brought myself and your cover photo and take-out Chinese food, too," Collie teased as I stood there ogling five-month-old Bailey.

"She already eats takeout Chinese?"

"What kind of a mother do you think I am?" Collie hip-butted me out of the way and proceeded into my office, setting the baby carrier in a chair. "The Chinese food is for us. I knew when I got here you'd tell me you didn't have time to go out to lunch, and then you'd want to steal my picture and pat me on the head, and 'Oh Collie, you're the best friend an editor could have'—yada yada yada and a few other sappy things like that, and then you'd kick me out the door and not call me until the next time you're desperate."

"I would not. You know I love you." I glanced at the cover photo in her hand. Perfect. "But you are the best friend an editor could have."

"Um-hmm." Looking skeptical, Collie smoothed stray tendrils of curly red hair back into her barrette. "I know you can't resist take-out Chinese. I've been to Hyung Sao's, so now you're going to have to sit down and tell me what in the world is going on with you and Dale."

"Lindsey called you, didn't she?"

"She was worried, that's all."

Pressing my fingers to my forehead, I leaned against the door frame, closing my eyes, trying not to get upset about Lindsey and Collie talking behind my back. Ever since we'd roomed together in college, Lindsey, Collie, and I had made an odd triangle. "She shouldn't have called you."

"Yes, she should have. She's a thousand miles away, and she was worried about you," Collie said simply. I could hear her unzipping the baby's diaper bag and rummaging around in it.

I opened my eyes and looked at her. "That's why you brought the cover photo in person. You didn't have a doctor's appointment, did you?" The molars started grinding in the back of my mouth as I imagined Lindsey and Collie on the phone last night. *Laura's having a breakup, or a breakdown, or something. You'd better rush right over there and check on her. . . .*

"I did have a doctor's appointment. It just wasn't in Austin."

I growled under my breath.

"Cut that out. Get over here and eat Chinese with me."

"Oh, all right." I pushed off the door frame. "Let me hand off these page layouts to Kristi."

As I turned away, Collie held up a cellophane bag with red Chinese lettering. "Cheer up. I've got fortune cookies."

"Oh, great," I grumbled. Collie had take-out Chinese and fortune cookies. We both knew what that meant. I would have to spill.

Everything.

By the time I returned, Collie had unpacked lunch and was busy getting the baby out of the carrier.

"Hey, would you get that bottle out of the diaper bag?" she said over her shoulder as she fiddled with the car-seat straps. "It takes a certified contortionist to undo these things."

I reached over to help Collie unhook the car seat. "Look how much she's grown," I said, happy for the distraction.

"Well, you haven't seen her in two months—since you were down for your mom's funeral, remember?" Collie wrapped a bib around Bailey's neck. "She's already starting to get up on her hands and knees and try to crawl."

"This early?"

Smiling, Bailey waved her arms, and we both paused to smile back. "Yeah, True's mom says he was crawling at six months, so I guess it's genetic."

"How is True?" I asked, cleverly leading the conversation astray. I'd met Collie's husband only a couple of times since she'd moved to Texas and gotten married.

Bailey gurgled and smiled again, like she recognized

the sound of her daddy's name. For an instant I was
struck by how perfect she was—with big blue eyes and
a fluff of curly red hair, soft baby skin, and tiny hands
with a roll of pudge at the wrist. Some emotion I
couldn't put into words grabbed my heartstrings and
yanked.

"True's fine," Collie cooed in a goo-goo voice meant
for the baby. Shaking her head and clearing her throat,
she repeated, "True's fine. Sorry, sometimes I forget
when I'm talking to an adult."

"There are worse problems to have," I said, wondering if Collie ever regretted choosing to get married and
move to Texas. Did she ever miss D.C., and all the rush
of being on top in a career she loved? Did she ever regret sacrificing the success she'd worked so hard for?

Elbowing Collie out of the way, I reached into the
carrier and lifted Bailey out. "Here, I'll feed her."

Collie gave me a sly sideways glance. "Oh, no, you're
going to eat Chinese and tell me what's going on with
you and Dale, remember?"

"I will, I will," I groaned, whisking Bailey away and
sitting in my chair with her. "Just let me spend a minute
or two with Bailey first. I never get to see her. You
know, I am her godmother."

Collie shut the office door. Tapping a fingernail
against her chin, she took a seat across from me. "So
what's going on, Laura?"

"I don't know, Coll. I really don't. There's so much to
it, I wouldn't even know where to start."

Collie stirred the lo mein noodles like there might be
an answer there. "How about at the beginning?"

"I don't know where the beginning is." That much was
true. I didn't know when things had started to change
between Dale and me. Had our relationship changed, or
had what I wanted from it changed?

The baby spat out her bottle and whimpered, distracting me from the question.

Scooting her plate onto the edge of my desk, Collie reached into the diaper bag and handed me a burp rag, then picked up something off the floor—the blue gingham napkin from the Crossroads.

Lifting Bailey onto my shoulder, I patted her back until she let out a very unladylike belch.

"You're pretty good at that," Collie observed.

"I've had lots of practice with my nieces and nephews," I reminded her. "Don't look so surprised." I thought of Kristi, who let me know without saying it that everyone in the office thought I was some kind of android.

"I'm . . . not," she lied.

"And look who's talking, anyway. Who would have thought two years ago that you'd end up in Texas doing the marriage-and-mommy thing." *The marriage-and-mommy thing* . . . A knot tightened inside me. Those were Dale's words.

Collie gave a helpless shrug, then looked into the napkin. "So what's this? There's a dried-up biscuit and a cute little jar of jelly in here."

In spite of the conversation, in spite of the baby in my arms and all the unspoken choices her presence there implied, I smiled, then started to laugh.

The next thing I knew, I was spilling the story to Collie. All of it. I started with Dale's phone call, and ended with me pouring coffee for the commuters at the Crossroads Café that morning.

When I was finished, Collie looked at me over her empty carton of Chinese food. Eyes wide with fascination, she whispered, "Laura, there's your Hometime feature. You tell me how to get to this place, and I'll write it for you. I'll have it ready tomorrow."

Chapter 8

ALL afternoon I wondered how Collie was doing at the Crossroads. I pictured her finding her way there, drifting into the parking lot, surprising Hasselene and Mernalene in the middle of a quiet afternoon, asking for an interview. I knew Collie would get the interview, and not just any interview. She would ask exactly the right questions to ferret out the quirky down-home stories that made perfect Texas fluff. And I was sure the Crossroads was full of stories.

What stories would Collie unearth? My mind was so caught up in wondering that I could hardly concentrate on my work. Every so often I realized I was staring out the window, wishing it were me at the Crossroads gathering old stories.

By five o'clock my office had started to feel like a cell, and I was ready to make a jailbreak. I'd been on the phone for hours, hashing out last-minute details about typesetting and printing, wheeling and dealing on the final ads, then calling Richmond to deliver the news that we anticipated almost breaking even on the first issue and moving into the black on the second. My boss was pleased. In fact, he was almost giddy, and Royce was never giddy about anything. His over-the-top reaction left me with an uneasy feeling that something was going on at the home office.

"Anything new up there?" I asked.

Royce cleared his throat, bringing his voice back to its usual monotone. "No. Nothing." But I could tell there *was* something. Royce had a secret. "Get the fires put out down there. You'll be out of that rat hole before you know it."

That was a clear tip-off. The only reason Royce would pull me out of this rat hole would be to send me to another one. "The company buying something new?" My mind started flipping through the possibilities, trying to figure out what small magazine Landerhaus Publishing might be swallowing up now, and where they might be sending me next.

"Nothing I can talk about yet." Royce's answer was quick and clipped. I knew I was on to something. "Have to make a meeting. Talk later."

A surge of adrenaline went through me as I tried to guess what secret plans might be in the works. One thing I loved about Landerhaus was that it was a company on the move—always changing, lots of opportunity. "Royce, wait, at least tell—"

"Gotta go. On my way out the door." Click. As usual, he didn't bother to say good-bye. Royce wasn't much for niceties.

"Jerk," I muttered, just as some intern from the circulation department came in and set a stack of spreadsheets on my desk. She pretended not to hear me, and quickly hurried out the door. Kristi came in behind her with layouts sent up by the production manager, Don, who was pulling double duty as sales manager, since the other one quit when Landerhaus bought the magazine.

Instead of starting in on the paperwork, I sat there and stared at it, dreaming again about making a jailbreak, which wasn't like me at all. Normally I would have been dying to pore over the circulation figures, compare them against my own preliminary estimates, e-mail the circulation manager and make suggestions. . . .

What in the world was wrong with me, anyway? All this mental meandering wasn't normal. Maybe I was coming down with something. But then, I didn't have time to be sick, either. I had a mountain of approvals to do, and no time for daydreaming, so I went back to work.

By six I still hadn't found the top of my desk, and my mind was wandering again. I pictured Collie heading home, and the Crossroads filling up with commuters stopping in for supper or coffee. I wondered if Graham had shown up yet, and if he was really going to explore the old mill building tonight. What would he find there . . . ?

I wondered if the sisters' meat loaf was as good as their biscuits. . . .

The next thing I knew, I was packing up everything I could possibly take with me and heading out.

At the sound of the office door, Kristi skidded her chair backward so fast she hit the edge of the plastic runner and almost tipped over. "You going home?" Her eyes widened, drooping on the bottom like a puppy's, begging, *Please say yes*.

"Yes. I'm going take the rest of this home with me."

Kristi's eyebrows knotted together in the center. "Ms. Draper, are you all right today?"

"I'm fine, I just . . ." *Think, Laura, think of a good excuse. Quick.* ". . . want to . . . go by the Crossroads and check on the Hometime feature, see how the interview went."

"Ohhh." Kristi was greatly relieved that I was leaving work to do more work. It fit in our normal scheme of things. " 'Kay, then. I'll see you tomorrow."

"Yes, see you tomorrow, Kristi," I said, in a hurry to be out the door. "Thanks for holding things together yesterday. You did a good job. Sorry I wasn't here."

Kristi nodded, surprised by the compliment.

"Thanks." Smiling, she stood up and began gathering her things. For the first time that day, she looked like she had the wind in her sails. "Have a good night."

"You too," I replied, then headed for the nearest door, hoping no one else would stop me on the way out.

I wasn't that lucky. Don, the production manager, caught me at the door with a printout of style sheets a mile long.

"Need you to approve these," he said in his usual I-hate-your-guts voice. Don had been on the staff of *Rural Texan* magazine for ten years, and he resented the fact that the publishing company had put that magazine out of print in order to start up the glitzier, hopefully more profitable *Texcetera*. He resented that the company had fired the old editor and brought me in temporarily instead of letting him take over as editor, and he resented my wanting to get a thumb on everything.

Only right now, I didn't want to. I glanced at those style sheets and all I felt was dread. It would take hours to look through all of those details, and at the moment I didn't care how we dotted our Is and crossed our Ts, and whether we put periods in O.K. or wrote OK or okay.

It occurred to me that, in truth, I never should have insisted on seeing the style sheets in the first place. That was the production manager's job, and Don was the production manager. Sticking my nose in it was obsessive, and it was no wonder that Don and everyone else thought I was a harpy. I'd spent my entire month here obsessing over *Texcetera* details so I wouldn't have to face the bigger issues in my life.

I thumbed through the stack of papers. "Have you checked these over, Don?"

Surprised by the question, he didn't answer at first. "Uh . . . yeah."

"And are you all right with them?"

He gave an uncertain sideways glance. "Yeah, I'm fine with them. I've checked them through twice."

I signed my name in the bottom corner of the page. "All right, then. If you've checked them over, there's no reason for me to."

Don drew back slightly, the sagging skin around his cheeks lifting as he took the papers back from me. "All right . . . er . . . all right, then I'll just get on with things."

"That's fine. I'm on my way to check on the Hometime feature and then go home, so if you need anything before tomorrow, e-mail me or call my cell."

His bushy gray eyebrows rose, then lowered. "You're leaving?"

"Yes, I am."

"Now?" Accompanied by a skeptical glance at his watch.

"Yes, I'm—"

Allen Parker rushed out of the composing room nearby and walked by me, saying, "Red or blue for subheads on the cover?"

"Blue," I answered.

"All right. Blue," he replied mechanically. "Gotta go pick up my kids at day care. I'll finish it up in the morning. Sidney said to tell you she went home, but she'll be in early to go over the layouts with you before the staff meeting."

"That's fine. I'll e-mail Sidney and tell her I got the message. I'm headed home, too." I leaned on the door to the downstairs parking garage, opening it a crack so that I could hear the street outside and smell the warm summer air. *Escape.*

Pausing at the corner, Allen glanced back at me, raising one incredulous eyebrow. Then he shrugged, shook his head, and went on.

When I turned around, Don had disappeared down the hall in the other direction, no doubt anxious to make a getaway before I changed my mind about the style sheets or gave him something else to do.

There wasn't much chance of that. I was out the door as fast as I could go.

"Hey, where are you going?" Sheila called as she and John Robinson headed across the parking garage carrying a pizza box and soft drinks.

"Home!" I hollered, exasperated with all the questions.

Their voices echoed in a whisper as I climbed into my car, ". . . think the power's out again?"

"She never leaves at six o'clock. . . ."

I closed the car door, shutting out their voices, trying to ignore the haze of conscience settling over me. Guilty or not, I started the car, pulled out of the parking garage, and headed out of Austin.

Twenty-seven minutes later, I had reached the Crossroads. I rolled the window down and drank in the soothing feeling of the breeze and the soft scent of a summer evening. In the trees, insects churred lazily, their songs mingling with the rustle of the car tires on the gravel as I pulled around to the front of the store.

The parking lot was not as full as it had been that morning. There were two shiny commuter cars, an SUV, a pickup truck, and a minivan, but no HAZMAT truck. I drove around to the side of the parking lot so I could see into the alley behind the gas pumps. Empty. A vague disappointment registered in the back of my mind as I parked in the corner of the lot and turned off the car. Suddenly my rush to get out of the office seemed silly. What was I doing here, anyway? What did I think I was going to find?

Turning the key, I started the engine again, feeling foolish.

You need to go home and check on Dad, then get busy on the work you brought home. By now there are probably a dozen e-mails in the inbox.

Gazing into the dappled evening shade, I tried to resign myself to the idea of going home, telling myself I had no real business here. Collie had the Hometime feature well under control, and there was no need for me to check on it. I was just making excuses to . . . excuses to . . . to what?

To see Graham Keeton? Was that what I was doing?

No. Of course not. That wasn't it at all. I was interested in the place, in the history of the mysterious coffee. That was all it was. And besides, I'd promised to return the napkin.

I turned off the engine again and silence floated in the windows as it shuddered to a halt. Leaning my head back, I let my eyelids drift downward, enjoying the cool evening breeze and the soft twitter of the leaves. Somewhere nearby a dove cooed, and farther away a whippoorwill called for its mate.

I smiled to myself. I could start for home in a little while. There was time to return the napkin, maybe have a slice of meat loaf and a piece of pie.

See if Graham Keeton shows up . . .

That thought came out of nowhere, and I sat bolt upright. *All right, this stops here,* I told myself. *Whatever kind of midlife crisis you're having, it's not, repeat not, going to include some kind of rebound romance. Don't have time for it. Don't need it. Not going to go there.*

Frustrated, I shoved the door open, grabbed the Crossroads napkin, and got out. I'd be quick about this. I'd give the napkin back, ask how the interview went, go home, and get to work. No biscuits, no coffee, no small talk. Just business.

I repeated the litany to myself as I walked across the parking lot—right up until I stepped onto the porch and nearly collided with Graham Keeton as he was coming out the door.

Something unwelcome fluttered through my stomach. Anticipation? "Oh, it's you," I heard myself say, the words sounding breathy, flirtatious. I cleared my throat, pretending to be occupied with surveying the parking lot. "Looks like this place is hopping again tonight."

Graham nodded, looking over his shoulder at the screen door. "It's chicken-fried steak night. More yuppies in there than you can shake a stick at." His tone changed on the second sentence, making it clear that, along with the army haircut, Basic Daily Uniform jacket, and olive drab T-shirt came a certain attitude. Graham liked chicken-fried steak. Graham did not like yuppies. Or maybe he didn't like all the non-Crossroaders intruding on his space.

Which made me wonder why he stayed there talking to me, since I was one of *them*.

Then again, I didn't have a good explanation for why I was hovering there talking to him, either. Growing up, I'd had enough BDUs and crew cuts to last a lifetime.

Though I had to admit that Graham Keeton looked pretty good in his. . . .

Jerking my attention away, I climbed the last few steps onto the porch. "Sounds good. Guess maybe I should go have a chicken-fried steak with all the other yuppies."

Graham gave me a sly smirk, not missing the fact that I had classed myself with them. "I didn't figure you for the chicken-fried steak type." There was a challenge in the words—bait that I couldn't resist nibbling at.

"Oh, really? What type *did* you figure me for?"

The smile spread into a grin, white and even against his tanned skin. Shaking his head, he looked down at his shoes, leaving the question unanswered.

The screen door swished open, and both of us jerked upright like we'd been caught at something.

Hasselene stood in the opening, looking first at Graham and then at me, doing a little mental math—adding up two and two and getting a twosome. "Well, there's Laura."

"I brought your napkin back." I held it out like an excuse, so she wouldn't think what she was obviously thinking—that I was there mooning after her nephew. "And I wanted to see how the interview went this afternoon. Did Collie Collins make it here all right?"

"Oh, it was fine. Lovely. That baby was absolutely darling." Taking the napkin, she folded it and put it in her apron pocket. "And we had such a grand afternoon talking to your friend. She told us all about . . ." There was a pregnant pause, during which I had the mortifying feeling they had been talking about *me*. Surely Collie wouldn't reveal anything. "Your magazine."

But I could tell from the acute look in Hasselene's gray eyes that, under cross-examination by the sisters, Collie had told them things about me. What things? "That's good." *No, it's not.* "So the interview went well, then?"

"Very well." She looked frightfully pleased. Worse than that, she looked at me as if she *knew* me, as if she knew what was going on with me.

I took a step backward, suddenly feeling very uncomfortable there. "Well, I guess I should be going. I . . . have a lot of work to do . . . at home."

"You don't want to do that." Hasselene moved forward so that she stood between me and the stairs. She hovered there, clearly trying to invent a reason for me to stay. "Graham was about to go see the old mill. I thought you'd like to go along to see it for your magazine article." Batting her eyes, she tried to make the suggestion seem innocent. "It's very historic."

Graham pushed off the porch post, giving her a reproachful look. "Aunt Hass, she said she's got things to do." I wasn't sure if he didn't want me along, or if he was trying to defend me from Hasselene's less-than-subtle attempt to throw us together.

Aunt Hass shot him a scathing glare. "Don't be such a stick-in-the-mud, Punky." Painting on an encouraging smile, she turned to me. "Of course she wants to see the mill."

Graham hung his head and crossed his arms over his chest, looking tired, looking like this had happened before, and he was weary of it. "Aunt Hass . . ."

Touching his arm, she stopped him, speaking quietly. "It's all right to enjoy things again, Graham. There's no need to keep this misery going forever."

I stood very still, watching, feeling that I shouldn't be there. Yet I was interested. I wanted to know—misery? Misery about what?

Turning away, Graham walked down the steps, shedding the emotion like water off oilskin. When he stopped at the bottom and turned back, he was smiling. "All right, then, it's up to you, Laura. You in a hurry to get home, or you up for an adventure?"

I looked from him to Hasselene, trying to catch up with the emotional boomerang they seemed to be riding. "I might be."

Any hint of pensiveness was gone from him, and there was a teasing glint in his eyes. "You sure? The trail's probably pretty rough. Can't drive down there in your Beemer."

"Very funny." I smirked. "I can walk just fine, thank you, and it's a Lexus."

Giving the car a quick look of dismissal, Graham pointed at my foot. "You might mess up your little red shoes."

I glanced down at my midheel pumps, about as far from hiking boots as you could get. If Graham Keeton hadn't been standing there goading me, I might have reconsidered the wisdom of rock climbing in pumps. Instead, I lifted my chin and said, "I can make it." *I hope.*

Graham clicked his tongue against his even white

teeth, his thick, dark lashes lowering skeptically. "Lots of overgrown vines down there. Might mess up your nice suit. Maybe pop a button . . . or something."

Gasping, Hasselene wagged a finger at him. "Graham! Really!" She glanced at me apologetically. "You'll have to ignore him. He's a real *rascal* sometimes." Leaning close to me, she added in a whisper, "He's always that way when he likes someone."

Undoubtedly, at that point, I turned as red as my suit. Somewhere in the back of my mind there was a little voice telling me that tromping down the hill in pumps and a suit didn't make sense, that none of this made sense. But I had gone beyond sense. I was incensed . . . in a playful sort of way.

Hasselene motioned to my shoes. "You'll have a hard time in those. I could loan you my gardening boots, maybe. They might fit."

Getting a mental image of myself in a suit and gardening boots, I shook my head. "I'll be fine." I handed my purse to her for safekeeping, and strode down the steps to where Graham stood. "In fact, I'm ready when you are."

Graham gave me a look of respect and reached into his jacket pocket, pulling out a small flashlight. "Then here's your flashlight."

"We're going to need flashlights?"

"Could be." He shrugged toward the mill building. "It'll be dark in there this time of day."

"You two have fun," Hasselene chirped, then went back into the café, her mission accomplished.

Graham waited until the door slapped shut, then gave me an apologetic look. "Sorry about that. They're a little daffy, in case you haven't noticed."

I chuckled. "It's all right. I think they're sweet."

"Sweet?" Graham scoffed. "Don't let them fool you.

They'll dance you around like a puppet on a string. It's what they do."

"I sort of sensed that," I admitted.

He glanced toward the café, his eyes catching the amber evening sunlight. "Now's your chance to make a run for it. You can probably make it to the car before they catch you."

"No way." Broadening my stance, I braced my hands on my hips. "I want to see the mill. And besides, they have my purse."

Graham grinned, clearly pleased with my decision. "All right then, Laura. Let's see what's left down there."

We started across the parking lot together, pausing at a blue pickup, which I assumed was Graham's. Taking off his BDU jacket, he threw it in the back, then rummaged around in the toolbox, coming out with another flashlight and what looked like an army machete in a holster. He looped the strap over his shoulder, the machete laying against the curve of his back, where he could grab it easily.

I realized I was staring. Obviously, so did he.

Clearing my throat again, I pretended to examine my flashlight. "Why do I get the small flashlight?" I meant to ease the lull in the conversation, but the words came out sounding suggestive.

Graham leaned close to me and held out the other flashlight. "Take your pick."

I took the big one and handed him the small one, just to stir things up a little.

He pointed at me with the flashlight I had left him with. "You are a stubborn woman, Laura Draper." He seemed to appreciate that.

"Sometimes." My gaze met his and every muscle in my body tingled.

"I bet more than just sometimes." He smiled, then

turned and started toward the tree line. Taking a deep breath, I tried to clear my head as I followed.

I immediately began to regret my stubborn streak. Any way I played this, I was going to end up looking like an idiot. There's no way to gracefully scale a cliff in a suit and pumps. I could barely navigate the parking lot.

This is a bad idea. . . .

Graham reached the edge of the trees and glanced over his shoulder.

I don't know why, but I smiled confidently and raised my flashlight, giving the *onward ho* signal as I tried not to wobble on the gravel.

He pulled the machete from the scabbard and hacked a hole in the thick stand of brambles that guarded the fringe of the parking lot. He looked good doing that. Good in a slightly dangerous sort of way, like a cross between G.I. Joe and the grim reaper.

The thought made me chuckle. He frowned sideways at me and pulled the brambles back, holding open the newly cut hole in the brush so that I could pass through.

I pushed my shoulders back and swaggered forward. Stopping short of the opening in the vines, I peered inside uncertainly. It looked surprisingly dark and cobwebby in there. An enormous spider ran up a broken strand and disappeared into vines overhead.

Eeewww. I glanced at Graham, realizing that my lip was curling. "There's a spider in there the size of my fist."

Rolling his eyes, he shifted his weight so that he could continue to brace up the foliage. "It's only a golden web. They're harmless."

"It's huge," I countered, peering into the vines where the spider had stopped to watch me, no doubt waiting to pounce when I got close enough. "That thing ought to be in a zoo."

Graham rattled the vines, and the spider ran higher, disappearing, which only meant that I didn't know where it was.

"Where's your sense of adventure?" he challenged.

"Well, I . . ." I tried to think of a good excuse, all the while feeling like a ten-year-old who'd just been hit with a double-dog dare.

"I could be wrong, but when you were trying to crawl through that hedge this morning, I would have sworn you'd do practically anything to see what's inside the old mill." The muscles tightened in his arms as he raised the vines a little higher, widening the doorway.

"Curiosity killed the cat," I muttered, bending down and inching closer to the hole in the bushes. *I can do this. I can. It's only a bunch of cobwebs and one great big spider. Hiding God knows where.*

Leaning down, Graham peered into the curtain of underbrush, which looked like it thinned beyond the entrance he had cut. "Maybe you'd better stay here." He seemed to reconsider the wisdom of cajoling me into tromping through the brush. "You really are going to mess up your suit going through this."

"Nope." Taking a deep breath, I covered my head and barreled forward. A heebie-jeebie ran through me as the vines clutched at my suit, and something soft and stringlike and sticky wrapped around my face. *Spiderweb.* "Ah-ihh-haa-ickh!" I heard myself squeal as I pressed blindly forward. Something dropped on the top of my head and clung there, burrowing into my hair. Letting out another guttural utterance, I exited the curtain of underbrush and stood up, hopping around and clawing wildly at the sticky strings on my face, trying to shake the crawly thing from my hair.

"Sounds like *The Last of the Mohicans* in here." Graham's voice was filled with laughter as he crashed through the brush.

"It's crawling on my head!" I shot back, frantically picking the sticky strands off my face with my eyes closed.

I heard Graham stop beside me. "Hold still." His fingers wrapped around my arm. "Here. Let me get it before you fall of the cliff. It's only a little stinkbug. You saved it from being spider lunch." His fingers touched my hair, then brushed my cheek, featherlight, as he freed the imprisoned insect and cleared away the last of the sticky strands.

I opened my eyes and for a moment we stood closer than should have been comfortable, his gaze meeting mine, his lips still holding a hint of a smile. An electric sensation vibrated through me.

I froze, uncertain.

"Better?" His voice was throaty and deep. It seemed to surprise even him.

I nodded, because I knew if I said anything my voice would be like his. Passionate. Inviting. Expectant.

All the wrong things.

A bird cried shrilly overhead, and we stepped apart. Graham cleared his throat, seeming nervous, caught off guard. "There's a trail down here," he said finally, gesturing ahead. "Years ago there were steps cut into the rock, and a walking path down the side of the cliff to the mill, but it's pretty much just a watershed now."

I leaned to the side, trying to see around him.

From where I stood, it looked like we were about to walk off the side of a cliff. "Are you sure there's a trail there?"

He moved forward a few more steps. "There always has been." He sounded doubtful as he pulled out the machete and smoothly cut through a tangle of vines, then holstered the knife again. "It looks a lot rougher than it used to be. I haven't been down here since I was a kid." Glancing at me, he made a quick survey of my attire, looking worried. "We might be better off going for that chicken-fried steak instead."

I didn't like the way he said that, the way his look said that I wasn't up to the challenge because I was a female, or a yuppie, or both. "Oh, no. I didn't climb through that spiderweb for nothing. I want to see what's at the bottom of this hill," I heard myself reply, sounding completely confident. *No problem, I'm Wonder Woman, I can do anything.* "You go first, Superman."

"You just want me to catch all the spiderwebs."

"Ex-actly," I replied, picking up a stick in case there should be a spiderweb that missed Graham.

"Wait here a minute and let me see how bad it is." He started down the cliffside trail, his boots sliding on loose rock, his form disappearing over the edge with each step.

Possessed by some insane desire to prove I could navigate the path, I took a deep breath and forged ahead, tiptoeing unsteadily over the rocks, alternately checking the trail, watching out for spiderwebs, and regretting that I had refused to go to Girl Scout camp.

Reaching the edge of the cliff, I stopped on the precipice, trying to decide whether to continue, and if I did continue, whether to go down forward, or backward on all fours. The trail was steep, cluttered with gravel and overturned rocks. It was only two or three feet wide, cut into the side of the cliff. It had probably once been wider, as evidenced by a few broader portions bordered by a crumbling handrail made of rock pillars and heavy, rusted chain. Leaning down, I glimpsed the bottom of the trail as Graham reached the valley floor, ducked beneath the overhanging branches of a tree, and disappeared into the foliage.

Not willing to be left behind, I took a step down the trail, and then another, then started to slide like I was on skis. Waving my arms, I muttered, "O-o-oh shoot!" then caught my balance, grabbing a sapling that was growing out of a crack in the cliff face. Peering over the side into the valley, I felt my head reel. It was at least thirty feet down, far enough that I was looking through the tree-tops. Too far to fall.

It occurred to me then to wonder what in the world I was doing. Trying to go down the side of a cliff in pumps and a pantsuit was, well, nuts. Come to think of it, so was tromping around in the woods playing Tarzan with some guy I didn't even know. I was a city girl, not exactly the woods-tromping type. All of this was nuts.

And I liked it.

Chapter 9

I was inching down the trail, clinging to the side of the cliff with my fingernails and tiptoe-sidestepping on the loose gravel when Graham reappeared at the bottom. I glanced over my shoulder at him, noting with no small pleasure that he seemed surprised to find me already halfway down the path.

"Need some help?" he called, trotting up the incline like a mountain goat. I think he did that just to annoy me.

"This isn't the easiest thing." I didn't say yes, didn't say no. Common sense was whispering to me in one ear, and pride was whispering in the other. "It's these darned . . ." I took a misstep and slid a couple of feet, ending up in the closest thing to the splits I'd done since high school cheerleading.

Graham had the audacity to laugh and make the baseball sign for *safe*.

"It's not funny." Wedging my front foot against a rock, I tried to raise my center of gravity.

"Need some help?" Graham repeated.

"Nope. I've got it." I wasn't usually one to ask for help until the situation got desperate. It was one of the things my mother had always sought to reform in me. *Laura, you're so stubborn,* she'd say. *You shouldn't be so stub-*

born. That's only pride talking. Mom was sure she was right about that flaw in my personality, even after that pride, or stubbornness, or whatever it was, had taken me through a journalism degree and an MBA in only five years, and into a successful editorial career.

The rock under my foot gave way, and my feet slid farther apart. "Oh, shoot," I muttered. Clutching the cliffside with a white-knuckled grip, I hung there, feeling like I was in some very ungraceful yoga position. "Darn." I sighed, resting my forehead against my arm, staring down at the huge gap between my feet. Not a good position for a thirty-six-year-old, slightly out-of-shape woman to be in. At my best, and without high-heeled pumps or the ground giving way beneath my feet, I couldn't have gotten up from that position.

"You're in a fix, huh?" Graham drawled.

I got a sudden mental image of how I must look, and a puff of laughter chugged past my lips. "Yes, I think I am." I began laughing in earnest. "I'm a magazine editor, not a mountain climber."

Graham laughed with me. "Well, that explains the shoes, then."

I laughed harder and my feet slid farther apart. "Stop making me laugh!" I wailed, somewhere between humor and desperation.

My partner in crime laughed so hard I thought he was going to fall off the cliff.

"Quit that!" I pleaded, sliding another inch, and another. "You're making it worse."

"All right. All right." He caught his breath "Sorry. It's been a while."

I glanced over my shoulder, wondering what he meant by that, but then at the same time I knew. *It's been a while since I've laughed like that.* That was what he meant.

"Me too," I whispered, the words lost in the crunching of gravel as he braced his feet, then reached for my hand.

"Here, take my hand and I'll pull you up."

Some strange emotion shivered through me, and I hesitated, only for an instant, but long enough that he gave me an intense look.

"Don't be stubborn, Laura," he said, or at least I think he said it. I heard it somewhere deep within me. Clenching the rock a moment longer, I fought the instinctive doubt that comes the moment you let go of something solid and reach for something uncertain.

Our hands met with a slap, and Graham wrapped his fingers around mine, giving a quick tug, which deftly set me on my feet, wedged between him and the face of the cliff. We stood like that, making moon-eyes at each other.

"Ready?" he said finally.

"Um-hmm." *Ready.* I definitely felt ready . . . for something.

He released my hand, and I caught my breath, dusting myself off. Looking around, I realized the daylight was getting thin. Graham seemed to notice it, too, but neither of us said anything.

"Guess we'd better get going." All of a sudden I was determined to continue on. Rocky trail or no rocky trail, I wanted to see the old mill—not just because I was curious about the building, but because I was curious about him.

He extended a hand, offering to help me, and I waved it away. In the business world, feminine weakness was death.

"No, I'm fine. I've got it," I insisted, and proceeded to follow him down the trail, hanging on to roots and vines and rocks and anything else I could find to get myself to the bottom. By the time we reached level ground, I felt like I'd been through a war. My shoes were scuffed and

covered with white limestone dust, and the little strip of
decorative alligator skin was coming off.

Leaning against a tree, I paused to empty the pound
of dust and gravel that was sharing space with my feet.
"Next time, I'll wear the right clothes." I realized right
away that I'd said *next time,* like it was something defi-
nite. Odd that it seemed perfectly normal to say that, to
fall into step side by side as we continued along the
path, which, on the undisturbed valley floor, joined an
old stone road that was surprisingly clear. I pictured a
troop of youngsters from the nearby town, Graham's
town, riding their bikes along the old road, like the lost
boys on an adventure in never-never land.

Graham started to whistle as we moved closer to the
mill. The music echoed into the quiet air of the canyon,
rebounding against the rock cliffs, mingling with the
song of a brook not far away. As we walked, the sound
of water grew closer, eclipsing even the evening churring
of the insects, so that there was only the music of the
water and the soft notes of Graham's song. Overhead,
beams of sunlight filtered through the thick canopy and
glided silently to the forest floor in shades of amber and
crimson, lighting the valley like the gallery of an ancient
church, giving the feeling of hallowed ground.

"What is that tune?" I asked. "I've heard it somewhere before."

"It's an old song." He paused a minute to think. "You
know, I'm not sure of the title. It's an old Texas folk song."

"It's so familiar," I said as we walked a little farther
and he started whistling again. The road ambled along
the edge of the stream, and all at once I realized why
that tune was familiar. I had dreamed about it. I had
dreamed about all of this last night—the notes of music,
the song of the brook, the soft whisper of the breeze
among the live oaks.

But how could that be? How could I dream about a

place I'd never seen and a song I didn't know? Yet as I looked around, the place seemed familiar, perfectly serene and hushed, like something from the last moments of a dream, something almost, but not quite, part of the world.

Rounding the bend in the stream, we stopped as the mill came into view. Stretching from the valley floor into the treetops, the old building looked wise, and enormous, and ancient, its white limestone blocks discolored by time, bearing the nesting mud of swallows and the resin of trees. Yet it seemed perfect that way—timeless, untouched, enchanted, a castle worthy of the exploits of imaginary knights and young cowboys.

Studying the imposing limestone blocks of the building's base, I imagined little boys with bath-towel capes jousting with their shadows there. In the breeze I could hear their laughter, see them scampering like elves through the bed of dead leaves. I could see their faces in the uneven reflections of the tall arched windows that lined the bottom story of the building. Thick with the patina of age and neglect, the glass showed nothing of what was inside, but instead mirrored the gnarled live oaks that stood like titans around the castle.

"It's incredible," I murmured, walking closer, watching my reflection in the tall windows. "I never would have guessed all this was down here. It doesn't look so large from up above."

Graham's reflection in the window raised a hand and gestured upward. "All you can see from up there is the tower. See up there where the light is hitting the building? That's the alley beside the store. The mill used to be connected to the store by a granary building, but they tore that down when I was little."

"Is that when the mill was closed down?" I asked, thinking about the magazine story and hoping that Collie would include the old mill.

"It's been closed as long as I can remember." Walking to one of the windows, he tried to wipe away the grime to see inside. "The aunts sold it to a farmer down the road forty years or so ago, and he used to store hay in here until he passed away. Now his estate owns it, I guess." He peered through the window. "You can't tell it from here, but there's a dirt road on the other side that leads up to the highway."

I crooked an eyebrow at him. "I thought you said there was no way to *drive* down here."

"Did I say that?"

"Yes. Right before you sent me through the spider hole. You said something like, 'Can't drive down there in your Beemer.'"

He cocked his head to one side as if I were speaking Greek. "It's a Lexus, isn't it?"

"Very funny," I grumbled, tempted to throw something at the back of his head as he looked in the window again. "Is there really a road that comes down here?"

"Technically . . . yes." He focused on something inside the building. "But it's the long way around."

If I hadn't been so interested in whatever he was looking at, I might have killed him. "You are not *nice,*" I said, elbowing him out of the way.

He grinned wickedly. "I never claimed to be."

Cutting a glare in his direction, I tried to see through the window, but the interior was cloaked in shadow.

"Better hurry before we lose the light," Graham urged as I stood studying the windows. "The front is around the other side, facing the creek." He motioned toward the front of the building, and together we walked around the corner. I stopped there, breath catching in my throat.

The area in front of the mill was like a scene from an artist's painting—beautiful, serene, bathed in light. Above us, the canopy of trees opened. The forest floor was carpeted with clover crowned with tiny white blossoms that leaned toward the setting sun and the passing stream. The water, clear like molten glass, sat idle in a pool above the mill, then tumbled over a waterfall into the stream below, weaving effortlessly through a maze of giant boulders. Beyond the boulders the brook continued on its journey, disappearing beneath the overhanging branches of a giant live oak. The tree, ancient like the rocks and the water, crouched low over the surface, keeping the remainder of the water's journey a mystery.

Walking a few steps farther into the glen, Graham braced his hands on his narrow hips and surveyed the old mill wheel, which sat silent now, the trough having long since rotted away. "Doesn't turn anymore," he muttered thoughtfully.

I watched my reflection in the high arched windows as I walked up the stone footpath that led from the creekbank to the mill and climbed the wide stone stairs to the front porch, stopping in front of the heavy wooden front doors.

"Are you sure no one will care if we look inside?" Even as I asked, I was pulling the latch and pushing the doors apart so I could peek into the building. The lure of the unknown was too much to resist.

The interior was dark, the dusty windows allowing in only a muted ghost of the evening sun. Reaching for the flashlight in my pocket, I pushed the door open further and shone the beam inside.

Something rustled within, and I jerked back, rethinking the idea.

"Hey, better watch out in there." I heard Graham coming my way. "Could be snakes."

I hesitated, then stepped in the door, just to prove that I could. A shiver ran over me at the idea of snakes.

"Or raccoons." I heard Graham's boot heels on the porch.

"I'm not scared of raccoons," I said, taking another step inside.

"Or big, big spiders." He was right behind me now. His voice, not much more than a whisper, echoed into the room.

I gave him a narrow-eyed glance. "All right, Rambo, you go first."

He looked disgustingly pleased, and not the least bit ashamed for having scared me out of the leadership position. Clicking on his flashlight, he moved forward carefully, silently, as if we were on some army mission in enemy territory. I had a feeling he was doing that to add to the spooky aura of the place.

I clomped after him in my pumps, the sound echoing through the building.

He glanced over his shoulder, lowering an eyebrow at my shoes.

I shrugged. "If there's an animal in this building, I want to scare it away, not sneak up on it."

"Good point."

"You army boys don't know everything, you know," I quipped, moving past him into the room.

He gave my statement a look of surprise.

I motioned to his outfit. "The clothes and the hair pretty much give you away."

He thumped himself in the forehead and gave me a look that said, *Duh,* then narrowed his eyes like he was still surprised I'd noticed.

I pointed to myself and explained, "Army brat," though I hadn't identified myself that way in years.

He made a silent *oh,* nodding, then raised a hand in a gesture of eureka. "Ah, an army-brat magazine editor." Fanning an eyebrow, he added, "The worst kind."

"The worst kind of what?"

"Trouble." He laughed, then disappeared through the

doorway of another room and left me standing there alone in the darkening shadows.

"Very funny," I said, and clattered across the floor to catch up. Trouble or not, I didn't want to be left alone in the darkening building.

"Hey, look. Bats," I heard him say from the next room. "There didn't used to be bats in here."

Bats. On second thought, alone wasn't so bad. Alone without bats was better than together with bats.

"Come look," he called.

"I'd rather not."

"There must be hundreds of them." Apparently he thought that would entice me, but instead it sent a heebie-jeebie through me and I considered running for the door.

"I'll take your word for it."

He peeked out the doorway. "Sure you don't want to see?"

"Umm . . ." Tapping a finger to my lips, I pretended to think about it, then added, "No."

Graham smirked at me. "They're harmless."

"I'll just wait outside." I started backing toward the door. A rustling noise shuddered through the building, and I looked around, noticing how dark it had grown. I thought about bats. Bats and nighttime, and what bats did when nighttime came.

And then I realized why, exactly, I didn't like bats. I remembered my parents taking us to Carlsbad Caverns once when Dad was stationed at Fort Bliss in El Paso. Dad insisted that all of us stay at the entrance to the cave as evening fell. Lindsey and I got into a fight because we were tired and hungry.

And then as the last of the sunlight disappeared below the hills, the mouth of the cave started to rumble and the air began to vibrate, and a massive, dark cloud of screeching creatures flew from the entrance, swooping over our heads and filling the air.

Lindsey and I screamed and ran to the car. . . .

"Oh, geez." Looking around, I realized that the last of the light was disappearing from the building. "Graham! We need to . . ."

The rustling in the other room intensified, and the building began to vibrate, filling with the slapping of wings and the screeching of thousands of tiny creatures.

"Go!" Graham finished my sentence for me. He crossed the room in a full run, the leading edge of the swarm of bats right behind him. Catching my arm without slowing down, he dragged me into motion as the air around us filled with bodies.

Screaming, I covered my head, my heart racing as we ran through the door and down the front steps without slowing. In a blur of motion, we dashed across the glen and into the trees as the forest filled with bats in flight.

We reached the cliffside trail, and if the high heels were a problem, I don't remember it. At that moment I could have climbed the mountain blindfolded and on stilts. Graham had a white-knuckled grip on my hand, and half pulled, half carried me the last twenty feet.

We reached the top as the bats cleared the trees and took to the open air.

I looked at Graham and he looked at me, and we burst into wild laughter, doubling over and bracing our hands on our knees, alternately laughing and trying to catch our breath. I wasn't sure how long we kept at it— long enough that the last of the bats had disappeared and the air was quiet, except for our laughter.

When I finally composed myself and stood up, Hasselene and Mernalene were watching us from the front porch of the store.

I sobered, but Graham kept right on laughing. Tossing the machete and the flashlight in the back of the truck, he said, "Now *that* was an adventure," loud enough that I was sure the sisters heard him.

Self-consciously, I reached up to smooth my hair into place, then realized it was full of leaves and I'd lost my hair clip. Glancing down at my suit, I noticed I was covered head to toe with leaves and white limestone dust.

I suddenly got a total picture of how I looked, and a pretty good idea of what the sisters must be thinking. All the physical evidence pointed to the idea that Graham and I had been for . . . well . . . a romp in the woods. I don't know why that bothered me, but it did. I was trying to dust off my suit when Graham reached up and touched something in my hair.

"I think you've been dive-bombed by a bat."

I forgot all about being embarrassed and moved straight to grossed out. "Oh, you're kidding. Yuck."

Graham had the nerve to look amused as he leaned in for closer examination. "Looks like bat guano to me."

Shuddering violently, I put my hands up, then down, then up, trying to decide whether or not to touch it. "Oh, that's . . . eewww . . . that's just . . ."

He attempted to conceal a chuckle by clearing his throat. "I wouldn't touch it. It'll smear," he said like he was some sort of authority on bat droppings. "Messy stuff. Let it dry and it'll flake right out of there."

I couldn't tell if he was baiting me or not, and it really didn't matter. "No *way*!" I gasped, mortified by the idea of keeping company with the bat droppings until they dried. Spinning around, I proceeded across the parking lot in search of a bathroom as fast as my pumps would carry me.

The ladies were waiting at the bottom of the porch steps. They smiled at me, then looked past me at Graham, seeming frightfully pleased.

"Well, my goodness, it looks like you two have had a good time," Hasselene observed.

Mernalene took in my hair and clothing with a calculating expression, clearly trying to figure out exactly how far the adventure had gone. "Not really dressed for hiking, are—"

Hasselene elbowed her and the words ended in a soft *ooof;* then Hasselene smiled at me again. "Come on in for supper. We've got chicken-fried steak and some of last night's leftover meat loaf." She nodded toward the parking area in front of the store, where only one car remained. "We've a little buttermilk pie left too, though we've had so many new folks in and out of here tonight, they've gone through most of it."

My stomach rumbled with surprising enthusiasm. Unfortunately, my conscience began to rumble, too. *Of course, the fact is, Laura, that you need to get home.* "That sounds good." *You've got Dad to check on and a ton of work to do.* "I'd like some, but first can you tell me where the bathroom is? I've got bat poop in my hair," I said, like it was the most natural thing in the world.

No one seemed surprised. Mernalene motioned toward the side of the building. "It's out back."

Hasselene elbowed her again. "Mernalene! You can't send her to the *outhouse.* For heaven's sake, how's she going to wash the droppings out of her hair there?"

"Oh, all right," Mernalene acquiesced, none too happily. "It's through the kitchen, through the red door beside the stove, down the hall, on the left. *Third* door." She emphasized *third*—an unspoken signal not to enter any of the other doors.

Hasselene frowned at her. "Use anything you need back there, dear. We'll get some supper put together for you in the meanwhile."

"I'd probably better take that to go," I said reluctantly.

Hasselene didn't hear me. She was busy trying to get

Graham's attention as he was closing the toolbox in his truck. "Woo-hoo, Punky. Don't forget about your meat loaf dinner."

Punky started toward the café, and Hasselene ushered me in the door. "Use anything you need back there," she repeated. "There are towels, soap, shampoo."

"Oh, I don't think I'll need shampoo or anything like that."

"Let me know if you need help," she replied sweetly.

As the screen door closed behind me, I heard Mernalene add, "That bat guano is messy business."

Chapter 10

MERNALENE was right. Bat guano was messy business. Its chemical makeup, as far I could tell, was somewhere between superglue and chewing tobacco. It also had a few of the properties of hair dye.

As I stood in the bathroom, which I quickly discerned was the sisters' personal bathroom in their living quarters, I began to understand that wiping the bat poop out of my hair with a tissue wasn't going to be possible. All the tissue did was spread the guano in a narrow brown streak down the side of my head.

I wet a washcloth with soap and water, then scrubbed the streak, then rinsed it as best I could without sticking my whole head in the sink. I'd have to wash my hair when I got home. Gee whiz, what next?

You should never ask a question like that unless you're prepared for the answer. As I rinsed out the washrag and moved to hang it on the towel bar beneath the old claw-footed tub, something jumped in the window I'd opened to thin the guano smell. Fresh from my encounter with the hoard of bats, I screamed and stumbled backward, bumping into the door of the linen closet.

A cat. Slapping a hand to my chest, I looked at the huge orange tabby on the windowsill. *It's only a cat.*

The cat gave me a cool sideways glance, jumped from its perch, crossed the bathroom, stood up on its hind legs, and, with its front paws, opened the slide latch on the door, then proceeded into the hallway.

I stood there wondering if somewhere during the adventure at the mill, I'd fallen down a rabbit hole. I was beginning to feel a little like Alice in Wonderland again, as the cat trotted down the hall in the opposite direction of the red door. I followed a few steps, calling, "Here, kitty, kitty," thinking it would be best if I caught the cat and put it back outside, since I was the one who had let it in.

Glancing back at me, the cat disappeared through an open doorway at the end of the hall.

"Shoot," I muttered, looking back toward the red door, then walking a few more steps to the end of the hall. I felt like an intruder there, a cat burglar, so to speak.

Reaching the end of the hall, I stepped through the open doorway into what was clearly the living room, though if it hadn't been for the old console TV at the other end, the room could have been a museum display or an old movie set. From the Queen Anne sofas to the heavy velvet drapes, nothing had been changed there in years. The tapestry covers on the furniture were faded, but immaculately clean, as was everything else in the room. The walls were filled with black-and-white photographs in all manner of antique frames.

Taking another step into the room, I studied the pictures, which read like an almanac of visitors to the Crossroads, a who's-who of American days gone by. John Wayne, Theodore Roosevelt, Lyndon B. and Lady Bird Johnson, Clark Gable, Judy Garland, Charles Lindbergh, Dolly Parton, Robert Kennedy, Willie Nelson with short hair, Will Rogers, John Glenn holding up an astronaut helmet, Greta Garbo, Humphrey Bogart,

Lauren Bacall, Buddy Holly. The list went on and on. Even Elvis had been there.

In almost every picture stood the twin sisters, sometimes younger, sometimes older, always smiling as the moment was recorded for posterity.

The cat jumped onto an end table, distracting me from snooping as he rubbed against a Tiffany-style lamp, then tipped over a picture frame.

Rushing across the room with my arms outstretched, I caught the lamp, then scooped up the cat. "I don't think you're supposed to be in here," I said as he rubbed against my chin and started to purr. "You bad kitty." Tipping the picture upright, I leaned closer, consumed with curiosity, studying the image of Hasselene and Mernalene as young women—slim, tall, beautiful, dressed like early-day movie stars in chic flowered dresses with matching hats. They stood smiling in the center of the photo, holding hands with two dashing young men in uniform.

Below the image, a handwritten caption read, *Our engagement party, 1944, a perfect day*. In the background was the mill wheel and the waterfall, a magical setting for a special time. Staring at the picture, I imagined the event—the area around the mill neatly mowed, a table of food set out, friends and relatives coming to wish the young couples well. The specter of war loomed somewhere near that perfect day, I knew. How difficult had it been for them to make a commitment in a world that was falling apart? What kind of faith had it taken? How long had they been married before they were widowed? A lifetime, a few years, a few months?

Setting down the picture, I turned to leave the room, stopping at the bathroom to release the cat, who jumped happily onto the windowsill, then bounded into the darkness. Closing the window, I left the bathroom and hurried down the hall, out the red door, and through the kitchen. The sisters were nowhere in sight, so I crossed the kitchen and went into the store.

The room was empty except for Graham sitting in one of the booths and a woman with a gray beehive hairdo standing by the door holding a pie. They stopped talking as I entered, and I had the distinct feeling I'd interrupted something private.

Graham stood up to make introductions. "Laura, this is Puff. She owns the beauty shop down the road in Keetonville." He motioned vaguely toward the crossroad. "Puff, this is Laura Draper."

Puff peered over the top of her glasses, clearly waiting for more of an explanation of my presence. She shot Graham an irritated look when he didn't fill her in.

Crossing the room, I extended a hand. "My magazine is doing an article on the Crossroads," I explained.

"Ohhh." Puff was impressed, and no small bit interested. She studied me over the top of her glasses as she shook my hand. "I heard about that. Not much goes on around here I don't hear about. Comes with ownin' the beauty shop." Her face became animated. "You ought to come on down sometime. The stories I could tell about this old place, well, they would fill a book. Anyone tell you about the time Elvis came here?"

I shook my head, not sure whether I should get her started on the story. I had a feeling Puff could talk for quite a while.

She took a deep breath. "Well, I . . ." Pausing, she glanced at Graham and then at me, and then at the table in front of Graham, clearly set for two people. Snapping her lips closed, she pointed a finger at me. "Know what? I'd better let you two get to your dinner—it'll get cold, and that old story will keep. Come by the shop sometime and I'll show you the jar with the Elvis hair."

"I'll try to do that," I said, but I doubted I ever would. In a couple of days I'd be gone. I'd probably never see the jar with the Elvis hair. "Nice meeting you."

"You too," she said, then turned to Graham with a purposeful look. "It's good to have you back, Graham. I know your mom and dad sure enough missed you while you were gone. We all did."

Nodding, Graham shifted in the seat so that he was turned away from her, clearly trying to close the conversation. "Yeah. Thanks, Puff."

She exhaled loudly, drawing her lips to one side and studying his back. "You remember what I said—let go of it. OK?"

"Um-hmm."

"We'd love to see you in church on Sunday."

"We'll see. G'night, Puff. Dark out—watch for deer on the road."

"Oh, I think I'll stay a little while and watch the domino game on the porch before I go. Have a good night, Graham." Standing in the doorway for a moment, she gave him a sad look, shaking her head.

Graham didn't see it, but I did. I wondered what it meant.

I thought about it as I walked across the room and sat down opposite from him at the embarrassingly intimate table—two plates of meat loaf, potatoes, green beans, cute gingham napkins, and a partially used Christmas candle burning in a mason jar in the center. Overhead, the lights on the ceiling fans had been turned off, so that the dim wall fixtures filled the room with a soft orange glow.

Graham stood while I took my seat, then sat down again, looking embarrassed or irritated, I couldn't tell which. "Sorry about all this." He motioned toward the candle in particular. "People around here don't mind their own business very well. I think Aunt Hass got the wrong idea about us when we came out of the woods."

I think Aunt Hass had ideas long before that, I thought, but I didn't say it. I couldn't help noticing that the sisters had left everything we would need for our meal—two glasses of tea, two cups of coffee, and two slices of buttermilk pie with . . . heart-shaped strawberry slices on each?

Following my gaze, Graham shook his head. "Sorry. They do things like this." Clearly the evidence of match-making bothered him.

Why didn't it bother me? It should have. In the first place, I didn't know anything about Graham. In the second place, he wasn't my type at all. In the third place, I would be leaving Texas in a few days. And in the fourth place, there was Dale, and the whole ugly issue of re-bound relationships.

Two little old ladies trying to match me up with an ex-army man was the last thing I needed.

Graham looked like he felt the same way. *An army-brat magazine editor from Virginia is the last thing I need. . . .*

I picked up my fork and looked at my plate, embar-rassed.

Graham cleared his throat. "Guess we'd better eat."

"Guess so." I stabbed a chunk of meat loaf and started to raise it toward my mouth, then glanced at Graham and realized he was . . . saying grace. I didn't react quickly enough to set my fork down, but sat star-ing at him instead.

He glanced up and gave me a quick wink, then said, "Small-town Texas boy."

My curiosity reared its ugly head. "So you grew up down the road in Keetonville?" Taking a bite of my meat loaf, I tried to seem only casually interested, but the truth was, I wanted to know about him. The incident on the porch with Hasselene, and now with Puff, drew me into the mystery of him. What was the chink in his armor that everyone else knew and I didn't?

"Grew up right down the road. The family's had a ranch down there since 1867. The folks still live there, but they're gone visiting my sister right now. My nephews are in some kind of baseball play-offs this week." He took a bite of the meat loaf, savoring it like fine French cooking.

The meat loaf might have been good, but curiosity was needling me so insistently I could barely taste my food. "So what kinds of things does your family raise on their farm?"

"Hay on the irrigated land along the creek. Cattle in the hills." Graham answered casually, as if he hadn't noticed I was probing. "My parents both retired from teaching school last year, but even with both of them home, it's hard for them to keep up with the ranch work at their age. They can't quite give up that dream of the next generation living there, you know? It's always been that way. There's a house at each end of the place, and the generations just swap back and forth, one in one house and one in the other. They thought my sister would live there, but she married a computer programmer from Houston, and his job is there. I think after she left they kept hanging on, hoping that if I ever left the army, I'd move back."

"So are you?" For some reason, my stomach tightened. "Moving back, I mean?"

Graham focused on his plate, so that I couldn't see the expression in his eyes. "A lot of things are up in the air right now." The sound of voices floated in through the screen, and he glanced toward the door, frowning. "It's a pretty small world around here, you know?"

I didn't know. I didn't know anything about this small

world or why he didn't like it, but I nodded anyway. "How long have you been out of the army?"

He looked up, his dark eyes narrowing slightly. "About two months." Clearly he realized I was trying to ferret out information.

"Cavalry?" I asked, because the bulk of the units stationed at Killeen were cavalry.

"Aviator." Cocking his head to the side, he gave me a calculating look.

"Oh . . . flyboy?" I said, trying to look casual.

"Used to be." He pointed at me with his fork and I knew he'd let me delve into his past as far as he was going to. "So, what about you, Batgirl?"

I rolled my eyes at the joke.

"Spider-woman?" he teased.

I laughed, even though I knew he was turning on the charm to get me off the subject. "Did you come up with all of that while I was in the bathroom?"

Nodding, he asked again, "So what about you? What's in Richmond?"

"My job." *Condo, boat, car, friends, ex–soul mate . . .*

He gave me a speculative look. "How does an army-brat magazine editor from Richmond end up in the hill country?"

Weird luck. "My job," I answered, and he cast an interested look, waiting for me to elaborate. "I work for a publishing conglomerate that owns a lot of regional magazines. Normally I edit *Southern Woman* and *Shore Life,* based out of the home office in Richmond, but when things come up with other magazines based other places, I go there, too. We recently bought *Rural Texan* in Austin, and we're in the process of retooling it into a new glossy called *Texcetera.*" The story was much more complicated than that, but I didn't go into it. "It was good timing for me, because I wanted to come down here to check on my dad. He moved to Killeen a couple months ago after my mom died, and he hasn't been doing too well."

Graham's eyes met mine with a look of sincere understanding. "I'm sorry to hear that."

"Thanks." I stirred some sugar into my coffee, thinking out loud. "I'm really worried about him. He's supposed to be living in a retirement condo, and instead he's camped out at my grandparents' old farm. The place has been sitting vacant quite a few years. My brothers use it for hunting trips, and it's pretty rough. I think Dad's waiting to follow Mom to the grave." My eyes burned, and I looked out the window, taking a sip of coffee. "I'm sorry. I don't know why I'm telling you all of this."

"No, it's all right." Pushing his plate aside, he stirred his coffee, the clink of the spoon echoing a soulful sound through the room. "I understand. We had the same problem with Pap when Mam died. He laid down in the bed and we thought we never would get him back up and into life. I was a kid in high school at the time, so I don't guess I understood it all completely."

"So did he ever?" I was afraid to ask, in case the answer was no. "Come back, I mean?"

Graham slid his pie into position, then laughed at a memory. "Yeah, he did. He lived ten years after that, and he ate plenty of buttermilk pie. My mother promised she'd make him one every week from Mam's recipe, as long as he didn't try to check out on us again." Graham laughed softly. "I guess that was enough. Mam had always said buttermilk pie was how she hooked Pap in the first place."

I looked at my slice of pie and my heart ached. "I wish I could figure out what would do that for my father." Meeting Graham's gaze, I felt my soul tumbling into the words. It seemed like the most natural thing in the world, the two of us sitting there together in the old store, sipping coffee as the night insects chirred outside the window.

Graham's eyes were sympathetic, soft, understanding. Wise in a way that didn't fit with his hard-chiseled looks. "Give it some time," he said quietly, reaching across the table and taking my hand in his. "It's hard for an old army grunt to ask for help." A warm sensation that had nothing to do with the coffee traveled through me. "We have to head-butt all the walls before we're ready to let someone tell us where the door is."

I didn't miss the fact that he said *we*. I wondered what walls Graham was running into and who would show him the door. "Thanks for the advice. I'll try."

Silence fell over us as Graham finished his pie and I sat staring at mine, thinking I would take it home to Dad, and perhaps it would work a miracle. . . .

The sound of cars passing in the darkness and the hum of voices on the porch reminded me that I needed to get going. It was late, and I hadn't checked on Dad or started on any of the work I'd brought home. *I should call Lindsey, check my e-mail from the office, play the message machine at the condo. . . .*

The reality crept onto my shoulders like a hundred-pound weight, and I realized I hadn't thought about those things in hours. I didn't want to. I wanted to stay right where I was. Of course, that wasn't possible. *This place is an illusion. It's a dream, a fantasy, and you know it.*

Gathering my resolve, I said, "I really should go."

"Yeah, me too . . ." The sentence had the feel of something unfinished. He met my gaze, and I saw a mirror of my own emotions.

"I really enjoyed this," I said softly. He turned his hand over and mine lay lightly within it, a nice fit. My resolve evaporated like the steam from the coffee as his thumb stroked the outline of my palm. I looked up and he was watching me. He had beautiful eyes.

His hand left mine and traveled upward, brushing back the dampened strands of my hair, stroking the curve of my cheek, cupping my chin, and drawing me forward. My eyes drifted closed, my body floating, heady, unaware, yet smoldering as I felt the space between us closing, his lips brushing mine, drawing forth the flame waiting within me.

A chair scraped across the porch outside, and we jerked apart like a couple of teenagers caught necking. In unison we looked toward the screen door. The voices outside hushed to a whisper, and all at once I knew they were watching, whispering about *us*. Graham must have realized it too. He looked embarrassed, and I blushed like a schoolgirl.

"I'd . . ." Blinking hard, I tried to clear the fog from my senses. "I'd really better go."

"Yeah, me too," he said for the second time, then stood up.

I did the same, picking up my uneaten slice of buttermilk pie with the heart-shaped strawberry on top and carrying it with me to the cash register.

Hasselene and Mernalene came in the door right on cue, more evidence that they'd been watching us all along. The ladies met us at the counter, looking frightfully pleased with themselves.

"Did you two have a nice dinner?" There was more than a subtle hint in Hasselene's sticky-sweet tone.

"Everything was great." I blushed again, realizing that by *everything,* I meant more than just the food. "Can I have a box for my slice of pie? I thought I'd take it home to my dad."

Reaching behind the counter, Hasselene handed me my purse, then pulled out a roll of aluminum foil. "I'll wrap it up right there on the plate. Good food shouldn't be eaten out of anything that goes in the trash afterward."

Mernalene added gruffly, "Makes it taste like plastic."

Graham chuckled and said, "Amen, sister."

I protested, "I hate to take your plate."

Hasselene clucked her lips as she wrapped up the piece of pie. "You'll bring it back."

"The biscuits and jam were wonderful this morning, by the way."

"And the coffee?" both of them said at once.

When I looked up from my purse, they were staring at me. I thought about my Crossroads coffee nirvana that morning and said, "Amazing."

The ladies shared conspiratorial smiles.

"So you'll be by in the morning, then?" Hasselene asked, but it was more of a statement than a question. She knew I'd be by.

Strangely enough, I knew I would, too. "Bright and early," I said.

Merna finished ringing up my tab. "That'll be five-ninety-five."

Reaching into my purse, I sorted through the disorganized wad of receipts, business cards, and dollar bills. "For the pie and everything? That doesn't seem like enough."

"It's plenty," Hasselene insisted, cutting off whatever response Mernalene would have given.

I was pulling out a ten when Graham reached around me and put some money on the counter. "I've got it, Aunt Hass."

"No. Really," I protested, glancing at the twenty on the counter, but Graham was already heading toward the door.

Picking up the money, Mernalene called after him, "Wait. At least take your change, Punky."

Punky winced at the nickname, waving us off. "I'll get it in the morning. Coffee's on Laura tomorrow." Then he opened the door and walked out without another word.

I wasn't sure, but it sounded like we had a date for coffee. There was a soaring feeling inside me that shouldn't have been there.

The ladies were so pleased that their faces crinkled like carved pumpkins a week after Halloween.

"Well, here's your pie." Giving me the plate, Hasselene patted my hands. "See you tomorrow." The ladies flanked me and herded me toward the door like livestock, seeming afraid that if I thought about it, I'd change my mind about coming back in the morning.

"All right . . . ummm . . . good night," I said as they shooed me out the door and followed me onto the porch. As they shut the door, I realized the sign had already been flipped over to read, *Closed.* No wonder Graham and I had the place to ourselves.

On the porch, an elderly couple and Puff were sitting at a table eating pie and playing dominoes. They smiled and waved, and I could tell that every one of them knew exactly what was going on.

"We'll be right there," Hasselene called, then clued me in, saying, "It's domino night. Sometimes we have as many as eight players. Kind of a light crowd tonight. There's a potluck VFW in Keetonville."

"Saturday night is music night at the Crossroads," Merna offered, which surprised me because Merna wasn't usually so friendly. I wasn't sure, but I thought I saw her elbow Hasselene.

"Yes, Saturday is music night," Hasselene picked up. "We'll have pickin' and grinnin' out back. You should come."

"Oh, I . . ." *am sure I'll be working,* I meant to say, but something in their expectant expressions made me say instead, ". . . think that sounds like fun." *It did? Pickin' and grinnin'?* Was I losing my mind? "I mean, I'll have to see how my dad is. I want to spend some time with him this weekend."

"Bring him along," Hasselene suggested.

"He's not up to doing much since my mom passed away." Short of hiring henchmen, I couldn't imagine how I'd get my dad out of the house and to the Crossroads.

"It'll be just what he needs," Mernalene coaxed.

"I'll think about it." Maybe it would be good for him, if I could somehow talk him into it. Maybe some of . . . whatever was happening to me would rub off on him. "Thanks."

"You're welcome," Hasselene said. "We told your reporter friend to come, too."

I realized suddenly that in my mountain-climbing, bat-hunting, meat loaf–eating frenzy, I'd completely lost track of my original reason for coming there. That wasn't like me at all. "I meant to thank you for being so gracious about the interview. I'm sorry I didn't ask ahead of time about doing an article. The idea came up suddenly, and we're up against a deadline. The magazine goes to print tomorrow."

Smiling, Hasselene nodded. "Yes, yes, we had such a nice chat, and that baby is a doll. She took our picture— your friend, I mean, not the baby. Been a few years since anyone has taken our picture. It used to happen all the time. . . . Oh, but that's a long story and you need to get on your way."

"Yes. I really do," I agreed reluctantly.

Hasselene patted me on the shoulder, and I think Mernalene gave me a shove toward the steps. Clearly they were through sharking me for one evening and were ready to move on to dealing dominoes with the crowd on the porch. "Have a good night, Laura," they echoed in unison.

"You too." I crossed the parking lot, dark except for the glow from the Crossroads porch and one flickering light on a telephone pole.

Somewhere in the shadows, a vehicle pulled onto the road and picked up speed. I imagined that it was Graham, driving off into the night, headed . . . somewhere.

As I climbed into my car, I tried to imagine where he was going, and what he would do tonight, and who he would spend time with, but I couldn't.

For some reason, that bothered me.

Chapter 11

DAD was asleep on the sofa when I got to the farm-house. There was little furniture in the bedrooms, so when he slept at all, he slept on the old sofa or recliners my brothers used for their occasional guy weekends. Being older, Mark and Daniel could remember visiting my grandparents at the farm, and they shared a sentimental attachment to the place that hadn't filtered down to Lindsey and me.

Standing there looking at my father asleep on the threadbare couch, I wondered if I should give up and have some furniture moved in for him. He was so steadfast in his determination not to return to the retirement village, and even if he did, he'd probably do the same thing he was doing here—sit around waiting to die. We couldn't force him to take up golf, or go to the potlucks on Saturday nights, or the wood-carvers' circle on Tuesdays, or learn to function in a world without Mom.

In all of my life, I'd never considered the depth of the bond between them. I couldn't remember ever, not even one time, having heard my father tell my mother he loved her. Yet there was a way they looked at each other, as if each knew the other's heart without having to ask, without having to search or wonder. They were two parts of one person, bonded through sixty years of army towns, four children, countless tours of duty that took him far away, yet never separated them. And now here we stood, Mom gone, Dad asleep on the sofa in three-day-old clothes, and me wondering why I'd never realized that my parents were in love.

Maybe I'd never thought about what love really meant. Maybe it wasn't about fighting to preserve yourself, or your space, or your "me" time. Maybe it was about wanting someone so much you fell in all the way. Headfirst. Every bit. About caring for someone else so much that you wanted that person's happiness more than you wanted your own. About not being able to imagine how you would breathe in a world you didn't inhabit together.

Dale and I had never had it. We had romance. We had desire. We had vacations. We had tug-of-war—my time, your time, our time. We never had love.

"Oh, Mom," I whispered into the dim, silent air, feeling the tingling of tears that so often came when I thought of her. "I wish you were here. I wish you could tell me what to do now. Everything's falling apart."

There was more truth in that statement than I was ready to face. Mom was the glue that held the whole spoiled, self-centered bunch of us together. Mom took care of the holidays and the birthday cards and gatherings full of food and grandkids. She gave Lindsey and me and my brothers advice on love and marriage, while we laughed behind our hands and called her ideas old-fashioned. We never considered that, just maybe, she understood all of it better than we did.

Now we were like planets with no sun to orbit, drifting in space.

Setting the plate of pie on the table, I leaned over Dad and pulled the blanket away from his face. He muttered something in his sleep as I folded it back against his chest, still broad and thick despite all the weight he'd lost these last months. Even at seventy-five, he was an imposing figure, his chin strong and stubborn, his thick silver hair shaved in the burr that went back as far as my memory. He was a statue in my mind, always the same. Always untouchable.

I never would have guessed he'd have such a hard time with Mom's death. Mark, Daniel, Lindsey, all of us thought he'd get right up and soldier on, unchanging and unchanged.

Of course, I'd thought I would, too.

Dad caught a ragged breath in his sleep, and rose up slightly, as if he were looking at something. Laughing softly, he whispered, "Paddy . . . she's . . . all right."

He always called my mom Paddy. We never knew why, and neither of them would say.

What was he dreaming about? Was Mom in his dream? I wished she were in mine. I wanted her to come to me in diaphanous gossamer white, and touch my face, and tell me she was fine. I wanted her to tell me what was on the other side of the door, that there was another side. . . .

I turned and walked across the room, rubbing my eyes.

"Don't be sad, Lauralina. Don't be sad." The words drifted into the air like mist, and I spun around, surprised to find Dad still sleeping.

Mom was the one who called me Lauralina, a takeoff on Thumbelina, because I was always a head shorter than Lindsey. A whiff of cool night breeze drifted in the window, carrying the scent of honeysuckle. I felt Mom there. I felt her all around me.

Running my hands up and down my arms, I moved to the old green recliner that had been hers when I was a little girl. Her Bible was lying in the seat, where Dad must have left it. Even that was strange, because the last time I'd seen it, it was at the condo. Picking it up, I stroked my fingers across the cover, then sat down in the chair next to the window and hugged the Bible to my chest.

Dad whispered something I couldn't understand, then said my mother's name again.

I closed my eyes, wishing I could slip inside his dream and be with her again. I had so many questions I wanted to ask her—about life, love, what things should matter, which path I should choose.

But my mind traveled to the Crossroads, to Graham and me at the old mill. The air was cool and filled with the scent of honeysuckle. Graham reached for my hand, and I slipped my fingers into his. Pulling me close, he kissed me as we stood in the soft green grass at the edge of the stream, gazing back at the mill. On the side of the building, a movie was playing, shining against the white rock wall like a drive-in screen. John Wayne in *Rio Bravo*. People were watching, just standing in the grass, all the people from the pictures on the wall of the Crossroads, young and vibrant and happy.

The crowd parted like a sea, and at the center I saw her. "Mom?" I cried, reaching for her.

She smiled and waved me away. "See where the stream leads." The words were only a whisper, like a thought passing between us.

Turning, I gazed at the stream, watching the water flow, thinking of all the unknown places it would pass. What would happen if I followed that wandering path?

Losing myself in the play of light and shadows, I stood for a long time, staring into the water, listening to the song of the brook, wondering whether I had the courage to follow beyond what I could see. Finally Graham's hand tightened around mine, and I remembered that I wasn't alone. A sense of comfort washed over me like cool, sweet water flowing from the place where we touched.

"Laura," he whispered, but it was not his voice. His hand parted from mine, and the stream and the mill, all of the people, and *Rio Bravo* vanished like vapor before a flame.

"Graham," I called, trying to find him in the darkness that remained.

"Laura. Laura, wake up." The voice was weak and raspy, not deep and musical like Graham's. "Laura, wake up. It's Dad."

I jerked awake, and something heavy tumbled from my lap, landing on the floor. Staring at it, I tried to make my mind come to reality.

Mom's Bible. I remembered all the times I had seen it in her hands. In all the different towns, in all the different churches, chapels, houses, whether Dad was home or away with his unit, Mom and that Bible were always the same.

I read the verse Mom had underlined at the top of the page in Jeremiah 6.

This is what the Lord says: "Stand at the crossroads and look; ask for the ancient paths, ask where the good way is, and walk in it, and you will find rest for your souls."

Beside it, she had written, *Find the right way.*

Picking up the book with one hand, I lifted it into my lap, staring at the verse. *Stand at the crossroads and look.* . . . When had she underlined those words—a few months ago, a few years ago, maybe in some long-past Bible study on some army base on the other side of the world before Lindsey and I were even born? *Find the right way.* Which way was the right way?

"Dad?" I whispered, choking on a lump of emotion. "How did this get here? How did Mom's Bible get here?"

"Laura, are you all right?" I realized Dad was still holding my hand. His brows were knitted in a worried expression, something other than his usual scowl.

"Yes." My voice was scarcely a whisper. "How did Mom's Bible get here?"

Dad glanced at the book with a befuddled expression. "I don't remember." The glitter of some old memory moistened his eyes, and he took the book from my hands, setting it on the end table. "It's three in the morning. What are you doing here in Mom's chair?"

"I guess I fell asleep." I leaned forward so that the footrest snapped down. My legs were heavy and numb, testifying to the fact that I'd been there awhile. "What time did you say it was?"

"Three in the morning," Dad repeated.

The aura of tranquillity vanished, and I jumped to attention like a soldier asleep on watch. "Three in the morning! I've got to get home. I've got work to get done yet tonight."

Dad eyed me critically, his scowl melting back into place. "What kind of work can a person do at three in the morning?" He groused like I was a teenager trying to go out past curfew. *Young lady, what kind of decent activity starts after nine o'clock at night?*

I took a deep breath, determined not to get started with him. "I brought home a stack of papers from work. We're up against deadline and it's touch and go as to whether we'll make it. This is Friday morning, and our print run is scheduled for tomorrow, six A.M. I'm still one article short, I haven't seen the final mockup of the cover, and I have a load of things in my briefcase that need to be signed off." Why I was telling him all that, I wasn't sure. Maybe to help get it straight in my own mind. Dad had never cared beans about my job, which he always described to people as, "Working on those ladies' serials."

Pressing his lips together, he crossed his arms and barred the way to the door. "No kind of sane person goes driving around town at three in the morning. Not safe. Asking for trouble."

"Oh, for heaven's sake, Dad, I'll be all right." I didn't mean to, but I huffed and rolled my eyes, feeling sixteen years old again.

Sidestepping to the coffee table, he began searching through the stack of newspapers piled there. "What if you have a flat tire, or the car breaks down in the dark? What about that? Right here in the paper, there's a story about a woman who got attacked in her car outside the grocery store last weekend. Army sergeant. Knew self-defense. Only reason she survived, and . . ." He left the sentence unfinished and turned his concentration to finding the article. We both knew the rest of the sentence anyway: *And if that could happen to a woman who's good enough for the army, what in the world could happen to a poor, pathetic magazine editor?*

"I'll be all right, Dad." I picked up my purse.

Yanking a newspaper from the stack, he stood up. "You can just get your work and bring it in here." He faced me with his feet spread apart and a newspaper dangling between his fingers. "Safer that way. When it gets light, you can go on home then."

I fumbled through my purse, trying to find my keys. If I stayed I wouldn't end up getting half as much done. "I can't. . . ." A movement in the corner of the room caught my attention. It was nothing significant—just the play of moonbeams in the darkened hallway, but I stopped to stare at it for an instant.

Silhouetted against it was the shadow of my father, a reflection thinner and more stooped over than the man casting it. I turned and looked at him—sad, lonely, too proud to say so.

I realized that was the first time all week he'd actually asked me to stay. Usually he tried to coerce me into it by losing things he needed, or misplacing his medication, or messing up the MediMinder, so that I would have to go through and arrange all the pills again. I, on the other hand, had tried hard not to spend time at the farm, because I didn't want to encourage Dad to stay here.

So far my approach wasn't working. "All right, Dad." I set my purse down beside Mom's chair. "I'll go get my stuff out of the car."

Dad looked more pleased than he had in a long time. I didn't know whether it was because I was staying or because he'd won the argument.

He hustled stiff-legged to the door to slip on the old shoes he kept there. "I'll help you carry things in."

"No. No, it's all right. There isn't that much," I insisted, worried that he'd trip and fall outside in the dark. He wasn't very steady when he awoke at night.

Dad followed me out the door anyway, and together we divided up the papers and the laptop and carried them up the steps into the old frame house. Plugging in my computer next to Mom's old chair, I sat down with that and my pile of *Texcetera* and logged on to my e-mail first. The article from Collie was waiting there. *Crossroads,* the header said, *received at twelve-forty-five A.M.*

"Thank you, Collie," I whispered.

Dad took a step closer, then hovered beside my chair, looking at the computer screen. I glanced up and he backed away a step, raising a hand palm-out in a placating gesture. "I'll leave you alone. Won't even know I'm here. Go read my paper until I get sleepy again."

With a quick shuffle-shuffle-shuffle-turn, he crossed the room to the sofa and began noisily rearranging the newspapers on the coffee table, unearthing the foil-wrapped plate from the Crossroads.

"What's this?" he barked with the usual resentment he showed when I tried to force food on him.

Turning back to my computer, I punched up Collie's

article. "Oh, that's from a little café I passed on the way to work. It's buttermilk pie."

"Buttermilk pie?" he repeated as he began unwrapping the edges of the foil. "Buttermilk pie . . ." Pulling off the foil, he held up the pie as if it were a gold nugget. "And on a real plate. Won't taste like plastic."

I chuckled. "That's what the lady said who gave it to me."

"I haven't had a slice of buttermilk pie in years— since before I married your mother. When I was in Germany after the war, there was a little old German grocery. Pretty little German girl worked there, and she served up the best buttermilk pie. . . ." He trailed off, but there was a twinkle in his eyes that said there was more to the story.

Sitting back in my chair, I waited to see if he would continue, but he snatched a fork off a dirty plate on the end table, swished it in the stale glass of water beside the plate, and stabbed the tip of the slice, saying, "Buttermilk pie . . ." with an air of reverence.

"Dad!" I protested. "I would have gotten you a clean fork."

"Don't need it. This one's fine." He punctuated the sentence by taking the first bite and swilling it around in his mouth.

I pointed a finger at him. "You're going to get botulism."

"Already had it," he replied matter-of-factly, then stabbed a second bite of pie with more enthusiasm than he'd shown for anything in months. "Fort Bliss mess hall, 1969. Bad batch of chili," he added, and under the influence of botulism and buttermilk pie, my father actually smiled.

A puff of laughter stole past my lips as I turned my attention back to my e-mail. On the other side of the room, Dad continued to loudly appreciate his slice of Crossroads pie.

Gratitude overwhelmed me. I was thankful for that simple moment, him on the couch and me in Mom's chair. Not complaining, not fighting, not mourning. I was grateful for the slice of buttermilk pie and the memory it brought. I was grateful that Hasselene hadn't put it in a plastic to-go container.

Sometimes things work out the way they're supposed to.

Collie's article was another act of divine providence. If I could have conceived the perfect article for our Hometime feature, Collie's "Crossroads" would have been it. From the first paragraph:

> There are places just beyond the map, but not beyond memory. The old Crossroads on FM 47-B between Austin and Killeen is such a place. For eighty years, since their father purchased the Lone Star Café and millworks in 1922, twin sisters Hasselene and Mernalene Goodnight have been serving up homemade sourdough biscuits, hot lunches, supper six nights a week, and legendary coffee, the secret ingredient for which is rumored to have come up the Goodnight-Loving trail with their great-great-uncle, Charles Goodnight.

To the last sentences:

> Now crumbling, with peeling paint and rusted advertising signs from an era gone by, old Lone Star Café has the look of a place that has seen better days. Perhaps therein lies the attraction for the harried commuters who have recently unearthed this hill-country treasure. In these times of impersonal service and Styro-enclosed food, there's

something particularly charming about entering through a torn screen door, settling into a recycled church pew next to a picnic table, and watching the ceiling fans turn lazily overhead while biscuits come to your table in a gingham-lined basket with a jar of homemade jam. There's something irresistible about down-home service and a place where the only two plates on the menu are today's main dish and yesterday's leftovers, if they've got any. It could be the home-baked pies that are winning a new generation to this nearly forgotten landmark, or just the rare chance to forget the modern world and take a trip back to better days.

Then again, the magic attraction of the Crossroads may not have anything to do with friendly service, or quaint atmosphere, or down-home Texas cooking. Perhaps the lure isn't the food at all, but that rumored secret ingredient in the coffee.

Collie had captured the essence of the Crossroads—the sense of bygone times that I could never quite put into words. Even the pictures she attached to the e-mail were perfect—Hasselene behind the counter, Mernalene taking biscuits out of the big oven beside the fry grill, both of them standing in their living room, surrounded by old photos of famous visitors.

"Perfect," I murmured, pushing the send button to forward the article on to the copyeditor.

"What?" Dad inquired from across the room, startling me from my thoughts. I'd forgotten he was there. Actually, I'd forgotten where I was altogether. Collie's writing could do that to me, even when I didn't know the place she was writing about. Her article about the Crossroads was pure magic, and I knew that *because* I'd been there.

"Oh, this article. It's perfect."

Dad grunted, or said "Um-hmm," I couldn't tell which.

"It's about the place where they make the buttermilk pie."

"Uh?" he said with greater enthusiasm. "Sounds interesting."

I almost fell out of my chair. That was the first time ever, *ever* in my life Dad had said those two words in connection with something I'd done. It felt good. It felt like for once we were connecting. "Well, I'll tell you what," I said. "As soon as the first issue of the magazine gets back from the printer I'll get a copy of the article for you."

"No need," Dad said, and my balloon deflated. "I'll buy one when I'm at the store."

There were several different ways I could have interpreted that, but I chose to take it as a sign of support. Dad wanted to buy his own copy. "That sounds good," I answered. Dad grunted an affirmation, got up, and headed into the kitchen. I went back to work.

Two hours later it was getting light outside. I had finished most of what I'd brought home, and I'd taken care of my e-mail list. Folding the laptop and packing my briefcase, I wrapped the used pie plate in the foil, balanced it on top of my stack, and went looking for Dad. I found him sitting on the porch drinking coffee.

"Coffee," he said. I couldn't tell if it was a statement or a question.

"No, thanks. I need to run home, take a shower"— *wash the bat guano out of my hair. Gee whiz, I haven't even done that yet*—"change clothes"—*go by the Crossroads to meet Graham Keeton for coffee*—"and head to the office."

Dad nodded with a pitiful expression that let me know he was about to lay on the emotional blackmail.

"Dad, it's five-thirty. I have to go get dressed and go

to work." Bolstering my determination, I started down the steps.

Behind me, I heard him standing up from the porch rocker. "Bring me another piece of that buttermilk pie." Not quite a statement. Not quite a polite request.

It reminded me of something I'd forgotten to tell him. "Listen, Dad, I'll have to check on you by phone tonight. Our deadline is six A.M. Saturday and we're behind, so we'll be pulling an all-nighter at the office in Austin." Dad did not look happy, so I added quickly, "You have my number if there's a problem, and you can also call Mr. and Mrs. Olsen at the retirement colony. All right?"

Dad grunted, turning his face away, slumping back into his chair.

"I'll be back first thing in the morning, though, as soon as we get the magazine to press." Dad still wouldn't look at me, so to sweeten the deal I added, "I'll stop by the Crossroads café on my way home and get another piece of buttermilk pie for you. All right?"

That promise won me a nod and a quick, "Watch the road. Early yet, and there's dew on the pavement. Could be deer on the roads."

"Yes, sir," I answered, a habit from the past when everything was "Yes, sir" and "No, sir," and we stayed at attention whenever he was around. Looking at him now, crumpled in his chair, puckered and faded like an old quilt, it was hard to imagine.

I hurried off the porch, feeling guilty, feeling pressured to get to the office and get the magazine on track for deadline.

I went through the steps in my head as I rushed across town to the condo. Even though I'd been to print hundreds of times with larger, more complex magazines, I couldn't shake the feeling that I was forgetting something, that something would go wrong, and it would be my fault. Everything that had happened lately had me off balance.

You're being paranoid, Laura. You're a little out of sorts, that's all. On time to press, and you'll be back in the game again.

I told myself that over and over as I showered, washing my hair several times to rid it of the real or imagined crusty feeling where the bat had dive-bombed me. Unfortunately, when I got out of the shower and cleared the steam off the mirror, I could still see it there—a very clear brown streak where I had smeared the bat doody while trying to remove it the night before.

"Great," I muttered, then grabbed a hair clip, combed my hair straight back so the streak wouldn't show as much, and inserted the clip at the nape of my neck. *Not too bad,* I thought as I put on makeup and dressed. I looked a little better today, a little less pale, less stressed, surprisingly enough.

Would Graham notice?

Rolling my eyes at the woman in the mirror, I slipped on my jewelry. What was I thinking? What was I doing obsessing, or flirting, or whatever it was, with some Texas guy I barely knew?

You're here to work, I reminded myself, brushing the questions off like lint, then giving my blue suit a last once-over before heading for the door.

On the way to the Crossroads, I tried not to think about Graham, or wonder if he would be there for coffee. I tried not to wonder if he'd have some crazy adventure in mind this morning.

No matter how tempting, you have to tell him no, Laura. You can't stay. You can't hang out, go mountain climbing, visit the bat cave, or anything else. You're stopping by for a quick cup of coffee. To go.

. . . And maybe a biscuit. Or two.

. . . Maybe a quick chat.

. . . But that's it.

I added force to the words with a determined nod and a straightening of my shoulders as I reached the old leaning stop sign. Shaking back and forth in the wind, it made a scornful sound I could hear even through the closed car windows. *Tsk, tsk, tsk, tsk . . .*

Even the stop sign knew I didn't have an ounce of resolve where Graham and the Crossroads were concerned.

Something jumped from my stomach to my chest and fluttered around as I pulled into the parking lot, past the side of the building to the front, noticing that it was even more crowded than the morning before. Graham's HAZMAT truck was near the gas pumps, and he was standing on the steps, leaning against the railing, talking to a couple of locals in straw cowboy hats like his.

Raising his coffee cup, he waved at me as I crossed the parking lot, carrying the used pie plate. I caught myself grinning from ear to ear and waving madly in return, and I admonished myself, *Stop acting idiotic. Be . . . dignified.*

Yes. Dignified. So far Graham hadn't seen my sophisticated side. If it still existed.

When I reached the porch, he excused himself from the conversation and motioned to the domino table, where a second cup of coffee waited. "Got some coffee for you," he said as we met on the steps. "Crowded in there this morning. They're out of biscuits already."

"Wow," I said, peeking through the glass and noting the line at the counter. "Thanks for getting me in ahead of the rush. Let me hand in this plate and I'll come back out here."

Inside, I threaded through the crowd. The seats were full, and the line at the counter was three-deep. Puff, the beauty operator, was serving coffee while Hasselene worked the cash register.

Puff stopped and gave me a look of particular interest. "Good morning, there. Did you find Graham? He had a cup of coffee for you."

I nodded. "I saw him. Thanks." Slipping through the crowd, I set Dad's used pie plate on the counter.

Looking frazzled, Hasselene waved at me and said, "Good morning, Laura. How are you this fine day?"

"Great." For the first time in months I meant it. "My dad loved the pie, and he was very glad it didn't come in a Styrofoam container. Thanks."

Nodding, she counted change to HOUSHNTR, who gave Hasselene a huge smile and slid the change back across the counter, waving her hand palm-down, displaying a fine manicure and saying, "Oh, goodness, you keep that." She sidestepped and leaned forward, cutting off the conversation between Hasselene and me, and saying in a low voice, "So, did you and your sister talk any more about the retirement village on Inks Lake? Those apartments are going fast, but I can still get you into one—so many wonderful activities there for active seniors." Reaching across the counter, she patted Hasselene's hand as the old woman picked up the change and dropped it into a jar by the cash register. "And don't worry one bit about the listing on this old place. I can handle that for you. Oh, of course there is some work to be done here, but I have good buyers for quaint country properties like this one. All I have to do is bring the listing papers by, and—"

"We're not interested," Mernalene barked as she rounded the kitchen doorway and set a tray of hot biscuits on the counter. Narrowing her eyes at the real estate lady, she turned to Hasselene and repeated, "We're *not interested*."

Hasselene flushed and gave HOUSHNTR an apologetic smile. "We're not interested." She reached for my father's used pie plate and turned to me, clearly looking to escape the heavy-handed sales pitch. "I knew your father would appreciate our buttermilk pie. Our pie cures a multitude of ills."

I chuckled. "That's what you said about the coffee."

She winked at me. "And it's true, isn't it? By the way, Graham has your coffee outside."

I might have imagined it, but I thought HOUSHNTR's ears perked at the sound of Graham's name. Hasselene gave her a peeved look and said, "If you can wait over there, I'll take care of these folks' checks and be right up with your biscuits as soon as they have a minute to cool."

HOUSHNTR glanced over her shoulder toward the door, looking like she was thinking of waiting outside. With Graham.

"It'll only be a moment," Hasselene insisted. "Wait *right here*." She glanced at me and made a hand motion that said, *Shoo, shoo, shoo.* So I did.

Graham was waiting at the table with our coffee. There was only one chair, and he stood up, motioning for me to take it.

"Oh, that's all right," I said. "I can't stay long."

"Me either." He motioned again to the chair. "Have to go inspect an anhydrous storage facility in Taylor this morning, and then do an asbestos screening on a building downtown." He didn't sound excited about it. It occurred to me to wonder again exactly what kind of work he did, and why he wasn't a pilot anymore. Most of the guys who left the army with their wings went on to take jobs with airlines. I wondered if that had anything to do with the deep dark secret I'd tried to ferret out the night before.

"So what is HAZMAT exactly?" I asked, trying to sound casual, polite. Sophisticated. "I mean, what does it involve?"

Shrugging, he scooted an overturned crate toward the

table and sat on it, his hands braced on his knees. "Hazardous materials," he said matter-of-factly, his face hidden beneath the brim of his hat as he sipped his coffee. "Anything toxic, explosive, flammable, or unidentifiable."

I focused on my coffee long enough to stir in some sugar, thinking about what to say next, how to subtly probe into his past. I wanted to know what the deep, dark thing was—the thing that everyone told him he should leave in the past and forget, the thing I saw behind his easy smiles and lust for adventure.

When I glanced up, Graham was looking at my hair.

He grinned, his eyes twinkling. "Didn't wash out, huh?"

I rolled my eyes. "It makes pretty good hair dye."

He had the nerve to chuckle. "I know where you can get some more."

"No, thanks. I think I've had all the guano experience I need."

"Chicken," he challenged.

"Hardly!" I defended, and then both of us laughed.

The screen door slammed and we looked up as HOUSHNTR stepped onto the porch. She was pleased that we had noticed her entrance. She glanced around like she was looking for a chair, then paused when she saw there wasn't one. "How are you this morning, Graham?" she said finally, then glanced at me and added, "And . . . umm . . . my gosh, I don't think I ever got your name. I'm Evie."

"Laura," I said, and stood up, extending a hand as she stepped closer.

Shaking my hand, she gave me what seemed like a genuine smile, and I felt guilty for having harbored less-than-kind thoughts toward her. "Oh, you're the magazine editor," she said. "The ladies were telling me earlier that you're doing an article on their place here. I think that's absolutely wonderful. This is such a quaint old stop in the road, and the coffee ... well, it's to die for."

"It is that," I agreed.

The three of us stood silent for a moment, and finally Evie had the grace to bow out. "Well, I should be getting on the road." She gave Graham one last glance, quick but intimate. "See you soon. Oh, and will you let me know if there's anything ... well, you know ... anything I can do?"

If I had been wondering about Graham before, that really made me wonder. What exactly was his game? Did he flirt with every woman who came through the Crossroads, and if so, what did he want with me? I wasn't any more his type than he was mine. Then again, neither was HOUSHNTR. I drew a perverse sense of satisfaction from that observation.

When I looked back at Graham, he was studying me—not looking at me, studying me—like he'd been thinking the same things I'd been thinking. There was a question on his lips, I could tell, so I beat him to the punch. "So how many years were you in the army?"

"Twelve."

He didn't offer any further explanation, so I tried to sound casual. "Why did you decide to get out?" *And what is the big secret everyone around here is hiding?*

Some emotion flashed across his face, and he looked away, his eyes reflecting the gathering morning sunlight. "Long story." His gaze cut to me, the frown lifting, the pensive expression still in his eyes. "Why did you want to know?"

"I ..." The parry of question for question caught me off guard. "I was curious. . . ." *That sounded bad.* "Interested ..." *Even worse.* "I just wanted to get to know you better." *Open mouth, insert foot.*

Cocking his head to the side, he looked at me, stroking his finger and thumb along the curve of his bottom lip, catching a drop of coffee. "It's not a very interesting story." Pausing again, he leaned back in his chair, dark lashes lowering slightly over his eyes. "But I can think of one that would be interesting."

My heart slowed its hurried rhythm, beating in time with the measured stroke of his thumb along his lips, back and forth, back and forth. "What would be interesting?" I heard myself say.

His gaze held mine, warm, strong, unwavering, the cool blue of a darkening sky. "It would be interesting to know why a magazine editor from Richmond sits in a parking lot all day while a hailstorm beats holes in her Lexus." He lowered his hand slowly, poising it on the table between us like a cat about to pounce on a canary. "That would be interesting to know." His lips raised slightly—a smile? A challenge? "Since we're asking questions."

Swallowing hard, I rocked back in my chair, feeling blindsided. I don't know why I should have. I'd done the same thing to him. That was what he was pointing out with his question, wasn't it? "It's not a very interesting story, either."

Nodding, he took a sip of his coffee, the intense look fading. "Then we're just two regular folks with no interesting stories to tell, sounds like."

I chuckled at the foolishness of it all—Graham and I acting like a couple of actors in some high-drama soap opera about hidden secrets and dangerous pasts. Yet, I did want to know about him—no, not know *about* him; I wanted to *know* him. "It's a little early in the morning for all of that, huh?" I didn't want to dissolve the conversation altogether, only to postpone it.

Nodding, he swilled his coffee, staring into the dark liquid. We sat silent for a few moments, not uncomfortable really, just listening to the sounds of the morning—the breeze rustling through the leaves, a dove cooing somewhere in the cedar bushes, the hum of voices inside the café, a dog scratching out a wallow in the damp dirt beneath the porch steps. The scent of lilacs drifted from somewhere not far away.

"It's a beautiful day." I realized that, until that moment, I hadn't even noticed.

"Yes. It is."

A clock chimed inside, working its way slowly into my consciousness. Half past the hour. If I didn't get on the road now, I'd be late. "I should go," I said.

Seeming as reluctant as I was, he nodded. "Yeah. Me too."

As we started toward the steps, Hasselene opened the screen door and held out two bundles in blue gingham napkins. "Here, take some biscuits." She handed them to us in a rush, without letting the screen door shut behind her. "You can bring the napkins back when you come for the pickin' and grinnin' Saturday night." She glanced from me to Graham. "Both of you *are* coming for the pickin' and grinnin' Saturday night, aren't you?"

"I hadn't thought about it," I replied.

Hasselene patted my arm. "Well, you come, and bring your dad." She pointed a finger at Graham. "And you come, and bring your guitar." She gave me a sly look. "Graham learned how to play and sing right here on this porch with all of us old folks. He was such a cute little thing, singing those old songs, and yodeling like one of those Swiss mountain climbers." Then she disappeared through the doorway and the screen door slapped shut.

I looked at Graham as we walked down the steps. "Yodeling?" I said. "Guitar?"

He ducked his head. "Don't expect much. I haven't played that thing in years."

Graham's a musician, I thought, and suddenly he took on a whole new dimension. *An artistic type who plays the guitar. Who would have thought?* "But you're going to play it Saturday, right?"

He nodded as we parted ways in the parking lot. "I'm guano try."

I groaned at the bad bat joke. "That was sad."

"I know."

"See you later, Graham."

"Have a good day, Laura. Good luck with the deadline."

I glanced over my shoulder as he climbed in his truck. *He remembered the deadline. Wow.*

Chapter 12

AT six-thirty-seven A.M. Saturday morning, the first issue of *Texcetera* went to press. A cheer rose through the office as we sent the last of the files to the printing company. We stood in the parking garage hugging and high-fiving for ten minutes like we'd won the Super Bowl.

Even Don stopped scowling long enough to take part in the revelry for a minute or two before he replaced his scowl and headed for his car, saying, "I'm tired. I'm going home."

I hovered between thanking him for his hard work and just telling him to have a good weekend. "Have a good weekend," I said finally, afraid that the thank-you might come off as me rubbing it in that I was his boss.

"Uh-huh," Don grunted over his shoulder. "I won't be in on Monday."

"I don't blame you," I replied before he was out of earshot. In spite of the fact that Don didn't like the new concept for the magazine, and didn't like my being there, he had put in dozens of hours of overtime in the past month to make sure we met deadline. "See you Tuesday."

Waving over his shoulder, he got in the car. The rest of the staff stood waiting for him to leave the parking lot, then sent up another cheer, turned around, and headed back into the building or toward their cars.

Beside me, Kristi reached into her purse for her keys. "I am *so* out of here. My apartment's a mess, and I've got a date tonight with Rick—you remember, the guy I met on the Internet?" She jittered in place. "He's so cute in his picture. I'm cooking us dinner tonight at my place."

I frowned, feeling parental, though I wasn't sure why. Kristi was twenty-three years old, an adult, and I barely knew her. "Do you think that's a good idea? I mean, you hardly even know this guy, except for a couple of phone conversations. Maybe you should get together some-place public the first time or two." This from a woman who was recently seen exploring the bat cave with a complete stranger.

Kristi seemed surprised that I'd offered a personal comment, something I usually tried to discourage. She had a bad habit of standing around in cubicle doorways talking about dates and parties. I'd tried to get across that we didn't have time for that. Now here I was giving her dating advice.

Rolling her eyes, she said, "I'll be careful."

"Good. You know, the Internet isn't the safest place to meet guys these days." *And probably neither is the parking lot of a gas station . . .*

Crossing her arms, she swung her hips petulantly to one side, then gave me a mock sneer. "That's easy for you to say. You're gorgeous, and thin, and you have a boyfriend."

I swallowed hard, wondering how the conversation had turned to me. "Look, all I meant was, be careful. I was worried about you, that's all."

Kristi's mouth dropped open. "Oh . . . uhhh ... all right," she stammered. We stood there in uncomfortable silence for a few moments, having crossed the customary lines between us. Kristi sorted through her keys and finally grasped the car key between her thumb and forefinger. "So . . . uhh . . . what are you doing this weekend?"

You wouldn't believe me if I told you. "Nothing special." *Lie, lie, lie.*

Frowning, she gave me a sideways glance. "Are you here through next week, then?"

"Probably through midweek, anyway. It depends on how long things take." Suddenly midweek seemed far too soon to be leaving.

Kristi jiggled her keys as if she were testing the weight of them, or thinking about whether to probe deeper or exit gracefully. The staff had probably paid her to find out how soon the dragon lady would be gone. "Is everything all right, Ms. Draper? The last couple days . . . I just thought . . . well . . . maybe something was wrong since that day we had the big storm here."

I turned away. Was my breakdown that obvious, or did Kristi, for all of her lack of common sense, just happen to have a special sense about people? "No, things are all right," I answered finally. "Everything's right on schedule." But then, schedules weren't the problem. "Have a good weekend."

She shrugged. " 'Kay. You too."

"I will," I returned, and headed back into the office to get my things.

The corridors and cubicles were emptying quickly. There was a sense of jubilation in the air, and by the time I'd gathered my belongings and headed to my car, I'd caught a dose of it. The first issue of *Texcetera*, which had been hopelessly behind a month ago, was in the hands of the printer. Another victory. The corporate office would be thrilled.

I decided to celebrate by stopping for a three-dollar cup of coffee at the cappuccino bar on the corner and a haircut at the walk-in salon down the block.

The lady behind the cappuccino counter was rude, and the cappuccino machine was uncooperative. Taking my money, she told me it would be a minute on the cappuccino—they were waiting for the machine to warm up.

Too tired to argue, I sank down on a bar stool and rested my chin on my hand, closing my eyes and sinking into a catnap as I listened to the waitresses talking behind the counter.

The discussion was about Internet dating sites. Kristi would have liked it.

I nodded off, thinking about Graham, about what he might be doing, and if he was at the Crossroads this morning, or someplace else. It was Saturday. What did he usually do on Saturday mornings?

My mind wandered to our conversation the morning before. *It's not a very interesting story.* But I was interested. I wanted to know. What was the big, dark thing in his past that Hasselene said he needed to let go of?

. My chin fell from my hand, waking me. The conversation behind the counter had turned to the latest news on the interstate bridge contractor scandal. ". . . reopened the interstate today," the waitress was saying. "I don't think it's safe. If one bridge can fall down, it could happen to any of them, I say."

"Well, now," the cashier replied, "I heard they'd found out that bridge got hit by a crane sometime back and the workers didn't report it and that was what made it fall down. I heard they might send some people to jail over it. The governor was on TV saying that the cracks they found in the other bridges were only surface cracks, and those bridges are right as rain. He said it's perfectly safe."

Snorting, cappuccino lady stuck a straw in my cup. "I don't believe it for a minute. I don't think it's safe. You won't catch me getting on the interstate. I'm not in that much of a hurry to get anywhere." She plunked my cup down in front of me, splashing drops of foam off the top. "There you go." She didn't smile, or tell me to come back, or give me homemade biscuits in a little gingham napkin.

Stepping out the front door, I stood on the sidewalk, trying to decide whether to walk or drive to the Hair Hut I'd spotted down the block. No matter how tired I was, I wanted to get the brown streak removed before the picking and grinning that night at the Crossroads.

The Crossroads . . . My mind hit on an idea.

Puff. Puff, the beauty-shop lady, knew Graham. She knew Graham's past, and she knew the secret. And she liked to talk.

I hurried to my car and left Austin behind, heading toward the Crossroads, and Puff, and I wasn't sure what else. A measure of guilt began to needle me on the way, telling me I shouldn't be nosing into Graham's background—that what he didn't want to tell me, I should leave alone. Why did I feel the need to know, anyway? We'd shared one kiss and a couple of very unusual adventures. That didn't amount to much.

Except the kiss was like no other kiss I'd ever experienced in my life, and the adventures felt like pages from a fairy tale . . .

By the time I'd found the town of Keetonville, a few miles down the road from the café, I'd lost the urge to probe into Graham's background. It wasn't the right thing to do, I told myself as I drove down Main Street, taking in the smattering of old limestone buildings. Slowing the car, I looked for the beauty shop, absently cataloging the buildings in my mind—grocery store, hardware store, church, farm and ranch supply, church, city hall, old bank building, church, secondhand store, constable's office, church, gas station, restaurant, dry-goods store, antique store, several storefronts sitting empty, and finally the high school, where a group of young football players was finishing up practice and preparing to cross the street. I stopped at the crosswalk, watching them, wondering if, once upon a time, Graham was like them, a Keetonville High School football star.

I rolled down the window as they came closer. "Excuse me, can you tell me where the beauty shop is?"

"Puff's Pooferé?" one of them asked.

"Yes, that's it."

They pointed back down the road. "Take a right on B, two blocks."

Thanking them, I rolled up my window, then sat at the crosswalk watching as the team filed past. I imagined Graham as one of them, growing up in that school, in this town, a peaceful-looking place where life probably centered around Friday-night football games and Sunday-afternoon church socials. It was the kind of place where people knew everything about each other, where people not only knew you, but they knew your parents and your grandparents, your aunts, uncles, and cousins. What would that be like? It was such a different life from the one I'd had, growing up in army towns, moving every few years, making new friends and going to new schools and having new neighbors, until my last few years in high school, when we finally ended up in Maryland while Dad finished up his last few years before retirement. In Maryland we finally had a taste of what it was like to put down roots, to know you were going to stay in a house long enough to plant flowers and put in trees.

It wasn't that ours was a bad life. We experienced lots of places, met different kinds of people, grew to be self-reliant, learned to succeed in unfamiliar surroundings, saw most of the country. It was an exciting kind of life—one that conditioned us to hold the constant expectation of something new and different just around the corner.

But now as I studied this town, Graham's town, I felt the tug of something old, some long-forgotten piece of me that used to look out the back window of our station wagon as we departed once again, and wonder what it would be like to stay in one place.

The football team finished crossing the road, and I made a quick U-turn on the shoulder, then headed back to B Street. I found Puff's Pooferé two blocks up and pulled into the empty parking lot of the tiny pink portable building. The sign said, *Open,* but I couldn't decide whether or not to go in. Puff made the decision for me when she opened the door and waved at me. My conscience went into a hyperactive fit as I got out of the car and walked up the steps. I wouldn't ask about Graham's past, I told myself. I'd get my hair done and go home.

Puff seemed delighted to see me, and for a moment I thought she was going to hug me right there in the doorway. She settled for ushering me inside, asking, "What can I do for you?"

"I was hoping you could give me a trim and do some highlights." I tried to sound like it was completely natural for me to drive to Puff's Pooferé in Keetonville, Texas, to get my hair done. "I haven't had time to get it styled lately."

"Well, sure, Laura." I was surprised that she remembered my name. She said it as if I were someone she knew and liked. It made me wonder if she'd been talking to Hasselene and Mernalene. "Come on over here." She hustled me to the beauty chair in a way that worried me. Puff seemed much too anxious to get her hands on me.

I tried to relax as she draped a towel over my shoulders and dampened my hair with a spray bottle. "What is this stuff?" she asked, frowning at the brown streak as she began trimming the shoulder-length bob into shape.

I smiled at our reflections in the mirror, glancing at Puff's four-inch beehive and hoping I didn't come out looking like that. "You wouldn't believe me if I told you." Closing my eyes, I relaxed in the chair, trying to ignore the desire to ask about Graham.

Puff took care of most of the conversation, telling me about the town and the new football coach, who was sure to win more games than he lost this year, which would be a change for Keetonville. The last winning football team the town had was, surprise, surprise, the year Graham played as a senior. "He was quite the hometown hero," she said. "Of course, that was before he went off to college and the army. After that, we didn't see him much. He was always gone someplace he couldn't talk about, doing somethin' he couldn't talk about, and when he did come home on holidays, once in a coon's age, he wasn't supposed to talk about where he'd been. His daddy understood it, of course, bein' as he'd been in the army, but oh, Lordy, his mama hated it. He'd been a mama's boy all his life, and she didn't like the ways the army changed him one little bit. He used to tell her everything, and all of a sudden everything about him was a secret. She kept hoping he'd get the army out of his system and come home, move into his grandmother's old house there on the ranch, and help take care of things.

"The Keetons have a lot of land around here. Some of it even came from original land grants awarded for fighting in the battle of San Jacinto. His mama sure hated the idea of not having a Keeton living in the other house on the ranch. She wouldn't even rent it out or anything. They left that old house empty until a couple months ago, when Graham moved back home. It's a darling little place, on down the road a couple miles south—white house with a wraparound porch. You might have seen it. Sits back off the road a ways, big pecan trees in the yard."

"I came from the other direction. From the Crossroads," I answered, my mind rushing to compose an image of Graham in white house with pecan trees in the yard, as Puff put the plastic highlighting cap over my head, muffling the sound of her voice.

She went on talking and began pulling tufts of hair through the holes in the cap. "Graham's mama sure didn't like that house being empty one little bit, no, ma'am. Oh, I think she was happy when Emily got married, but she hated that they moved to Houston, and now the grandbabies are there. She was proud Graham had made a big success of hisself in the army, but that didn't ease the pain of havin' him gone sometimes a year at a time without a visit."

Puff didn't look at me as she spoke, and I wondered if she even remembered who she was talking to. I stared at my feet as she tugged and colored. "She spent a lot of hours on her knees praying for that boy, and I guess her prayers were answered. I mean, I don't think she would have wished for all of that stuff to happen the way it did with the helicopter crash, you know, but it was because of that he decided to get out, and he came back home."

She sighed, pausing, resting her hand atop my head. We looked at each other in the mirror, and I realized from her expression that she thought I knew what she was talking about. I glanced away.

Puff interpreted that as my commentary on the *stuff,* whatever it was, the helicopter crash, that had happened to Graham. She sighed. I closed my eyes, wishing I'd never come in. I felt guilty, and the sadness in Puff's eyes told me the secret was big and tragic. No wonder Graham reacted the way he did when I'd asked why he left the army.

"I'm glad to see him get interested in . . ." Pausing, she seemed to realize she might be saying too much. "Well, I mean it's good to see him . . . doing things. He's been here these last couple months, but he hasn't been *here*, you know? That HAZMAT job keeps him off on his own most of the time, and I think that's why he took it, instead of just staying home taking care of the ranch. That's not good for him, not natural, I mean. He used to be the friendliest kid in town, always jokin' and cuttin' up and—"

The door opened, and she looked up. "Hi, Miss Mazie, how are you?" she greeted the new customer. "Have a seat right there and let me finish up this young lady." Glancing at her watch, she said, "A few more minutes, hon," then walked over and discussed perm-rod sizes and the upcoming fire department chili supper with Miss Mazie before coming back to rinse and style my hair.

When Puff was finished, she spun me around, and I looked in the mirror at the new me. She looked startlingly like the old me, like the person I used to be a few short months ago. Staring at the reflection, I remembered who she was. I felt like her.

"Is there a quick way to hit the interstate from here?" I asked, feeling strange about everything she'd told me about Graham, and tired, and ready to get home the quickest way possible.

"Sure. Just hop on the road here, go south two miles. Turn left on 512—that'll be a bit past the Keeton ranch main entrance." She took the fifty-dollar bill I handed her and gave me change. "Follow FM 512 about fifteen miles and you'll run smack into the interstate."

The new-old me in the mirror was relieved. She knew that taking the interstate home would be much faster, and the cell phone would have good reception the entire trip. She knew she could spend the drive time checking on Dad by phone, returning other phone calls, catching up with Lindsey to tell her Dad seemed a little better yesterday, calling Collie to thank her for once again pulling her editor friend's neck out of the noose.

The Laura in the mirror saw the opportunity to multitask for the next hour, and she couldn't wait to seize it. She left Puff's Pooferé feeling in control, charged up about the possibility of getting things accomplished during a stretch of downtime, and determined not to let personal matters take the focus off work.

My sense of purpose wavered as I passed by the gates of the Keeton Ranch, two miles south of Keetonville. Slowing the car, I gazed at the long stretch of white pipe fence that led to an entrance, where the sign overhead read KEETON RANCH EST 1895. At the end of the long driveway I could see the old white house with the wraparound porch. Graham's house. I slowed almost to a stop, surveying the yard, imagining I'd see him there, mowing the grass beneath the towering pecan trees. I'd stop, say hi, pretend I was just happening by . . .

But the driveway was empty, and I realized how silly the idea was. I was acting like a love-struck high school girl, not like the new-old me from the mirror at Puff's. That me would never be caught doing drive-bys on the house of a man I'd only just met.

Feeling foolish, I stepped on the accelerator, turned onto FM 512, and proceeded the quickest way possible to the interstate. It wasn't until I was actually on the superhighway that I wished I'd traveled on 47-B instead. I felt lonely and out of place zipping along the sterile stretch of road, passing gleaming industrial buildings and enormous billboards. I missed the tall yucca stalks beside the road, their lacy white crowns swaying in the wind. I missed the overhanging branches of the live oaks, and the car traveling through patches of sun and shade, sun and shade, crafting a soothing rhythm of light and shadow.

"Oh, for heaven's sake," I grumbled at myself, then picked up the cell phone and started making calls. I told Dad I was going home to get a little sleep and I'd see him later in the day. I told Collie all about our all-night session getting the issue to print, and I left a message for Lindsey. I called the printer to check on last-minute details for the print job and left voice mails with various outlets telling them we would be delivering the first issue of *Texcetera* on time and that the cover photo of the first family at the ranch would be a knockout on the shelves.

By the time I got home, I was exhausted, but I felt good. I had almost extinguished the nagging guilt about going to Puff's Pooferé, and the lingering questions about what she'd told me. Guilt was little more than a whisper in the back of my mind as I fell into bed.

Long afternoon shadows were drifting across the room when I awoke. Jerking upright, I looked at the clock, wondering how long I had been there. *Four-thirty.* I felt like I'd just lain down, but the entire day had passed.

It's almost dinnertime at the Crossroads.

Jumping up, I ran to the bathroom, washed up, slipped into a pair of khaki capris and a white T-shirt, grabbed a banana and a Coke to have on the way, and rushed out the door. I hurried across town to the farm. The gate, luckily, was open and Dad was sitting on the porch. He looked up as I skidded to a halt, jumped out of the car, and trotted up the steps. I expected the typical, *Where have you been, why did it take you so long to get here, I can't figure out my medicine, and I haven't eaten all day.*

Instead I got, "You bring me another slice of that buttermilk pie?" and a pair of gray eyebrows rising into an expression that could only be called hopeful and expectant.

"You know what, Dad?" I said, opening the door and starting into the house to get his medicine case. "We're going to go right to the source. Put some shoes on. We're going on a little adventure."

Behind me, I heard Dad sputter, cough, and say something that sounded like, "B-b-but," and then the rocking chair squeaking as he got up.

I didn't stop to argue, just hurried into the kitchen, pretending I didn't hear him protesting behind me. I rolled my eyes heavenward, and of all things, prayed. *Please, God, if you're listening, just make him come along. I have a feeling about this. I really do.*

Stopping in the kitchen doorway, Dad spread his feet like he was bracing for a battering ram. "I'm not dressed to go anywhere."

I glanced at his faded striped overalls and old plaid shirt—his *farmer outfit,* as Lindsey and I laughingly called it. After so many years of seeing him in uniform, we couldn't get used to it. "You look fine. You'll fit right in."

"Got all my medicines to take yet."

"We're taking them with us." Slipping the box in my purse, I continued moving around the kitchen, stacking dirty dishes in the sink and throwing away trash, hoping that sheer force of movement would put him into motion. *Please, God, make him give in this once. He'll sit in this house until he dies, if he has his way.*

"Hamper's full in the bathroom. I got . . ."

I stopped. Turning slowly, I met those faded, stubborn eyes, pointed toward the door, and said, of all things, "If you want buttermilk pie, you'll quit arguing and get in that car."

Dad opened his mouth, then closed it, then did a shuffle-shuffle-turn and vacated the doorway. I heard him in the living room putting on his shoes.

Thank you, God.

Fifteen minutes later we were in my car headed for the Crossroads. Dad leaned forward and inspected the half dozen tiny, star-shaped cracks in the windshield. "What the hell happened here?"

"Dad!" I scolded, without even thinking. Mom always scolded him when he cussed. *Hardy!* she'd gasp, like she'd never heard a cussword before—unlikely if you're an army wife—*Your language!*

Dad looked chagrined, but he continued peering through the windshield, commenting on the damage to the car. We had a benign conversation about hail dents, which served to get us across town and onto old 47-B before Dad thought to ask where we were going.

"I remember this road," he said as I slowed to accommodate the hills and curves of the narrow highway. "Used to travel this road to Austin on Saturday nights when I was a young GI, back before your mom and I married."

"You did?" I held my breath, not wanting to break the fragile thread of memory.

"That was a lot of years ago." He sighed and looked out the window, smiling wistfully to himself, lost in the past.

I wished he would share it, but I didn't know how to ask. We passed the rest of the ride in silence, the car moving silently through light and shadow, through the present and the past, until finally we reached the leaning stop sign.

Dad sat up and looked around as we drifted through the intersection and pulled into the parking lot. "I remember this place," he muttered.

I barely heard him. I was focused on looking for the HAZMAT truck. Not there. My hopes sank. "What did you say, Dad?"

"I remember this place. They used to show twenty-five-cent movies down the hill on Saturday night. There was a big building down the hill—an old granary or some such. You brought your twenty-five cents and your folding chair, and you could come watch the picture show on Saturday night. If you had a date, you brought a blanket instead."

"Dad!" I gasped.

He actually grinned and fanned an eyebrow. "I was quite a young rounder, once."

"Dad!" I said again, laughing. Never, ever in my life had I heard my father talk like that. It was actually kind of ... well ... cute.

Dad must have realized what I was thinking, because he straightened in his chair and put on his curmudgeon face. The facade cracked again as we parked behind two rows of farm trucks and pickups, intermixed with a smattering of shiny commuter vehicles. Dad leaned forward and pointed excitedly through the canopy of trees. "Look! The old building's still there. You can see the old tower through the trees."

"I was down there the other day," I offered as we got out of the car. "A bat pooped on me."

I think Dad smiled at my joke. "We didn't mind the occasional bat in the belfry. Made those gals cuddle close to their fellas." He stumbled over a piece of gravel, and I slipped my hand under his elbow, focusing on the ground as we crossed the parking lot.

"It's more than an occasional bat now. There's a whole colony of them. Graham and I got mobbed down there."

Dad looked up at me. "You and who?"

"Graham ... Keeton. It's a long story, Dad."

Dad made an *ahhh* sound, then observed, "You were calling his name in your sleep. Guess you were dreaming about the bats."

I swallowed hard. "Guess so."

"So who is this Graham fella? Never mentioned him before."

"He's . . . I . . ." *Ay, ay, ay.* How in the world was I going to answer this?

He's this guy who helped drag me out of the bushes on the worst day of my life, and then he held me up with a caulking gun, and the next day we went mountain climbing and were attacked by bats, and since then I think about him all the time, and I'm not sure why, because he's not my type, and Dad, if you can explain all this to me, please go right ahead, because I'd like somebody to tell me what's going on. . . .

"Graham is—"

"Right here."

Looking up, I realized that Graham was at the top of the steps and we were at the bottom. How much of our conversation had he heard? "Hi, Graham," I said lamely as he descended the steps. He motioned to my new hair, winked, and gave me an *OK* sign.

I didn't want to get into the bat story, so I quickly introduced my father. "This is my dad, Hardy Draper. Dad, this is Graham Keeton."

For a moment I thought Graham was going to snap to attention and salute, but he settled for shaking Dad's hand and saying, "Sir," in a way that sounded very military.

My dad liked that. Straightening his stance, he cleared his throat, then tugged on the front of his overalls as if he were straightening his dress uniform. "Glad to meet you, Graham," he said very formally, then added in the same matter-of-fact tone, "My daughter's been talking about you in her sleep."

I coughed like I had a peanut stuck in my throat, gasped, "Dad!" then blushed from head to toe.

Graham raised an eyebrow at me. "Oh, really?" he said, focusing on my dad. Together they turned and started up the steps, shoulder-to-shoulder, looking much too friendly. "What'd she say?"

I choked on another breath and followed them up the steps.

"Not quite sure," Dad answered, the faint lilt in his voice telling me he knew what he was doing and he was enjoying it. "Think it had something to do with bats."

Graham reached for the screen door and held it open. "Hope you're hungry," he said with enthusiasm. "It's catfish Saturday."

Stepping through the doorway into the interior, we stood in the golden glow of the late-afternoon sunlight. Dad took a deep breath, his eyes cloudy and faraway as he looked around. "I remember this place," he said so softly that the words hung suspended in the air like dust.

Graham motioned to the corner of the room. "There's an empty table over there."

I slipped around Dad as the aunts appeared in the kitchen doorway. Hasselene moved from behind the counter and came across the room. "Hello, Laura, how are you this evening? We're so glad you came. Graham's been wondering where you were."

I glanced over my shoulder, and this time it was Graham who looked embarrassed.

Hasselene fixed her attention on my father.

Stepping in, I made a quick introduction. "This is my father, Hardy Draper. Dad, this is Hasselene and Mernalene Goodnight. They made the buttermilk pie you liked so much."

"Oh, a fan of our buttermilk pie," Mernalene observed from behind the counter.

"How wonderful!" Hasselene said, shaking my father's hand. "We're so glad Laura brought you to us. We have catfish tonight."

"And buttermilk pie," Mernalene added.

My father cleared his throat and straightened the front of his "uniform" again. "Ladies, that sounds like exactly what the doctor ordered." He actually sounded a little suave.

The ladies seemed thoroughly charmed.

"Dad says he remembers this place from years ago," I interjected. "He remembers the movies down the hill in the old mill building."

Hasselene's lips parted in a surprised smile, and Mernalene pressed a hand to her chest, and both of them said, "Is that so? How wonderful."

Hasselene snaked an arm between my father and me. "Why don't you come on up and sit at the counter with us?" She glanced over her shoulder at Graham and me. "That way the kids can have a romantic dinner. Alone."

Chapter 13

ROMANCE over fried catfish, corn fritters, and buttermilk pie. It doesn't get much better than that. Not in Texas, anyway. By the time Graham and I had finished supper, I had a heady sense of . . . something. I felt jittery and fluttery, like I'd been drinking, but the only thing in my glass was tea. All the same, I could feel myself slowly letting down my guard, becoming more comfortable. Losing my sense of judgment.

And I absolutely didn't care.

Graham and I swapped stubborn-dad stories and talked about our moms, who sounded a lot alike—old-fashioned apple-pie types, family oriented, softhearted, yet strong and capable. I told him about the marathon session at the office, and about sending the first issue of *Texcetera* to the printer only seven minutes past deadline. He told me a little about his twelve years as an army special-ops pilot, which had included tours in some of the world's worst trouble spots—missions, as Puff had described it, that he couldn't talk about even now. There was a sparkle in his eye when he described flying, a weariness when he talked about what he'd seen on the ground. He looked out the window, faraway and thoughtful. I had a feeling he hadn't talked about those things with anyone until now.

Watching him, I balanced on a thin line between guilt and curiosity. What would he say if he knew I'd been to Puff's, and she'd told me that his reason for leaving the army had something to do with a helicopter crash, a tragedy that made Puff's eyes grow moist when she talked about it?

He'd be angry. You shouldn't have been snooping. It wasn't the right thing to do.

"Do you miss it?" I asked quietly.

He met my gaze, the somber mood leaving as quickly as it had come. "Not right now."

I shivered somewhere deep inside, and the muscles tightened in my stomach. "Why not?"

He grinned and I felt like I was melting. "Your turn to answer questions."

Blinking, I tried to clear the heady fog from my mind. Right then I would have told him anything he wanted to know. "Like what? There isn't much else to tell."

He rubbed his thumb and finger slowly along his bottom lip, like he had during our morning coffee repartee. "Really?"

"Yes, really." The words were breathy, passionate-sounding. I realized we were leaning close across the table.

Slipping his fingers around mine, he looked at my hand, where a wedding ring might have been. His voice was deep and contemplative, "Army brat, magazine editor, two brothers, twin sister . . . and what else?"

"What else?" I repeated, growing uncomfortable, growing tempted. What would he say if I told him everything? Would he think I was on the rebound, looking for some kind of vacation romance as a quick fix? Would he think I was the kind of person who jumped in and out of relationships without thinking?

"What brought you here?" His eyes cut upward with an intensity that took me back.

"My . . . my job . . . and my dad," I answered, but I

knew that wasn't what he was asking. He was asking what brought me *here,* to the Crossroads. It was the same question he'd asked yesterday morning.

Some emotion flashed across his face, then disappeared. Disappointment? Why did I feel like I should tell him? Why did I *want* to tell him *everything?* Did that make sense when he remained a mystery to me?

"Graham, I—"

A clatter arose on the other side of the room, and I jumped, looking up to find Mernalene beating on a cookie sheet with a spoon. "Kitchen's officially closed," she said loudly. "There's coffee in the pot if anyone wants more, and it's time to head out in the parking lot for the pickin' and grinnin'."

Hasselene punctuated the sentence with a little "Yee-haw!"

I realized that the room was nearly empty. My father had left his stool at the counter and, presumably, gone outside with everyone else.

Graham and I smiled at each other, the spell between us broken. I wasn't sorry. I wanted to enjoy the time with him without getting into my reasons for ending up at the Crossroads, and his reasons for quitting the army, and all of the other things that might ruin it.

I wanted to pretend that the past didn't exist, and as we walked out the door into the spill of moon shadows beneath the oak trees, it seemed possible. Our hands brushed and our fingers intertwined as we crossed the fringes of the parking lot. It seemed natural, perfect. Perfectly natural.

"Walk with me to get my guitar?" he asked. The shadows hid his face, but I could tell he was smiling.

"Sure," I replied, and squeezed his fingers, because there weren't words to express how I felt right then, how good it felt to be there with him, whether it was logical or not.

Tipping my head back, I looked through a gap in the trees, where stars were scattered like pearls in a blue-black sea. They seemed close enough to touch. I leaned against Graham's pickup and gazed upward as he released my hand and opened the door. "It's beautiful out here," I whispered.

"Yes, it is." But he wasn't looking at the sky—he was looking at me.

A warm, sensual feeling slipped over me, and I met his gaze. For a moment there was no parking lot full of cars, no people moving nearby in the darkness, no circle of lawn chairs forming in front of the store, no soft refrain of bluegrass music drifting into the night. There was only Graham and me.

No past. No future. Only that moment, and it seemed like enough.

Graham leaned close to me, his hand sliding warm and soft into my hair, his thumb tracing the outline of my cheek just before his lips brushed mine, lightly at first, then with growing intensity, until my head reeled and I felt the ground shifting beneath me. The sounds of the music and the night faded, and all I could hear was the beating of my own heart. He pressed closer, and I felt the beating of his.

I fell into the kiss, forgetting everything. It was like nothing I had ever experienced, like no other kiss, as if my soul felt a connection my body was only now discovering.

His lips parted from mine, and I met his gaze, my mind cloudy with passion. I breathed his name into the night like a question unanswered.

"Ssshhh." He pressed a finger to my lips and shook his head, the look in his eyes saying, *Don't question this.*

But somehow I could tell he was as bewildered as I. We clung to each other, awed by the power of the moment, until finally the plaintive cry of a violin drew us apart.

Clearing his throat, he reached into the truck for his guitar. "Guess that's my cue."

I smiled, disappointed to be joining the group, yet relieved to have time to regain my senses. I wondered where my father was and what he was doing, and if anyone had seen Graham and me kissing in the parking lot. Then again, why did I care? We were grown-ups, after all.

Grown-ups with all the grown-up problems, and secrets, and histories.

Graham closed the truck door and reached into the back, pulling out a couple of lawn chairs. "You ready for this?"

I wondered if he was talking about the music circle, or the other thing, whatever it was, that was happening between us. "I don't know." It was an honest answer to both. "I'm ready if you are."

His eyes glittered, telling me he liked that answer. "Then let's go."

And so we did. I grabbed the lawn chairs, and Graham carried his guitar, and we walked across the parking lot together, looking, I was afraid, more like moonstruck lovers than casual acquaintances who'd met only a few days earlier.

A lump rose in my throat when I recognized Puff settling into one of the chairs in the circle. If we sat near her, she might mention that I came into her shop, and it wouldn't take long for Graham to put two and two together. I was glad when he changed course and headed for the other side of the gathering, near his aunts. I followed, but I knew it was only a temporary stay. Sooner or later, Puff would mention having done my hair.

Before I left tonight, I needed to tell him about my

conversation with her. It would be worse if he heard it
from Puff instead of from me.

Hasselene and Mernalene waved us toward their side
of the circle when they saw us coming. Between them, a
man was sitting in a lawn chair, bent over a violin. As we
came closer, and my eyes adjusted to the light of the fire
burning in a huge clay chimenea, I realized that was my
father sitting there, plucking the strings of the violin and
then turning the keys, as if he knew how to put it in
tune.

I stood gaping at him as Hasselene moved her chair
away from Dad's, opening up a space in the circle that
she had clearly reserved for Graham and me. As I set up
the lawn chairs, Dad finished tuning the fiddle, pulled
the bow across it, then handed it to Mernalene. Tucking
it under her chin, Mernalene hit a bluegrass lick that
was worthy of an episode of *Hee Haw*.

"Wow. That was great," I said, looking from her to my
dad. "Dad, I didn't know you knew how to tune a violin." Never in my life had I seen my father pick up a musical instrument of any kind.

Dad tucked his head and crossed his arms, looking a
little embarrassed. "Had to do something to pay for my
slice of buttermilk pie," he said, obviously pleased to
have been included.

Graham and I slipped into our seats, Graham ending
up beside my father, and me between Graham and Hasselene. Bracing his guitar on his knee, Graham slid his
hand to the strings, checking the notes. Dad leaned forward to watch, and Graham glanced sideways at him,
saying, "I think you'd better tune mine, too. It's been in
the case a few too many years."

Dad raised his hands palm-out. "Nope. Nope. Don't
know anything about a guitar."

Hasselene leaned close to me, giving my father a sly

look. "He does, too. Maybe we'll get him to play something later."

Wide-eyed, I glanced sideways at her. How, in the space of an hour over dinner, had she found out things about my father that I hadn't learned in a lifetime?

Standing up, Mernalene clapped her hands, and the various tuning and picking around the circle stopped. "Y'all know the rules—well, y'all know we don't have any rules at the Crossroads pickin' and grinnin', except no profanity and no rock and roll, which is pretty much the same thing. As y'all know, it's been a busy week here with the interstate closed, and we're pleased to have some guests with us tonight." Nodding toward the other side of the circle, she acknowledged a group of well-dressed people standing outside the ring, looking like they weren't sure if they should unfold their lawn chairs or run for their lives.

I noticed HOUSHNTR among them, looking ready for a Wild West evening in tall red snakeskin boots, a long black broom skirt, and a designer straw cowboy hat with a leopard-skin hatband. She'd brought the restaurant guy from Austin as her date, which made me wonder why she was looking at Graham like she wanted him to notice her. Was it him she was after, or another chance to try to talk Hasselene and Mernalene into selling their restaurant? She definitely looked like she'd come for some reason other than the music. That sent a twinge of apprehension through me, or maybe it was jealousy.

Mernalene beckoned enthusiastically to the newcomers. "Y'all come on in. Spread the circle out over there, make room. Well, look, there comes our favorite magazine writer." She waved into the darkness, and I recognized Collie and her husband, True, walking in from the parking lot. Collie shuffled the baby onto one hip and waved, while True unfolded their lawn chairs. Surveying the group with the keen eye of a reporter looking for an interesting story, Collie noticed my father in the chair beside Graham, and she nodded, giving me the thumbs-up.

Merna continued talking to the crowd. "If you've got an instrument, don't be shy. We go around the circle, and if you've got a song, tell the key it's in if you know it, then start up and other folks'll join in when they can. If you can sing and play, we like that even better, but we'll take whatever we can get." She pointed across the circle to the man I'd met at the gas pumps a few days before, the mayor of Keetonville. "Robert, you start. But I'm warnin' you, none of them off-color songs about gamblers and naked females."

The mayor picked up his guitar and obliged by saying, "Yes, ma'am. 'Red River Valley' in the key of G." He played the first few chords alone, and one by one people around the circle joined in—an old man with a huge bass, a barefoot woman who played a mandolin and looked like a poet, Puff on a dulcimer, a boy who couldn't have been more than nine and played a harmonica, his father on the guitar, and Mernalene on her fiddle, sending long, plaintive strains into the quiet night air.

The mayor began to sing in a deep, resonant voice that sounded like it should have been crooning to the cattle in some old Western movie.

> *From this valley they say you are leaving*
> *We will miss your bright eyes and sweet smile*
> *For they say you'll be taking the sunshine*
> *That has brightened our pathway a while. . . .*

My mind drifted away from the song. Beside me I heard Graham begin to pick out the melody on his guitar, the notes floating upward like steam rising from water in the chill of evening. As the chorus came again, Graham sang along with the words.

Come and sit by my side,
If you love me.
Do not hasten to bid me adieu,
Just remember the Red River valley,
And the cowboy who loves you so true.

I didn't hear the voice from the other side of the circle. I only heard Graham's. I watched his hands caress the strings, coaxing forth the music from thin bands of steel. He leaned low over the guitar, the hard, military lines of his body softening, his ear turned toward the strings, his eyelids drifting downward in a sweep of dark lashes against his tanned cheeks.

He didn't look like a soldier anymore. He looked like an artist caught in the mystery of his art, like a lover adrift in the passion of a perfect interlude.

Something powerful and compelling welled inside me—a sense of contentment, of not wanting the moment to end. A sigh passed my lips as the song faded. The other guitar fell silent, and Graham's fingers trailed the last notes of melody into the air. He glanced up, his gaze finding mine, and I saw a mirror of my own emotions, a sense of being lost in the moment, of forgetting everything that lay outside it. He smiled, his eyelids slightly lowered, the light of the chimenea reflecting in his eyes like a rising moon in a deep velvet sky. My gaze traveled from his eyes to his lips. I wanted to kiss him. I didn't think I'd care who saw. He leaned closer, and I knew I wouldn't care. . . .

Someone on the other side of the circle hollered, "Awww-haww!" and struck up a tune on the fiddle, and Graham and I jerked away from each other. He started strumming his guitar along with the music, and I looked around the circle to see if anyone had been watching us.

Collie was staring at me with her eyebrows knitted together and her mouth hanging open.

I tried to evade the look by being nonchalant, hoping she would think she was imagining something where nothing existed. I wasn't ready to answer questions about Graham and me. I could imagine what she'd think. Only two days ago we were talking about my breakup with Dale. Tapping my foot along with the music, I pretended to be engrossed in the show.

Collie went back to watching the musicians, as well—with one eye, at least. The other one, I had a feeling, was still on me. She wasn't the only one looking my way. HOUSHNTR was staring at me like a cat sizing up her next meal. Beside her her date gawked upward into the trees, then around the parking lot, then into the darkness near the mill, uninterested in the music or in her. Tapping a knuckle against his chin, he surveyed the store building and the parking lot in a slow, calculated fashion, as though he were mapping something out in his head. It occurred to me to wonder if he was the buyer HOUS-HNTR had said was interested in the Crossroads, but that didn't make much sense. The place was small and old, and even if he did like the biscuits and wanted to know about the secret ingredient in the coffee, surely he wouldn't be interested in running a tiny café in the middle of nowhere. It was more likely that he was hoping to make nice with Hasselene and Mernalene and con them out of more recipes.

HOUSHNTR caught me looking and gave me an artificial smile. I didn't smile back, but returned a puzzled look, a little hint that I was wondering what they were up to. She leaned over and bumped her partner on the shoulder, then pointed toward the fiddle player, so that both of them were again focused on the music. I turned back to the show as well, but I had a feeling she was watching me. Or maybe she was watching Graham. It was hard to tell.

Beside us Mernalene picked up the tune and started

playing second fiddle, and next to her my father leaned forward in his chair and clapped his hands to the rhythm. Halfway around the circle, two men began playing an accompanying hambone on their knees and thighs. Never having seen the hambone done outside of old movies and reruns of *Hee Haw,* I gaped at them.

Graham glanced at me and then at the hambone players and grinned. "Texas Saturday night," he whispered close to my ear.

"I guess so."

With a quick head jerk, Graham motioned over his shoulder, and I glanced past him, my mouth falling open. My father—*my father,* my father the *sergeant major*—was doing the hambone right along with them. Just like on *Hee Haw.*

I gaped at Dad as he closed his eyes and went at it while Hasselene looked on, terribly impressed. Opening his eyes a crack, he glanced in her direction, and I couldn't tell for sure, but I thought he winked.

I sat staring, feeling like I had dropped through one of those wormholes they talk about in science-fiction movies, and landed in some alternate universe, where I was desperate to kiss a man I'd met only a few days ago, and my father played the hambone.

He didn't just *play* the hambone. He was *good* at it. He could keep a rhythm and wink at the ladies at the same time. And what was even stranger was that I thought he looked great sitting there in his old overalls, bouncing his knees up and down and slapping his hands, palm-up, palm-down, to the rhythm. I was proud of him.

A sense of wonder came over me as I watched Dad transform into a person I'd never known. He looked happier, freer than he had in months, years, maybe ever. I couldn't remember a time when he would have let himself go like that. I wondered if Mom had known that side of him. Even if she hadn't, I knew she was seeing it now from somewhere, someplace high overhead in the glittering night sky.

Wrapping my arms around myself, I leaned back in my chair and gazed into the canopy of ancient branches. The leaves twittered softly in the breeze, stars glittering among them like Christmas lights, so bright and so near they seemed more a part of earth than of heaven. I felt Mom close, and joy filled me like the scent of the smoke and the sound of the music. All of the stress, all of the things I had been worried about, faded away. I felt that I could close my eyes and drift into another world and never return to the one I'd left, that I could finally let go of all my illusions about what my life should be and just let it be what it was. *Stand at the crossroads and look . . .*

The song faded, and the circle grew quiet.

"Favor us with a song, Graham," I heard Hasselene say. "We haven't gotten to hear you play in years."

"Let someone else go ahead." There was a sigh in Graham's voice, a sadness. "I've forgotten all those old songs."

When I looked up, Mernalene was turning to Graham, her eyes dark with some hidden message only he could read. "Those old songs are in your blood, Graham. To forget them, you'd have to forget who you are."

I noticed that no one in the circle was making a sound, not the whisper of a voice or the clinking of a coffee cup or the disconnected notes of an instrument being tuned. The onlookers waited, breathless, as if this were some sort of test.

Graham didn't look at them—he looked at me, his eyes meeting mine with an unreadable expression.

"Play the one you were whistling when we were down at the mill," I said quietly, in hopes that would help. I could tell it was hard for him to be here like this, among all these people who, like Puff, knew what events had brought him back home, who whispered sympathy behind their hands and wondered if he would ever turn back into the smiling high school football star they remembered. When they looked at him, they saw a ghost of whoever he was before. Maybe that was why he liked me—because I didn't see the ghost. I only knew who he was now.

The cloud lifted from his expression, and he leaned over the guitar, finding the notes, coaxing forth a melody that was familiar to me for some reason I couldn't explain.

"This is an old Texas folk song." The same thing he'd said at the mill when I asked about the tune. His gaze found mine and he added, "About falling in love."

I looked away. No wonder he hadn't told me more about the song when I'd asked. *Falling in love* . . . Was that what we were doing? How could that be possible in so little time?

From across the circle, Collie was giving me the look again. Hiding her hand behind her crossed knees, she pointed at Graham and blinked at me, mouthing, *Who's the guy?* I pretended I couldn't understand her, and she pursed her lips, giving me an irritated scowl. She knew I understood perfectly well.

Graham started singing, and my attention turned to him.

Spanish is the loving tongue, soft as music, light as spray,
'Twas a girl I learned it from, livin' down Sonora way
Well, I don't look much like a lover, but I sing her love
  words over,
Mostly when I'm all alone, mi amor, mi corazón. . . .

The plaintive wail of a violin trembled into the air as Graham played the bridge between verses. Glancing up, I realized the violin player wasn't Mernalene. The hands, trembling slightly as they drew the bow across the strings, were my father's. A memory rushed through my mind with startling clarity—my father in his wood-shop, whistling that song, my mother walking in with a sandwich for him, him swinging her, plate and all, into his arms, dancing her around the garage as if it were a ballroom, finally singing those last words, *My love, my heart,* in Spanish. I was watching through the window. I couldn't have been more than two or three. . . .

A sense of wonder came over me again as Graham met my gaze and sang the second verse.

> *Late at night when I would ride,*
> *She would listen for my spur,*
> *Throw that big door open wide,*
> *Lift those laughin' eyes of hers.*

Winking at me, he smiled and shook his head almost imperceptibly, as if the words were about me.

My heart tumbled from my chest and I realized what some small part of me had known all along. Whether it made any sense in the outside world or not, here, now, at the Crossroads, I was falling in love.

Chapter 14

THE music continued as the night grew deep and still around us, separating the circle from all that lay outside the firelight, beyond the violin's cry and the soft refrains of the guitar. On the other side of the fire, little Bailey slept curled in her father's arms. Watching her there, her tiny head resting against True's chest, the fluff of her red hair brushing his chin, I was reminded that all things are possible. Collie and I had been friends most of our adult lives, but I would never, ever have guessed that she would end up in Texas, married to a cowboy, doing, as Dale so crudely put it, the marriage-and-mommy thing.

Collie wouldn't have guessed it, either, and that was what made it beautiful. That was what made it real and perfect. It wasn't a dream she invented, some new life she created because she wanted it. It just happened. It was meant to be.

Watching Collie watch True, I found myself wishing I could ask her, *When did you know? How did you know? How do you know what's real? Did you think it through? Is there logic to it, or is it all a matter of following your heart and taking a leap of faith?*

But looking at Collie, seeing the love and rapture on her face when she watched True and the baby, I knew it didn't matter how she figured it out. What mattered was that she did. She saw destiny passing her way, she grabbed it and went along for the ride. . . .

On True's shoulder, the baby awakened and started to fuss. Leaning close, Collie whispered something in his ear, and he nodded, patting her knee and standing up. Bouncing Bailey on his shoulder, True murmured soothing words as he carried her away from the circle. Collie gathered their things, then came around the circle, thanked Mernalene and Hasselene for having them, complimented my father on his violin playing, then leaned close to my ear and whispered, "You'd better call me tomorrow, girlfriend. You've got some explaining to do."

Ducking my head, I gave a halfhearted groan.

She patted my shoulder, then grabbed the back of my hair and tugged playfully. "Call me or you can't have the rights to my cover photo." Collie had a way of hitting me where she knew it would hurt.

Laying my fingers over hers, I nodded and muttered, "Tyrant."

Beside me, Graham glanced over, set his guitar aside and rose from his chair. Extending a hand, he gave Collie a curious look, smiling and saying, "I don't think we've met."

Collie covertly raised a brow at me, impressed by the display of manners, then turned to Graham with the enormous smile she always used when she was about to charm information out of a victim. "I'm Collie. I'm an old friend of Laura's." She emphasized the world *old,* almost as an invitation, I thought, for him to ask *old* questions about me.

Seeming to read the invitation, Graham glanced from Collie to me and back with an interested look, saying, "Really?"

For a mortifying instant, I had the feeling that they were going to start talking about me right then and there, so I stood up and made a quick show of giving introductions during a break in the music. "Collie, this is Graham Keeton. Mernalene and Hasselene are his aunts. Graham, this is Collie Collins McKitrick. She's the one who interviewed your aunts for the magazine article."

Giving me an acute look, Collie tapped the end of a finger to her lips, then pointed at Graham. Fortunately the music started again before she could start interviewing him, which was clearly what she was about to do. Reporters are dangerous people—especially dangerous as friends.

Mernalene gave us an impatient look, motioning for us to sit back down and rejoin the audience.

Giving Collie a quick wave, Graham smiled that wide, friendly, natural smile that I loved, and said, "Nice to meet you, Collie. Glad you stopped by tonight," then sat back down in his chair and picked up his guitar.

Across the parking lot, a set of car lights came on, and Collie glanced in that direction. "Looks like True has Bailey buckled in already," she said apologetically, letting me know she wished she could stay longer. "Bailey's not in the best mood today. I think she's cutting teeth."

"Oh, I'm sorry." But I really wasn't. As much as I loved Collie, the last thing I needed right now was a game of Twenty Questions. Twenty logical questions would be enough to diffuse the mist-and-gossamer fantasy I was building in my head. "I hope she feels better."

"She will. You know babies—sleep a little while, wake up in a whole new world."

I rolled my eyes, because I knew she was talking about me, intimating that I was in some whole new world, and had neglected to tell her about it. "I'll call tomorrow," I said quietly, then leaned closer and pleaded, "But please don't call Lindsey. I really don't want to get into this with her."

Collie nodded, and said, "All right," as Mernalene gave me another reproachful look, and I slid back into my chair, still half-turned toward Collie.

Slipping an arm around my shoulders, Collie hugged me. "I can't wait to hear this," she whispered against my ear, and then, "By the way, cute guy. Nice . . . umm . . . smile."

Graham glanced our way suspiciously, and I hissed, "Ssshhh!"

Collie wasn't placated. "You know," she whispered, "as soon as your dad talks to Lindsey, he's going to spill the beans, anyway. He tells Lindsey everything."

I felt myself going pale as Collie patted my shoulder. *Oh, God, I hadn't even thought of that.* All of this was getting more complicated by the minute. If Lindsey found out, she'd probably call Dale and try to do some kind of relationship rescue. Lindsey liked to take control of situations. Lindsey didn't like impulsive decision making. If she got wind of what was happening at the Crossroads, she'd be all over it like a wet blanket, sure she was doing me a favor by butting in.

Giving my shoulder a quick squeeze, Collie disappeared into the night. I felt the stress melt away with her. I wasn't going to let myself worry about little things like logic and commitment, not right now. For once I was going to live, and do, and be in the moment, and enjoy.

The moment lasted until late in the night. One by one the members of the circle grew tired, and packed up their lawn chairs, and drifted away into the darkness as the heavy orange moon washed white and rose high into the night sky, bathing the parking lot in a celestial glow. In his chair, my father started to nod off, and I began to face the fact that the evening would have to end.

Starting awake in his chair again, Dad gave me an addled look as the last group of participants packed up their instruments, and the few remaining onlookers, Evie and her date among them, took their designer lawn chairs and headed for their cars.

Clearing his throat, Dad blinked drowsily into the darkness. "Reckon I'd better go sit in the car and rest my eyes awhile."

I glanced sideways at him. I'd never heard my father say *reckon* in my life. Of course, I didn't know he could play the Texas fiddle, either. "I'll help you, Dad."

"Nope. No, ma'am," he said placatingly, popping out of his chair more quickly than I would have thought possible. "I'm fine myself. You two young folks sit here as long as you like." With a quick shuffle-turn, he headed off in the wrong direction. "Don't hurry on my account."

As if on some unspoken cue, Mernalene and Hasselene stood up and started after him, Hasselene saying over her shoulder to us, "We'll walk him out there," and then to my father, "Hardy, your car's the other direction, hon. This way, see? If you keep going that way, you're gonna walk off the cliff and end up in the river."

Taking my father by the elbows, the sisters turned him around and guided him toward the store, Mernalene saying with unusual tenderness, "Why don't you come on in for a minute, Hardy? We can wrap up that last slice of buttermilk pie for you to take home. We're closed on Sundays, so no sense leaving it sitting around. It won't be any good by Monday."

"Well . . . all right," my father grumbled, obviously tired but unable to resist the lure of buttermilk pie to go.

Watching him, I smiled, shaking my head. "I think your aunts have made a fan."

"I think it's mutual." Graham replied, still absently picking notes on the guitar. "Your dad's quite a fiddle player."

I thought about that for a minute, staring into the dying flames in the chimenea. "You know, I never knew that about him." A sense of gratitude welled up in me. I wished Lindsey and my brothers could have been there to see Dad playing the fiddle and doing the hambone. "It was a good night. I'm glad we came." Resting my head against the back of the chair, I gazed into the heavens, taking a deep breath of the cool, sweet air.

Graham set the guitar aside and leaned back in this chair, his long legs crossed in front of him and his head resting near mine. We sat for a minute, not talking. "Yes, it was," he said finally. "I can't remember the last time I did this."

"Did what?" Turning my head to one side, I looked at him.

Some earnest comment was in his eyes, but he gave a quick grin and said instead, "Sat under the stars with a pretty girl."

I tried not to act like I was charmed by such an old line but, of course, I was. "Did you learn that line from a John Wayne movie, cowboy?"

"Jimmy Stewart, actually."

I smiled at him. "Ah, an old-movie fan, huh?" Which was odd, because I loved those old, classic, larger-than-life movies. My movie watching was one of those habits Dale always teased me about. I had the feeling that Graham and I could sit and talk all night about old movies, and bats, and buttermilk pie, and never run out of things to say.

"Overseas, the old ones are all you can get most of the time. You haven't lived until you've seen John Wayne face off against the Culpepper gang, put his rifle in one hand and his pistol in the other, and start speaking Japanese." He chuckled under his breath.

"Oh, my gosh, I've seen that one," I said, laughing. "In the airport last year when we went to Osaka." I realized instantly that I'd said *we,* as in Dale and me. A sick feeling traveled to the pit of my stomach.

Pausing, Graham gave me a speculative look. He hadn't missed the *we,* either.

The firelight caught his face, and I wondered if I'd ever seen eyes like his before—deep, mysterious, like a window to an inner self I wanted to touch, but couldn't quite see through the shadows on the glass. I realized that if I wanted to know him, I was going to have to let him know me. "Graham, you know the other day when you asked me how I ended up here?" I heard myself say. "There was a reason why I didn't want to tell you." Looking into his eyes, I knew that I could tell him how I'd come to end up at the Crossroads, about Dale and me, and he would understand.

He let out a long breath. "Yeah. I guessed that." He looked worried, tired suddenly, like he was afraid I was going to tell him something he didn't want to hear. Leaning forward in his chair, he braced his elbows on his knees, gazing toward the smattering of stars over the blue-black hills in the distance. "Laura, look . . ." Leaving the sentence unfinished, he pointed toward the horizon as a meteor streaked across the sky. "Falling star."

"Oh," I breathed, leaning forward, my arm brushing his and an electric sensation tingling through me.

Inside, the clock chimed midnight. Graham smiled, his eyes twinkling in the firelight. "You know what that means."

He leaned closer, so close I could have kissed him, but instead I said, "It means my coach is going to turn into a pumpkin?"

The breath of his laughter touched my cheek, sending a shiver through me. "It means if you make a wish, it'll come true," he whispered against my ear, as if it were a secret between us.

I wish there were no pasts to talk about. "How do you know?"

"It's guaranteed." His voice was still only a whisper, his nearness radiating heat against my skin, filling my mind with a heady desire, erasing the hesitation that had been there only an instant before, driving away my urge to talk about the past.

"How do you know?" I whispered against the curve of his neck. I thought I might just kiss him and stop the ridiculous discussion about falling stars and wishes.

"I heard it from Kermit the Frog." His voice was a mixture of passion and laughter. "In Japanese."

"Then it must be true."

Closing my eyes, I made a wish, asked for a single, impossible thing. *I want this to be real.*

Then we sealed it with a kiss.

For once we weren't interrupted. The kiss was long and slow. My mind and body fell into it until I didn't know where I was, and didn't care. I only knew I'd never been kissed like that before. Ever.

Breath caught in my throat as our lips parted. "Wow," I heard myself say.

"Yeah," he agreed, his fingers trailing the length of my arm. "Wow."

He smiled and I smiled, and under the influence of honeysuckle, and smoke, and a Texas full moon, I felt as if I were floating.

When the café door opened, we were still sitting in our lawn chairs making moon-eyes at each other. Graham shifted slightly at the sound of my father and the ladies coming out, and we stood up, starting slowly across the parking lot toward the car.

"So what about tomorrow?" he asked.

The knot reclenched in my stomach. All of the questions inside me spun through my mind, and a rush of words came out. "I don't know. I mean, it's all so complicated. I'm only here for a few more days, maybe a week at the most. I didn't plan to get . . ." What should I call it, exactly? What was the right word? "I wasn't looking to . . ." *Fall in love?* "It's complicated and—"

"Laura," he stopped me. I looked up at him, and he was laughing. "I really just meant, how about lunch tomorrow?"

Groaning, I covered my face with my hand, muttering, "Insert foot," and wishing I could evaporate like smoke. When, oh, when had I become so inept at romance? I used to be pretty good at coy conversation and subtle wordplay. But when I looked at Graham, it was as if my brain went out of my head and I blurted out whatever I felt. There was something so different about him, about him and me together.

Graham chuckled under his breath, glancing toward the café, checking the forward progress of my father and the ladies, who were descending the porch steps. Stopping near the base of one of the trees, he tugged my hand, pulling me into the moon shadow with him. The darkness hid his face, a rim of moonlight silhouetting his form. I could feel him looking intensely at me. His hand touched my cheek, his fingers combing into my hair, holding me riveted.

Leaning into his hand, I felt my heart immerse itself in his nearness, pushing away the questions and warnings in my mind.

"Don't worry about all the rest of it," he whispered, as if he sensed that I was about to bring up difficult realities. "All I need to know right now is that this was the best night I've had in a long time."

"Me, too," I whispered, half truth, half lie. It was the best night I'd had in a long time, but I felt a faint sense of disappointment that he was once again unwilling to step beyond the present, into the past or the future. If there was to be a possibility of anything more than a few stolen moments between us, we would have to move forward and move back, talk about where our lives had been and where we wanted them to go. Why did he remain such a closed book, even now that I was ready to open myself to him?

His body pressed warm against mine, and I could tell he was going to kiss me. I raised my face toward his, toward the shadow of him silhouetted against the moon. Tomorrow would be soon enough to worry about all the rest. We'd go somewhere quiet for lunch, somewhere with no aunts looking on, where we could really talk. . . .

My thoughts fled, and I let myself slip into one more moment stolen away from reality, one more stolen kiss.

Voices were coming near as our lips parted. Graham stroked a hand over my hair, and we started walking toward the car in silence.

He groaned under his breath, muttering something to himself, then saying out of the blue, "So how do you feel about barbecue?"

"Barbecue?"

"For lunch tomorrow. How about barbecue?"

"Umm . . . I like barbecue." Finally, a question I could answer easily—one with no life-altering implications.

Stopping beside my car, he winced, and I could tell something was up. "How do you feel about *lots* of barbecue?"

I had the sinking feeling a lamb must get while being led to slaughter. There was more to lunch tomorrow than just barbecue, I could tell. "OK, I guess. Why?"

Raising his brows apologetically, he opened the car door for me and leaned against the frame, giving me his most winning grin. "Because I just remembered that tomorrow at noon I'm supposed to be heading up the judging for the Kittery Creek Barbecue Cook-off. It's a Keeton tradition, of sorts."

It may have been a Keeton tradition, but he didn't sound thrilled about it. I had the sense that he felt this was another one of those tests from the past—like Mernalene asking him to sing one of the old songs in the music circle. The look in his eyes told me he really wanted me to be there, so I said, "I don't know a thing about barbecue, but I'm game. Sounds like fun."

A wicked twinkle lit his eyes, making me wonder what I was in for. "Good. Where should I pick you up?"

I had an image of Graham coming to the retirement village to pick me up, while the old folks on their way to the Sunday potluck watched, and speculated, and stopped us to ask questions. "You know what—I have to go into the office for a while in the morning to work on some distribution issues. Why don't I meet you at the cook-off?"

"All right." He seemed a little bothered that he couldn't come pick me up. I wondered if he thought I was hiding something. "It's six miles down the crossroad to Keetonville, turn left on B street, and go two miles or so to old Kittery Creek Church. The park is out behind, by the river." Pausing, he glanced over his shoulder in the general direction of Keetonville, then added, "You sure you don't want me to pick you up?"

I shook my head. "No. I can find it. Not much chance of me getting lost in Keetonville."

Cocking his head to one side, he studied me quizzically, and I realized I'd slipped up. Graham, of course, didn't know I'd gone snooping around his hometown, or that I knew Kittery Creek Church must be about two miles down the road from Puff's place.

Think of something, quick. "So . . . what time does this barbecue thing start?" I realized suddenly that my father and the ladies had reached the other side of the car and were standing at the passenger door, watching us with interest. Clearing my throat, I gave a quick head bob in their direction, and Graham glanced that way, seeming unconcerned. Apparently he was no longer worried about discouraging his aunts' matchmaking efforts.

He only glanced at them, then grinned at me. "Better be there by noon. They swear in the judges at twelve-thirty." Pausing, he pulled a business card from his pocket and handed it to me. "Here's my cell phone number, just in case." He stepped back, gallantly ushering me into my car while my father climbed into the passenger seat with a big, tired groan.

"All right. I'll be there," I agreed.

On the other side of the car, Hasselene closed the door, then peeked in the open window, saying, "Well, how lovely, Laura. You're coming to the Kittery Creek reunion day tomorrow?"

"Yes," I said uncertainly, wondering if the barbecue cook-off and the reunion day were the same thing. "I guess I am."

Closing my car door, Graham gave the open window frame a friendly pat, saying, "Sure she is. She's the newest Kittery Creek barbecue judge," as he backed away from the car.

Barbecue judge? "What?" I glanced toward Hasselene, then back toward Graham, but he was already striding away, looking far too self-satisfied.

Hasselene rolled her eyes heavenward, muttering "Oh, Lord," while backing away from the car.

I leaned across Dad's seat so I could see her. "What's he talking about?"

Hasselene just smiled, then elbowed Merna so that she smiled too, and in unison they said, "Have a good night, you two."

Dad was completely oblivious to the devious barbecue dealings going on right under his nose. He benignly held up his buttermilk pie. "G'night, ladies. Thank you for the care package."

Waving, the ladies turned around, their heads huddled together. I heard one of them mutter, "She doesn't know anything about barbecue," and the other add, "Lord, Lord, Lord. Wait until Jud Puddy finds out about this. There'll be hell to pay."

I looked toward Graham's truck as it started and roared toward the crossroad, in a hurry, no doubt, to leave before I could turn down my appointment or ask any questions about Jud Puddy and why there was going to be hell to pay.

Beside me, Dad took in a breath, then exhaled a long, satisfied sigh. "Well, let's get on home, young ma'am. This has been some day. Can't remember the last time I stayed up past midnight. Reckon I'll have to sleep until noon tomorrow to make up for it."

Frowning, I glanced at him. There it was again, *reckon*. I'd never heard my father use that word, or talk with that little Texas twang in his voice.

Sliding back into my seat, I buckled the seat belt, started the car, and headed toward home. "Dad, how is it that you never told us you played the violin?"

Relaxing in his seat, he squinted thoughtfully. "Oh, don't know. It was one of those things I learned from your grandpa. It's a shame you never knew your Grandpa and Grandma Draper. She played the squeeze box, and he was the best fiddle player in four counties." He smiled, remembering, then deflated with another long sigh. "That was a lot of years ago, the last time I had a fiddle in my hands. Your brothers can probably remember me playing the old one I had back then. Think we lost track of it when we moved back from overseas, back before you and Lindsey came along. Never really thought about getting another fiddle after that. Too much else to do." He paused thoughtfully, then added, "Wasn't any kind of secret, if that's what you're thinking. I guess no one ever asked me about it, that's all."

A pang of regret went through me. In all our years together, I couldn't remember a single time my father and I had really talked about anything that mattered. By the time Lindsey and I had come along, he was wrapped up in the past, in old wars and old wounds, and he barely saw us there. He wasn't into hugs and kisses, and all that mushy-gushy girly stuff. He was interested in good grades and good manners, lectures and military-style discipline, so we dodged his notice as much as possible.

We wrapped our lives around Mom, and Dad was an orbiting satellite, sometimes closer, sometimes farther away, always out of reach. It wasn't until I was older that I realized how much Mom suffered over it. She yearned for a close family, one that could talk and share and love easily. She wanted to be able to talk to my dad, but she couldn't open the box he kept himself in. Yet she loved him still, so much that she spent her life searching for the chinks in his armor.

Now I wished I would have tried harder to get to know the man behind the uniform. There was so much about him that I had never seen. Somewhere in my past there was a history I knew almost nothing about—his history. There was a connection to the grandparents I'd never known, to that farm my father grew up on and the young man he used to be, to this rugged hill-country land, where my ancestors had come as pioneers when the area was still wild and dangerous and new.

All of that was within me somewhere. I'd never thought about it before, but I felt it now—something deep, instinctive, permanent. Of all of the places I'd ever been, this was the only one that felt like home.

Chapter 15

ALL morning long, I thought about barbecue. I awoke at four-thirty A.M. with it on my mind, and couldn't go back to sleep. I thought about it as I dressed, surveying my clothes, and finding nothing that looked barbecue judge–ish. Just slacks and suits, two pairs of shorts, and a pair of jeans. No fluffy Western skirts and tall Western boots like HOUSHNTR had worn to the pickin' and grinnin'. That was how a barbecue judge should dress. Jud Puddy would probably like a barbecue judge who dressed like that.

There was nothing like that in my closet, which only proved I was highly unqualified for the job. On TV, the weatherman was warning that today would put an end to the unseasonably mild weather—ninety-five degrees and breezy, he was saying.

I settled for a blue shorts outfit with a waist-length top that was sort of denim-ish, a pair of chunky sandals with midheels and silver bangles, simple loop earrings, and a string of silver beads. Pronouncing the outfit as good as it was going to get, I fixed my hair, grabbed a banana for breakfast, and stood in front of the entry-hall mirror. I didn't look at all like a barbecue judge, but I didn't look too bad. Puff had done a good job on my hair, and there was some color in my face, probably from the little bit of time I'd spent outdoors at the Crossroads.

Grabbing the business card with Graham's cell phone number on it, I hurried to the car and headed to the interstate to take the fast lane to the *Texcetera* offices. No Crossroads coffee, unfortunately, since the Crossroads was closed on Sunday, so I made the sterile, uninspired trip to the office in relative silence. Propping Graham's business card beside the speedometer, I toyed with the idea of calling him, just to wake him up and razz him about having conned me into becoming a barbecue judge.

A giddy feeling slipped through me like bubbles from champagne, and I found myself giggling and squealing like a high school girl. Pretty foolish behavior at thirty-six and all grown up, but I didn't care. In the privacy of my car, I let myself engage in the silliness of being completely smitten.

Beside me, the papers I'd stacked on the passenger seat rustled like reality whispering in my ear. Glancing down, I felt real life slipping over me like a cold, wet blanket. In my mind, there was the question again—did all of this really make sense? I would be leaving Texas next week—either for whatever new opportunity Royce had up his sleeve, or else to go home. Home to my real job, and the condo, and the complicated question of sorting through the wreckage of a three-year relationship. It was bad enough that I was involved in an impossible mess with Dad down here in Texas. What was I doing getting wrapped up with a man I didn't really know, who wasn't my type, who lived a thousand miles from where I lived?

Panic gripped my stomach, and I rolled the window down further, wishing it away, picturing all the uncertainties cast into the breeze. Gone. The questions slowly faded as I took in a deep breath of the clear hill-country air, then exhaled, then took another. I wasn't going to think about it. I wasn't. I was going to go to the office, spend a few hours handling what *Texcetera* business I could on a Sunday, then go to Kittery Creek to judge barbecue. I was going to enjoy the day and pretend the rest of the world didn't exist.

I arrived at the office and buried myself in distribution and other details essential for a smooth release of the upcoming issue of *Texcetera*. I promised myself that I would not, repeat *not*, obsess about personal issues.

By eleven o'clock the office was starting to feel like a cell. I was jittery and frustrated, and I wasn't sure why. Other than my own self-doubt, everything was going fine. The distribution reports looked good, more new retail outlets had committed to giving *Texcetera* space on their racks, and I had a couple of e-mails from the printer, saying that we could expect to see the prep run of *Texcetera* on time. There was even a JPEG of the cover on my e-mail. Collie's photo of the first family looked wonderful with the *Texcetera* logo and blue subheads. I tried to call her to compliment her on the cover, and maybe have a little girlfriend talk about Graham and me, but she wasn't home, and I had to settle for leaving an answering machine message about what a knockout the cover was.

Any other time, seeing the first cover of a brand-new magazine would have been enough to give me the rush that always came with completing a project against all odds and having it turn out perfect. But today all I could think about—all I wanted to think about—was finding Graham and getting away from the real world.

So I got up and started packing my briefcase. The phone rang on my desk, and I thought about not even answering it. But since it was Sunday, and there was no one else in the office, I figured it had to be for me, and it might be that Dad, having finally awakened after sleeping late, was calling to check in.

I was unprepared for my boss's voice on the other end of the line. "Thought I would find you there," he said. "Anybody else in your office right now?"

"No." It still occasionally amazed me that Royce didn't seem to grasp the concept that normal people didn't work on Sunday. "Why?"

"Got some interesting news. Didn't want anybody else listening in. It won't be public until Monday." Royce sounded positively gleeful, which, for him, was unusual. He was paid to be an emotionless workaholic, which was pretty much what he was. That had always been fine with me, because I didn't have much of a personal life either, and being around Royce made me feel all right about that.

A spark of interest lit somewhere inside me and fired the editorial jets into high gear. If Royce was tracking me down on a Sunday, sounding like that, this was something big. "What won't be public until Monday?"

Royce let the line buzz for a minute, just to hold me in suspense, then said, "The Western Limited Press deal just went through. We just took over the seven biggest magazines on the West Coast."

"Holy crap, you're kidding." A blast of adrenaline zinged through me like a hyperactive Ping-Pong ball. The takeover of WLP would nearly double the size of our publishing company. WLP put out Hollywood tabloids and upmarket glossy magazines with huge circulations. "I wish I could be there when they announce that at the press conference on Monday."

Royce laughed, pleased with my excitement. "Too bad you can't be here for the announcement, since the deal involves you."

"Wha . . ." I muttered, sinking back in my chair, my mouth hanging open, my heart leaping up and jumping around in my throat. "Royce, are you telling me . . ."

"They're sending you out there," he finished. "With

the eventual plan of putting you in as publisher. Old Walters wanted somebody good, said he wouldn't sell us the company unless we could send someone good out there to learn WLP and take it over."

For an instant everything around me dimmed, and I thought I might be passing out. A scream traveled through the empty office, and I realized it was coming from me.

"Draper," Royce barked impatiently, "just keep it under wraps until after the announcement tomorrow. The new editor for that little Texas rag can't get out there until the end of the week. Just leave her your notes and bring her up to speed by e-mail. I'm sure she can handle it."

A green-eyed twinge shot me out my seat before I realized what was happening. Just short of protesting into the phone, I gathered my wits and said, "Is she good?"

"Good enough. That's not *Time* magazine down there, you know."

"Maybe not, but it is *my* project, and I want someone who's going to know how to bring it on." The words came out with more force than I intended, almost argumentative.

"Getting a little territorial, aren't we?" Royce laughed, but it was an irritated laugh.

Turning toward the window, I quieted my tone. "Sorry." I glanced over my shoulder at my office, imagining someone else settling into my chair, making herself at home, editing the next issue of *Texcetera*. A nerve pinched in the back of my neck, and I rubbed the spot. "So who is she? Where was she before?"

"Name's Portia Randolph. She used to be with First Street in New York, got laid off when the company was sold out, so she's been on the market looking for a place to go. She's only got a couple of years' magazine experience, but I liked her portfolio. I think she'll be good."

Slapping myself on the forehead, I sighed into the phone. "And let me guess. She's blond, about five-six, short skirt, and she's your boss's niece." Royce gave a snort that told me I was right. "Geez, Royce, she applied a couple of years ago, and you said no way."

I could almost hear him rolling his eyes. "The old man pushed it pretty hard this time. And her portfolio really did look good. She'll be fine."

"In other words, this is a nice, out-of-the-way place where she can get her feet wet."

"Pretty much."

"Great," I muttered, thinking about how hard I'd worked to get *Texcetera* going, and how the staff had fallen in behind me. I'd thought they would get somebody good to take over the magazine, not the twenty-something niece of our company vice president. "Does she *know* anything about Texas?"

"Do you?" Royce scoffed. "What's your problem today, anyway? You ought to be kissing my feet about now. You're headed for the big stuff, remember?"

"Yeah." The end of the word trembled, and I swallowed hard, hoping he didn't hear it. "Been a long month with my father and the magazine, that's all."

As usual, Royce didn't ask after the personal stuff. He didn't like to validate the existence of anything that kept people from slaving away for the company. "They want you out there by Wednesday night. Pack your bags, kid; you're going to Hollywood. Land of dreams and pink stucco." He paused, and when I didn't answer right away, he added, "Get on the plane. You'll feel better."

"I'm sure I will." The words were filled with forced enthusiasm. Royce didn't notice. He told me to have a good trip and hung up without waiting for an answer.

I sat listening to the buzz in my ear, then returned the phone to the cradle, my hand starting to shake as the reality of what he'd told me hit home. *Publisher.* "Oh, my God." I cupped my hands over my mouth, trying not to hyperventilate. *Publisher.* This was what I'd been dreaming of, hoping for, working toward for fifteen years, and it was finally coming true. This was huge. It was unbelievable. "Oh, my God, oh, my God!" Jumping out of my chair, I grabbed my briefcase, danced around the office with it like it was my waltz partner, then floated out the door, images of Hollywood and West Coast glossies dancing in my head.

I was halfway to the Crossroads before I came back to Earth, looked around, and realized where I was, and thought about the implications of Royce's news. Aside from all of the good things it meant for my career, it also meant that I would be leaving in two days, and I wouldn't be coming back. It meant I'd be too busy for a long-distance relationship, or taking care of Dad, or anything else that wasn't directly related to WLP.

It meant I'd be saying good-bye to everything here. For good.

As hard as I tried, I couldn't get my mind around that idea, and the closer I came to the Crossroads, the more unreal it seemed. I couldn't imagine myself saying good-bye to Dad, and Hasselene and Mernalene. I couldn't imagine not starting my workday with a cup of Crossroads coffee . . . and Graham, not ending my workday with dinner at the Crossroads and Graham. In some logical part of my mind I knew that didn't make sense— that a career you love and have worked for all of your life should supersede a relationship with someone you've known only a few days. I knew that, if I insisted, I could probably get Lindsey and my brothers to help settle the situation with Dad. Maybe if I worked at it, I could even convince Dad to come out to California with me for a while. A change of scenery would probably do him good.

I knew that they had perfectly good coffee in California, and I would find a new favorite coffee shop, and life would go on. If anything long-term was really meant to happen between Graham and me, we would somehow keep in touch . . . wouldn't we? In spite of the demands of the WLP job, I could try to find time to visit Texas soon. . . .

Or maybe once I left, all of this would fade from my consciousness the way the beauty of a vacation fades from memory. Maybe I would look back on it someday and shake my head and realize that all of this wasn't right for me anyway. . . .

I thought about it as I pulled into the empty parking lot of the Crossroads, then passed the oleander bush that hid the words on the wall, if, indeed, the words were actually there and not something I had dreamed. Even that might not be real, I reasoned, feeling like a junkie coming off some powerful drug, as my spirits crashed from the rush and I landed in the real world. In the real world, life was not all sunshine and rainbows and buttermilk pie. It was hard choices and painful decisions. *Either/or,* not *and.*

As I pulled onto the county road and headed toward Keetonville, I made the only decision I could live with right then. I told myself I wouldn't think about it. I'd let the news settle, let myself drift back to solid ground, then assess the situation logically. Later. For now, I would just let the day take me where it would, and try to enjoy it.

I had, of course, no problem finding B Street, and other than a momentary pang of guilt when I passed Puff's place, I made the trip to Kittery Creek Park without a hitch. Passing the old white-rock church, I slowed the car and gazed at the stained-glass windows, crafted of thick colored squares and mortar in some bygone time when things were made by hand. Like the old mill,

Kittery Creek Church had a timelessness that gave it a hallowed feeling. Stopping the car in front of the building, I rolled down the window and did something I seldom ever bothered to do. I read the historic marker.

KITTERY CREEK CHURCH

CONSTRUCTED IN 1869 BY PIONEER FARMERS IN THE KITTERY CREEK COMMUNITY, KITTERY CREEK CHURCH SERVED AS A SCHOOL, CHURCH, AND COMMUNITY CENTER FOR RESIDENTS OF GERMAN AND NORWEGIAN DESCENT, WHO SETTLED ALONG KITTERY CREEK AND ITS TRIBUTARIES IN THE PRESTATEHOOD ERA OF TEXAS. FOR OVER ONE HUNDRED YEARS, THE CHURCH WAS IN CONTINUOUS USE, THOUGH NEVER WIRED FOR ELECTRICITY OR MODERN CLIMATE CONTROL. TODAY THE CHURCH IS ONLY USED FOR WEDDINGS AND OCCASIONAL SPECIAL SERVICES. IN 1975, AFTER A PETITION FROM LOCAL RESIDENTS, THE CHURCH WAS OFFICIALLY LOGGED ON THE REGISTER OF TEXAS HISTORIC BUILDINGS.

Below that, there was a plaque that listed the names of the original elders of the church, as well as the builders, and the architect, T. Oleg Draper. A chill ran over me as I read the name again, considering the idea that perhaps that long-ago architect may have been an ancestor of mine. How strange, if that were true, that I would end up here now, over a hundred years later, reading his name on the sign.

Smiling at the thought, I gave the building a last look, imagining that I could see the ghosts of those hardy immigrant builders reflected in the light and shadow of the old windows. They were there, I thought, in mortar and stone and glass—in something permanent that had stood the test of time. I imagined them traveling with me as I continued along the lane that circled the church and led to Kittery Creek Park, in the valley below, where what looked like acres and acres of tents, wagons, and canopies had been set up among the smattering of ancient trees. Near the entrance, a sheriff's deputy waved me toward a parking spot among rows and rows and rows of cars on the hillside.

As I exited my car, I quickly realized that I had completely underestimated the magnitude of the event. The valley floor along both sides of the clear-running creek was filled with what looked like elaborate campsites centered around enormous iron barbecue smokers on wheels. The campsites were decorated with waving Texas flags, strings of bandannas, twinkle lights shaped like chili peppers, cow skulls, and various other barbecue paraphernalia. Moving in frenzied activity were teams of barbecue chefs in large cowboy hats and colorful aprons bearing team names and slogans like, *Say no to sauce, Nice to meat you,* and *You wanna piece o' meat?* The chefs laughed and talked and sang and cussed as they fed stacks of wood and slabs of meat to their iron giants, causing them to roar and belch puffs of sweet-scented smoke that hung over the valley like a cloud.

As I walked slowly through the fray, it occurred to me that I looked horribly out of place, and that I didn't know how in the world I was going to find Graham. There were probably a thousand people there, and I didn't have a clue where he was. The look of a lost lamb must have been obvious on my face, because a passing barbecue chef took pity on me. Tipping his enormous white cowboy hat, he asked me if I was lost, little lady.

"Well . . . yes . . . actually." I wasn't exactly sure what to ask. He probably didn't know Graham, and Graham hadn't told me where to meet him. "I'm trying to figure out where the barbecue judges go."

Cocking his head to one side, he stroked his gray mustache and rocked back on the heels of his tall cowboy boots, counterbalancing an ample waistline that looked like it had sampled many a batch of barbecue. "You a judge?" He raised a brow and eyed me incredulously, all the way from my beaded and bangled sandals to my newly-colored hair.

"Yes." He frowned harder, and I changed my story. "No. Not really. I just need to know where the judges go."

"You with one of the barbecue teams?" His squint looked slightly suspicious. "No team members allowed to fraternize with judges. Against the rules."

I shook my head quickly. "No. I'm just here to meet up with one of the judges . . . Graham Keeton. Do you know where he is?"

"Um-hmm." His demeanor changed in the space of the instant it took me to say Graham's name. Suddenly he was looking at me with more than casual interest, and I wondered why. "He's over there at the judges' tent. Here, let me show ya the way." Sticking his hand out, he grasped mine in a handshake that nearly dislocated my shoulder. "I'm Jud Puddy, by the way. Nice to meet you."

"Laura Draper." *Great. Here for only five minutes, and I've already run into Jud Puddy.* "Nice to meet you too. Thanks for helping me find Graham."

"Why, sure. It's no problem. Happy to oblige." Looking me over again, he frowned. "You ain't from around here, are ya?"

I shook my head. "Richmond." He looked confused, so I added, "Virginia."

To which he nodded, as if that explained a lot of things. "So what brings you out here to the cook-off today, little lady?"

Chewing my lip, I tried to decide what to say next, as, *She doesn't know anything about barbecue,* and *There will be hell to pay when Jud Puddy finds out,* ran through my mind. "Oh ... well ... it's ... a long story," I hedged, raising onto tiptoe and trying to see ahead, hoping that we were near the judges' tent, where I could find Graham and clear up this mess. Jud may have been a little geriatric, but he was a big fellow, and obviously very serious about barbecue. I didn't want him mad at me.

Much to my relief at that point, Jud Puddy pointed to a large blue-and-white-striped tent as we rounded the end of the aisle and came within sight of Kittery Creek again. "There's the tent," he said. "Looks like the mayor's here and they're just about to swear in the judges."

Swear in the judges? A chuckle tickled my throat, but then I realized that Jud was serious. "Oh," I said, scanning the crowd gathered in front of the tent. "There's Graham."

Graham spotted me at the same moment I spotted him. He seemed surprised to find me walking with Jud Puddy. If it worried him, though, he didn't show it. Grinning, he strode through the crowd, gave Jud a quick greeting that once again led me to wonder what was going on between them, then grabbed my hand and said, "Come on, Laura, you're going to miss the swearing in."

The next thing I knew, I was standing in a line of a dozen would-be barbecue judges, solemnly facing His Honor, the mayor of Keetonville, with my right hand in the air, swearing that I had not been coerced, bribed, blackmailed, or preprejudiced in any way, and that I would, to the best of my ability, faithfully execute the office of barbecue judge for the sixty-second annual Kittery Creek Reunion Barbecue Cook-off. Amen.

Not far away, Jud Puddy was lodging a protest with the county sheriff. He was trying to be discreet about it, but he had the kind of voice that carried, and I could hear him muttering, "... can't just bring a judge in from out of nowhere. He was supposed to line up folks from in town. *Keetonville* folks."

The sheriff raised his hands helplessly, saying, "Jud, I can't help it. Since Graham's daddy's out of town, it's Graham's job to get the judges together. You know the Keetons always head up the judging. He can do whatever he wants, as long as it ain't against the rules."

I glanced uncertainly at Graham, and he leaned close to me, whispering, "We've got Jud on the run now. He buys off the judges every year. Doesn't like to lose this thing."

"Oh," I said, getting a mental picture of the small-town barbecue treachery going on right under my nose. "Well, my vote's not for sale."

Graham chuckled. "I didn't figure it would be." He smiled at me and I smiled at him, and we stood there for a minute just ogling at each other. He looked really good in his official Kittery Creek Cook-off T-shirt, jeans, and straw cowboy hat. The blue in the shirt just matched his eyes. . . .

When I came to my senses, I realized that Hasselene and Mernalene were standing with us, and the mayor had been talking, and I hadn't heard a word he'd said. "... hotter than a fly on a griddle." The mayor nodded toward Jud Puddy, who was headed our way with the sheriff and what looked like a lynch mob. "Graham, this'll be worse than that time you put that bull snake in his desk drawer at the Ford dealership." The mayor raised his hands like a parent pleading with a child to behave. "Lord, Graham, sooner or later you're gonna aggravate that fat old man right into a heart attack."

Graham's eyes sparkled mischievously, and I caught a glimpse of the hometown boy Puff remembered. "Are you kidding, Uncle Robert? He lives for this kind of stuff."

Mernalene nodded, seeming to enjoy the excitement. "Oh, Robert, you know they've always gone at it like this. Jud's been moping around ever since Graham moved off and he didn't have anyone to harass."

Hasselene rolled her eyes and put a hand to her face, whispering from the side of her mouth, "For heaven's sake, Merna, don't encourage him."

But Mernalene remained undaunted. Bracing her hands on her hips, she threw her chin up with a satisfied smile. "It's just good to see folks"—I didn't miss her quick glance at Graham—"having some fun around here."

Graham then turned his attention to Jud Puddy as he came within striking distance and shook a finger at Graham.

"Graham, you can't just come in here and bring in any old"—he glanced toward me and said, "Pardon me, ma'am," then continued talking to Graham—"any old *out-of-towner* in here at the last minute. Old Mrs. Gann is supposed to be the twelfth judge. I talked to her last—" He snapped his lips closed, realizing he was just about to say too much.

Crossing his arms calmly over his chest, Graham raised a brow. "Must be you didn't talk to her *yesterday,* after she went in for emergency gall bladder surgery. She said to tell you she was real sorry she couldn't judge your barbecue, but she's sure grateful for that big discount on the new car, anyway."

Wide-eyed, Jud Puddy make a choking sound, and the sheriff turned red.

Looking perfectly in command, Graham went on. "And so, in the absence of Mrs. Gann, Laura here has graciously agreed to step in at the last minute and provide us with another *completely* impartial judge."

Jud gagged a second time, and I think at that point he might have swallowed the plug of tobacco in his lip.

Frustrated, he took off his hat and slapped it against his leg. "She know anything about barbecue?" He turned to me and repeated the question. "You know anything about barbecue?"

Squaring my stance, I lied through my teeth. "Yea-absolutely. In fact, I have always wanted to judge a barbecue contest." Beside me, I heard Graham swallow a laugh. "It's a secret dream of mine, and I want to thank you and the rest of the cooks for helping it come true."

Jud actually looked flattered. Putting his huge white hat back on his head, he gave me a look of respect and said, "I believe this little lady does know barbecue. What did you say your name was?"

"Laura Draper." I introduced myself again, feeling suddenly very important.

Jud thought for a minute. "Draper . . . You any relation to Melvin Draper, or Don Draper, or Hack and Harlan Draper?"

The last names rang a bell, and I pointed a finger at him, saying, "My grandfather's name was Harold, but I think everyone did call him Hack, and I think my father did have an uncle named Harlan."

"Well, I'll be!" Jud stuck his hand out and shook mine as if I were the prodigal daughter returning home. "If that don't beat all. My father did business with the Drapers for many a year, over there at the dealership in Killeen, back before the town got so big and Dad moved out here to Keetonville. Dad had a lot of stories about Hack and Harlan, and the rest of them Drapers. There were seven of them boys, all cousins. Well . . . heck, there's still more Drapers around here than you can shake a stick at." His eyes met mine and narrowed purposefully. "And you know, them Drapers, now, they knew barbecue. They knew that it ought to be made with just enough mustard seed to give it a little twang . . . a little twang of mustard, know what I mean?"

I started to nod, but Graham stepped between the barbecue king and me. "All right, Jud, quit trying to give her clues. If you're going to win this thing this year, it's going to be fair and square."

Pressing a hand to his chest, Jud effected a look of great offense as Graham led me away toward the judges' tent. He leaned close to my ear and asked, "Your vote still isn't for sale, is it?"

"No." I whispered. "And incidentally, I hate mustard. I've always hated mustard."

"Good. That's my girl." He patted me on the head like a puppy. "Have to say, I've never seen anyone handle old Puddy quite so well." Clearing his throat, he did a fair imitation of my voice. " 'I've always wanted to judge a barbecue contest. It's a secret dream of mine.' "

I rolled my eyes and smacked his hand away. "Very funny. And by the way, if *someone* would have told me about this more than twelve hours ahead of time, I might have been able come up with some clothes to fit the occasion." Reaching up, I flipped the brim of his hat. "I don't have a really big cowboy hat." I kicked a little gravel at his boots. "Or way cool—what are those?— lizard-skin boots, or a nifty barbecue cook-off T-shirt, or anything. How in the world am I supposed to judge barbecue dressed like this?"

Stopping, Graham took in my outfit, his expression sending chills from the tips of my toes to the ends of my hair as he said in that Texas twang he could turn on and off at will, "Darlin', you're the only thing in here looking hotter than the barbecue." Then he swept his hat off his head, plunked it on mine, and added, "There, now, cowgirl, feel better?"

"You betcha." I laughed, adjusting the hat, then looking up at the brim to see if it was straight. "I kind of like this thing. Can I keep it?"

He tweaked the brim of my new hat, still talking in

that Texas twang that sent shivers through me. "Sweetheart, you can have anything you want."

From inside the tent, I heard the mayor hollering at us, "Graham, quit fraternizing over there and get her to the table. We've got to get this thing started."

Leading me into the enclosure, Graham pulled out a chair at a long table already filled with serious-looking barbecue judges. Sitting down, I frowned when I realized mine was the last empty chair at the table. "Where are you going to sit?"

He took a step backward, a devious twinkle in his eye letting me know there was at least one more thing he hadn't told me. "Afraid you're on your own at this point, Batgirl. I'm only *in charge* of the judging. You *are* a judge." He started toward the tables at the head of the tent, where countless pans of barbecue were waiting, then he glanced back over his shoulder and added, "Enjoy the barbecue, darlin'."

Enjoy the barbecue, enjoy the barbecue, enjoy . . . I heard that over and over and over again in my head as pot after pot after pot of barbecue was brought to the table by Hasselene, Mernalene, and a few other ladies. Mernalene gave me encouraging nods, and Hasselene cast sympathetic glances my way, while I did my best to live up to my solemn oath as a barbecue judge.

Just as we had been instructed, I used a new plastic utensil for each taste, passed the pan to the next judge, then engaged in the all-important cleansing of the pallet, otherwise known as eating a grape or two between samples. I did not fraternize with the judge on my right, nor my left, nor the one across the table, an elderly woman who kept giving me odd looks like she was trying to figure out if she knew me. She stopped Hasselene and whispered in her ear, and I could tell they were talking about me, probably discussing my lack of qualifications as a judge.

I tasted until I was certain that if I saw one more pot of barbecue, I would be sick. Then I tasted fifteen more, including the one with the mustard seed. I went above and beyond the call of duty—was a model example of the barbecue-judge code of conduct, which was more than I could say for a few other people at the table, who were not above whispering to each other, and theorizing about whose entries where whose, and occasionally were so busy talking that they forgot to eat their pallet-cleansing grapes between samples.

Even though I was the only one in the room following the rules, the mayor spent most of his time standing behind *me,* looking over *my* shoulder, and seeming unaware of the people whispering at the other end of the table. Mernalene and Hasselene didn't appear to notice, but I couldn't help wondering if the mayor was on Jud Puddy's payroll, and was trying to intimidate me. To make matters worse, Graham disappeared halfway through the judging and left me there alone, wearing his hat. It could have been the dirty looks I was giving him that drove him away. After thirty or so pots of barbecue, I was no longer thinking friendly thoughts toward the HAZMAT man.

The woman across the table looked like she felt sorry for me. When we'd finished the last pot of barbecue, she leaned across and patted my hand, asking, "You're the one who's a Draper?"

"Yes," I answered, feeling a little defensive, since the mayor had been looking over my shoulder for the last hour and a half. "Why?"

She wagged a finger at me, studying my face. "Now, are you Hap's daughter or Hardy's?"

A sense of curiosity prickled through me. "Hardy's. Do you know my dad?"

She nodded, tossing a fluff of gray hair that looked like it might have been created down the street at the

Pooferé. "Know him? I'm your dad's cousin Nette. Hap, Hardy, and I grew up just down the road from each other, went to all the school dances together and such, whenever we didn't have a real date. We was like the Three Musketeers right up until Hardy and then Hap went away to the army. We kept in touch for some years after that, sent Christmas cards and pictures, but somewhere in all those times your family moved, we lost track of each other, I guess. Then after your Grandma Draper died and Hap died, we didn't get any more news through them, either. I guess that must have been right around the time you and your sister were born. The last picture I saw of your family was your mama with you two babies in Easter bonnets. I think your folks were stationed in Germany then. Your brothers were maybe ten, twelve years old or so."

"I never knew all that. I'll have to tell him I ran into you," I said, fascinated with the idea of having family members here whom I'd never even met. We'd always been closer to my mother's family, keeping in touch and getting together for holidays when we could. Not much was ever said about Dad's family after his mother died. We'd all been surprised when Dad decided to have Mom's burial in Texas in his family cemetery.

"How are your folks doing?" The woman's face lifted into a pleasant expression. "I was by your grandparents' old farm the other day and saw some activity there. I thought maybe your brothers were in, hunting."

"Dad's staying there," I said solemnly. "Mom passed away two months ago, and he hasn't been doing too well."

She leaned closer, touching my hand again, her eyes warm with understanding. "Oh, I'm so sorry. We didn't know. We've just lost touch with your folks for so many years now. I'll make sure to get by and visit your dad just as soon as I can."

"That would be good," I said, thinking that the visit might raise Dad's spirits.

The woman pushed her chair back and stood up, and I realized there was someone behind me. "Hey, Graham Ray, how are you doin'? Haven't seen you since you got back in town. I'll tell you, you look just as happy as a warm pig in cool mud." She didn't wait for him to answer, but pointed a finger at me and went right on talking. "You tell your daddy that Cousin Nette said hey, and that I'm gonna drive over to see him soon, OK?"

Picturing Graham covered in cool mud, I waved a quick farewell. "All right. Thanks. I'll tell him. Nice meeting you."

She said good-bye and then hurried across the room to talk with some of the other judges. Swiveling in my chair, I grabbed the front of Graham's shirt, pulled him close, and growled, "You owe me. Big-time."

He tugged the brim of my new hat and sat down beside me, trying to make nice, saying, "Good-lookin' hat."

I gave him my best evil eye. "Don't even *try* to flatter me. You, sir, are a lousy date."

He looked down at his boots, doing a poor impression of chagrin—poor, because he was grinning. "So I've been told."

I supposed he thought that would make me go easy on him, but I didn't have much sympathy. I doubted if Graham had ever been told he was a lousy *anything* before. "If you were going to stick me here to overdose on barbecue, the least you could have done was stay around and feed me grapes or something."

He chuckled at the image, cutting me a wry glance. "Now, how would that look—me fraternizing with an official barbecue judge like yourself? People would think I rigged the competition against Jud Puddy." He leaned close to me, adding in a hush, "Especially since we just finished counting the ballots, and Jud is no longer the barbecue-beef king of Kittery Creek."

"You're kidding," I breathed. "Please don't tell me he lost by—"

"One vote." He finished the sentence for me.

Covering my face with my hand, I groaned. "Oh, no." Visions of angry mobs stormed through my mind. "Are they going to come after me with a hangin' rope?"

Graham clicked his tongue against his teeth melodramatically. "Don't know. How'd you vote on the one with the mustard seed in it?"

Lowering my hand, I tasted the sweetness of revenge. "Can't say. Barbecue judges never tell." I grinned back at him, and he shook his head, then tweaked my hat.

"You'd better come with me, little lady." He did a perfect imitation of John Wayne, or Jud Puddy, which was pretty much the same thing. "Best we head for the hills before they finish up judging chicken in the next tent and the mayor announces the results of this here contest."

"Why, yes, sir, Sheriff." I did a not-half-bad Texas twang myself, then put my hand in his and we started toward the door. Together we walked out and, under cover of the crowd, slipped right past Jud Puddy and his henchmen.

We were halfway down the row of barbecue canopies when a gasp and then a cheer went up, and we knew the winners had been announced. Stopping, Graham put a hand to his ear and made an exaggerated display of listening, then smiled and said, "My work here is done."

"You're enjoying picking on poor old Jud Puddy way too much."

He rolled his eyes. "Poor old Jud Puddy's been cheating for years. All I did was level the playing field. If they didn't want things to be fair, they shouldn't have asked me to head up the judging."

Something in the way he said that told me he was talking about more than just the barbecue cook-off. I eyed him curiously, saying, "Oh, Boy Scout, huh?" and watching his reaction.

His expression turned serious, grave in a way that I couldn't read, and for a moment I was sorry I'd said it. "Yeah." Then, as quickly as the emotion came, it was gone. "So what's next?"

It took me a moment to catch up with the emotional ricochet, and just that one little hint of something hidden left me feeling off balance. It reminded me that there was still so much about him I didn't know.

Somewhere not far away I could hear music playing. *Just enjoy the day, Laura,* I told myself, and turned my attention to the music. "I don't know. Think it's safe to stay here and listen to the music, or is Jud going to come after us?"

Graham shrugged confidently. "No. It's fine. Jud will get over it. If you want to stay, we'll stay." There was a faint undercurrent that said he didn't want to stay, and I wondered if he felt the way he had last night at the music circle—as if everyone were looking at him, expecting . . . something.

"It's up to you. Really. I'm game for anything." I realized that was true. I didn't care what we did or where we went. I just wanted to be with him. Remembering our last big adventure, I added, "Anything that doesn't include bats or spiders."

Snapping his fingers, he gave me an *aw-shucks* look, and said, "Darn," then grinned that slow smile I'd come to love, slipped his arm around my shoulders, and said, "Let's go listen to some music, then."

So we did. We retrieved the lawn chairs from the back of Graham's truck and walked to the hillside, where a music festival starring local artists from two to ninety-two was going on. I recognized some of them from the Crossroads pickin' and grinnin', and to my surprise, people seemed to recognize me. I could only guess that Hasselene and Mernalene had been spreading the word, because most of them seemed to know about the magazine article on the Crossroads. I was a bit of a minor celebrity for doing it, and for helping to turn the tide in the barbecue contest, and for being a Draper.

Throughout the afternoon, people seemed to make a particular effort to stop and talk. It didn't take me long to figure out that wasn't because of my newfound celebrity status—it was because I was with Graham. Everyone was clearly watching and wondering, not about me, but about him. But no one asked. Instead they gave him searching, sympathetic looks, and greeted him with obtuse comments about how well he seemed to be "doing." It made me wonder all the more what was going on.

Yet, at the same time, I didn't want to get into all of that. It was such a perfect day, with the wide, cloudless blue sky, the dappled shade of the trees, the hot, dry breeze that smelled of grass and just faintly of the passing creek, the music drifting upward, and the rustling of people setting out picnics on the ground. I wanted to just enjoy all of it, to be swept away in it, to leave the hard conversations for some other time.

Graham shifted in the chair next to me, eyeing someone else's picnic. "That fried chicken looks good. You hungry?"

I cut him an evil sideways glance. "I'll never be hungry again." The very idea of fried chicken made my barbecue-stuffed stomach roll.

He must have noticed me turning green, because he actually looked like he felt sorry for me. "How about a soda, or a lemonade, or . . . Alka-Seltzer?"

"Very funny. Bring me back a Coke, smart guy."

"Yes, ma'am," he drawled, and batted the brim of my ten-gallon hat so that it fell down over my eyes.

Hopelessly charmed, I smiled what I'm sure was a stupid, giddy smile, peered under the brim of the hat, and watched him walk away. I couldn't help it. I liked everything about him, including the way he walked—a little military march, a little swagger, a little careless abandon. Just right.

A shadow fell across me, and I realized someone was standing by my chair.

"You two look like you're having a fine time." I recognized the mayor's voice.

Pushing my hat brim up, I straightened in my chair, wondering if he was going to question me about the barbecue judging. "The music is great," I said, hoping to lead the conversation in another direction.

The mayor nodded, his round face lifting into a friendly smile beneath thick, graying eyebrows. "So you're enjoying our little barbecue festival today?" He glanced toward the concession stand, then slid into the chair beside me and extended a hand. "We didn't meet properly earlier. I'm Graham's uncle Rob."

"Nice to meet you." I leaned to the other side of my chair, feeling odd about his being there, because he seemed to be there for a reason. "The festival is . . . great. I've really had a wonderful time."

He surveyed the crowd, trying to look casual as he commented, "Seems like Graham's having a fine time, too. Glad to see him out enjoying himself. Sure is good." He met my gaze and fanned a bushy eyebrow. "Looks like you've put a spark in that boy."

I blushed, looking around and wishing Graham would come back. Spotting Hasselene passing by, I half stood in my chair and waved, hoping she would come over and interrupt the conversation with its heavy undercurrent.

To my great relief, Hasselene made a beeline for us, her lips tightening into a thin line of concern as she reached us and the mayor stood up. "Robert, you're not haranguing poor Laura about the barbecue judging, are you?" She wagged a finger at him. "You tell that Jud Puddy to just let it go and behave himself."

Taking a step back, the mayor made a placating gesture. "Now, Hass, don't get all bowed up on me. I wasn't saying anything about the judging. I was just saying it's good to see Graham out enjoying the day ... *with someone*." The emphasis on the last two words wasn't lost on Hasselene, and clearly conveyed a meaning they both understood. "I was going to tell Laura that she ought to get Graham to take her by the church before she leaves. There are some Drapers named on the plaque. Could be some of her ancestors."

"That's a fine idea." Hasselene gave him a quick nod as someone called for the mayor over the loudspeaker. "You go on and tend to things, Robert. I'll sit here and keep Laura company until Graham comes back."

Nodding, the mayor excused himself, and Hasselene took his place in Graham's chair. "So you're having a nice time." She reached across the space between us and patted my arm.

"Yes." The dreamy sound of the words surprised me. I was looking toward the concession stand, and Graham had just slipped into view, putting mustard on a hot dog and juggling two sodas.

Hasselene followed my line of vision, chuckling. "It's a little hard to say who's more smitten here."

I looked away, embarrassed. "I'm sorry. I'm usually not like this."

"Neither is he." She studied Graham with a thoughtful crinkle over her brows. "You wouldn't know it by looking at him now, but it's been a full year since I've seen him smile. He hasn't shown interest in anyone or anything these two months since he came home, and believe me, it's not because folks haven't tried to get him back on his feet. We just couldn't. First time I saw him laugh about anything was that day you and I fell in the bushes." Smiling to herself, she slanted an embarrassed glance toward me. "Right then and there, I knew. Oh, I guess I knew even before that, when we saw you out there in the storm. I knew then. Sometimes I just know."

Her eyes, the pale gray of a dawning sky, met mine, and I remembered that day when she knew I needed help, even before I knew it myself. "Be a little patient with our boy, Laura." Her voice was little more than a whisper, so that no one could have heard but her and me. "He's just now realizing it's all right to go on and have a life." She patted my knee, then used it to push herself up, groaning as she added, "Here he comes with your drinks."

She was gone before Graham made it to his chair, but he didn't miss the fact that she'd been there. He watched her suspiciously as he popped the last bite of his hot dog into his mouth and finished it, then handed me my soda. "What was Aunt Hass doing?"

"Matchmaking, I think."

If that bothered him, he didn't show it. He leaned close to me so that our arms were intertwined. "A little late for that."

"Guess so." Snuggling in my chair, I rested my head on his shoulder and listened to the last two sets of music, thinking that I couldn't imagine a more perfect day. I thought about what Hasselene had said, how she seemed so certain that Graham and I were something special together. *Sometimes I just know.* What would she say if she knew I was leaving for California in three days and didn't have the courage to tell them?

The light around us grew dim, and one by one the audience thinned as the evening sun drifted below the crowning hills of the Spanish Rim, throwing soft purple shadows over the valley. Finally the musicians announced the last song, and Graham smiled and said, "Guess that's it."

"Guess so," I breathed, intoxicated by the drifting twilight breeze, and the calls of the mourning doves on the hillsides, and the final strains of the music. Even though I knew I needed to be heading home to check on Dad and get a little of the laundry done, I found myself not wanting my day with Graham to end. "Your aunt told me that I should see the old church before I go," I said as we stood up and started down the hill, Graham carrying the lawn chairs on his shoulder.

He changed course so that we were headed toward the old structure. "Want to see inside before it gets too dark?"

"Really?" I felt the lure of history, the connection to those long-ago pioneers who may or may not have been my ancestors. "It's not locked or anything?"

He raised a brow, as if that were a strange question. "Never has been." Shifting the lawn chairs off his shoulder, he set them down and ushered me up the stone steps to the heavy wooden door.

"Nobody ever comes out here and bothers the place?" I asked as he pulled a cord, raising the latch inside so that the door swung open.

"No one ever has." His voice echoed into the sanctuary as I slipped across the threshold. "It's sacred ground."

"It's beautiful." I breathed in the scent of old wood and dust and the idle coal-burning stove in the front corner of the chapel. Thinking of those early-day settlers, I gazed around the small sanctuary, its ancient pews bathed in long strands of colored light from the squares of red, green, and blue glass in the windows. Overhead, candle chandeliers swayed slightly in the breeze of the open doorway. My mind rushed back in time, imagining the candles burning, the pews filled with women in long dresses and men in dark woolen frock coats. Somewhere in my imagination I heard them singing hymns, and I felt that connection again—the one that told me I belonged to this place.

I turned, and Graham was watching me. He touched the familiar name on the brass wall plaque. My last name. "Looks like you've come home."

Smiling, I moved closer to him, drawn by the pull of his gaze and that sense of wanting to belong, to this place, to him. "It feels like I've come home." Standing beside him, I touched the letters on the plaque, trying to connect with the past, with the essence of my ancestors.

Graham's hand slid over mine, warm, solid, tender, and my musings flew out the window. I turned around just as the last streams of amber light caught his eyes, and all I thought about was him.

Chapter 16

THERE are times when you wake up on Monday morning with the feeling that everything you remember from the weekend couldn't possibly be true, and you must have been in bed since Friday, dreaming it all. When the phone rang at five-thirty A.M., I felt that way. For a change, I wasn't up tapping away on my laptop. I was in bed, asleep, dreaming of something wonderful that I couldn't quite remember after the phone rang.

Maybe it was being startled awake that left me with a sense of dread.

Dad was on the other end of the line when I answered. "Dad?" I whispered, my voice hoarse. "Is everything all right?" It seemed like it had been only an hour or so since I left him at the farm, after staying there late doing two loads of laundry while he slept in his chair.

"Wanted to make sure you didn't forget me this morning." He sounded unusually cheerful. "Got my tools out. Had my coffee. Ready whenever you are."

My mind took a minute to click, and then I remembered the strange conversation I'd had with him the night before—the one in which he suggested that I should pick him up in the morning and drop him at the Crossroads on my way to work. He said he was going to take his tools and help "fix some things around there."

"Dad, are you sure about this?" As glad as I was to see him interested in getting out of the house, I was worried about dropping him there all day. I was afraid he might strain himself, trying to do too much.

"Already called the ladies and told them I'm coming. Got it all figured out. I'm gonna work for my meals." He'd argued with me the night before, too. "Won't hold you up much. Got all my tools ready. Figured you were headed to the Crossroads for coffee with Graham this morning, anyway, but if you got other things to do, I can drive myself in the old truck."

"No, that's all right. I'll come get you," I rushed, because I didn't want him driving himself there, and I was, indeed, going to the Crossroads for coffee with Graham. A warm feeling slipped over me as I thought about standing with Graham in the doorway of the old church the night before, talking about meeting for coffee. Morning had seemed ages away, too long to wait to see him again. "I was planning on going that way."

Dad made a sound that might have been a chuckle. "Figured that." He seemed pleased. I wondered if he was in on the matchmaking scheme along with the ladies and Graham's uncle Rob. "I'll be waitin' on the porch." *Click.* I didn't even get a chance to say, *Dad, it's five-thirty in the morning and the phone woke me up. It'll be a while before I can get there.*

I don't suppose it would have mattered much anyway. If I told Dad it would take me an hour to get there, he'd sit impatiently waiting on the porch. At least he was out of his chair and looking forward to doing something. I hoped he didn't hurt himself trying to do repair work at the Crossroads. It was a much more strenuous job than he could handle in his present condition. I'd have to explain to Hasselene and Mernalene that, even though their pie seemed to have worked miracles on Dad, he was still quite frail and he probably wouldn't be able to do much carpentry work. It was hard to imagine that he would even have the energy to gather up his tools.

But when I got to the farm, there he was, waiting on the porch steps with a toolbox, a bucket of secondhand nails, and a crate loaded with various saws, hammers, levels, and a crowbar. He was trying hard to hide it, but he was obviously pumped up about his new work-for-food deal. I didn't have the heart to argue with him about it, so I just helped him load his things, and together we drove to the Crossroads.

Dad was in a talkative mood, and we chatted back and forth about the picking and grinning Saturday night, and the food at the café. He told me the story of the German girl who had first introduced him to buttermilk pie, and how he'd continued to write to her after the war and even considered proposing marriage—until he met Mom, he said, and then he knew Mom was the one. Two weeks later he asked her to marry him.

"How did you know?" I heard myself say. "I mean, how did you know it was right?" I realized that the person I really wanted to ask was Mom. It was unusual enough for Dad and me to converse, much less talk about emotions and mushy-gushy stuff like true love.

For a minute I thought Dad wasn't going to answer. He looked out the window, moving his lips like he was chewing on something.

Disappointed, I turned my attention back to the road. I missed my mom. I wanted to sit on the bed and giggle with her, and tell her about Graham and how he made me feel. I wanted to ask her if it made any sense after only a few days. I wanted her to tell me how she knew so quickly that what she and Dad felt was real.

"I knew because I talked about her in my sleep." When I glanced back at Dad, he was trying to hide a wry grin.

I laughed, and blushed, and muttered, "Geez, Dad."

We finished the rest of the ride in a comfortable silence. Graham and the ladies and about a dozen coffee-starved commuters were already there when we reached the Crossroads. Dad settled in at the counter, and I went out to the porch to have breakfast with Graham. He was talking on his cell phone when I came out the door with two cups of coffee and some biscuits. He looked grave and tired, completely different from only a few minutes before, when he'd smiled and told me good morning. Now he didn't seem to notice I was there. Hunching forward with the phone pressed to his ear, he rubbed his forehead, his eyes falling closed, creases of pain forming at the corners.

I wanted to step forward, to comfort him, but I was frozen in place. I saw for the first time the broken man that Hasselene, Uncle Rob, and Puff had described. I saw the suffering he kept locked beneath the surface. My heart wrenched, and more than anything, I wanted to take that pain away, to lessen the burden, to know exactly what had caused it.

"I'll be there," he said. "I'll do the presentation." He finished the conversation, but didn't move or open his eyes or lay the phone down. He just sat there, rubbing the creases on his forehead, his dark lashes lowered against sun-browned cheeks.

The sound of voices coming from the side of the building distracted me, and caught Graham's attention. He stood up suddenly, seeming to realize where he was. Together we looked toward the alley as Evie and the restaurant guy from Austin walked around the side of the building. Evie was laughing and flirting, touching his arm and delivering a parade smile as she said, "Oh, Randal, you don't have to do that." Leaning close to him, she whispered something that I couldn't hear.

"Absolutely," he answered, as they started toward the steps. "Evie, you are a wealth of good ideas."

"I know," she chirped, in a tone that said, *Go ahead, flatter me some more.* "So you owe me a steak dinner, Randal."

"Anywhere you want." It sounded like he was talking about more than just dinner.

Evie noticed Graham as they started up the steps. "Oh, hi, there." Letting go of Randal's arm, she stepped between Graham and me and touched Graham's shoulder, saying, "How are you doing today, Graham? Are you all right?" with a note of sympathy, and an emphasis on the word *today* that told me, whatever was going on with Graham, she knew about it.

A pang of jealousy flared hot inside me.

Graham moved so that her hand dropped off his shoulder. "Fine, Evie, thanks," he said flatly, glancing at her and then the restaurant guy. "You two out taking a walk this morning?"

Evie's giggle was like the jingling of a wind chime. "Yes, oh, you know, talking real estate. I never stop."

"Mm-hmm," he muttered, crossing his arms over his chest, clearly ready to end the conversation.

In one swift movement I stepped around Evie and set the coffee on the table, saying, "Got the coffee," with exaggerated cheerfulness. I slid into my chair as if I hadn't a clue that Evie was hanging around trying to start up a conversation about something Graham didn't want to talk about. "Ready for breakfast?"

"More than ready." Graham excused himself with a quick nod toward Evie and her companion, and sat down across from me.

Left with little choice but to move on, Evie said, "Well, have a good breakfast. I'm glad to hear you're doing all right, Graham." She reclaimed her grasp on Randal, and they continued through the door into the café.

When they were gone, I turned to Graham, trying to

hold back the raging whirlwind of questions within me. "What was that all about?"

He gave the screen door a narrow look as it vibrated to a stop. "I think she's got some scheme in her head about getting my aunts to trade off the restaurant for some kind of retirement apartment on Inks Lake." The words were clipped, his gaze hard. "I told her the day she brought it up to me that it'll never happen. Aunt Hass and Aunt Merna have been here all their lives. They'd die before they let go of this place. The family has tried over the last few years to talk them into closing down the café and moving into town, and they won't budge. They sure aren't going to let some real estate agent from out of town waltz in here and sweet-talk them into selling it off."

"No, I guess not." I barely heard what he said. I focused, instead, on the expression on his face. There was something different about him this morning. Something strained and troubled. Angry. Taking a deep breath, I plunged forward into that sea of uncharted issues we hadn't yet discussed. More than anything I wanted him to open up to me, to move past the barrier between us. "But I really meant, why was she asking about you? Is something wrong?"

A flicker of emotion crossed his face, a hint of something deep. Sliding my hand across the table, I touched his arm, and he lifted his hand to intertwine it with mine.

"No," he said, the darkness lifting like a veil. "There's nothing wrong now."

"But, Graham, if there's something ... if I can help ..." *I know there's something wrong,* I wanted to scream. *Why won't you talk to me?* For the first time, I understood how my mother must have felt all those times my father remained strong and silent, shutting her out.

"Laura, you have no idea how you've helped. Every

minute I spend with you, nothing else matters." Graham's eyes warmed until I felt it in every part of my body.

Everything around me stood still. There were no voices drifting through the screen door, no birds, no breeze, no floating bits of shadow from the live oaks. There was nothing but Graham and me.

Nothing else matters, I tried to tell myself. *Let the questions wait. Give it time. Be patient.* But in the back of my mind there was a fear that I was setting myself up for a fall, that he would continue to keep me at arm's length.

"I guess we should have breakfast, then," I said finally, choking on a mixture of emotions, both bitter and sweet.

"Guess so." He smiled, and let go of my hand, then opened our biscuit bundle. "So what's in store for your day?"

We went on from there, making perfectly benign conversation as we ate breakfast and finished our coffee. It was what he needed right then, I told myself. This wasn't the time to question him or to talk about my job promotion.

But in the back of my mind, there was a nagging little voice buzzing like a fly determined to find a place to land. It was telling me that time was running out. Even if this morning wasn't the time, tonight had to be. I had to tell him I was supposed to be leaving for California the day after tomorrow, and that Puff had told me some of what was going on with him, and that I had some past history of my own. If we were going to have any hope of developing a relationship from this pixie-dust beginning, we were going to have to be honest with each other.

"Guess it's time to get going," I heard him say, and I slipped from my thoughts.

Glancing at my watch, I realized I was going to be late to work. "Wow, time flies," I said reluctantly.

He nodded, clearly sorry to be leaving. "Yes, it does."

"I'd better go in and tell Dad not to overdo," I said, and stood up. Graham stood with me and cleaned the mess off the table while I went inside.

In the café, Dad was, of all things, wearing an apron and serving coffee. I stood there staring at him for a minute, then walked to the counter and asked Mernalene to please make certain he didn't overdo it. Giving him one last, bewildered look, I went back outside and stood at the car, kissing Graham good-bye like it was good-bye forever. I wasn't sure why I felt that way. There was an uneasiness in me that I couldn't quite quantify.

"Have a good day," I said, wishing again that I knew what was happening, what his day would bring.

Cupping the side of my face in his hand, he kissed me on the top of my head, then stepped back. "You too." There was the slightest flicker of those painful emotions in him, then he turned around and headed toward his truck. I started my car and left for work, dragging all of the unanswered questions behind me like deadweight.

The day was busy, but without major disasters. First thing in the morning the employees got the interoffice memo that Landerhaus Publishing, which only a few months before had swallowed up their magazine, was now acquiring Western Limited Press. Around noon, the news was announced to the general public. I heard it on the TV in the break room, during the noon business report. A bolt of excitement zinged through me as the analyst reported that stockholders were thrilled with the deal. *Texcetera* employees, pawns themselves in one of our recent buyouts, looked anything but thrilled. At the table in the corner, someone grumbled, "Damn Landerhaus is going to own every midsize magazine and newspaper in the country pretty soon."

The guy next to him, a *Texcetera* Web designer whose name I couldn't remember, elbowed him in the ribs and nodded covertly toward me. Pretending I hadn't heard, I finished making my coffee, then went back to work making sure that Landerhaus Publishing would be happy with the successful release of its newest glossy publication.

Graham called late in the afternoon to tell me he'd be tied up and wouldn't be able to meet me for dinner. He sounded as disappointed as I felt when he said, "Have a good night, Laura. See you in the morning for coffee, all right?" I could tell he was down, and I wanted to ask why, but not over the phone.

"All right," I said, cradling the receiver on my shoulder and letting out a long, slow sigh. Tomorrow was Tuesday. I had booked a flight out on Wednesday, and I hadn't even told him yet. "See you in the morning."

"Night, darlin'."

"Night," I whispered, and then I realized he'd called me *darlin'*. All my mental dialogue about airplane flights and possible long-distance relationships evaporated and I sat there feeling giddy and thinking about Graham and all of the little things I loved about him.

That night I woke up talking about him in my sleep. I said his name even after I was awake. For an instant my mind hovered in some fantasy in which he was there in the room with me.

Then I realized the cell phone was ringing on the nightstand, and the fantasy evaporated like a puff of smoke. Fumbling for the phone, I thought of Graham as I put my thumb over the button, illuminating the display. Maybe he was up late, traveling back from wherever he'd been. He'd laugh when I told him about how my dad had fixed the porch railing at the Crossroads that day, and how I'd found him and the sisters sifting through ancient cans of paint, trying to find one that wasn't dried up, so they could paint the new rail. . . .

An instant before I would have answered, I looked at the glow on the screen and saw the caller ID: DALE DAWSON. 236-4231. The condo phone number. A sick feeling twisted in my stomach, squashing the butterflies that had been there only a moment before. Dale was back home. And he was trying to call me.

Rubbing my thumb back and forth over the button, I read his name again, DALE DAWSON, DALE, DALE, DALE. . . . The phone rang insistently, three times, four. *If you don't answer it now, Laura, the voice mail will pick up.*

My thumb quivered on the button—the key that could unlock the door to all that had been, to everything black-and-white and certain. If I told Dale about the WLP deal, he would cheer me on. Dale would love the idea of Hollywood. He'd tell me I deserved this job, that I'd worked hard and I was good at what I did, and that I deserved the promotion. After all, I'd given the company fifteen years of my life. . . .

I tossed the phone onto the floor, and it slid into the corner, out of reach, then quit ringing.

Lying back on the bed, I covered my face with my hands as tears squeezed from my eyes. Why was Dale home, and what did that mean? A simple change of plans? Maybe the next overseas assignment didn't materialize? Or had he come home looking for me? At some point I was going to have to deal with going back to Richmond and dissolving the life Dale and I had built—splitting up the things, moving out of the condo. What would Graham think about all of that? What would he say if I told him that, back home, I was effectively still living with someone I'd once thought was my soul mate?

If I told him that what I felt for him was something

completely different, would he believe me? Would I be able to describe it, when I didn't even understand it myself? How had everything gotten so complicated in the space of a few days? A week ago I was living with someone and we were talking about houses. Only a week ago. Now it felt like another lifetime. Someone else's life.

Oh, God, I can't think about this now. The future. My past. Graham's past. Too much gray area, too many questions. I didn't want to try to figure it all out. I wanted to slip back into sleep and forget it all.

Except that right now, the past was probably leaving a long message on my voice mail. Wherever I went it would be there, waiting. And the future, one possible future, was somewhere in the little town of Keetonville, perhaps just now on the way home, perhaps passing by the old rock church where my name was engraved in stone, or perhaps pulling up to the old white house inside the Keeton Ranch gate. The other possible future was coming by express mail tomorrow: a plane ticket to California.

Rolling over on the bed, I pulled the pillows against my ears and cried myself back to sleep. I dreamed of the old mill and *Rio Bravo* playing on the side of the building before a crowd. I was standing beside the stream with Graham again. My mother was there, urging me to follow the stream, to see where it led. She tried to speak, but a plane flew overhead, the roar of its engines masking her voice.

When I awoke, the television in the bedroom was playing *Rio Bravo*. Startled, I darted a confused gaze around the room, trying to separate the dream from reality. The gray light from the window told me it was nearly morning.

On TV, the music rose to a crescendo as John Wayne galloped on horseback across the screen. Jerking upright in the bed, I fumbled around on the nightstand, trying to find the remote. My leg touched something solid in the folds of the bedspread, and the picture on the TV wavered off, then on again. I realized the remote was tangled in the covers and that I must have rolled over on it while I was sleeping.

Taking a deep breath, I swallowed to calm my racing heart. Mystery solved. I untangled the remote to turn off the TV, but sat there with it in my hand instead. The movie was the same one in my dream. Odd, because I couldn't remember ever watching *Rio Bravo*. I supposed I probably had, on some long-ago Saturday afternoon when my father was resting in his chair, or one of my brothers was home from college. How odd that the details of that old story were stored somewhere in my mind, waiting to be the stuff of a dream. . . .

The cell phone rang, and I jumped, glancing toward the shadowed corner of the room, remembering Dale's call the night before. Or had I dreamed that, too?

Throwing the covers aside, I stepped unsteadily from the bed and grabbed the phone, looking at the display. COLLEEN COLLINS the caller ID said, and below that, VOICE MAIL—1 MSG. Dale's. Not a bad dream, but reality.

I answered Collie's call as the music on *Rio Bravo* rose dramatically and echoed through the bedroom. Collie said hello, and all I could hear was the music, and then John Wayne hollering.

"Collie?" Pressing the phone closer to my ear, I fished around for the remote. "Hang on a minute. I can't hear a thing." I hammered the button and turned the sound down without even picking up the remote. "There, that's better," I said, still watching the screen, strangely fascinated with John Wayne.

Collie laughed. "What in the world are you watching?"

"Some old movie. I must have left the remote on the bed last night. The TV woke me up this morning."

"Oh," Collie said, and I could tell it wasn't old movies she wanted to talk about. "Sorry to call so early, but since I was up with the baby, I thought I'd catch you before you got off to work. I heard about the Western Limited Press deal yesterday. That's big news."

"Yes, it is," I agreed, and a spark of excitement tingled through me. "Royce just called me Sunday. He said they want to send me out to Hollywood for the transition."

"And?" Collie knew there was more to the story.

I paused, not sure what I wanted to say next. On the one hand, I wanted to tell her about the possible promotion to publisher-in-charge, but on the other hand ... well ... on the other hand, there was everything she had seen going on at the Crossroads. If I started telling people about the publisher position at WLP, then it would become real. I would feel more committed. "And I guess we'll see after that. I don't know. I'm still adjusting to the news."

"Be-caaause . . ." Collie stretched out the word, leaving it open, like a question unfinished. She knew something was going on with me.

"I don't know." I sighed, climbing out of bed and pacing the room impatiently.

"Yes, you do."

"No, I don't."

"Yes, you do, but you don't want to say." Her voice was steady, confident. "So, spill. What's going on with you lately?"

I sighed, sitting on the corner of the bed near the TV, watching while John Wayne mounted his horse and sent it into a gallop in one swift movement. I liked the way he did that. It made me think of Graham. "Midlife crisis, I guess."

"Oh, one of those." Collie gave a regretful sound into the phone.

"Yeah, I think so. I guess I wasn't ready to leave yet."

"Hmmm." The baby whimpered, and I heard Collie moving blankets around. In the background True said something, and Collie whispered, "No, it's all right. Go back to sleep, hon." She came back on the line, and again said, "Hmmm . . ." and then, "Have anything to do with the handsome guitar playing cowboy with the great . . . umm . . . voice?"

"God," I muttered like a prayer, letting my head sink into my hand. Now it was really out in the open, and Collie would want to help me analyze it.

"Mm-hmm!" Eureka, she had found the truth, and she knew it. "So that's what's going on, huh?"

"Yes, I guess it is." If anyone, *anyone* on the planet could understand what I was going through, it would have to be Collie. This was so much like what had happened to her, it was like we were living parallel lives. If I told her, would she think I was doing all of this out of some bizarre desire to compete with her—as Dale had insinuated—out of some twisted jealousy over Collie's marriage and new family? "Collie, I want you to know this isn't me trying to live out some twisted fascination with your life. I swear. I didn't come to Texas looking to . . ." *Gulp.* I swallowed the last three words, *fall in love*.

Collie *tsk*ed into the phone. "I know that. Since when have you ever followed anybody's lead?"

We chuckled together, and then I thought of the day I'd called Collie, two years ago, when she was down in Texas secretly falling in love with True, and I'd told her there was a big story in D.C., and she had to come home. "You know, Coll, I'm sorry I pushed you so hard when you didn't want to come back to D.C. I should have spent less time judging and more time being supportive. I'm glad you didn't listen to me."

"Oh, cut that out." Collie's voice quavered with emotion. "You were fine. You helped me think things through, and I needed that at the time."

"No, I talked you into going back home, and I shouldn't have."

"So you're saying that you shouldn't go home? It *is* you we're talking about, isn't it?"

Pounding a fist on my knee, I stood up again. "I'm not saying that. . . . I don't know. . . . How could anyone possibly know after only a few days?" The music on TV rose again, and I walked closer to hit the mute button.

Collie drew a quick breath. "Oh, my gaaah . . . What are you watching?"

"*Rio Bravo,* I think. Why?"

Collie gasped, then whispered, "It's a sign."

Openmouthed, I stared at the screen. "What . . . are you . . . talking about?"

"That's what I did." She sounded stunned. "That's what I did the week I was falling in love with True. I sat in my cabin at the bed-and-breakfast and watched John Wayne movies. Not for any reason I could explain. All of a sudden I was fascinated with cowboys. I watched *Rio Bravo* three times." She halted the rush of words, then repeated, "It's a sign."

I wasn't sure whether to laugh or call a psychiatrist, so finally I settled for chuckling and saying, "Collie, this conversation has just entered the Twilight Zone." I had a feeling she was toying with me to see if I would take the bait and admit I was in love with Graham, or John Wayne, or both.

"I know." She seemed completely serious. "Hard to believe you'd turn into a John Wayne junkie, too." Then she made a ghostly "Wooh-eee-ooo" into the phone and added, "Pretty strange."

"You're pretty strange," I joked. "I doubt if I'm watching John Wayne movies because I'm in love with Graham Keeton."

"So you *are* in love." *Snap.* Collie closed the trap.

I reminded myself never to engage in word games

with an ace reporter. Collie knew how to sniff out the truth. "I don't know."

"Yes, you do. You just don't want to admit it."

"I don't know, Coll. It seems kind of impossible. Last week I was breaking off a three-year relationship, and this week I'm in love with some guy I just met—in Texas, no less. Doesn't that seem a little weird to you?"

"Well, not to me, but I've been there. I kept telling myself I couldn't be in love with True after only a few days, but, hey, look where I ended up."

"I don't know if this is the same thing as you and True," I admitted. "It's all so fast, and to tell you the truth, I don't know that much about him. He doesn't talk about himself. I know he was an army aviator, special ops of some kind, and he got out a few months ago. The lady at the hair salon in Keetonville told me his leaving the army had something to do with a helicopter crash. There was some kind of scandal involved. He doesn't want to talk about it, I know that much. So far he's a closed book. It's a little hard to base a relationship on that. Of course, I haven't told him about Dale, either. He doesn't know that back home we're effectively still living together. How bad does that make me look?" I realized suddenly that Collie wasn't answering. In fact, there was dead silence on the other end of the line. "Collie, are you still there?"

"What did you say his name was?" I could tell she had something on her mind.

"Graham Keeton. Why?"

"Geez," Collie rushed. "I knew he looked familiar."

"Collie, what are you talking about?" My heart lurched against my chest and froze there. For an instant I had the urge to tell her I didn't want to know.

"The helicopter crash last year. It was on the national news for a while, and it was a big story here. Eight soldiers were killed, and a bunch of senators came down to investigate. I did a four-part story on it for the Dallas paper."

"Oh, my God." Vague images of news footage came to my mind. "Graham was involved in that?"

"Laura, he was the c.o. Those were his soldiers. He blew the whistle on his own program. It was because of him that the senate investigated and found out the crash wasn't due to pilot error. It was due to a design flaw in the choppers, and the helicopter company knew about it. They'd had problems with some of the prototypes and almost killed a test pilot two years before. It was a huge scandal. There were some pretty important people wrapped up in it. When all was said and done, they never did prove exactly who knew about it ahead of time, and who was taking payoffs, but they got quite a few people. It put a stain on the whole chain of command and grounded a fleet of very expensive new helicopters. It's no wonder Graham doesn't want to talk about what happened. He lost eight young soldiers, and the scandal ruined his career."

"I remember," I whispered, staring at the blank white wall, suddenly understanding everything. Now I knew the secret, the thing from the past that Graham hadn't figured out how to live with yet—the loss of eight men under his command. "Listen, Coll, I'd better go." Suddenly I didn't want to talk anymore. I said good-bye and hung up the phone, feeling like I'd just awakened on the surface of the moon.

Chapter 17

I thought about Graham as I dressed and drove across town to pick up Dad, then headed to the Crossroads. Dad was in a good mood, actually trying to make conversation. The problem was that I didn't feel like talking. I felt like going to sleep, winding the clock back, and waking up two days ago—before Royce called about the West Coast deal, before Collie told me details Graham didn't want me to know.

I understood what Graham was going through, but I wasn't sure how to tell him that. Growing up in an army family, I knew what the loss of fellow soldiers meant, especially soldiers under your command. My father had lost young soldiers during Korea and Vietnam. It was one of the wounds that stayed with him, one of the things he never wanted to talk about. He felt the burden, always, of the wives and children left behind with no fathers, and that burden stood as a wall between him and us. He didn't feel he had a right to still be here, home with us, watching his children grow up when others would not.

Now I understood the reason Graham didn't think he deserved a new life. Even though a year had passed and the public inquisition was over, the private inquisition continued within him.

Every minute I spend with you, nothing else matters.
His words made sense now. When he looked at me, he
didn't see a reflection of the questions that were inside
him, because I didn't know about his past. The problem
was that when he saw me now, I wouldn't be able to
hide the questions. How would I feel if he, like my father, wasn't willing to talk about them?

"Everything all right?" Dad asked as we neared the
Crossroads. "You're a little quiet this morning."

I sighed. "I have a lot on my mind." I realized I hadn't
even told him I was leaving tomorrow. "It's kind of a long
story, Dad, but I'm due to fly out midday tomorrow."

A quick look of disappointment crossed his face before
he turned his gaze out the window. "Suppose I shouldn't
be surprised. All you kids ever do is come and go."

I sank against my seat, wounded in a way I hadn't
thought possible. For the first time in my life I really
cared what my father thought. We'd opened the doors
to each others' hearts these past few days, and now I
could feel them falling closed again.

"Dad, I'll be back." Would I? Once things got rolling
in California, there wouldn't be time for vacations. "It's
business, Dad. There's a big promotion at stake. If I
don't go now, I'll lose my chance."

He turned to me, his gaze long and soulful. "Suppose
you'd better go, then." For an instant I thought I was off
the hook, but his tone said otherwise, and he added, "If
that's what's important to you."

I coughed in disbelief, turning to him as we came to a
halt at the leaning stop sign. "Well, isn't that what mattered to you, Dad?" I spat, slamming shut those doors
inside me. How dare he criticize me for putting my work
first. How many times had he left us for months, years,
picked us up and moved us here and there because it
would keep him on the promotion track? "Isn't that all
that ever mattered? Because it sure seemed like it."

Sighing, he deflated like a raft losing air, sinking, as he squinted toward the Crossroads. "Seemed like it mattered at the time," he agreed. "But lately I realize it isn't the army I miss. It's your mother. I'd trade a lot of things for one more day with her. It comes to my mind that we could have had a lot more days together in our lives, but I decided to spend my time on other things. In the end, your life is all about those little decisions you make." Fingers bent and trembling, he raised a hand and tapped the window glass like a bird pecking at a cage. "When you're young, you don't think of time as a limited currency. But it's like the dimes in that old coffee tin my mama used to keep on top of the refrigerator. You reach up and take out a few, and you reach up and take out a few more. You spend them here and there— they're only dimes, after all. They don't mean much. You never take down the jar to see how much is left. One day you reach in and your fingers hit the bottom. The jar's empty, and there's nothing you can do about it. You realize they were only dimes, but altogether you've squandered a fortune."

Tears choked my throat. I reached across the car, slipping my hand over his. I couldn't remember my father ever saying something so profound, ever expressing regret for keeping himself apart from us. "Dad . . ." I whispered, wishing I hadn't brought up the bitterness of the past.

He shook his head and went on, squeezing my fingers. Outside, I heard the stop sign swinging on the crooked post, but inside the car we sat frozen in time, somewhere between the past and the future. "I wish I would have spent more of my dimes on things I could keep—you know, bought some memories, some treasures for my old age. I wish I'd put more into you kids and into your mom. I wasn't much of a family man. It was easier for me not to be."

"It doesn't matter now, Dad. That's in the past." How many times had I yearned for him to say exactly that, to admit that he needed us, after all, that he had missed out on something valuable.

He nodded slowly, looking sad, old, poor. "I guess it doesn't. I guess all of you are fine." But the way he said it told me he didn't believe that my brothers, who were both workaholics, were fine, and he didn't think Lindsey, still bitter from her divorce five years ago, was fine, and he didn't think I was fine.

A car pulled up behind us. I turned my attention back to the road and continued through the intersection. As we turned into the parking lot, a terrible longing twisted inside me. "Dad, are you going to be all right when I leave?" Even as I asked the question, I knew what a part of me, that part where the longing grew, wanted. That part wanted him to say, *No, Laura, you can't go. If you leave me, I'll curl up and die. Stay.*

Slipping his hand away, he patted mine, then twined his fingers together in his lap. "Oh, I reckon. Nette called and said she'd start coming by to look in on me every few days, and I've got the work here at the Crossroads to keep me busy now. The ladies are sure glad for the help, and with that story to come out in your magazine they'll have more business than you can shake a stick at. They're going to hire Puff's daughter to help in the kitchen. They said they'd pay me for my time and keep me in meat loaf and buttermilk pie. I guess that's all I need." He gave me a slow, sad smile that was filled with emotion. "If you leave . . . are you going to be all right? You haven't been getting on too well since we lost Mom."

My eyes watered. "Yeah, Dad, I'll be all right. The job will keep my mind off . . . things. Anyway, I don't know if I'm going for good. If I don't like the job out there, I may just come back." Pulling the car into a parking space behind a row of vehicles, I turned the key. "Guess we should go in."

"Wonder what the ladies have for breakfast this morning." Dad straightened in his seat and opened the door, ready to shake off the heavy cloud of emotions. One leg out the door, he turned back and frowned at me, looking suddenly gruff. "I want you to know there's no hanky-panky going on here."

Dropping my jaw, I said, "W-what . . . Dad?" The switch from *life is like a can of dimes* to *hanky panky* caught me unprepared.

Dad was impatient with my lagging behind his train of thought. "I want you to know there's nothing . . . well, nothing . . . unseemly going on between the ladies and me. I wouldn't do that to your mother. The ladies need help here and I've taken the job. That's it."

Clearing my throat, I pinched a hand over my lips so he wouldn't see me trying not to smile, trying to get control of myself before I answered. "I know that, Dad," I choked out. The grin tugged at my lips as I climbed from my seat, and I turned my back to him, catching a few quick breaths, surprised that I suddenly felt like laughing.

By the time Dad came around the car, I had myself under control, but he frowned at me anyway, barking, "You can tell your brothers and your sister that, too. You know Lindsey is always suspicious about things. You just tell her there's nothing racy going on here. Just friends helping each other out."

I nodded. "I'll tell her to mind her own business."

"That'd be fine, too." The corners of his lips twitched, and for a moment we were partners in crime.

I wondered if there was any interest between him and either of the Goodnight sisters, or if there would be in the future as they got to know one another. Right now, Mom's death was still so new. How would my brothers and Lindsey feel about it if something developed in the future? "Dad," I said quietly as we drew near the porch steps, "Mom wouldn't want you to be sitting at the farm alone. She would want you to be happy."

He nodded, his lips set in a thin, straight line. "I know. I'm trying."

I slipped my arm around his shoulders, the first time I could ever remember doing that. He didn't feel as thin as he had a few days ago, and his body didn't tremble as he moved. "Good for you, Dad."

He only gave me a *humph* and moved away from me as we reached the new, improved porch railing. "Looks like the ladies went down and wrangled some paint off Jud Puddy." Leaning down to read three shiny new gallon cans, he added, "Looks like they decided to paint the porch white again." He shook one of the gallons, then set it down. "Oh, I forgot to tell you—you don't need to come get me tonight. I'm going to ride over to Killeen with Jud Puddy in his flatbed truck and pick out lumber and such at the big lumberyard. When we're done, Jud'll drop me at home."

"That sounds fine," I commented, glancing around and noticing how much better the Crossroads was already starting to look. "Just promise me you're not going to try to do too much."

The café door opened, and HOUSHNTR stepped out dressed in a silky gold suit and thick iridescent jewelry.

Dad smiled and hurried forward to hold the screen door for her. "Mornin', Evie," he said, as if she were an old friend.

Giving him the beauty-queen smile, she leaned forward and gushed over him, telling him how great the porch railing looked, and what a wonderful carpenter he was, and how, when he was finished at the Crossroads, she had some carpentry work she needed done at her house, and would he be interested?

Clearly flattered, Dad stuttered out an answer in the

affirmative, then told her to have a good day and slipped a little farther in the doorway to wave at someone inside, while still holding the door for me.

Evie stopped next to me. Dad went inside and let the screen door close. Evie reached out and put her hands on both of my arms, her voice tinkling like a wind chime as she said, "I saw the article about the Crossroads on your magazine's new Web site last night. It was just wonderful."

"Thank you." I stepped back, a little embarrassed, because I didn't even know the *Texcetera* Web site was up. The last thing I'd heard, the designer was having trouble getting the pages to load correctly.

Evie didn't seem to notice my less-than-enthusiastic response. Flipping her hands in the air, she gestured amazement and flashed another wide, square smile that showed every tooth in her mouth. "I can't tell you how well that Colleen Collins captured the ambiance of the place. The article had such an earthy feel. When the magazine hits the shelves, my goodness, tourists will be showing up by the dozens."

For some reason, that possibility bothered me. I hadn't considered that in publicizing the Crossroads, I would be changing the very thing I loved about it. I loved the fact that it was a place strictly off the map. Now it wouldn't be any longer. Of course, I wouldn't be here to see that happen. . . .

"Well, usually the hype from an article is fairly temporary," I said, trying to comfort myself, and perhaps to discourage any ideas she might have about talking the Goodnight sisters out of their café. That thought still unnerved me, and I wasn't in the mood for Evie's plastic merry-sunshine this morning. "Well . . . it was good to see you." I sidestepped toward the door, trying to politely end the conversation.

Her eyes darted toward the entrance, then back at

me. "Graham's not in there," she informed me abruptly, with a little too much gloat, I thought. I wondered again at her keen interest in him. "He doesn't seem to be anywhere this morning. I wanted to see how he was doing . . . if he needed someone to talk to, I mean." She leaned closer to me. "You know, this is the first anniversary of the helicopter crash. I'm sure he gets tired of everyone making such a big deal about that, but it's bound to hit him again . . . on a day like today, I mean. There's a memorial service later at the army base—congressmen coming down to be with the eight families and the little kids who lost their daddies. It'll be really sad. The noon news is going to show some of it."

I nodded, feeling a huge lump in my throat. I didn't think I could talk, and I wished Evie would go away.

She glanced toward the parking lot, then back at me, raising a finger thoughtfully. "You know, that would make a terrific article for your magazine—the memorial service. *Everyone* would love to know how those poor families are doing a year later, how they're coping with the loss. And Graham, my goodness, *everyone* wonders about his side of the story."

Heat boiled from somewhere deep within me, and I clenched my fists at my sides, trying to keep my cool, since we were standing right next to the open screen door. "You know what, Evie—"

She looked past me and gave a quick wave. "Well, my goodness, there you are, Graham. Laura and I were just talking about what a heart-wrenching magazine article the memorial service would make."

I spun around unsteadily, catching my breath in a quick gasp. The instant I saw Graham's face, stone-cold and rigid, I realized exactly how it looked, him finding me here with Evie, talking about him and magazine articles.

Evie blinked at me innocently, then waved enthusiastically toward an SUV coming into the parking lot. "Oh, there's my client." She bounded down the steps, climbed into Randal's passenger seat, and together they sped away. •

Graham remained on the bottom step, arms crossed tightly over his chest, lips set in a hard line. "So is that what's going on? A magazine article?"

"Graham, no, I . . ." I didn't know what to say. *I'm sorry?* I was. The look on his face made me ache inside. "Evie just said that to make trouble." I moved closer to him. "What happened between us had nothing to do with magazine articles. Come on, you have to know that."

He cocked his head to one side, his eyes a deep, unreadable blue, stormy like a windswept sea, wounded. "That why you went by Puff's the other day? Doing a little research?"

Closing my eyes, I let my body collapse against the porch post. My fingers gripped the railing, seeking something solid. "You have to know I wouldn't do that. Graham, surely you know I wouldn't—"

"Investigate? Satisfy your curiosity? Try to get the *real story?*" He filled in the blank with quick, angry words. "You can count on Puff to tell you everything you want to know."

"That's not how it was." I searched his face, not certain how to feel. How could he accuse me of something so terrible as secretly investigating him for a magazine article? "Surely you know I wouldn't do that. Surely you know me better than that."

"How would I, Laura? How would I know who you *really* are? I don't even know why you'd spend all day sitting in a parking lot in a hailstorm. But at least I had the decency not to go asking around behind your back about it." His gaze met mine, punctuating the sentence with a hard, unwavering stroke. "Some crazy game of let's-pretend we've been playing, isn't it?"

"It wasn't a game." I swallowed my tears like broken glass. "I wasn't playing a game, Graham. Yes, to tell you the truth, I was embarrassed that the day I met you, I was having a mini-meltdown. I'd just broken off a three-year relationship over the cell phone, and I didn't want to tell you that. I wasn't sure you'd understand."

He descended the bottom step, increasing the distance between us. "Don't give me much credit, do you?"

"It's not that. Everything was so good between us. I didn't want to do anything to mess it up."

"Like write a magazine article?"

Frustrated, hurt, growing angry, I threw my hands in the air. No matter what I said, he would use it as an excuse to move farther away from me. "There *was* no magazine article, Graham, and if you knew me at all, you would know that. And as for not giving you any credit, how in the world would I know whether or not to give you credit? You, with all your mantras about not living in the past, but you *are* living in the past. You've got it wrapped around you like a fortress, and I can't find the gate." He didn't answer, so I went on, my frustration, my anger flaring up. "Since we're getting real here, let's get real about this. You're not mad because Puff told me some things about you, or because you *really* believe I was doing a magazine article about the helicopter crash. That's just your excuse. You need a reason to push me away, like you push everyone away, and now you've got it. Congratulations. You can go back to being the legendary iron man around here. Isn't that what you want?"

He didn't answer, and his silence twisted the knife inside me. My temper, my wounded pride, demanded that I force a reaction from him—something other than his staring at me stone-faced, as if we meant nothing to each other. "It's good timing, too, because I have a flight out of here tomorrow. I've been offered a promotion to a publisher's job in California." I fell silent, my heart hammering in my throat, my hopes suspended on a thin ribbon. I wanted him to say something, to push down the wall finally, to tell me he didn't want this to be the end of things.

We stood for a long moment, the world around us silent except for the faint flowing out of everything that might have been. The café door opened, and a woman walked out with biscuits and coffee, glanced quizzically at both of us, then hurried to her car.

When she was gone, Graham slowly turned an unreadable gaze my direction. "Sounds like a great opportunity," he said flatly. "Guess we both knew this would happen sooner or later. The real world calls, right?" He turned to go, saying as he started away, "I have memorial services to get to. Take care, Laura."

A chill settled over me, and I stood there feeling like I had growing up, the times I tried to make contact with my father and he turned me down and marched off like a soldier to his own private hell. As I watched Graham walk away, out of my life, his arms rigid at his sides, his stride stiff and unwavering, I did the same thing my mother always did. I didn't try to stop the soldier. I just stood there and let silent tears fall.

When he was gone, when the sound of his truck had faded into the distance, I walked to my car, got in, and left the Crossroads behind.

Chapter 18

THE day was a blur. I went through the motions numbly, thinking not about the first issue of *Texcetera*, but about Graham, where he was and what he was doing. I knew I shouldn't be. I knew, somewhere in my logical mind, that I should be trying to let go and focus on the future. Life was about to take me in a fabulous new direction—Hollywood, a publisher's position at WLP. Everything I'd ever dreamed of.

Almost. Somewhere in that dream life I'd painted over the years there was a happy hearth and home that coexisted perfectly with ambition and career. In my head there was a place that needed success, and in my heart a place that yearned for someone to share it with. My sudden attachment to Graham, my dad, the Crossroads, and the people I'd met there was born out of that need, I told myself. It was more about me than about any of them—the yearnings of a lonely heart and an overactive biological clock. If I could fill up on enough success, maybe that hunger would go away. Once I got to California, these last few days and the yearnings they had brought would be a distant memory.

By four o'clock I had myself convinced. I told Kristi to call the airlines and get me on a flight tonight, rather than tomorrow. Just leave me enough time to get home, pack my things, and say good-bye to Dad, I told her.

She gave me a sad frown as she turned to leave my office. "I'm going to miss you," she said in a way that squeezed the knot in my throat.

"Me too." For an instant I thought both of us were going to cry, then I realized how silly that was, and added flippantly, "I'm sure everyone else around here will be glad to see me go."

Kristi had the good grace to look shocked. "Oh, no. Everyone thinks you're amazing. You pulled us through deadline. You don't know what a mess it was before you got here. We all figured we were . . . like, about to lose our jobs."

I smiled, the flattery buttering my wounds like salve. If nothing else in my life was constant, at least I was good at my job. "I don't think that's too much of a worry now. *Texcetera*'s going to be a hit, I can feel it." *That is, if Royce's little rich girl doesn't screw things up.* Jealousy pinched me again at the thought of her taking over my office. My magazine.

Kristi straightened her shoulders, looking like she had the wind in her sails. "I hope the magazine is a hit. I like this job."

"You're good at it." I realized how true that was. Despite all of her immature quirks, Kristi was becoming fine editorial stock. "Now go get me that plane ticket, all right?"

"All right." Sagging again, she paused in the doorway, then finally she left.

Thirty minutes later, she buzzed me and told me she had scheduled a late flight to California. I felt sick to my stomach, and my body went flushed and hot. I rushed to the bathroom and stood in front of the mirror spritzing water on my face, my mind spinning with questions.

What was wrong with me? Why was I having a panic

attack now? Why was I still thinking about Graham, and clinging to some impractical fantasy that he would call? Why wasn't I ready to leave?

After I left, would I dream about Mom anymore? What was she trying to tell me?

What did I really want from life?

There was no answer, only the empty hum of the air-conditioner vent overhead and the soft sound of the water spilling from the faucet, flowing down the granite sink into the drain. The sound reminded me of the brook by the old mill. *Follow the stream. See where it leads.* . . . Twice Mom had said that to me in a dream.

Where did the stream go?

Shaking my head, I turned off the faucet, yanked a paper towel out of the dispenser, and dried my face. This was ridiculous. I wasn't making any permanent life decisions. I was going to California on a business trip to begin the transition after the WLP merger. If, after that work was done, I hated it out there, I could tell Royce I didn't want the California position permanently.

But even as I told myself that, I couldn't imagine doing it. Royce would think I'd lost my mind. He'd been doubtful of me these last two months since Mom's death. He could tell I was off balance, letting personal problems interfere with my work. *Texcetera* was a test, and I'd passed. One misstep, and he'd be wondering if I still had what it took. I wasn't going to give him that opportunity. I'd worked too hard to prove myself at this level, and I couldn't step back now.

I left the rest room and walked to Kristi's cubicle. "If I'm going to make the flight, I'd better get the ticket and get going."

Kristi winced, and I thought she was going to start up with some more sappy talk about not wanting me to leave. She took a breath. "There's a problem."

"What?" I groaned. *Now what?*

"The travel agent just called and she couldn't get you on the flight after all, and you'll have to take the one tomorrow. Sorry," she rushed. "Everything's full until then."

"Great." But I wasn't as disappointed as I should have been. "That's all right. That'll give me time to wrap up some things today, and to come by here in the morning and check on the shipments before I go to the airport." I walked back to my office, closed the door, and proceeded to bury myself in phone calls and reading submissions for the rest of the day.

After everyone had gone home for the evening, I stood looking at the empty office, trying to decide what to do next. *I can work through the dinner hour, leave late, and go see Dad around bedtime, or I can leave now and go by the Crossroads. Maybe Graham will be there. . . .*

I was packing my stuff before I had time to consider the thought. The briefcase fell off my desk and landed on the floor, spilling papers, pens, and a half dozen business cards. My cell phone and a piece of fabric landed under the feet of my office chair. I picked up the fabric first, then sank into the chair holding it. Blue gingham. One of the napkins from the Crossroads. I didn't even know how it had gotten there.

Regret spiraled around me, tangible like the sting of a sudden slap. I thought about everything I'd seen and done and experienced at the Crossroads. These last few days had been peaceful, sweet like the scent of honeysuckle that clung to that place. This time with Graham had made me feel alive—vital, passionate, giddy. In love. Even if so much of it was an illusion that could exist only within the pixie-dust sphere of the Crossroads, there was still something special about him, about him and me together. Wherever I went, whatever happened next, I would always miss that feeling.

What if I never find it again? What if I never find it with anyone else?

Tucking the napkin into my briefcase, I picked up the cell phone, glancing at the message bar. VOICE MAIL—2 MSGS.

Graham, I thought. *It must have rung while I was in the bathroom.* A flutter started in my throat as I pressed the menu button.

The flutter died as the message menu came up. Not Graham. Dale. Another message from Dale, at home in Richmond. Stroking my thumb back and forth over the button, I wondered again why he was calling, and what message he'd left on the voice mail. Again, I didn't delete the message, just tucked the phone back into my briefcase. *Not now,* I thought. *Not yet.* Then I reached in and turned off the phone. I'd call him tomorrow from the plane. Whatever he had to say, I wasn't ready to deal with it yet.

Packing my briefcase and my laptop, I finished gathering my personal things into a box, then went to drop off some papers at Kristi's desk. A pink "While you were out . . ." slip puffed from the tabletop and drifted to the floor. Picking it up, I read the message: Laura, Dale called, three-fifteen P.M. Strange that Kristi hadn't brought the message to me. It wasn't like her to forget things like that. . . .

But then I realized I really didn't care. I walked back to my office and grabbed my things, then took one more look around. This was my last day here. I wasn't sure why that bothered me. *Texcetera* was nothing special. Just another little magazine in some nowhere part of the world.

I was going to miss it.

Those feelings enveloped me as I left Austin. I felt myself slipping into what my mom would have called a blue funk, and no matter how much I tried to focus on

the California trip, and the idea of a move to Hollywood, and the new magazines, I couldn't make the funk
go away. It grew thicker, like fog, the closer I came to
the Crossroads. I considered whether I should stop or
not. Dad had probably already gone to Killeen with Jud
Puddy in the hardware truck, so there wasn't any real
need for me to go by the Crossroads. If Graham was
there, I wasn't sure what I was going to say to him. If he
wasn't, that meant he didn't want to talk. I didn't know
which would be worse.

I wasn't ready for the good-bye scene with Hasselene
and Mernalene, either. My father had probably told
them I was leaving. They would be disappointed that
their matchmaking scheme hadn't come to fruition.
They might try to talk me out of leaving. . . .

Even as I thought it, the car was angling into the
parking lot on autopilot. I pulled into an empty space by
the front steps, near a *Wet paint* sign that guarded my father's newly refinished railing. He had repaired the
screen door also, putting in new screening and carefully
painting around the McCaughey's Better Bitters sign.
The screen door opened, and a man in a business suit
stepped out with two little girls trailing behind him. Balancing a stack of food to go, he hustled the girls down
the steps as the door swung shut. The sound was different, one solid, tight-fitting slap. When Dad fixed something, he built it to last. The man with the food didn't
notice the difference, just gave a quick glance over his
shoulder and continued to his car.

I gazed after him, looking for Graham's truck. But as
I surveyed the parking lot, my hopes sank. Graham's
truck wasn't there. I didn't want to think about what
that meant, but I couldn't help it. It meant that, wherever he was, whatever he was doing and thinking, I was
shut out of it.

The disappointment inside me was familiar, the ache

of an old wound, never quite healed. How many times had I seen my mother with that same yearning in her eyes, while Dad hid behind his newspaper, or his woodshop, or his tours of duty?

I didn't want my mother's life. I didn't.

I had to let go, to stay focused on reality, on the task down the road, my job in California. At least that was something predictable. Something solid. Graham was an unknown quantity, even to himself.

The porch lights flickered on as I gave the building one last look. Through the window, I saw Mernalene bringing food to the table under the A in *café,* and Hasselene moving past the C with a pot of coffee. For an instant I thought she saw me there, as I put the car in reverse, but she didn't wave, and I realized she didn't know I was outside looking in.

The image of them stayed with me as I drove to Killeen, then across town to the farm. I'd go by the Crossroads tomorrow on my way to the airport, I told myself, return the cloth napkin I'd found in my briefcase, tell everyone good-bye.

Everyone? Graham. *Tell Graham,* was what I meant. I couldn't lie about that, even to myself.

"What's wrong with me?" I muttered as I parked in front of the farmhouse and walked up the steps. No one answered, of course. Inside, Dad was dozing in his chair, his cheeks flushed, his nose a little sunburned. He looked well fed and happy, so I didn't wake him. I kissed him on the forehead, then left him a note telling him I'd come by in the morning. My eyes stung as I turned around and left, wondering if I was doing the right thing, if he was really going to be fine here on his own. I could call my brothers, tell them how things were and that they needed to come down as much as they could. I could tell Lindsey to fly in for some long weekends. . . .

Would they see the changes in him? Would he tell

them the story about the German girl and buttermilk pie, and how he fell in love with Mom? Or would he be the same with them as he had always been? When I came back to visit, would this new bond between us be gone?

The questions followed me home to the condo, whispering in the silent air there as I packed my suitcase and cleaned up the place. We probably needed to do something about terminating the lease. Dad wasn't going to be moving back, and there was no point draining his retirement income. Now that he was feeling better, he'd probably be all right at the farm. I could call in the mornings and check on him long-distance. . . .

Trying to convince myself that it all made sense, I walked to the bathroom and fished for my robe on the back of the door without flipping the light switch. When I turned around, something familiar was waiting on the counter—Mom's Bible with a note tucked in the pages, sticking out far enough so that I could see my name. *Laura*—written in Dad's handwriting. Laying the book open on the counter, I took out the note and held it close to the dim glow of the nightlight.

Laura, it said in handwriting that trembled slightly, *I think Mom wanted you to have this.*

He hadn't signed the note. In fact, it seemed unfinished, as if he had wanted to say something more, but couldn't find the words, or maybe he'd been rushed to bring it over before I got home. Looking down at the pages, I read that verse again: *Stand at the crossroads and look. . . .*

And beside that, in Mom's handwriting: *Find the right way.*

I wondered if Dad knew he was putting the marker on that page, or if he'd simply slipped it in wherever the book fell open. Was he trying to send me a message or simply giving me a piece of my mother to take with me?

Slipping into my robe, I clutched the book to my chest and walked to the bedroom, hit the button on the remote without even thinking about it, and slipped into bed. John Wayne was playing on the Cowboy Channel again. Curling my body around Mom's book, I laid my head against the pillows and watched until I fell asleep.

I dreamed about my mother at the old mill again. She was telling me to follow the stream, to see where it led. As before, I asked her what that meant, and she wouldn't say. She only smiled, as if I should know already.

When I woke in the morning, I was talking to her, telling her in soft whispers about Dad and the Crossroads. I felt peaceful, rested, safe, as if she were right there in the room with me—until I rolled over and looked at the clock, and realized I'd slept until nearly six-thirty.

The thought jolted my nerves and sent me rushing from the bed. If I didn't get going in thirty minutes, I wouldn't have time to go by the Crossroads on my way to the airport.

And one thing I knew for sure—the *only* thing I knew for sure that morning—was that I didn't want to leave without going to the Crossroads one more time.

Chapter 19

SOMETHING was wrong. I didn't know what—it was just a feeling that needled me as I got out of bed. Dad called before I was even in the shower to tell me he had his truck all packed and was headed for the Crossroads to get some work done before it got too hot. He seemed in good spirits, laughing a little as he told me he'd treat me to a cup of Crossroads coffee to say good-bye. I told him to be careful on the drive, and he promised he'd be all right. He had new tires on the truck, and she was running like a top.

All of that seemed fine, and I realized as I hung up the phone and went through showering and dressing and loading my things that it wasn't Dad I was worried about. It was something else. There was something I couldn't quite put my finger on that kept me uneasy as I finished up at the condo, then got in the car and headed toward the Crossroads. I wondered if it was the prospect of seeing Graham that was bothering me. Or the thought of not seeing him at all.

By the time I reached the leaning stop sign, my nerves were standing on end, and my heart was fluttering like I'd just had a near-miss car accident. Even the steady *creak-creak* of the sign swaying back and forth wasn't soothing, more like a ratchet torquing up that anxious feeling inside me. The cell phone rang on the seat, and I grabbed it, answering in a hurry.

"Laura?" My heart skipped a beat at the sound of Dale's voice, faint as if it were coming through a long tunnel. I didn't answer, but sat there at the deserted intersection with my mind flashing back to the day he'd called me at the Crossroads and changed everything. "Laura, are you there?"

He'd said those exact words to me that day. Closing my eyes, I tried to regain my composure. Anger seeped through me like thick, black ink. "I'm here, Dale." The words sounded low, steady, almost a growl. "What do you want?"

"I'm guessing from your tone that I'm still on your bad list." He sounded perfectly calm, maybe a little patronizing.

Bad list. Funny term for it. "I don't have time to talk now, Dale." *I don't want to talk now, or ever.* I realized suddenly how true that was. My life with Dale seemed long ago and a million miles away. I wasn't going back. "I'm on my way to catch a plane to California. The company's sending me out there for the WLP merger. I'll call you about getting my things moved out of the condo, or put in storage, or something."

"Laura . . ." I let my foot off the brake and the car idled forward through the intersection. Dale's voice disappeared into the ether, then came back. ". . . going to meet you out there and we can talk."

The car rolled into the back parking lot of the Crossroads, past the spot where I'd sat in the storm while he abandoned my dreams, and I begged him not to. "I don't want to talk, Dale. I don't. Not about us. Not now, not later. You made everything perfectly clear. It's over."

"Laura, listen, I . . ." Whatever else he said, I didn't hear it. My mind and body went numb as I rounded the corner of the building, and all at once I realized what was wrong. No cars, no lights, no voices, no sound. Nothing. No one. Not my father's truck or any other. The Crossroads looked abandoned.

"Dale, I have to go." I clicked the button without waiting for an answer, then parked the car and rushed up the steps, knocking on the door and peering into the darkened interior. No signs of life inside. My mind rushed with terrible possibilities as I ran from window to window, then down the steps and around to the back of the building to look in the windows of the living quarters. No lights on. No one inside. What if there had been an accident? What if something had happened to my father, Hasselene, or Mernalene . . . or Graham?

I called their names, pounding on the window. No one answered. Nearby, a minivan pulled off the road, circled the parking lot, then headed back toward the highway, the driver giving me a confused look as I hurried around the building to my car. Yanking the car door open, I grabbed my cell phone, then pulled my briefcase onto the driver's seat, digging through the stack of business cards. Where was Graham's number? He'd given it to me and I'd put it in my briefcase. It had to be there.

I remembered spilling my briefcase on the floor at the office, and all at once I realized that must have been where I had lost it. Drumming impatiently on the top of the car, I tried to think of what to do next. I'd have to go into Keetonville and see if anyone there knew what was going on, or how I could get in touch with . . .

"Graham." I whispered his name like a sigh of relief as the HAZMAT truck appeared on the county road. Waving my hands, I hurried across the parking lot to make sure he was stopping. I was breathless when I reached the truck, and it skidded to a halt. "What's going on?" I gasped. "There's no one here. My father should have been here an hour ago. Is everyone all right? Did something happen?"

The grim look on his face told me something was very wrong. "Everyone's all right. Something happened," he said quickly, then reached across and opened the passenger door for me. "I've been trying to call you, but the call wouldn't go through."

"What's happened?" I said as I climbed in and he drove us across the parking lot, stopping beside my car. "Graham, tell me what's going on. When I got here and saw the place empty . . . I was scared to death. I thought there had been an accident or something." I realized my hands were shaking and there were tears in my eyes.

"Everyone's fine," he said again, his voice steady and reassuring. "Take a deep breath. You look like you're about to faint. Everyone's fine, I promise."

"I'm sorry. All kinds of terrible things went through my mind."

He combed his fingers roughly over his hair, looking tired, looking like he hadn't slept all night. "Your dad's fine, Laura. He went with the mayor and my aunts to Austin."

"Austin?" I repeated. "What are they doing in Austin?"

"They're trying to protest a zoning hearing." He squinted out the window. "I should have figured it out. I should have seen it coming."

"Seen what coming? What's going on?"

"A real estate deal." He ground out the words from between clenched teeth. "Involving Evie and Randal. They bought the old mill from the Lowell estate. They're going to turn it into a great big restaurant and bar—bring the Austin nightlife to the country. Just what we need around here, a bar."

I followed his line of vision to the wall of trees that hid the old mill—our secret place, the place where my mother spoke to me in dreams. "They can't do that . . . It'll—"

"Put the Crossroads out of business." He finished the

sentence for me. His gaze met mine, and I could see that
he knew what I was only now figuring out. This would be
the end of everything that was magical about this place.

"They can't do that," I whispered again.

That hard expression glazed his face again. "They
can, and they're going to. Randal's got money, and he's
apparently got political pull, and he's going to steamroll
the paperwork through on this thing. I got a call to do a
HAZMAT inspection on the building first thing this morning. That never happens. We're weeks behind on inspections. Always."

"What . . . what happens after the inspections?" I
looked at the old café, thinking of Hasselene and Mernalene. This place was the heart of their lives.

"They bring in dozers and start clearing for a parking
lot and a paved road down there, and all the rest of it."
He pounded the steering wheel with a fist, the muscles
in his arm corded with frustration. "The zoning hearing
won't do any good, either. I already called and had a
friend at the courthouse look up the zoning on the mill.
It's commercial property from way back, so anyone can
move in there and start a restaurant, or bar, or anything
else. The zoning was never changed thirty years ago
when my family sold the building to Lowell for hay
storage."

The connections began to form in my mind, and I realized Evie had been planning this for a while. "I knew
something was going on." I let my head fall forward,
pounding my forehead with the heel of my hand. "I
should have figured it out—the way she was so interested in the *Texcetera* article. She kept talking about
how it was going to put this place on the map, bring in
lots of people. I wondered why she kept showing up
here all the time. I thought she was after you." I snapped
my mouth shut, embarrassed.

Graham swiveled his head my way with an incredulous look. "Evie's not my type." The twinkle in his eyes was irresistible.

For an instant I forgot all about the fight we'd had the day before, and the problem with the Crossroads, and we just sat looking at each other.

A car pulled in and circled the parking lot, and reality came creeping back to my thoughts. "Graham, I don't want to leave things the way we did yesterday. I want you to know I never planned to do a magazine article about you or the helicopter crash. I wouldn't do that to you."

His body sagged as he exhaled, staring thoughtfully at his hands. "I know that, Laura. I shouldn't have reacted so strongly. Yesterday wasn't my best day."

"I understand that, Graham, I really do," I whispered. "I understand how painful it is to have lost young men who were under your command. I understand about questioning yourself and wishing you'd done things differently. I understand being loaded down with grief and guilt. But why would you want to bear that burden alone when you have family, a whole community of people who love you?" *I love you,* I thought.

Intertwining his fingers on top of the steering wheel, he rested his chin on his hands and sat perfectly still for a long time, staring out the window, thinking. I could see the armor coming off, piece by piece, and suddenly he wasn't a soldier. He was only a man filled with grief. "It was the only way I could get through at first," he said finally. "Shut out everyone and everything. I didn't want people trying to make me *feel* better, telling me it wasn't my fault, telling me I did the best that I could. The fact is that I didn't do well enough. If I had, there wouldn't be eight dead soldiers. I keep asking myself, Why didn't we figure out there was a problem with the helicopters? The crews had suspicions, but the manufacturer was giving us downdraft stats that told us everything was fine.

Why didn't I dig deeper? Why wasn't I on top of it? We were so wrapped up in showing what the machines could do that we pushed the helicopters to the limit. We pushed too far."

Tears pressed my eyes, and I blinked hard to keep them away. "Graham, you can hide yourself away and ask those questions for the rest of your life, just like my father did, and there still won't be any answers. It won't change anything. It won't bring those men back. It'll only take you away from the people who need you here." I reached over and laid my hand on his arm. "I know that no one can tell you how your grief is supposed to feel, and I know that no one can take your grief away. But I also know that hiding from it, trying to soldier on and pretend it doesn't exist, won't help either. I know that because it's what I've been doing these last months since Mom died—just ignoring the pain, trying to go on like nothing happened, like everything was fine. Not feeling anything, not admitting to anything, not crying, not eating, not sleeping. Not living, just existing. In the end it landed me here, the day Hasselene and Mernalene found me, and I met you. I hardly knew who I was or where I was—I only knew I couldn't face one more minute of one more day. Then you called me that night about my dad's checkbook, and your voice sounded so good on the phone. When I came here the next morning, you made me laugh. I couldn't wait to return that evening and find out what was in the old mill. All of a sudden I felt myself starting to breathe again, starting to taste the air and look forward to things and want something from life."

He moved his hand and interlaced his fingers with mine, turning slowly to look at me, his expression filled with meaning. "And what is it that you want from life, Laura? What is it that you want from life now?"

I felt a tear spill from my eye and trace a line down

my cheek. I had asked myself that question so many times; now suddenly I had the answer. "I want to let go of all the bitterness and the sadness, the missed opportunities and the paths I didn't take. I want to turn them all over to the past, and to God, and accept that this is the road I've taken so far, and that's all right. This is where I am now. I want the future to be different. I want to really live. I want life to move forward from here to someplace better."

He slipped his hand free and raised it to wipe the moisture from my cheek. "And forward for you is California?"

I wasn't sure. I wasn't sure about California, or anything else. "I don't know," I admitted. *Find the right way,* Mom had written in her old Bible. Which was the right way? "I guess I won't know until I go. It doesn't have to be for good."

"I don't want to be the one who keeps you from it, if it's what you want, Laura." His eyes were tender, soft, and filled with understanding, with love. "If it's the right thing for you, we can work something out." But I could tell by the way he said it, by the tone of *something,* that he had no idea what *something* might be. His life was here, his family, his home, his town. Would he really give them all up? Was it right for me to ask him to?

Yet he was offering what I had thought I needed—freedom from the choice between him and my job, the possibility of having both. Still, I was afraid, and I knew why. "Graham, the problem with us isn't California. The problem is that we have to be able to talk, *really* talk to each other."

"I know that too, Laura. I do." His eyes, so serious a moment before, began to twinkle with sudden mischief. "I will if you will. You go first, Spider-woman."

I remembered saying that to him when we explored the bat cave. *You go first, Superman.* In a rush, the feelings of that day came back to me. I wanted to fall into the old pattern, be tempted and charmed, and forget the real issues. "Graham, I'm serious."

"I know." He gave me an earnest if slightly exasperated look. "Ask me anything you want to know. I'll tell you. Laura, I don't—" The cell phone rang in his pocket, and he answered. "Yeah. Hi, Uncle Rob. Tell Hardy Laura's here with me. I'm going to do the building inspection now. What's the news down there?" He paused to listen for a moment, then said good-bye and straightened in his seat, turning back to me. "They're at the courthouse now waiting on the hearing. They don't have an exact time, but they think it'll be sometime around noon."

"I'm going to Austin." I said the words before I thought about the fact that I was supposed to catch a plane in a few hours. "I'm going to see if there's anything I can do to stop this. It was my magazine article that helped give Evie the idea this was valuable real estate. There has to be some way to stop Randal. What about the inspections? What happens if the building doesn't pass?"

He clearly thought I was suggesting he not pass the building through inspection. "It'll pass. The building is solid."

"Then we'll have to find another way. The building is a bat habitat. Maybe we can do something with that. Maybe there's some kind of endangered-species law that applies. I'll get the *Texcetera* staff on it and see if we can come up with anything, maybe even as a follow-up article to the first Crossroads piece. Our staff has all kinds of connections at the courthouse. They may have ideas." I stepped out of the truck, not knowing where I was headed or exactly what I planned to do.

"I thought you had a plane to catch."

"I can get a flight later. Right now I'm on a mission.

Are you going to make it to the courthouse for the hearing?"

"I'll try to be there," he replied.

"See you then." I closed the door, feeling that, as a team, Graham and I were invincible—like the heroes in the old John Wayne movies. Somehow we were going to drive out the invaders and save the Crossroads.

I started making calls as soon as I was close enough to Austin to get cell phone reception. I put the *Texcetera* staff on the project of researching the bat colony and poking around the courthouse looking at old records, then I called the courthouse to get information on the zoning hearing, which was set for eleven o'clock.

I was pulling into the courthouse parking lot when the cell phone rang with Graham's name on the screen. I answered, and the tone of his voice told me right away that something was very wrong.

"We've got a bigger problem than the zoning hearing," he said, his voice grim. "I just took field samples. There's friable ACM—sorry, asbestos containing material—in the attic of the mill, and there's asbestos in the dust throughout the ceiling."

"What does that mean, exactly?" My mind flashed back through occasional magazine stories we'd done about asbestos in old buildings.

"In this case, it'll mean a half million dollars in cleanup, at least. It'll nix the restaurant deal. Randal will never want to put that kind of cash into the place."

I jumped in my seat, a jolt of hope running through me. "Then that's good. That's what we wanted."

The phone line went silent, and I could tell there was something else he didn't want to say. "Laura, the buildings used to be connected through the granary in the alley. If there's contamination in the mill building, it's in the Crossroads store, too."

My stomach fell. "Oh, my God." In the space of a

heartbeat, I realized the implications. When asbestos was found in a public building, the building had to be shut down immediately. And if cleanup at the mill would be expensive, so would cleanup in the store.

"There's no way Aunt Merna and Aunt Hass will be able to pay for the asbestos abatement on the store building, and they won't be able to stay open if the building isn't decontaminated," Graham said, reading my thoughts. "As soon as I file this report, no one's going to be allowed to go back in there."

"Graham, how can that be? They've lived there all their lives. If the building were contaminated . . . well, they're both so healthy. I mean, asbestos is dangerous. It's carcinogenic."

"It's only dangerous when it's airborne, when it's disturbed and inhaled," he explained. "This stuff could probably lie up there in the attic and between the ceiling timbers for another hundred years and not bother anyone. But the regulations are what they are, and there's always a risk of storm damage, any renovations, even normal cleaning, releasing the material. When the report goes in, the records are going to show that the buildings used to be connected, and both buildings will be sealed until there is a satisfactory asbestos abatement plan."

"Oh, Graham," I whispered, realizing how hard this had to be for him. "I'm just pulling into the courthouse now. Do you want me to go in there and tell them?"

"No." He let out a long, labored sigh. "I already have a call in to the judge. I'm already on my way and I'll try to get there before the hearing so I can explain it to Aunt Merna and Aunt Hass. I want them to hear it from me, not the court. It's going to be really hard for them. Laura, you should have seen them this morning when they heard about the real estate deal. Aunt Merna was furious because they'd been nice to Evie and Randal, and Aunt Hass kept muttering about how Randal and Evie were good customers, and they wouldn't do such a thing. This asbestos business is going to kill them both."

"I know," I whispered, wanting to save him the pain of having to tell them. "Are you sure you don't want me to tell them?"

"No," he said quietly. "I'll be there in fifteen minutes."

"I'll be here. I'm parked by the south door."

I hung up the phone and sat thinking about how he must be feeling. What were Hasselene and Mernalene going to say when he told them? The Crossroads was, had always been, their whole lives. All of their history, all of their memories were tied to that place. Where would they go now? How would they move on when everything had to be left behind? What about my father? He'd found a new sense of purpose there. Would he now drift back to where he was—just sitting in a chair, waiting to die?

The questions thundered through my mind as I called the *Texcetera* office and told Kristi to take everyone off the Crossroads research; there wasn't any point now.

"Are you sure?" Kristi asked. "You acted like it was pretty important. I mean, you know you're missing your flight and everything, right?"

"Yes, I know." I realized I hadn't even thought about it until that moment.

"Do you want me to book another flight later?"

I squeezed my forehead, trying to think. Go now? Go later? Don't go? Was I really willing to leave Graham behind, to take the chance of trying to build our relationship long distance? "Not yet," I said finally. It was the only thing I knew for sure. I wasn't ready yet. "Don't book a flight for me yet." Even as I said it, my stomach flipped over. If I wasn't in California by tomorrow morning, Royce would be furious.

"All right." Kristi sounded worried. Clearly she knew

that something was up. "Is there anything else I can do? Don's at the printing plant and he said the prep run is ready. Are you going to look at it, or do you want him to sign off?"

"I'll stop by the office when I get a chance. Tell him if he needs to sign off on it, to go ahead. I trust his judgment."

I heard a beep on the other end of the line, and she paused, then said, "Wait a minute. This is him on the phone. I'll put him through to you."

"All right."

Don was already talking by the time the line patched through. ". . . here looking at the prep run and everything looks good. Real good. I gotta say this thing is going to knock their socks off at the newsstands."

My jaw dropped. Don actually sounded excited. "I can't wait to see it."

"Thought you were heading to California."

I paused, not quite sure what to say. "I was, but I got caught up in something."

"This about that business with some restaurant tycoon trying to put a bar in next to that old store we featured in the Hometime column?" He sounded like he had more than a casual interest. "You know, I remember that place. Been around forever. Got any idea how old that building is?"

"I don't know," I answered, a little confused by the question. "A hundred years or more, I'd guess. Why?"

"I was just thinking about something. Let me do a little research and get back to you."

My hopes inched up, then crashed again as I thought about Graham's news. He would be here soon to deliver it. "Thanks, Don, but I doubt it would do much good. The bar going in isn't the problem anymore. The inspections this morning turned up asbestos contamination in the buildings." Why I was telling him this, I didn't know. I guess I was trying to reconcile it in my mind. It seemed so incredibly unfair. "The cleanup fee in itself will probably nix the restaurant deal, but the ladies who own the store won't be able to pay for the renovations on their building, either."

Don didn't answer, just grunted, "Hmmm," and then, "I'd better get back to work," and hung up. I leaned my head back and closed my eyes. In spite of everything, I felt a sense of relief, and I knew why. I'd missed my flight. I was still here, not on my way to California, and I was glad.

The squeal of tires punctuated my thoughts, and I startled as Graham's truck pulled up to the courthouse. Stepping out of my car, I waved, then hurried across the lot to catch up with him. He met me, looking grim. Neither of us spoke. I slipped my hand into his and we hurried up the steps into the corridor.

By the time we found Hasselene and Mernalene, sitting with my father and the mayor on a bench outside the courtroom, it was obvious that we were too late. The hearing was over, and they'd already gotten the news. Hasselene was crying inconsolably on my father's shoulder.

Randal stormed out of the courtroom, gesticulating wildly and yelling about breaking the real estate contract. Evie was trailing after him as fast as her spike heels would carry her, promising she would find him another property. Even that sight wasn't enough to lift my spirits as I looked at Hasselene and Mernalene, their faces fallen, eyes rimmed with tears. For the first time since I'd known them, they looked old and tired, defeated.

Graham knelt on the floor and took Hasselene's hands in his. "I'm sorry, Aunt Hass." He touched Merna's arm. "Aunt Merna. If I could have—"

Mernalene stopped him with a quick, angry stroke of

her finger. "Don't you say anything more, Graham Ray. You are not to blame for this. You'll not take it on your head, do you hear?" She turned away and cupped her body over her sister's shuddering form. "Don't cry so, Hassie. This problem isn't bigger than God's ability to solve it. We just have to pray. We'll pray for a miracle."

Hasselene sniffed, trying to swallow her grief. "Oh, Merna, we need a miracle. We can't lose our store. All of our memories are there. It would be like losing everyone again—Mama and Papa, Cam and John in the war. The last place we were all together was there, at our engagement party at the old mill. Remember that, Merna? That wonderful party before Cam and John went away to the war and never came back? Remember how in love we were? If we lose the store, all the ghosts will be gone."

Merna rubbed the bow of her sister's back. "Hassie, you have to get your mind together. You're not making sense, going on about ghosts. Your blood pressure's up. Look how red your skin is. You have to calm down. You'll give yourself a stroke." She looked helplessly at us. "We need to get her someplace where she can lie down. Somewhere quiet."

Hasselene collapsed into sobs again.

My father stood up and took charge. "I'm going to take them to the condominium at the retirement court. It's quiet there, and they can rest, stay the night, or however long they need. You can call us there if anything . . . changes."

"All right, Dad," I said. Hasselene looked like she was close to a total breakdown. It wouldn't do her any good to be there while Graham, Uncle Rob, and I talked about what would happen to the Crossroads buildings now, and whether there was anything we could do about it. "Are you sure you're all right to make the drive, Dad?"

He nodded, looking strong, determined, and capable,

like the sergeant major from my childhood days. "Call if there's news."

"We will, Dad," I said as Graham helped Hasselene to her feet and we all walked down the long corridor.

At the courthouse door, the mayor kissed Hasselene and Mernalene good-bye, vowing to return to Keetonville and begin taking up a collection to save the Crossroads. But I could tell by the look on Graham's face that he knew it wouldn't make a dent in the cost of the asbestos removal.

Hasselene laid her hand on Graham's arm as we helped her into my father's old truck. "Punky, you know we have to take care of the pictures," she said, her voice quavering and her eyes distracted and faraway. "You know we can't leave all our pictures."

"I know, Aunt Hass." Graham patted her hand tenderly. "Get some rest. Try not to worry until we see exactly what we're dealing with in the store building."

Hasselene nodded, but Mernalene's eyes said what all of us were thinking—it didn't feel like the exact report would make much difference. Barring a miracle, this would be the end of the Lone Star Café.

Chapter 20

I had a revelation as we were about to part ways at the courthouse—Graham heading to the Crossroads to secretly perform tests in the store building, while I went to my office. As I stood there with Graham on the steps, watching my father's old truck drive away, I knew that if the Crossroads crisis had resolved itself in the courthouse earlier, I still wouldn't have wanted to leave. I wasn't staying because of the crisis. I was staying because of Graham. This place, this life, he and I together felt right, whether it was logical or not. In one quick, certain rush of thought and emotion, I knew I didn't belong anywhere but here.

"Graham," I said quietly, while he was still looking into the distance, watching the truck disappear against the downtown skyline. "I'm not going."

"Hmm?" He turned to me.

"I'm not going to California." There, I'd said it out loud. "It doesn't feel right." My heart stopped in my chest. I felt like I'd leaped out over a chasm and was waiting for him to catch me.

He took my hand, gazing at my fingers. "I want you to stay, Laura, but be sure it's what you want—it's not because you feel guilty, or pressured, or because we're in the middle of a crisis right now. You'd be giving up a lot by staying. There's some publishing business in Austin, but it's nothing like you're used to. Nothing like California."

I smiled, breathing in the warm summer air, gazing into his eyes, feeling like I could float away. "I don't need California. I have a job here at *Texcetera,* and I've come to like it. California can't offer me anything I don't already have here. It can't offer me bat caves and mountain climbing and buildings with my ancestors' names on the plaques. My roots are here. My father is here. You're here. I never really wanted to go to California—my heart wasn't in it. My heart was here, from the very first day I met you. I know now that I'm not giving up anything by staying. I'm gaining everything that matters."

He brought my hand to his lips and kissed my fingers tenderly, then held them against his chest. "I guess you can see where my heart is. I'm not going to try to talk you into leaving again. You've had your chance."

"I took my chance," I corrected, and stood gazing at him, all the noises of the city fading away.

The door swung open behind us and a group of Girl Scouts came out, then began assembling on the steps so their leader could take a group photograph.

Graham glanced at me and grinned. "Guess we'd better go."

"Guess so," I agreed.

"See you in a while," he said, leaning over and kissing me quickly.

The Girl Scouts made "Ummm" sounds, and giggled.

"In a while." I turned away and trotted down the steps, laughing, giddy, lighter than air. In spite of all the bad news the day had provided, I finally knew what I wanted from life.

There was no question in my mind when I went back to my office, shut the door, and dialed Royce's number.

I blurted it out right after explaining to him that something had come up and I hadn't made the flight to California. "I want you to give me *Texcetera*," I said.

He laughed so hard I had to hold the phone away from my ear, then finally he hollered, "What?"

I repeated it again. "I said, I don't want the WLP deal. I want you to give me *Texcetera*. I have ongoing family demands here and the magazine has potential. I don't want to turn it over so Lander's niece can cut her baby teeth on it. It's mine. I built it. I want it."

For the first time ever, Royce was stunned into silence. After all, I was dealing in complex issues he couldn't understand—family, commitment, emotion . . . love. "So let me get this straight," he bit out sarcastically, and I could tell he was on fire. "You want me to let you *blow off* the California deal, your chance at the publisher's position, *and* your editorship here in Richmond so you can stay in *Texas?*"

I swallowed hard. The way he said it made it all sound completely ludicrous. And it would have been, if only the facts were concerned. But there were a whole host of feelings I couldn't describe to my boss. Staring hard out the window, I rebuilt my composure, one mental brick at a time.

"Yes, that's what I'm saying." It felt like I was jumping off a high wire without knowing if the safety net was real or a figment of my own hopes and dreams. "You know as well as I do there are a dozen people who'll jump at the California job, and no doubt you've already got my replacement picked there in Richmond. If you're so confident in Lander's niece, put her in there, where you can keep an eye on her. My staying at *Texcetera* isn't much more than a wrinkle in your plans."

"And a rip the size of Miami in yours," he shot back, his voice so loud it rang through the office and my brain. "What the hell is going on down there?"

"Nothing. Just an overdue change of priorities." The truth of that statement hit me like a shot of pure oxygen, making me bolder, more determined, more sure of myself. "You know I can do the *Texcetera* job, Royce. You know I'll bring this magazine to the top, and Lander will be thrilled, and pretty soon he and everyone else will forget I didn't take the WLP deal. Stop yanking me around. Send someone else to California."

He growled under his breath, and I could hear him tapping his pen furiously on the desk, one of the nervous habits he'd developed in thirty years of publishing magazines. "Take a couple days off and get your head together. I'll hold the WLP job. I'll tell them to expect you on Monday."

I realized that he was offering me a huge favor, and Royce didn't usually do favors. Normally, anyone who didn't go along with his way of thinking was out the door. The fact that he was bending for me made me feel even guiltier for turning down the WLP promotion.

Temptation whispered in my ear, telling me I could wait a couple more days, let things settle, leave the future in limbo for now. . . .

And then it would be that much harder to do what I knew I had to do. Royce would be more determined to send me to California, once he had time to think about things. Right now I had the element of surprise on my side. "A couple more days won't make any difference. This isn't about me needing to tie up a few things, or needing a couple days off. This is about the rest of my life."

He sighed hard, unwilling to give in. The line went silent, and I sat holding my breath, afraid of what the answer might be. Royce had a legendary temper. What if he told me to go to California or get out? What if he fired me? What then?

"Royce, please." I had to get the conversation over

with, get a commitment, before Royce had time to really work up a head of steam, or before he managed to talk me into something I didn't want. "I haven't ever asked you for anything. You *know* me. You know I don't go off half-cocked."

"I know you've been only about halfway up to par these last two months," he replied flatly, but underneath the purely business tone there was the faintest hint of compassion. "I can understand that, but I'll give it to you straight. Right now I wonder which half is coming up with this idiotic crap about life priorities and family responsibilities."

So much for tenderhearted understanding. My temper flared like a Bunsen burner in high school chemistry class. "Well, you know what? When you see the first issue of this magazine, on the racks *on time,* at *twice* as many outlets as that rag we bought out, you won't be thinking *idiotic crap.* You'll be thinking it's one heck of a job, and so will Lander."

Royce was silent for a moment, then he laughed. "All right. That sounds more like my rainmaker. Enough of this nonsense about Texas. When are you headed to California?"

"I'm *not!*" I hollered, and even though the door was closed, my voice must have echoed through the glass. Kristi's face poked around the edge of her cubicle, eyes wide. I turned my back to the door. "I want *Texcetera.*"

He growled into the phone, and I heard him slamming something against his desk. "This is one monumental error in judgment."

"Maybe so. But I'm staying."

"Circulation down there has a limited potential. Even if the magazine is good, it's still a regional publication. Once you get the kinks worked out, that's an eight-to-five job, at best. No special issues. No big challenges. You'll be bored within three months. Come on, Laura, think about how it'll really be. What are you going to do with your time?"

"Have a life." The words swept through my mind like the stroke of a painter's brush, changing vague images and diaphanous ideas into something real, tangible, visible. I wanted all of those things I'd put on hold these last fifteen years—home, family, community, roots, true love. I wanted time to get to know my father, to learn about my history. I wanted to be with Graham. I wanted to share all the normal, everyday things. I wanted to rake leaves and have backyard barbecues, mow the lawn and grow roses in the flower beds. I wanted to follow the stream to see where it led. My heart knew, even if my mind hadn't been able to comprehend it until now, that this was what I had been yearning for.

Royce roared on the other end of the phone, leaving me hanging on the line while he hollered, "Get out!" at some unfortunate sap who'd stepped into his office. When he came back, the fight seemed to have gone out of him. "All right. Have it your way."

"Thanks, Royce." Moving the phone away from my lips, I let out a long sigh, trying to loosen the knots in my stomach.

"Don't thank me. I just let you slit your wrists." *Click.* As usual, he didn't say good-bye.

When I turned from the windows, Kristi ducked back around the edge of her cubicle, and I realized that, even with the door closed, she'd heard the conversation. The news would be around the office in no time. The dragon lady was staying.

Kristi tried to pretend she hadn't been listening in, as she brought me the prep run of *Texcetera,* fresh from the printing plant. "I know you were listening," I said, leafing through the pages.

She stopped halfway to the door. "I didn't . . . I mean,

I wasn't . . ." With a guilty shrug, she faced me, crinkling her button nose. "I'm glad you're staying."

"Thanks, Kristi."

She didn't say anything more, and I was glad. The last thing I wanted was for anyone else to ask me why I was staying at *Texcetera*. I couldn't explain it, other than that I knew, I just *knew*, this was where I belonged.

After I finished looking through the prep run and making a half dozen phone calls, I told Kristi I was leaving for the day, and packed my things, even though it was only four-thirty. Graham would be finishing up at the Crossroads by now, and I wanted to know what he'd found there.

"See you tomorrow, Kristi," I said, heading out of my office.

Her smile was big, genuine, warm, and it made me feel good. "See you tomorrow, Ms. Draper." Then she grabbed a sticky note off her computer monitor, remembering something. "Oh, Don wanted to see you before you left."

"What about?" I felt a sliver of apprehension. Maybe Don was going to hand in his resignation, which would be a shame, because even though we often rubbed each other the wrong way, together we'd produced one heck of a first edition.

Kristi shrugged. If something ominous was in the wind, she hadn't sniffed it yet. "He called and said he'd be here in five minutes. He's been gone most of the day. That's all I know."

I turned away to hide a grimace. Gone most of the day probably spelled j-o-b interview. "All right. I'll catch him downstairs." I walked slowly around the corner and down the stairs, trying to decide what I was going to say to Don if he told me he was quitting. It would be hard to replace his kind of experience. Don had been in the magazine and newspaper business since the Kennedy era. He knew the business, and he knew Texas.

He met me at the bottom of the stairs, looking, as usual, like a basset hound having a bad day.

I let the stairway door close behind me, then glanced up and down the corridor to see if anyone was nearby. "Kristi said you were looking for me."

He nodded slowly, pausing for what seemed like an hour to pull a wad of papers out of his shirt pocket. "Had something to tell you before you left."

"Do we need to go back up to my office?" I tried not to sound as apprehensive as I felt. If he was going to quit, I didn't want anyone else to hear.

"No." A quick smirk told me he'd read my mind. "This won't take long."

"All right." I drummed my fingers nervously on my arm, watching as he leafed through the disorganized jumble of crumpled business cards, matchbooks, gas receipts, and folded papers.

"Got some information on that building you asked about," he said, so casually I wasn't sure if that was what he wanted to tell me, or if it was merely a side note.

I waited for him to continue, but he was focused on the wad of papers, sorting through them and grumbling to himself.

"And?" I asked.

He looked up like he'd forgotten I was there, then fished a business card from the pile. "That store and mill are historic buildings. You know what that means?" Leaning close, he looked into my eyes, his lips spreading into a slow, triumphant grin.

"Nooo . . ." I stretched the word out, playing along with this little game of cat and mouse. Inside, my heart started thumping like a bass drum. Whatever he was about to tell me, I knew it was big. I'd never seen Don smile before. "What?"

He held up the business card and dangled it between two fingers. "It means that the right person"—he cut his eyes toward the business card, then back at me, and I knew the punch line was coming—"won't have any problem helping the owners get federal and state funding for the renovations. And this right here is the business card for a county commissioner who's very proud of his record for saving Texas's historic buildings. It's his pet cause, so to speak. He helped save the McDaniel building downtown last year. I just spent an hour in his office, and he says the Crossroads sounds like just his kind of historic building—something with an interesting story and some publicity surrounding it."

I gasped, frozen in place, blinking numbly as the information sank in. "You're kidding."

"I might have also mentioned that a *Texcetera* article on the renovation would sure make him look good to the voting public."

"It will." I caught his drift and sailed on it. "David and Goliath. The little guy versus the restaurant giant, and the county commissioner is on David's side."

His grin broadened, seemingly in slow motion, revealing a mouthful of tobacco-stained teeth. "Guess Goliath and his real estate agent should have checked with the county commission before they decided not to buy the mill building, eh?"

I smiled back. "I doubt if Goliath or his real estate agent would have known who to ask."

Don's eyes narrowed slyly. "Fifty years in the journalism business, you learn a few things the young pups don't know." By young pups, I knew he meant me. "You hang around here long enough, you might learn a few things."

"I guess you heard I'm staying on at *Texcetera*," I surmised.

"Yeah. Kristi told me on the phone." He dangled the business card like a bone. "Guess this ought to be worth a few days' vacation."

"You got it." Lunging like a basketball player in a tip-off, I grabbed the card, and the next thing I knew we were inches away from a bear hug of pure exuberance. I caught myself just in time, and we stood gaping at each other, shocked and appalled.

Clearing my throat, I caught my breath as my apprehension over Don's quitting dissolved. He wasn't at a job interview all day. He was down at the courthouse trying to help me out. Wow. "Anything else?" I was almost afraid to ask . . . in case I was wrong. . . .

Studying me, he lowered his wooly brows. "Nope." One suspicious eye squinted. "Why?"

"No reason." I tried to sound casual, but I knew there was a look of pure relief on my face.

"What'd ya think I was gonna do—quit my job?"

I rolled my eyes, scoffing, "No. Of course not."

One saggy cheek twitched upward; then he rubbed his face, repairing the scowl. "I'm gone fishing until Monday."

"Good idea," I said, then rushed forward and beat him through the door to the parking garage. I might have let out a little squeal on my way to the car. I'm still not sure.

By the time I reached the Crossroads, I was about to come out of my skin. My mind had been spinning the entire time with thoughts of Graham and me, and with ideas for how we could save the Crossroads. I had come up with one wrinkle in Don's otherwise brilliant solution to the asbestos problem—the mill was still owned by heirs to the Lowell estate, who quite clearly had no interest in keeping it. As soon as the news of grant money came out, it would be only a matter of time before someone, maybe even Evie and Randal, bought the mill building. We had to find a way to get the mill building off the market, or else find a buyer who wanted to do something other than put in a nightclub.

The options were playing in my mind as I pulled into the Crossroads and circled to the front of the building. Graham's truck was parked next to my father's pickup and the mayor's flatbed farm truck. All of them were sitting on the porch with Hasselene and Mernalene. I knew right away what that meant. Graham had found asbestos in the store building. Otherwise, they would have been inside.

I parked my car and got out slowly, trying to decide what to say. I didn't want to dangle hope, especially not with Hasselene and Mernalene there, only to have to snatch it away. I walked up quietly and stood across from Graham on the steps. They were talking about the levels of asbestos in the store—not as bad as Graham had feared, mostly contained undisturbed in the attic, but he'd found a small number of dustborne fibers in two storage rooms, in a pantry in the kitchen, and near a crack in the ceiling timbers above one of the shelves on the store wall. Only a very small amount in the living quarters and no measurable levels in the air, which meant that the ladies probably had little to worry about, healthwise. Unfortunately, the attic was full of old asbestos-containing insulating tiles, probably put in sometime early in the twentieth century. The tiles were badly decayed, which meant that cleanup would be expensive. It also meant that the building couldn't be reopened without going through asbestos abatement.

Hands on her hips, Mernalene turned on them impatiently. "The fact is, we don't have the money." Uncle Rob started to speak, but she pointed a finger and silenced him. "And we're not going to get it by bankrupting the savings of our friends and neighbors, so you stop all that nonsense about taking up a collection." She moved the pointing finger to Graham. "And we're not going to get it by you selling off that parcel of land on Sand Creek, or any of the other property that came to you through your mama's family. That is yours, and you're a young man, and you should keep your stake to build a life for yourself. Hassel agrees with me on this. We've talked about it. We don't want to lose our place, but we're not going to be a burden to folks." Setting her mouth in a firm, straight line, she crossed her arms over her chest.

"I think I have a possible solution," I blurted, and the next thing I knew, I was digging the business card out of my suit pocket and handing it to Graham. So much for being careful of what I said and not getting everyone's hopes up. I plunged in as Graham gave me a quizzical look and handed the card to the mayor. "A staff member at *Texcetera* did some poking around today, and it turns out that the store is a historic building. That's the business card of a county commissioner who's willing to help with getting federal and state grants to save the buildings. He's apparently done it before for other historic buildings."

Everyone stood looking at me, openmouthed. Finally Hasselene grabbed the card and clutched it against her chest, muttering, "Oh, thank you, Lord." Giving her sister a narrow-eyed look, she added, "Answered prayers. See? Answered prayers."

"There's only one problem." I winced, preparing to throw cold water on Hasselene's answered prayers. "The mill. As soon as word of this gets out, someone will want to buy the mill. We have to find a way to get control of it."

One by one, they nodded and muttered agreement, growing thoughtful.

"Laura's right." Graham gave me a look of admiration, and I fell in for a moment. "As soon as the Lowell estate finds out the building is salvageable, they'll seek a buyer for the place."

The mayor tapped his pen on the porch railing, the

sound zinging down my father's tight row of new two-
by-fours. "We need a buyer who will do something good
with the place, who'll help bring some economic growth
to Keetonville, bring in tourists. We're drying up on the
bone here, and the town needs the income, but not from
some smarmy nightspot. . . ." He trailed off thoughtfully.

"Maybe it could be a movie house again," my father
offered, then frowned and shook his head.

"An antique store, or maybe one of those new bed-
and-breakfast inns?" Mernalene paced to the door and
back, watching her feet thoughtfully. "Guests could take
their meals here . . ."

Hasselene sucked air through her teeth. "Everyone
should be able to enjoy the mill and the old swimming
hole. Youngsters ought to be able to go down there and
play cowboys and Indians in the woods and pick mustang grapes by the creek. Folks ought to be able to have
gatherings." She regarded Graham and me with a mean-
ingful expression. "Young lovers ought to be able to put
pretty cloths over the old tables and have engagement
parties in the park, like we did all those years ago." Graham glanced at his feet, and I blushed as she went on,
her voice mixing with a breeze that twittered the leaves
of the live oaks, as if the place itself were speaking.
"That's the heart of this old crossroads. People leave a
little something of themselves, and take away a little
something they didn't know they needed. There aren't
too many places like that left in the world—the kind of
places that change people." Her eyes met mine, and I
knew she was talking about me as much as anybody. The
Crossroads had changed me in ways I could never have
imagined. It had lured me back, time after time, until finally I'd realized I was speeding down the wrong path.

The mayor clapped his hands together. "What about
a park? What if the city buys the building—there are
grants out there for the economic development of little

towns like ours, and Lord knows, we can show we need it. The city of Keetonville could buy the old place, create a park for swimming, hiking, reunions and weddings and such. We could renovate the old mill and rent it out, maybe put some shops inside for the tourists, maybe even leave the bats in the back end of the building and put up some kind of a Plexiglas wall. Down in Austin, hundreds of tourists come every day to see the bats fly out of Congress Avenue Bridge. Imagine how many would come to see our bats. We can breathe life into this town again."

Stunned, we looked at each other, each waiting to see if anyone was going to find a flaw in the plan. When no one did, we slowly started to smile, a little more, a little more, until we were like a circle of Cheshire cats.

The mayor bounded out of his seat and square-danced toward his truck. "I'm headed to the office. Before anyone else finds out about this, I've got to get with the town council and get plans and a letter of intent together; then we'll contact the Lowell estate and present a binding offer for the mill."

Hasselene and Mernalene started after him, speaking in unison. "We're coming with you." Descending the steps, they glanced back at my father like mirror images, and Mernalene added, "Come on, Hardy, let's go."

Jumping up, my father straightened the front of his farmer uniform with a quick tug, then hurried to the steps. As he passed me, he leaned forward and kissed me on the cheek, whispering close to my ear, "Reckon you better admit to that boy you been talkin' about him in your sleep."

"All right, Dad." I chuckled, watching him as he hobbled away after the Goodnight sisters. I'd never loved my father more than at that moment, wearing his farmer suit, using his Texas words, giving me advice about true love.

When I turned around, Graham was watching me.

"You're amazing." There was a world of gratitude and admiration and love in those two little words. I felt warm, like I'd stepped from the deepest shadow into a patch of sunlight.

I tried to play it casual, with a shrug. I hadn't, after all, forgotten *everything* I knew about romance. Never let a man know when he's got you wrapped around his little finger. "Well, you know—mountain climber, spider catcher, bat girl, barbecue judge, real estate mogul ... all in a day's work. Nothing to it."

Eyes twinkling the deepest blue, he clicked his tongue against the even white line of his teeth. "That so?"

He advanced a step, and I backed against my father's freshly painted railing. Wrapping my hands around it, I hung on. My head was spinning. "Sure."

He closed the distance between us with one quick, smooth step, his eyes meeting mine, a mirror of all my secret hopes and dreams and longings. I knew he felt it. Everything. Just as I did.

His lips met mine in a long, slow kiss, and every shred of doubt within me vanished like vapor before a flame. I understood how Collie knew True was her soul mate, how my father knew my mother was the one, how lovers have always known. I felt it with my heart, my soul, with every ounce of life in me. This was meant to be.

When the kiss ended, the world was silent except for the music of the brook passing the old mill below. I thought of my dream—of the message my mother had delivered to me three nights in a row. *Follow the stream; see where it leads.*

"Graham?" I whispered into the breeze, now scented with honeysuckle and beginning to cool with the coming evening.

"Hmm?" A soft sound, barely a breath exhaled.

"Where does the stream go? The one that passes the mill—where does it go?"

He considered the question for a minute, then stepped back to look at me thoughtfully, his eyes content, as when he was lost in the music of his guitar. "I can show you." He leaned closer so that only inches separated us, his gaze holding mine, a current running between my body and his. "You up for a little adventure?"

The ground seemed to shift under my feet. Life with Graham would be nothing if not an adventure. "The last time you asked me that, I ended up with bat doody in my hair."

He moved so close that I could feel his breath on my lips. "That a yes or a no?"

"It's a yes . . . I think." The words were heady, passionate. Right then I would have followed him anywhere.

"You *think?*"

I sighed, letting my eyes fall closed. "No, I *know*." I'd never been more sure of three little words in my life. We sealed it with a kiss, then set off to find that last thing I had been seeking at the Crossroads—the answer to the question my mother had planted in my dreams. Where did the stream lead?

The answer came to me long before we reached Keetonville, before we turned left onto B Street and drove slowly away from town, passing Puff's Pooferé, continuing down the winding road, moving through the overhanging live oaks, sun to shadow, shadow to sun. I held my breath as we crossed the waters of Kittery Creek and drifted to a stop before the ancient stone frontispiece of Kittery Creek Church.

Graham opened the car door and I followed. Together we walked past the church to the crest of the gentle hill that cradled the ancient chapel. He swept his hand to the valley below, where one stream flowed through the flatlands and another tumbled down the hillside, and the two became one. "This is where the stream leads," he whispered against my ear. "It doesn't come by the straightest path, but it ends up here."

"I don't think it matters how it came." I understood now where my dreams had been leading me—to this place, to Graham, to a new life I could never have imagined if I hadn't come to the Crossroads one extraordinary day. "As long as it ends up where it's meant to be."

"True enough," he agreed. "True enough."

He slipped his arms around me and we stood in the silence of that old place, a place with history, where my ancestors came to leave behind one life and build another. I suppose there were no crossroads then, long ago, when they traveled that wild, hilly country. Not roads as we know them. But still, I imagine that they came to a fork in the path, as I did in my life, as my mother did in hers, as everyone does, sooner or later. The trick when you get there, when you stand at that place where two roads separate, leading in opposite directions, is to stop for a minute, and follow that very last bit of advice my mother left for me—advice as timeless as the book from which it came.

Stand at the crossroads and look. Ask for the ancient paths. Ask where the good way is. . . .

And walk in it.

Don't miss Lisa Wingate's
new contemporary romance,
which completes the trilogy begun with

TEXAS COOKING
and
LONE STAR CAFÉ

coming in September 2005

National Bestselling Author
Lisa Wingate

Texas Cooking

No one is more surprised than Colleen Collins when she's offered a job writing a fluffy magazine article about rural Texas cooking. But after only a few days in the charming little town of San Saline, the big-city reporter is falling for the local residents, and finding it impossible to reisist the frustrating True McKitrick, a local-boy-made-good whose mere presence makes her feel alive—and at home.

0-451-41102-1

"WINGATE WRITES WITH DEPTH AND WARMTH; JOY AND WIT." —DEBBIE MACOMBER

"EVERYTHING ROMANCE SHOULD BE, YET SO MUCH MORE." —CATHERINE ANDERSON

NAL ACCENT

LISA WINGATE

Tending Roses

0-451-20579-0

While living in a remote Missouri farmhouse—and
struggling to care for her husband, baby, and aging
grandmother—Kate Bowman finds inspiration in the
pages of her grandmother's handmade journal.

Good Hope Road

0-451-20861-7

Twenty-year-old Jenilee Lane is the last person to
expect any good could come from the tornado that rips
through the Missouri farmland surrounding her town.
But when she rescues an elderly neighbor, her world
changes in ways she could never have imagined.

Coming January 2005:

The Language of Sycamores

Available wherever books are sold or at
www.penguin.com

Penguin Group (USA)
is proud to present
GREAT READS—GUARANTEED!

**We are so confident that you will love
this book that we are offering a
100% money-back guarantee!**

If you are not 100% satisfied with this
publication, Penguin Group (USA) will refund
your money—no questions asked!
Simply return the book before
April 1, 2005 for a full refund.

**With a guarantee like this one,
you have nothing to lose!**